When East meets West

When East meets West

K. K. Sudan

PARTRIDGE
A Penguin Random House Company

To order additional copies of this book, contact
Partridge India
000 800 10062 62
orders.india@partridgepublishing.com

www.partridgepublishing.com/india

Dedicated with great reverence to my parents
Bakshi Nand Lal Sudan and Smt. Rameshwari Devi.

ACKNOWLEDGEMENTS

I certainly do have for acknowledgement some persons who have a very special place in my life and deserve my sincere thanks for rendering their behind-the-curtain help and thus making the project a great success.

While the inspiration to write this novel comes from my Son Ravi Sudan after the debut of my first book 'Face to Face with Destiny' published in 2008, it is my youngest son Rahul Sudan on whose concept the present novel 'When East meets West' is based upon. Next come the names of Sunita Sudan and Prerana Sudan both my daughters-in-law and my grand-daughter Aarohi Sudan who had become instrumental in shaping up the sequences and had been a great help in making countless readings of the manuscript from time to time

The list of the persons who also deserve my thanks wouldn't be complete without the mention of their names, such as Ms Antoniet Saints my Publishing Consultant and her team who had always stood by me and helped me off and on with her valuable advice. A big 'Thank You' goes to M/s. Partridge India publishers as well for publishing the book with such an attractive cover thus giving it a presentable form.

When East meets West' is another book in the series by K.K. Sudan who had earlier made a debut with his book **'Face to Face with Destiny'**, in the professional world of authors. Written with a depth and sincerity, the book engrosses the reader from the first page to the last. It shows the intense insight of the human spirit which can triumph over the odds, which life is subjected to.

The story of a girl child who had to live in the disguise of a boy to hide her identity, reared by a man becoming himself a eunuch by accident at the cruel hands of fate, feelings of love, romance, struggle and tenderness, a fantastic and remarkable read professing enlightenment.

(Book – I)

CHAPTER – 1

⚭

She skipped to the bathroom. Her face in the mirror, fixed against the washroom, practically looked that of a stranger--- eyes too bright, hectic spots of red across her cheekbones. After brushing her teeth, she worked to straighten out the tangled chaos that was her hair, fixing up with the ribbon making a pony tail. She splashed her face with cold water. She had begun to be a little beauty-conscious in fact since the day she came into contact with Bob. It had become her habit as a general routine to make a survey of self before going out. She would stand before the mirror, make a critical look upon her dress, her make-up, her facial expressions, her hair style, her jewellery including her footwear. She was just nineteen with five feet three inches and had around fifty kilos of carefully monitored weight and looked quite slim and attractive. On that day she had chosen a particularly chic little outfit, a red dress with skirt, a cream cardigan and sandals with red piping. She wore simple earrings and artificial pearl studs and the gold-plated necklace.

Bob had been minutely observing her and said, "Wow! With the passing of time, you are becoming more beautiful day by day."

"You too look 'beau' and I could say the same for you as well." replied Somi, blushing a little, as like every day, Bob was beautifully dressed today also, with that effortless style--- she was sure he never gave a thought to it. All his suits were bespoke, of course, and his shoes, and shirts; she thought the only thing he bought retail were his ties. Today, like every day, the tie was perfectly understated, a dark red and white stripes.

"By the way, what's on agenda for today?" She asked.

"I've planned to explore Pahalgam today. The taxi was booked last night for the to and fro trip as usual. Anyway, if you are ready to go, I think we should have a quick breakfast before we leave," replied Bob. A little after, both of them were seen coming down the stairs. The kitchen looked bright, seeming to absorb their mood. Soon, they made themselves settled on the chairs.

"What's for breakfast?" Somi asked pleasantly.

"I'm not sure." Replied Bob and asked, "What would you like?" She made a quick glance over the tables, occupied by other young couples also, in that early hour like them, and found them feasting on omelette and toast, a light and mouth-watering dish quite fit for the breakfast.

"Butter toast and omelette one plate each for me. A cup of hot coffee afterwards would suffice." She ordered for herself and asked Bob, "What you would like to have?"

"Me too the same," replied Bob with a sweet smile as usual, in total agreement with his beloved as he had been doing throughout the long tour. And thus the order was doubled for two plates each. However, a bowl of cereal was also added which both of them could share, to be followed by a cup each of hot coffee afterwards.

'Pahalgam', the confluence of the rivers--- 'Sheshnag' and 'Lidder', was their next on the agenda of 'Bharat Darshan' tour. They didn't have to wait for long, as the private taxi had already been booked by the Manager of the hotel, like he had been doing daily, during the entire week, since the day, the couple had checked in. On the way to Pahalgam, both Bob and Somi had enjoyed the scenery of the valley soon after coming out of the main parts of the city. They passed over the bridge, the road winding northward, the houses flashing past them growing farther apart, getting smaller. The trees held their protecting shadow on both sides of the road. They had also seen scores of factories where skilled artisans and carpenters could be seen even on the roadside engaged in manufacturing the wooden Bats for Cricket as the forest surrounding that area had been thickly populated with the grownup trees which provide the raw material for them. Both Somi and Bob were too fascinated to capture the beauty of the valley and realized having reached their destination only when they could hear the sound of the river close by.

"Wow, what a beautiful view!" exclaimed Somi on seeing the beauteous greenery on all sides with mountains covered with snow.

"You like it?" Bob smiled.

"It, of course, has a certain charm," replied Somi.

He pulled the end of her pony tail and laughed quietly.

"Ready?" He asked, opening her door.

"Let's go". She tried to laugh but it seemed to get struck in her throat. She smoothed her hair a little on coming out of the taxi.

"You look lovely," said Bob and took her hand with a smile on his face, his thumb rubbed soothing circles into the back of Somi's hand. They walked towards the river 'Lidder'. The taxi was kept on waiting as they tracked along the riverside and reached a wooden over-bridge with the 'Lidder' flowing underneath. The strong current of water looked gushing out from the steep mountain at great speed. The weather became fine by the afternoon and the sun would be crossing over their heads in a short while. Taking a walk together, their fingers playing with each other, they reached the end of the bridge and took a small round descending below towards the left bank of the river. While tracking here, their attention was shifted to a solid huge rock near the bank of the river and they decided to climb over and sit upon it. A cool breeze was blowing to make the feelings more romantic. A little later, they found themselves experiencing the icy water when they trod toward the bank with the idea of having a little fun by dipping their feet into the water. Having enjoyed his swimming in the cold waters at sea-beaches during the tour, Bob was quite enthusiastic. Taking the lead, he entered first into the water. But to his dismay, had to rush out of the water on the spur of the moment as, to stand in even ankle-deep strong current of the icy water was certainly in no way less than a heroic deed. Later they enjoyed the 'pony ride' also. Looking for lunch, they found a number of eateries running by the riverside. A few young boys tried to lure them but Bob preferred a small restaurant toward the corner that looked neat and clean as compared to the others. Here again it was Somi who ordered a light meal --- fried dal, chapaties, mixed vegetables and salad. Having been in India for so many days, Bob too had, by now, developed a taste for the Indian food and started liking it to the amusement of Somi.

There was another holy place of pilgrimage known by the name --- 'Martand' (or Mattan). Here an ancient temple dedicated to the 'SUN' god is surrounded by a beautiful 'sarover' (pond). It is the most memorable work of king Lalitaditya (AD 693 – 729) a kshatriya from Surya dynasty. The Emperor got it built in (AD 693 – 729) now in ruins, situated on top of plateau, just 9 Km. on north-east from Anantnag. Utilizing the little time they still had, they made a dashing visit to see the 'Sun god' temple also.

They returned back to Hotel Lake View at Srinagar quite late in the night. They ordered for some light dinner and were pleased with the quick service. The beans were fresh and crisp, the salad dressing used lemon juice instead of vinegar, and they had added some fresh chopped herbs that made the whole thing smell like summer pudding. They also found that the potatoes were coloured with round sweet made of chocolate mixture covered with cocoa, and sighed with pleasure. At the end of the dinner they also enjoyed a cup of hot coffee and then ascended the upstairs towards their suite.

Retired to their bedroom, Somi found Bob in a romantic mood. He gently pulled her toward him and she sat on his lap as he kissed her. Their kisses were filled with tenderness and passion. And as he held her, for an instant he felt desire race through him like a tide that could not be turned back, and neither of them had any inclination to. The force of what they felt for each other was irresistible and overwhelmed them both. They were lying together. His lips were on hers and he began to undo the hooks on the back of her bodice. In a moment she stood naked and he lowered her gently down to the bed. And the passage from girlhood to womanhood became an exciting, soaring experience that made Somi feel more alive than she had ever felt in her life. *'I'll remember this moment forever'*, she thought. When they were spent, pooled and exhausted in the linen sheets of their cozy bed, she rolled around on the bed and he had a hand draped over her body. *'No woman could ever love anyone as much as I love this man,'* she thought once again. He pulled her to him, hard, and kissed her deeply again. She was his desire. He held her in his strong arms, and she wished she could be there forever. He felt himself in love; yet there was always that element of separation. They had thus got the first-hand experience of living like that during their stay in the valley of Kashmir.

They had undertaken the holy pilgrimages as also visited the other places of interest worth mention. Tracking in the Himalayas and riding a motor-boat in the sea had been the major attractions for Somi. She however had lamented for not having been able to enjoy the swimming at the sea-beaches like Bob, as she didn't know how to swim. Ironically, Somi wasn't aware of the fact that the time had come for both of them to depart whereas Bob had known it from the very beginning about his limited short stay in India, and yet he had deliberately refrained from telling her about the truth and kept her in the dark for fear of losing her whom he really had loved profoundly from the bottom of his heart.

"*The validity of my tourist visa is going to expire in a couple of days. So, this 'Bharat Darshan' tour should also come to an end like everything else,*" Bob was thinking fast lying in the bed. He had found himself unable to sum up the courage to tell her at that juncture about his expiring visa in next two days and that he'll have to fly to his home country positively. He was at a loss to know how to tell her about his compulsion of leaving India. If she asks why he hadn't told her in the beginning, what explanation he would give her. Anything he would say is surely to be considered as a bundle of lies and far from the truth.

"*It would definitely be hard to make her believe whatever I say and try to convince her about the truth. At this time, I'm not in a position to say whether I shall be able to make another trip to India or not. I do love her through the core of my heart but what purpose would be served with my confession of love when I can't live in India with her? I now find myself in a dilemma and do not know how to overcome the situation like this. Throughout the tour, I had never bothered to seriously give it a thought, fully knowing that at the end of the tour this problem will definitely come up, and perhaps at that time, I won't be able to find an appropriate solution to that whatsoever. How to cope with it now is a million dollar question for me,"* thought Bob.

"This has been the golden period in my life. In the company of Bob, my love, I have been able to visit almost whole of the country, right from Kashmir to Kanyakumari and enjoyed my life up to the hilt," Somi was thinking. Feeling extremely happy and free of any worries, she had her glass of bed-time-milk as usual and went to sleep with pleasant thoughts.

On the night of 31st March viz. before the morning he had to leave, Bob told the Manager of the hotel they had been staying at, that they would be checking out in the early hours of the morning and as such cleared all the bills. He had also told Somi to pack the luggage as they would be checking out the next morning. Bob had already got booked, on line, two air-tickets for the first of April, 1995, one for his 'self' to fly over to Humberside, England (Great Britain), his native country and the other for Somi to return to Poona (now Pune), her home town. At the moment a vague thought had just cropped up into his mind as to what the poor old man would have explained to his neighbours about the sudden disappearance of Somi. But it was of no use thinking about such a thing at that time. Anyway, he had tried to make himself sure that she would somehow manage to give some suitable explanation to her father. With his guilty conscious mind he didn't dare face Somi for his shameful act of deceiving her at that juncture. The inevitable wicked thought had frightened him down his spine. He had kept on scheming to find a way out to overcome the most critical situation he found himself in. Ultimately, he had thought about 'an idea' and finally had made up his mind to implement the same with an iron will. Though he still felt sorry with his bleeding heart in her sympathy yet he couldn't help it in any way.

Of course he didn't forget to mix the doze of the sleeping pills in her glass of milk before going to bed.

CHAPTER – 2

∞

After having a hearty sleep, Somi woke up quite fresh in the morning. She was immensely pleased to be such a lucky girl, for having enjoyed the company of Bob whom she loved through the core of her heart. *'He certainly has come like a god-given gift into my life'*, she thought in her mind and was happy to think again, *'He too loves me very much that had made it possible for both of us to visit almost all the major attractions of the whole of India, during the 'Bharat Darshan' tour, right from Kashmir to Kanyakumari, the feat which even remotely I could never have achieved in years.'*

While the weather outside had been a little cold in the valley of Srinagar, it was quite warm inside the room. Lying comfortably in the cozy bed, she fascinatingly looked up and caught the sight of the beautiful chandelier hanging from the ceiling of the room. On hearing a knock at the door she looked for Bob to open it as usual. However, thinking that he might be in the bathroom, she herself got up to answer the door bell. There stood the room-service-boy holding the tray for the bed-tea. He placed the tray on the table. While going out he said to somi: "Sahib had called for a taxi in the morning and had left for the airport," before closing the door behind him.

'So Bob has made me the First April Fool,' she thought in her mind with a sweet smile on her face as, per chance, that day just happened to be the first of April. Sipping her tea, she just noticed an envelope lying at the table. She couldn't wait to finish the tea and out of sheer curiosity picked up the envelope and opened it with gusto, hoping for a surprise

gift in it, like Bob had done many a time earlier also during the tour. *'Again a love letter perhaps,'* she had thought in her mind. It was only going hurriedly through its contents that she had fainted instantly and fell upon the bed. On attaining consciousness a little while after, she had tried to compose herself and gone through the letter with a cool mind once again which read:

"Dear Somi, my love!

Attached with this letter is the air-ticket booked in your name for Pune, your home-town. I'm also leaving herewith my wallet containing some money to meet your immediate needs. I have paid all the bills of the hotel and the Receipt is kept in the wallet. I'm sorry I couldn't tell you beforehand that the validity of my 'Tourist-Visa' is going to expire tomorrow. My guilty conscious too despises me for the injustice I have done to you. Believe me my heart still bleeds for you. It may be perhaps beyond your imagination that how strongly I wished to remain in India forever but had to go against my wishes forcing myself to act in accordance with the 'Law of the Land'. I couldn't dare face you for the shameful act of mine. I'm therefore left with no other option but to leave India by tomorrow morning. You may also leave before the check out time by the forenoon. I have no words to thank you for your love and the company you have given me during my short stay in India and I will always cherish your sweet memories throughout my life. God willing if I ever get a chance to visit India again, I would definitely like to see you. Please forgive me. Sorry once again. Yours etc.—Bob."
The letter was signed by Bob with the date of the previous day, the 31st of March, 1995.

Having recovered from the initial shock she wiped off her tears. Collecting her petty things lying hither and thither in the room she finally packed up her bag and checked out from the hotel in the forenoon itself, as directed in the letter. She had been thinking about her foolishness all the more as even having spent so much time with Bob she still vaguely knew that he belonged to some place in England (Great Britain) and nothing else. Being of a guilty conscience from the very beginning Bob too had never disclosed his real identity. Prima facie his sole purpose appeared to be just enjoying the tour in the company of Somi. He had become very fond of her at the first sight and succeeded in luring her by expressing his love for her. Strangely enough, the way he behaved during the tour by taking the holy dip and performing the pooja (worship) at certain places of the pilgrimage, he had tried to establish or rather prove himself a cent percent Indian and nobody could ever have imagined that he could do a thing like that. However, it was of no use crying over spilt milk any more.

During the tour a lot of travelling was made by air in order to save the precious time as Bob wanted to make maximum out of his tour before the expiry of his visa. That had greatly helped Somi to learn about all the customs and the formalities to be completed at Airports. Accordingly, Somi had reached the Airport well before the check-in time and presented herself at the counter. She was, however, told to wait for the arrival of the flight she was supposed to board. As for the luggage she had only a small bag and was told that she could carry the same with her to be kept in the luggage-duct above her seat in the aircraft. She had to wait for a couple of hours as the flight was delayed on account of the bad weather, as announced on the P.A. system a number of times. Finally after about two and a half hours, her flight had arrived.

While boarding the plane, the first thought that had come to her mind was about her father whom she had abandoned for no fault of his. *'He too could have deserted me at the railway platform'*, she thought, *'when I was just a little kid. What reward I have given him for his kindness and also bringing me up for so many years?'* Strangely enough, no such thought had come to her mind while leaving with Bob on the tour. She had started feeling sorry for her wrong-doings and didn't know how to repent.

"We are just starting our descent into Pune," said the captain's voice on the tannoy. "If you'll fasten your seatbelts, return your seats to their upright position......."

Somi was only too glad to oblige. She loved flying. The stewardess smiled obsequiously as she collected the cups of coffee that Somi had sipped during the journey; she had been fascinated by Somi's charms and was sure she was some kind of Indian royalty. Or may be a film star, someone she just didn't recognize. Who wore diamond studs like that? They were almost the size of pebbles.

She gazed uneasily out of the window as the plane came into land. On the one hand, the earth seemed horribly far below her; on the other she was foolishly glad not to be over water. She shook her head---stupid morbid thoughts. It was childish to have a fear of landing, wasn't it?

"Don't you worry, miss; it's a very safe way to travel," the stewardess said looking upon her gloomy face.

Somi smiled thinly. "I'm sure." She managed.

The plane grunted and shuddered as the wheels dropped down. *'All is over now.'* She tried to console herself with the thought, *'It could have been worse.'* She was here, and she was going to meet her father. The plane jolted. She pressed her head back against the soft cloth of her luxurious seat, but when she glanced outside, they had landed. A wave of mixed gloom and anticipation washed through her. *'How would I dare face my father?'* She thought. *'What explanation would I give him against his queries? Honestly, my act could be considered as elopement with a foreigner. It surely was a blunder on my part. I should have taken him into confidence and told him all about Bob. Possibly, he would have agreed and given his permission for the tour. But now it's all a mere speculation. It was my fault. Whether he would have allowed for my going on tour or not, is another matter, but at least I should have given him a chance to think over the proposed tour. What explanation he would have given to the neighbours, the band members of his pal Bhima and all other acquaintances, about my sudden disappearance? This is quite shameful for me and is unforgiveable at the same time. How am I to repent for such a disgraceful act of mine except that I'm feeling extremely sorry for all that happened.'* She would step off the plane and into a whole usual old life again. She came out of the airport and hired a taxi. As the taxi was approaching near her locality, she had become nervous and her heartbeat also was increased. She paid off the taxi driver and entered the street with a heavy heart. The crucial moment had come at last when she gave a knock at the door.

❧

CHAPTER – 3

'Who could be knocking at the door at this hour?' Mangal Sen had started guessing about the visitor. *'Dusk had fallen and the night would be approaching a little later. Bhima, had left just an hour ago and nobody else had ever bothered to visit me for weeks together except my help, who too had left after serving the meals to me a short while before.'* The knock, in the meantime, was repeated once again. Mangal Sen then, quite unmindfully, got up from the cot he had been lying on, and hurried through the courtyard to open the door.

As soon as the door was opened, Somi hugged her father with tearful eyes. He too, in a fit of joy had suddenly cried out so loudly that his 'scream' had instantly restored his lost voice. That was not less than a miracle which had enabled Mangal Sen to speak after a gap of such a long period. Sobbing, both of them, instead of going to their respective rooms, settled down on the cot itself. In anticipation of any queries her father was supposed to make, Somi, still unable to overcome her sobs, had wanted to explain the things herself. But Mangal Sen, caressing her forehead with fatherly love and trying to keep a check upon his emotions, asked her, "You must be feeling hungry I suppose?"

"No, they served the dinner in the plane itself." Somi told her father. "It was a direct flight from Srinagar (Kashmir)," she added.

"That, I think, could have been a long journey and you must be feeling tired. You better go to bed now and take rest. We'll talk in the morning," said Mangal Sen.

Having overcome her sobs by then and feeling a bit comfortable, Somi intended to make her father go to sleep. Surprisingly, she observed that he had been lying upon the bare cot without making the bed. In contrast to his being in a sound health when she had gone on tour, her father looked pale with a frail body and considerable weight loss. *'It's all because of me,'* she lamented. She then once again did feel guilty for causing her father an unbearable mental agony that led him torture himself like that and live with such an uncared-for life. She then drew the mattress, a bed-sheet and a pillow to make his bed and lovingly made him lie upon it comfortably. Finding it somewhat difficult to control her emotions, she too sat beside him for a few minutes, caressing upon his head and making him sleep like a child.

After some time, Somi went to her own room. She knew it beforehand that for years, both the rooms were very rarely locked. Of course, Mangal Sen must have used to lock them when she had been living in the Boarding School. She unlatched the door and as soon as she entered the room she had made a hasty retreat. In fact, she was greeted with a strange kind of smell that showed that the room had not been opened for a long time since she had left. In fact it was opened just once on a Sunday, after about a month of her leaving on tour, when Shyam Prasad, the Librarian, had called on, looking for a couple of missing books, Somi had borrowed from the library. Mangal Sen, then, having lost his voice, had gesticulated his 'help' to open her room and see if there were any books lying inside. It was at that time when Somi's letter, written to her father, explaining about Bob and her going on tour, was found from one of the books recovered from her room which had provided some consolation to the aggrieved father. It was deemed sure enough that, had that letter not been found by Shyam

Prasad, the survival of Mangal Sen had been jeopardized as the poor fellow had taken her disappearance to his heart. Anyway she had to keep the door open for a while to get the foul smell out and let the fresh air inside the room. Sweeping or dusting at that hour of the night, didn't look appropriate to her. She then resolved to do it the next morning itself. As for the night, she just made her bed and went to sleep in no time.

Back home in Humberside, England, Bob was having nightmares about Somi and felt unrestful for weeks together. He had realized of having been actually in love with her and lamented very much for abandoning her. He was ashamed for having betrayed her trust in spite of the fact that she had surrendered herself to him completely and gone to the extreme of even losing her virginity on the altar of love. And what did she get in return? Remorse, humiliation and disrespect from all corners. The sense of guilt had followed him everywhere. Not gone a day when he wouldn't remember her and the happy time they both had enjoyed. He would off and on turn to the album that contained the photographs taken together of the sweet memories

Somi looked absolutely stunning in her profile picture. He felt his gut clench and for seconds he was lost in that beautiful smile. *"I still love her."* The thought blind-sided his brain for a split second before better sense could dismiss it as a knee jerk reaction.

In that smile, he re-imagined a million memories. He remembered their first meeting in the library and how nervous he had been. Their first kiss...he still didn't know how he had summoned the courage to suggest it. She said no. He kissed her anyway. She didn't back off. He didn't know if he was doing it right. Then her arm wrapped around his neck and then the other. He loved her so much. The world couldn't have been more right. He remembered the day he saw her when he waited for her across the road. She saw him from the other side and smiled her widest smile. *That smile*, he thought, *I still love her*.

He had spent a very long time telling himself that he had moved on, but the memories of her always surprised him with the intensity and ease with which they pervaded his mind. His mind would spring into denial at these moments ignoring everything that followed the happy days and constructing a fairy tale of a future that could never happen. It was intoxicating, and he would allow his mind to run amok till he was rudely brought back to reality. His mind insisted on going all the way through the troubled times that followed.

It was quite late, after the sunrise, when Mangal Sen woke up. Poor fellow didn't have a sound sleep for weeks together. By the time Somi had finished the sweeping and washing of the house premises neat and clean. The things, in her room, were still lying in place as she had left them. However they were all covered with dust. Thanks to the help, the stove and a few utensils of daily use other than the frying-pan for preparing tea and the hotplate etc. were kept duly washed at the usual place in the corner, used as a permanent kitchen for years. On hearing a knock at the door, Somi inquisitively looked towards her father.

"He could be the help from Bhima's band," said Mangal Sen and added, "He used to come daily to take care of my needs and do the other household chores in your absence." She, then, unlatched the door. The help came in and was surprised to find that Somi had come back. Somi, at first, felt a little humiliated but then thanked the help for his services rendered to her father. Back to his band he told Bhima and others about Somi's comeback from the Bharat darshan tour as had already been revealed to them by Mangal Sen after the discovery of Somi's letter from the library's book. The whole of 'Bhima and party' then made a point to come and greet her at the expense of Mangal sen that night.

Mangal Sen's joy knew no bounds. He had been feeling as if having got a second lease of life. Looking at her he had felt once again that he had a purpose to live. Before that he always used to lament that he had saved so much money just for nothing. To him 'Somi' and only 'Somi' was everything. In fact his heart did beat only for Somi. Soon, the help was relieved of serving in the kitchen, as she had started to manage her daily routine of doing household chores herself, like she had been doing before.

Ever since the day, Somi had returned from her 'Bharat Darshan' tour, Mangal Sen had really been very happy. But the happiness didn't last for long. All his hopes were shattered when one morning all of a sudden Somi broke the news, taking her father in to confidence. She, with little hesitation, had revealed that she had become pregnant after having physical relation with Bob, her beloved.

CHAPTER – 4

❧

H e was born with the silver spoon in his mouth in Poona (now Pune) in the year 1958. His original name was christened as 'Mangal Sen' at the time of his birth. He had been very cute and handsome even in his childhood. His beautiful eyes looked as if having some kind of magnetic power to attract one and all. His face always adorned an enviable sweet smile on his lips. To the delight of his parents, even people from the neighbourhood had become quite fond of him and used to be trying to have a close look of the child on one excuse or the other. They would very often take him in to their lap, cuddle him and hug him lovingly. Drawn towards his charming physical gestures everybody would try to develop some kind of love or intimacy with the child whatsoever.

Veer Sen, his father, was a well known businessman and their residence was quite famous as 'Veer Sen-ki-Kothi' in the vicinity of the whole area. Perhaps, only the word 'huge' would fit appropriately to the Kothi. But its vast expanse had proved the main hindrance in its upkeep with the result that it remained for years in a very dilapidated condition. In fact it had been a shame watching what'd become of it over the last few years. All it ever needed was for someone to care for it. People seem to take it for granted that it won't ever change. Had a little attention were given, it would never have ended up like that in the first place. However, it's always better late than never. That was the time when Gyan Bihari, alias 'Gyanu', a well known contractor in horticulture business was engaged who had assured to

19

change the overall look of the Kothi's lawns and garden etc. with his professional expertise. He had summoned his team of gardeners. One could see a couple of nursery trucks also. He had got them parked in the drive-way. The workers congregated in groups, began to unload the bushes and low flowering plants from the trucks. They stacked them into wheelbarrows and rolled them to their appropriate spots. It was the rose garden that attracted the most attention. Gyanu himself grabbed a set of pruning shears and headed towards it, joining the half a dozen workers who were already waiting for him. Beautifying the garden struck him as the type of job where it was impossible even to know where to begin with, but Gyanu simply started pruning the first bush while describing what he was doing. The workers clustered around him, were whispering to one another, as they watched and then finally dispersed when they understood what he wanted. Hour by hour, the natural colours of the roses were artfully exposed as each bush was thinned and trimmed. Gyanu was adamant that few blooms be lost, necessitating quite a bit of twine, as stems were pulled and tied, bent and rotated, into their proper place. By the evening, everything began to take shape. Once the yard was mowed, bushes were pruned, and the workers started edging around the fence posts, walkways and the Kothi itself. Needless to say that Gyanu had really done a good job leaving the mark of his professional expertise all over the place.

Entering through the main gate one would find a green and well mowed grassy lawn. There was a hedge that looked trimmed to perfection. There were flowers everywhere in rows running alongside the hedge on all sides. The rose garden looked all the more beautiful which adorned in the centre. The Kothi was surrounded by the boundary wall made in brick-and-stucco, a kind of plaster or cement used for coating wall-surfaces or moulding into architectural decorations. Inside, the lobby, the drawing room, the living room etc. had been beautifully maintained. It was a double storey building with four bedrooms, one at the ground floor and three on the first floor, all of them with attached bathrooms and toilets. The whole building seemed like freshly painted. The large hall in the centre of the Kothi served the purpose of drawing room where a pair of sofa-set, was placed, one each quite opposite each other, against the walls in the north and the south. Likewise, a pair of beautiful central table duly polished light brown with a durable glass of standard thickness fitted artistically on the top were also placed before both the sofa-sets. The maid had standing instructions to change the flowers daily in the flower-vase which decorated both the centre tables in the drawing room. The floor-to-ceiling glass-windows, were fixed, one each, in the eastern and the western walls of the hall, meant for sunlight which looked as permanently closed and covered with heavy curtains of fine fabric. While there was a small pantry on the first floor to be used at odd hours, the main kitchen could be found on the ground floor in the south-east corner of the house. Outside the kitchen a round dining table of large-size, and that too with the heavy glass-top was seen with a set of six chairs placed elegantly around it. Quite adjacent to the left side of the building, there was a garage that looked spacious enough for parking a couple of vehicles. In the foreground there was a central roundabout surrounded by the approach way leading towards the portico.

Unlike his father, Veer Sen had been in good health with a robust athletic body since he crossed his adolescence. He had been very health conscious even in his childhood. He was a good runner and while in school he used to run race with his class-mates. Later on, being a fast runner, he had participated in a number of race-competitions as well and won trophies and shields which now adorn the shelves in his room. He was very proud of his achievements and often used to narrate the stories about the very tough competitions he had won, while attending to the dinner parties off and on with the persons of high profile. He had always wanted to look like a body-builder but didn't have time to go to the gym. Alternatively he had a small personal gym of his own on the back of the garage, fully equipped with an electric racing machine, dumb-bells for muscle-building exercise, a stationary bicycle and such other equipment and accessories required of a gym. He was a handsome, tall and fair-haired with startlingly light grey eyes. He looked young enough and would do a hundred push-ups and sit-ups daily. Though he has been in the habit of going to bed in the late hours at night, yet he would hardly miss his routine of going to his gym in the early morning itself. With the stoutly built body he possessed a charming personality as well. Very fond of wearing branded clothes, his wardrobe was full of bespoke suits and nice dresses. A dozen of matching designer ties could be seen hanging in it. He would manage with just half a dozen shoes that always looked freshly polished. He was in the habit of keeping himself tip-top and never looked less than a film star when coming out in his antique 'Ford'. A well educated person, he was a successful businessman also and had made his niche in the ranks of high society. He was, in short, quite capable of impressing anybody with his innocent good looks and was envied undoubtedly by young ladies.

Savitri Devi, his mother, was married to Veer Sen about nine or ten years back. She too was strikingly beautiful at the time of her marriage. She was tall, with black hair and gold-flecked brown eyes, set in almost perfect features. Her sleek dresses always outlined a firm, stunning figure. She had a creamy skin and a beautiful necklace adored her neck. Incredibly costly and delicate matching earrings dangled from her perfect lobes. Being a religious lady she would leave her bed early in the morning before sunrise. As per her daily routine, she would take her shower and devotedly say her prayers before the statuette of the deity installed in the niche of a wall in her room. Even after such a long period of her marriage she couldn't conceive and had been longing for a child to play in her lap. She would regularly give some amount in charity to help the poor and needy. On a particular day she would offer food to the roadside beggars with the help of her driver and also give alms to any mahatma coming at the door.

Maya Devi was the aged mother-in-law of Savitri Devi and possessed a weak and frail body. She was a staunch devotee of Shri Sai Baba of Shirdi. Having become old enough, she too had very strongly wished for a grandson at least, before her leaving for her heavenly abode. A few years back, she herself had been to Shirdi on a pilgrimage with a small group of devotees and paid her homage in the Samadhi Mandir of the Baba. She was obsessed with her strong faith in the supernatural powers of Shri Sai Baba. However, when even after four years of the marriage of her son Veer Sen, her wish of becoming the grandmother, didn't seem to materialize, she thought to have recourse to Shri Sai Baba and made up her mind to visit Shirdi and seek His blessings. She then had a talk with Savitri Devi, her daughter-in-law. Explaining about the supernatural powers of the Baba she told her the miracles she had heard from the people whose wishes were fulfilled by the blessings of Shri Sai Baba. She then coaxed her to think over it seriously and go for the visit to Shirdi. Savitri Devi then discussed the matter with her husband Veer Sen who promised to take the family to Shirdi next month as he had a very tight schedule for the time being. Thus the visit was postponed for a month. Well, he didn't keep his promise even after the month and came up with some other excuse to postpone the visit to the next week. Savitri Devi was very much excited at the thought of the ensuing trip and also asked her mother-in-law to keep herself ready for the pilgrimage. However, when Veer Sen couldn't make it once again, Savitri Devi got annoyed with the disappointment to the extent that she had decided to go alone with her mother-in-law. Accordingly, she had asked Veer Sen to at least spare the Ford for a day in order to facilitate their visit. Likewise the driver was also instructed to check the car, get it fueled, and keep it ready for the long journey.

The very next day, the car had come quite earlier than expected. Both, Maya Devi and Savitri had become ready with their bag and baggage, waiting for the car to arrive. And as soon as the sound of the car purring in the porch was heard, Savitri Devi hurriedly came out with her mother-in-law. The driver came out and opened the rear door of the car. The old lady was then helped to sit comfortably on the rear seat. She then asked the driver to check that the bottles of drinking water, a thermos flask with hot tea, snacks and biscuits, as well as the lunch packs for all the three of them, which had been prepared by the maid in the early morning, a pair of towels etc. was kept in place. Having satisfied with the arrangement, she made herself seated beside her. She then signalled the driver, enchanting the name of Shri Sai Baba and the car geared up towards the shrine. That was perhaps the golden opportunity in years for both the ladies coming out together. While the grandma had already been to shirdi once, a few years back, for Savitri Devi that was her maiden journey. to the Shrine. The whole of the journey was quite comfortable. On their way, Savitri Devi enjoyed the sceneries running alongside, as well as fresh air coming from the window. However, her mother-in-law dozed off after a little while.

On their way, they had to make short stoppages twice for a few minutes to have tea and snacks etc. and reached Shirdi well in time, just by the afternoon. Once inside the Samadhi Mandir, both of them bowed before the deity with full reverence. Savitri Devi then, with her mother-in-law, paid her obeisance with utmost devotion to Shri Sai Baba and prayed for His blessings for a child. She had also taken a 'vow' that she would come again with her child to pay her obeisance. On coming out of the Mandir, all of them were feeling hungry. They had their lunch packs which they had brought with them from home, while sitting in the car itself. There was a market selling various types of memorabilia of Shri Sai Baba. They had purchased a small statuette of Shri Sai Baba and then straightaway headed on their return journey. That was Savitri Devi's first visit to have the holy darshan (glimpse) of Shri Sai Baba. Reaching home, she placed the statuette of Sai Baba in the niche of her room. She also had become a staunch devotee and having too much faith in Him she started worshipping Shri Sai Baba making it henceforth her daily routine.

On an early morning, grandma noticed that her daughter-in-law was vomiting. She looked pale and complained of feeling some kind of nausea. Maya Devi was an experienced old lady. She immediately got alarmed and sensing about some good news, summoned Veer Sen, who was still at home, and told him about Savitri. She then asked him to either take her for a check-up or send for the doctor to come at the Kothi itself. *'It will take some time for the doctor to come,'* thought Veer Sen. So, instead of waiting for the doctor, he preferred to take her himself to the hospital. In a few minutes he got the surprising news. "Your wife is pregnant," said Doctor D'Silva. "She is O.K. and there is nothing to be worried about," added the doctor. Needless to say that the family's joy knew no bounds and Savitri Devi's faith in Shri Sai Baba had got further strengthened.

Chapter – 5

⚺

The last month of her pregnancy was quite difficult. She was down with fever and chest pain with a kind of infection in her lungs. However, with His blessings she gave birth to a healthy male child on maturity. Being the wife of a businessman of Veer Sen's stature, special care was taken for the safe delivery of her child. Poor obstetrician and the doctors had to experience much difficulty at the time of her delivery. At a certain moment they feared as if the patient was sinking. But thank God, they were able to retrieve her. They had literally gone through a hell of time to assist for the successful delivery of the child from such a frail and weak patient. At the end of the day, however, all of them heaved a sigh of relief, like all is well that ends well. Her faith in Sai Baba had increased manifold after the birth of the child. She remembered her vow taken at the Smadhi and resolved in her mind to go and pay her obeisance to Shri Sai Baba as soon as possible. But having been of a very weak body structure she had not been feeling well since the day of her delivery.

The child, by the grace of Shri Sai Baba, had become the blue-eyed boy of 'Maya Devi' his grandma, to the extent that out of sheer love and unequivocal affection for her grandson, she would always call him just 'Mangalu' for short as his nickname instead of Mangal Sen. Consecutively, the parents as well as others also had started calling him by the nickname 'Mangalu' with the result that within a few days, the originally christened name viz. 'Mangal Sen' had fallen into oblivion. As his mother Savitri had remained consigned

27

to bed for quite a long time after the birth of Mangalu, his grandma Maya Devi had to take care of the child. He would be taken to his mother off and on for breastfeeding only. Grandma had her room on the first floor of the Kothi where she had shifted after the death of her husband Dheeraj Sen long back. An elegant photo of Mangalu's grandfather in a golden frame adorned the front wall of her room. Maya had placed her bed against the window of the side-wall, for sunlight and fresh air to come through the window. She used to keep her clothes and other belongings in a small wooden almirah lying in one corner of the room. Recently a beautiful cradle, with side-bars, was specially purchased for Mangalu. One shelf in the almirah was reserved for keeping Mangalu's underwear garments, nappies, pears' soap-cake and oil for massage and other essentials of daily use like talcum powder etc. required for the child. After the breastfeeding she would take him upstairs into her room and make him lie comfortably in the cradle. The seat of the cradle is slung by a rope for swinging it on, with an easy flowing rhythm. She would thereafter make herself sit upon the edge of her bed beside the swing, holding its rope and rock it gently to and fro in such a motion to make him sleep. She would often recite a short musical poem in rhymed stanzas (more commonly called 'lori') while rocking the swing and with the effect of the movement Mangalu would just close his eyes and go to sleep instantly.

In the beginning Mangalu was supposed to have been enjoying all the comforts of being looked after lovingly since his birth. But that was far from any speculation as good luck didn't favour the child for long. Initially, down with the chest pain, Savitri Devi, his mother, had developed a delicate membrane that covers the lungs. Later on the doctors had declared that she had been suffering from 'pleurisy' viz.

inflammation of the pleurae marked by pain in the chest or side of the body accompanying fever etc. The patient had not been responding even to the best available treatment. She lingered on and on for quite some time but ultimately had to succumb to the disease. However, a day before she breathed her last, she had lamented for not been able to fulfill her vow and opened her mind to grandma--- her mother in law, asking her to see that the child is taken to Shirdi, once at least, in due course of time to pay her obeisance to Shri Sai Baba. Her critical condition, as declared by the family doctor, had gotten further deteriorated and she left for her heavenly abode the very next day. Poor Mangalu, thus, had lost his mother even before the lactation period was over and was left with no other option but to be bottle-fed by his grandma.

CHAPTER – 6

That was really a great shock to the family. For Veer Sen it was no less than a scourge. He lamented the loss of his beloved wife and suffered from acute distress. All his nears and dears were there praying for him and the family to give them the strength to bear the irreparable loss. They had tried to console him, to make him a little comfortable and overcome the great sorrow. To cope with the situation Veer Sen was used to be compelled day in and day out by his close relatives coaxing him for a second marriage with the sole object that the infant shouldn't remain neglected at that tender age. Having belonged to the so-called well-to-do family, proposals for a second marriage of Veer Sen had started coming even before the flames of Savitri's pyre had extinguished completely. There was, in fact, no dearth of offers coming his way from certain families of equal status who would prefer to give their daughter in marriage even to an aged widower and father of a young one from his previous marriage but Veer Sen had always declined to accept any of such marriage proposals.

The main reason behind his disapproval of the idea and becoming dead against his second marriage was that, apart from his having become a little old, he too had the general conception that stepmothers are usually prone to ill-treat the stepchildren at the cost of their own comforts. Since Mangalu had become too favourite of his grandma, Veer Sen had wanted her to keep the child under her care as he was sure that the infant would be looked after well by her only. There was no doubt that Maya, the grandma, had been quite affectionately looking after her little grandson to the entire satisfaction of one and all. However, in due course of time Veer Sen had realized that she had become too old and should be free from any such burden at that age at least. Fortunately, a fresh proposal had come once again. He was told that his would-be bride was beautiful, well educated and also belonged to a respectable family. That she would not only look after the child but would manage the other household affairs as well quite efficiently. He was also made to convince that the little one should not be deprived of his right to enjoy a mother's love. Ultimately, Veer Sen was forced to give way to the heavy pressure from his close relatives supposed to be his well-wishers.

So, to the amusement of one and all, the second marriage of Veer Sen was performed soon after the mourning period was over. Thus Mangalu did get his stepmother and his grandma had to remain just a silent spectator. 'Mrs. Rani Sen', the newly-wed stepmother of Mangalu, was undoubtedly an amazingly attractive girl. She looked pulled together and beautiful from all angles. Her nose, adorned with a gold ring, was classic, not tiny and even, and her figure was slim with fine curves and not large breasted. She was clearly in her late twenties. There were laugh lines around her eyes and mouth but she had a serious face, not one that had done much laughing. She belonged to a neo-rich family of jewellers, who had made a fortune when the prices of gold and diamonds and other precious stones were escalated considerably and gone sky high. They had sufficient old stock of gold ornaments, diamond-jewellery etc. of their forefathers that helped them raise their status. However, as it generally happens with the newlywed brides, they seldom get any time to attend to housework. Instead, their priorities consist of the things like dressing up, doing make-up, sorting out their wish-lists and scheming to execute their long cherished dreams which couldn't be fulfilled prior to their marriage and had remained pending since long. Needless to say that 'Mrs.Rani' the newly-wed bride, wasn't any exception. She would keep herself busy in one thing or the other, looking over her outfit, feeling more stylish, and more perfectly chic, wore a single emerald-cut sapphire suspended from a white gold chain, strappy sandals and an ivory cashmere cardigan thrown over her shoulders. She liked listening to her favourite music, reading novels, enjoying T.V. serials, etc. reigning over the Kothi with full freedom. She always felt a sense of pride of having literally become the 'Rani' (Queen) in the real sense of the word after winning the heart of Veer Sen who was very much against his second marriage. She had virtually left the housework to the sole discretion of the housemaid. The task of looking after Mangalu couldn't find its place anywhere in her list of preferences which was supposed to be the sole objective of the marriage in question. Ultimately, it was poor grandma who had to continue taking care constantly of her little grandson. There was no doubt that she had really become too old but her strong will-power and unfading affection towards her grandson had kept her alive during the coming years.

Veer Sen, presently the sole proprietor of the 'Dheeraj Spinning and Weaving Mills' had inherited a fortune after the death of his father Dheer Sen who had toiled throughout his life and risen from rags to riches. In the flashback, Veer Sen could still visualize the days of his childhood when his mother would lovingly call him just 'Veeru'. Their family used to live in a dilapidated rented tenement in a chawl. His father Dheer Sen had worked very hard to look after his small family consisting of his wife and a son, selling coarse cloth on the road-side corner of a pavement. He also could recall the weak body structure of his mother with a pale face wearing a cheap and inexpensive 'saree'. She had never made any complaint or demand of anything and carried on the household chores with the minimum necessities which could be made available to her. His father had got him admitted in a municipal corporation school as he couldn't afford to pay the exorbitant fees of a convent school.

Remembering his early school days, Veer Sen could still recollect about taking his studies very seriously. He was quite studious, very brilliant and always attained first position in his class. In such schools, the boys generally form their own groups. Thus a rival group always felt jealous of him and never missed a chance to humiliate him on one plea or the other. One of the boys once complained that his lunchbox was missing and accused Veer Sen for the theft, who denied it out-rightly. Thereupon all the boys were asked to stand outside the classroom. The class-teacher, then, under his own supervision, asked the class-monitor to make a thorough search of their schoolbags. Surprisingly, the lunchbox was found in the schoolbag of the complainant boy itself. Having been quite jealous of Veer Sen and provoked by his so-called friends, he had complained out of mischief and got the scolding as such. While searching, the class monitor fished out a matchbox also from another boy's schoolbag. The teacher got startled on the discovery of the matchbox as that was beyond his speculation that at such a tender age the boy could smoke. The boy was then summoned before him.

"This matchbox is recovered from your schoolbag. Is it yours? Or somebody else has mischievously put it into your bag?" Asked the teacher.

"This is mine Sir. I've brought it from my home," replied the boy.

"What do you do with the matchbox in the school," asked the teacher.

"Nothing Sir," replied the boy.

"Then why did you take it to school?" asked the teacher again. "Do you try to smoke in the school toilet? Tell me the truth, and I won't punish you," the teacher added.

The boy still didn't dare say anything for fear of punishment. However, on further assurance given by the teacher, the boy said, "Sir, this is my father's matchbox who is in the habit of smoking 'bidis' and my mother always objects to it. As a result both of them use to quarrel off and on. So, I took this matchbox in my schoolbag while leaving for the school. Now my father must be looking for it but without the matchbox he won't be able to light his bidis. That way I would restrain him from smoking and thus prevent him to make any quarrels with my mother," explained the boy. The teacher was literally taken aback on the innocence of the boy who had tried in his own way to make his parents avoid any confrontation with each other and live in peace and harmony. In fact, 'Innocence' is the God-given gift to children. Poor boy could never think beyond it that his father could purchase another matchbox in order to satisfy his urge for smoking and thus making his sincere effort as completely futile.

During his school days, Veer Sen had, throughout, remained the blue-eyed boy of all the teachers as also the Principal of the school. As far as he could remember, he had never tried to make excuses to bunk his class or ever skipped the school, except on one occasion when he was down with fever, which later on was declared as typhoid. It was Harnam, one of his friends, who used to visit him on alternate days to find about his progress as also to apprise him of the topics discussed during his absence in the classroom. That surely had helped him to update his knowledge while staying at home. And on other occasions, whenever he missed the Bus, he always preferred racing towards the school and would generally catch up with the morning prayers. Even from his childhood he was very much health-conscious, wanting to have his body like an athlete. His favourite exercise was doing push-ups, sit-ups and racing which he could never do in the morning lest he would be late for the school and as such always did it in the evening. In brief, contrary to his other friends of his age, he had lived a much disciplined childhood with no spare time to waste for unnecessary things.

Immediately, on his coming back from the school in the afternoon, 'Veeru' would rush to his father with the tiffin, prepared by his mother. She used to have the lunch ready in anticipation of Veeru's return from school. Till then, poor Dheer Sen used to keep on waiting for him and both the father and the son would share their lunch at the pavement itself. Thereafter, the boy would sit a little aside on a gunnysack and do his homework. In those times the family could hardly make their ends meet. The puzzle--- how could his mother was able to run the kitchen with such a meagre income of his father, still remained unsolved in his mind. Years passed by and Dheer Sen got a respectable job with the famous 'New Textile Store' engaged in selling all kinds of fabric. Dheer Sen had coined a popular slogan---"FABRIC--- You just name it, we have it" and displayed it in bold letters at a prominent place in front of the Store. Within months of his joining, the sales-figures had touched a new high with the result that Dheer Sen was given a handsome raise for his honesty, devotion and hard work in the best interest of the Store. Over the years Dheer Sen had acquired thorough knowledge about all kinds of fabrics as he used to visit certain cloth mills also for stock-purchasing himself and was in rapport with the owners of those mills as well. Sometimes during the ensuing discussions, they would have his expert opinion in selecting the saleable varieties of fabrics for mass production. It was at that juncture when one Mahendra Kumar, who owned the Mahendra Textile Mills, had been greatly benefitted with the expert advice of Dheer Sen and made a substantial gain in his textile business. Very much impressed with his expertise and the future vision regarding the textile industry, Dheer Sen was offered not only a handsome salary but a small share in his venture also. Consequently he left the 'New Textile Store', he had been working with previously, and joined to work full time with his new benefactor the Mahendra Textile Mills. And after that he didn't have to look back. In the next few years he was able to float his own company the "Dheeraj Spinning and Weaving Mills."

CHAPTER – 7

❦

Veer Sen's business commitments had never allowed him to spare any time to either look after or interfere in to the household affairs. It had become solely in to the hands of Mrs. Rani who would do everything according to her whims and fancy. As a result poor grandma was left with no option but to continue looking after the child as usual. Rather than his stepmother, Mangalu was now more attached with grandma whom he used to call 'Daadi-ma'. Veer Sen himself never had time or inclination even to ask about the welfare of his son as if his duty was over after remarrying. He was perhaps under the impression that Mangalu was being looked after very well by his stepmother and as such had never cared to find out the reality. Since Mangalu's real mother had left for her heavenly abode when he was still a lactating child, he didn't have the slightest idea that Mrs. Rani was his stepmother. Contrary to the general perception that Veer Sen's love for Mangalu was at the helm of his second marriage, had proved just a myth. Surprisingly, Mrs. Rani too couldn't conceive for a good number of years and enjoyed her youth and authority to predominate over the Kothi. In fact, she could have poured out her love and affection on her stepson on having failed to conceive herself but regretfully that was not to be her cup of tea.

Mangalu's Daadi-ma was a staunch devotee of Shri Sai Baba of Shirdi. After the untimely death of Savitri devi, Mangalu had been looked after by her, since his infancy for so many years, who always prayed for his wellbeing. She was not feeling well lately and became bed-ridden for a long time.

Lying alone in her room, she looked at the golden framed photo of Dheer Sen that hung upon the wall over her bed, a strange thought had come to her mind and she felt faintly as if time had come for her to get prepared for her union with her late husband. And nourishing such vague thoughts, she called her grandson by her side, only a couple of days before her death. Extending her wrinkled hand a little, she caressed him on his back and said, "Mangalu beta! Just try to understand it seriously that with such a precarious health condition in this old age, I won't be living for long. So, listen to me very carefully. As you know, your father, Veer Sen, had often remained occupied in his business commitments, it was your mother, Savitri Devi, who used to look after the household affairs before 'Rani' came in."

"Savitri Devi? You mean, 'Rani' isn't my mother?" Mangalu was shocked to hear that.

"She is, in fact, your stepmother who came in after your father got remarried," told Daadi-ma.

"And what about *'my'* mother? Tell me where is she? Was she divorced on some account? What happened to her after all?" Mangalu shot question after question raging his voice curiously without waiting for any answers from his Daadi-ma.

"Don't panic Beta. Just cool down a bit," she murmured with tearful eyes and added, "Let me tell you the fact that your mother hadn't been keeping well during the last month of her pregnancy. After giving birth to her son, that's *you*, she developed a kind of disease called 'pleurisy' and didn't show any signs of recovery whatsoever. Then came a time when she became critically ill and even with the best available treatment, her life couldn't be saved and she died just within a month after your birth,"

Mangalu was greatly shocked on hearing such a heart rendering news about his late mother and hugged his Daadi-ma in grief. She too wiped off her own tears and consoled her grandson as well, to overcome the shock. In his quest to know more about his mother, Daadi-ma told him, "Savitri too was very much devoted to Shri Sai Baba of Shirdi. Unfortunately even after ten years of her marriage, she couldn't bear a child to become a mother and had a very strong longing for the same. Once, it so happened, that she had an opportunity to accompany me to visit Shirdi where she had prayed and sought the blessings of Shri Sai Baba for a son. She had also made a *vow* to come again with the child to pay her obeisance to Shri Sai Baba. In fact, her visit to Shirdi had become due soon after your birth but it couldn't be made possible on account of her grave illness and untimely death thereafter. Your father also knew about this fact but so far he had never bothered about the *vow* of your mother which the family owed to Shri Sai Baba. Since this was the last wish of your mother, it becomes your duty to honour it and pay your obeisance to Sai Baba with full devotion on behalf of your mother, as also for yourself. Now promise me that you will visit Shirdi and honour her vow. I wanted to apprise you of these facts lest I die and leave for my heavenly abode to unite with your late grandfather."

"Don't say things like that Daadi-ma. You're not going to leave me alone," saying that Mangalu became too emotional and hugged her once again. "I love you Daadi-ma and give you my firm promise that I'll definitely visit Shirdi and pay my humble obeisance to Shri Sai Baba and fulfill the vow of my mother as well," he added. And after three days when Mangalu awakened in the morning, his Daadi-ma was no more. She died in her sleep, leaving Mangalu heart-broken in his grief.

"Yes doctor," Rani said, "I'll do that." And the next minute, she was on the telephone giving Veer Sen the breaking news about her pregnancy. Needless to say that he, at first, wouldn't believe in excitement, asking her to repeat the news once again to confirm that he has heard it right. *'Ultimately God has listened to my prayers after so many years,'* thought Veer Sen.

It was a difficult pregnancy and Rani spent much of the time in bed, weak and tired. She lay there hour after hour.

On an early December, precisely the 7th of the month, Rani's labour pains began at around 04.00 a.m. and her moans awakened Veer Sen. He began hurriedly dressing. "Don't worry, we will be going to the hospital immediately," he told Rani, and then immediately telephoned Doctor D'Silva also.

The pains were agonizing and unbearable. "Please hurry," Rani said.

In her heart, however, she was confident that God would not let anything bad happen to her. When Rani and Veer Sen arrived at the hospital, everything was in readiness. Veer Sen was escorted to a waiting room and Rani was taken into an examination room. Dr. D'Silva, the obstetrician took her blood pressure. She frowned and took it again. She looked up and said to his nurse, "Get her into the operating room --- fast."

In the operating room, the doctors were fighting desperately to save Rani's life. Since Rani was carrying twins in her womb, her delivery was very painful and difficult which posed serious threat to her life. Her blood pressure was alarmingly low and her heartbeat was erratic. She was given oxygen and a blood transfusion. It couldn't be made possible conventionally in the normal way and as such the twins were delivered by Caesarean section. The twins had

41

shared common umbilical cord. She was conscious and screaming when the first baby was delivered and the next minute the second twin was taken out. The Nurse who had assisted the doctor, was very quick and immediately tied the birth-mark tags upon the tiny wrists of the twins for easy identification of being the first and the second child.

Veer Sen heard a voice calling "Mr. Sen!"

When he turned, Doctor D'Silva came to his side.

"You have two beautiful, healthy twin daughters, Mr. Sen."

Veer Sen saw the look in her eyes, "Is Rani all right?"

"Of course, she is, but too weak and has to be hospitalized for more than a couple of weeks I suppose," said the doctor.

As soon as Veer Sen entered his office and settled in his chair, all the staff members came into his room to congratulate him on becoming father once again after so many years. "How did you all have come to know about the news?" He asked Ram Nath, his most trusted employee in the office.

"In fact, I had made a phone call at the Kothi," replied Ram Nath and added, "The maid servant had picked the phone."

"Is there any news?" I asked her.

"Sahib had taken Ma'am to the hospital after midnight, she informed me."

And after a short while I contacted Doctor D'Silva, the obstetrician at the hospital and asked her, "Is there any news about Mrs. Rani-Veer Sen?" Said Ram Nath.

"Yes, the couple has been blessed with the beautiful twin daughters," she replied.

"And that way, I was the first to know about the twins and disseminate the news to all the staff members. We had planned to visit the Kothi as well to congratulate her but learnt that Ma'am hadn't been discharged from the hospital as yet," said Ram Nath.

CHAPTER – 9

⟡

And so, by the time, Mangalu had two siblings---
his twin sisters. He seemed to be quite happy and
was also surprised to see that both of them looked very
much identical. Everyone agreed that they were the most
beautiful babies they had ever seen. There wasn't even a
small mole or some other identification mark on anyone's
body to distinguish one from the other. Of course, both of
them were healthy and unusually lively and the nurses at
the hospital had kept on finding excuses to go into Rani's
room and look at the babies. On the persistent requests
made by Veer Sen, just a week after the twins were born,
Rani was discharged from the hospital. However, Doctor
D'Silva had, as a special case, allowed Rani to go home
with the condition that she would take complete rest. A
resident-nurse had been arranged by the hospital who would
accompany her to stay in the Kothi itself for the time being.
She would be responsible for taking care of the twins as
also to timely administer the medicines prescribed for the
treatment, to the mother. In addition she would have to see
that the patient is given proper food as recommended by
the dietitian which was essential for her speedy recovery.
Strangely enough, no arrangement of such a kind was made
to look after Savitri in her illness when Mangalu was born.

Veer Sen didn't have time to accompany them. He
simply gave instructions to the driver to take them home
and hired a taxi for himself to rush to his office as he was in a
hurry to attend to some urgent work. When she reached the
Kothi with her twins and the staff nurse, it was the guard at

the gate who welcomed them first, and congratulated Rani, the 'mistress of the house', even before all of them came out of the car. Rani was shifted to the room at the first floor of the Kothi which had earlier been occupied by the grandma and was lying vacant for long after her death. It was a great surprise for Rani to see, when she entered the room, that it had been nicely decorated with ribbons and streamers and brightly coloured balloons. There were crudely lettered cardboard signs hanging from the ceiling which read: WELCOME BABIES. The room was filled with dozens of gifts, all of them beautifully wrapped. Rani could not believe her eyes. There was a rocking cradle, handmade bootees, embroidered woollen caps, and cashmere cloaks. There were French-kid button shoes, child's silver cups, gold-lined, and a comb and brush with solid silver handles. There were solid silver baby bib pins with beaded edges, a pair each of plastic baby rattles and rubber teething rings and a rocking horse painted grey with white spots. There were toy soldiers, brightly coloured wooden blocks and the most beautiful thing of all were a pair of silvery white frock-like dresses for the babies. It was beyond anything Rani could ever have expected. All the bottled-up loneliness and unhappiness of the past months of her pregnancy got vanished.

"Gosh! What a beautiful arrangement," exclaimed Rani. "Who has done all this?"

"It is Mangalu and the gang of his friends Ma'am, in whose company he remains all the while. Soon after receiving the news of his becoming the brother of the twins, he was seen rejoicing with his friends. And a day after, in anticipation of your coming home, they planned to do this thing. They bought the required raw material such as balloons, coloured streamers, ribbons, etc. needed for the decoration. Closing the door from inside, all of them got to work. They were busy throughout the day inflating the balloons of various assorted colours. However a good number of them had burst while blowing into them, one after the other, on very short intervals, making a resounding noise, as if something got exploded. Mangalu had asked me about the things which are usually required for the new-born babies and God knows where from he had got the money to buy all those gifts as well. Of course some costly gifts have been received from a few of the staff members of Sahib's office," explained the maid. Rani looked really touched on knowing about all that.

Inwardly though Veer Sen had a strong longing for another son, yet having become enlightened and a bit of liberal-minded with the passage of time, he wouldn't discriminate between a boy and a girl anymore. The twin daughters gave him another occasion to rejoice once again after a good many years since the birth of Mangalu. Messages continued pouring in from most of his relatives and well-wishers. On their moving into the Kothi, a nursery suite was set up for them which contained a large-size cradle also in addition to the one received as gift from Ram Nath, slung with a rope for swinging it in rhythmic flow of movement for rocking on the twins to sleep, like it was purchased for Mangalu a few years back. As it had become customary, a band of eunuchs did register their presence for their 'neg' (reward) for the new arrivals. They had sung and danced merrily for hours together like they had on the previous occasions, on Mangalu's birth, the first issue in Veer Sen's family, as well as Veer Sen's second marriage, a few years back and got a handsome reward which Bhima, the head of their band still cherishes very proudly. And now, once again, they proved their mettle. The rendering of latest film-songs and the music by the band --- Bhima and party, had factually made the evening unforgettable for the times to come.

So far, the small tags tied by the hospital-nurses as the birthmark, around the tiny wrists of the twins at the time of their birth, had served the purpose of their identification. The first-born was named Nandini and her twin Shalini. By the time, the small 'birthmark-tag' was substituted with a pair of silver anklet which adorned the feet of Shalini for easy identification of the younger one. Likewise, after a few weeks, Nandini too was made to wear a simple pair of tiny gold earrings after her ears were got pierced. In a few weeks Rani had observed quite uncommon and very strange characteristics of the twins despite the fact that they weren't the Siamese twins, except for the fact that both the twins had shared the same umbilical cord, she had been told. She then discussed the problem with Veer Sen and told him, "I have it keenly noticed that when Shalini, the younger one, cries on some account, Nandini too would follow suit immediately and start crying possibly on no account, without any valid reason or provocation. Likewise when one of them has a laugh or becomes happy the other too feels the same and acts like her." To look after both the young kids with such strange characteristics had indeed proved quite difficult for Rani, particularly when they would feel hungry and start crying simultaneously for the breastfeeding or otherwise.

"This is really something very strange and seems to be a matter of great concern," said Veer Sen. He further added, "I'm also a little worried to know about the strange natural phenomenon, yet I think that it could be just because they happen to be twins and are of too young age. Still I hope everything would become normal with the passage of time when they grow up in the years to come."

In due course of time Rani had further observed that Shalini, the younger one, seemed more responsive and was first to crawl on her hands and knees, which too was followed by Nandini. Similarly, Shalini was first to talk and walk as well, whereas her twin, Nandini had just followed her sister and tried to imitate everything she did. Out of her love, Rani got prepared same to same little identical dresses for both of them, the same fabric, design and colour. Wearing those frocks they would become lookalikes to such an extent that even Rani would get confused that who was Shalini, the younger one. Thus in order to distinguish between the two, she started dressing them differently in design and colours, in contrast to one another for an easy identification. But that didn't work for long. As soon as the kids started identifying the colours after a year or so, both of them would become stubborn to have the same dress which is worn by the other. If Nandini wears red, Shalini won't go for any other colour. Same was applicable upon their choice of the toys as well. Not only that; when one of them goes to sleep, the other would also follow suit. While playing or even otherwise, if one gets hurt her right knee and cries in pain the other would also catch hold of her own right knee and start crying with pain like her sister. Initially it was thought that she was just imitating her sister but when tears would roll down her cheeks, it was felt that she really felt the pain as if she too was hurt. Same was the case with their eating habits. At times, Rani would get totally bewildered with such kind of behavior of the twins. She would always spend as much time as possible with her daughters keeping an eye on them and minutely observing their childlike activities. Ironically, she never had time to look after her stepson Mangalu, when he was a little child and needed to be taken care of by her, which had been the sole purpose of her marriage. And consequently, poor Daadi-ma had been compelled to take the responsibility of the child in her old age.

CHAPTER – 10

❧

Though, her maid servant had also been there to help her, yet it had become a hell of a job to attend to each of them. Over the months when the problem became more acute Rani had a talk with Doctor D'Silva and discussed the matter in detail. She too got excited to learn about the things when Rani explained to her of the strange behavior of the twins. "For me, it's hard to believe in the first place, as this appears to be definitely the first and a rare case of its kind, ever reported in my life, even elsewhere, in the history of medical science so far," said doctor D'Silva. "However, one thing that comes to my mind is that because of the twins having shared the same umbilical cord, they might have shared the characteristics of each other as well and inherited the each other's common feelings, which are now seen in their behavior," she added.

On her advice, the twins were taken to the hospital also for a thorough check-up, where they were subjected to various types of tests, but no kind of any abnormality was detected. The doctors were baffled over the results to find that even the slightest indication of any ailment couldn't be seen throughout the whole exercise. Apart from a good number of physicians a couple of psychiatrists were also consulted to examine them but nobody could help or suggest how to overcome such a strange phenomenon. Consequently poor twins had to suffer off and on with no individuality of their own. In a way it seemed as if they happened to be having one soul bifurcated in separate bodies, a cruel joke of the destiny indeed. When one of them goes for peeing, the other would also wet her huggies. When one looked happy the other would feel delighted. If one feels sorrow the other would get depressed. Both the kids were extremely sensitive to each other to the extent that if Rani screws her finger to Nandini's armpit to stimulate her for a laugh, the other will automatically feel the same and would laugh uncontrollably even if put in a separate room down stairs.

Dr. D'Silva had personal regard for Veer Sen. On his persistent requests to see how to overcome a situation like that, she tried to explain to him, "There hardly seems to be a definite solution to such a strange problem, yet according to the final outcome of the mutual discussions I had with the doctors and the psychiatrists about the problem, I would like to suggest that the only remedy which comes to the mind is, that both the children ought to be brought up separately in different environments. The purpose behind such an idea is that the distance, such involved in their separation, may trigger some positive effect on their behavior. It would be better to get one of the twins, as such, be admitted to a good public school having boarding and lodging facilities. So, let's wait and see how it works. This is for the betterment of both, the children as well as the parents, equally, I hope."

When Veer Sen informed Rani what the doctors had suggested, she out-rightly rejected the proposal. She pleaded that both the children were her heart and soul and she couldn't think of living without them. She had made up her mind and showed her willingness to cope with the situation and face the challenges as they come, whatsoever. She was, in fact, unable to foresee the implications involved with the lives of both the kids for not having their separate identity in the long run. They could fight over each other's likes or dislikes on account of bearing the same feelings and attitudes, specifically with reference to the love or hatred about anybody or anything at any stage.

But the doctors had thought it otherwise. "It's not the question of their mother's willingness," said the doctors. "It is definitely the question of the twins who would have to live ahead a long life for which the parents ought to make some sacrifice for the sake of giving each of them their own individuality. Though that too, so far, is mere a speculation, yet the attempt to get it tried upon the kids, could be worthwhile, as also a unique experiment in itself which could make history if becomes successful." They had further opined, "In such kind of treatment, the faculty of forgetfulness could play a vital role in changing the behavior of those young ones positively who still happen to be at their vulnerable stage. On the other hand, once the child becomes grownup it would be all the more difficult to change his behavior with such a therapy of which he was supposed to have become hardened since his childhood. Moreover, once on becoming grownup with their behavior like that, they would definitely blame the parents as to why they were not taken care of at their young age,

Veer Sen was in a fix and didn't know what to do. He too loved the kids like Rani, but he had been wise enough to foresee the consequences in the near future for not agreeing to the proposal separating the kids for their own good. He then persuaded Rani and asked her, "Just think it over once again with a cool and calm mind. Perhaps that could be the only remedy which may change the life of the kids at that very young age which will ultimately help them to attain and enjoy their individual identity. And that it wouldn't be possible to achieve the positive results after the children become grownup."

"There seems to be another very important aspect which needs to be considered urgently. So far, the kids are too young to know or understand anything even if one of them is shifted to the hostel. But after the kid in the hostel becomes a little grownup she would ask certain questions and would like to know about her parents and at times may even insist on getting the requisite information. Just think over it as there must be some positive and convincing answers to the day-to-day queries of the child.

Though Rani had yet to make up her mind, it was hard for both the parents that which of the twins would be sent to the boarding school. While Shalini, the younger sister had her leadership qualities, Nandini never took initiative in anything and always followed Shalini. And that way Rani's choice was Shalini who would definitely adjust herself in the new changed environment. It was a very tough decision to part with one of the kids of such a tender age which was considered as essential for her future betterment. Veer Sen, then sought the help of his Office Assistant Ram Nath to make a survey and look for some good boarding school. Among the three schools they had short listed on merit, their first choice was the famous and well reputed Nanda Boarding School of Co-education. But unfortunately they didn't have any arrangement for children below four years of age. So the second choice fell upon the Vikram Boarding School for Children at Lavale located a little far off on the outskirts of the city. It was owned and run by Mrs. Kamlesh, the Principal. She had inherited a fortune from her husband lieutenant colonel Vikram Singh who had participated in World War II. After the war was over in 1942 he was supposed to be returning with his platoon but was declared as missing, on way back to his homeland, and since then there was no news about him. Kamlesh madam was considered a highly educated lady in those times. She loved children but unfortunately didn't have any of her own. She had observed that there was a dire need of opening a modern school which could provide boarding and lodging facilities to the young children, especially those of the working women, in the near vicinity. She happened to be a pious lady and to put her resolve in letter and spirit she began searching for an appropriate place which she found at Lavale, located at a little far off on the outskirts of the city. Soon her dream began to take shape and ultimately the school came up covering a vast area and equipped with all kinds of modern facilities whatsoever.

The Vikram Boarding School for Children was being run in a big newly renovated building with very spacious rooms. There were cradles and toys and a host of other material for children of different age-groups to play with. The air-conditioned rooms meant for the children were neat and clean. They looked superbly maintained with cradles fitted with side-bars. The teachers as also the nurses on duty in uniform looked smart enough. Special nutritious diet used to be prepared hygienically with changed menus daily in consultation with the resident dietitian. Only mineral water was used in the kitchen. The school had a small clinic of its own where a child specialist treats the children if there need be. A well maintained small playground with a boundary line of nicely mowed green hedge was also there. Overall it was a good residential school.

Veer Sen accompanied Ram Nath the other day. He had taken a full round of the school and was very much pleased with the arrangements. He had a talk with the Manager of the school and discussed the various formalities required to be completed before the admission of his daughter. She was hardly one and a half year old at that time. Fully satisfying himself, he explained to Rani about the school and the overall arrangements they have for the inmate children. But Rani insisted that she too would like to visit the school, once at least, to get the first hand information to satisfy herself before admitting the child in it. Being well educated herself she too had a brief conversation with the Manager. She discussed with the teacher and the nurse also and looked into their kitchen as well. She was really happy to see that such a residential school also exists apart from the normal schools run in the city. Only after that, she gave her consent to shift the younger daughter--- Shalini.

It had taken another couple of days to get her admission after completing the necessary formalities including the opening of a savings' bank account in the name of Shalini to be operated by Kamlesh Ma'am, the Principal, as her guardian. It would also be Ma'am Principal's prerogative to draw up to a limited amount for any undue extra expenses deemed fit to keep the child comfortable and happy due to her sensitive nature as explained to her. She was so touched and sympathized with the child's rare characteristics of sensitiveness, that she had willingly given her consent to be her guardian. Having no issue of her own, she also vouched to act like her mother with the firm assurance of keeping the parental secret about the child as long as possible.

"By the way, I would like to suggest you to get her sister also admitted here for which we could give fifty percent concession in the charges," said Mr. Raja Ram, the Manager.

"Thank you and I appreciate your generous offer, but there is a genuine problem with these babies for which they have to be brought up separately," said Rani. She had further added, "As I've already explained it to the Principal Ma'am, both the sisters, with some peculiar characteristics in their behavior, are very sensitive to each other. If, per chance, one

Chapter – 11

⟡

On the day of admission, both, Veer Sen and Rani accompanied the kid to the school. Shalini was very happy and so was Nandini at home. While Veer Sen sat in the office with the Manager, Rani herself had visited the room allotted to Shalini which was to be shared by three other children of shalini's age group. She also examined the strength of the cradles with side bars fixed for the safety of the children. She was allowed to taste the food that was being served to the children on that very day which was nutritious, tasty and hygienically prepared. On that day, Rani had shared the meals with Shalini. In a short while, she got quite emotional but forcibly checked herself from crying before her daughter at the time of leaving her. Of course tears rolled over her cheeks as soon as she stepped out of the school with a heavy heart. After they got settled in the car, she lost her control on herself and started crying bitterly. Thank God, Veer Sen was there to comfort her. He wiped her tears off and tried to console her. He had, then, asked her to just visualize a little, and see the bright side of the kid's future life.

On the very first night, before going to bed, she checked into the cradle with the pounding heart knowing well that Shalini wouldn't be there. She had a fear in her mind that Nandini may miss her sister. She, however, felt some contentment on seeing that poor Nandini was sleeping alone comfortably unaware of the fact that her sister wasn't sharing the cradle with her. In order to ensure the well being of Shalini in the Boarding School, it had become essential for Rani to see that come what may, Nandini must not feel unhappy on any account, fearing that it may have its effect on Shalini in the boarding school. So, all her demands, whatsoever, were to be met with a smile and without any hitch. In the morning, Veer Sen too looked worried about Shalini. However Rani told him, "I had a word with the Principal In-charge of the Boarding School to enquire about Shalini."

"She is quite hale and hearty and had comfortably slept in the night as well," Informed the Principal. "There hadn't been even a slight indication to show that she was missing her sister," she added.

Surprisingly, none of the kids felt the absence of the other. They were perhaps too young to take notice of any change. Initially, for a few days Rani kept on making enquiries on alternate days about Shalini. The frequency however got slackened to once in a week and so on, because of receiving satisfactory reports from the boarding school that the child had been doing par excellence as compared to the other children of her age-group. That hardly gave Rani any surprise as being a brilliant child that was expected of her. She was always up, to make some mischief at times with the sole purpose of just to make others laugh and enjoy. She would crack jokes, make stories with her own imagination and in her own way would reign over her friends. Even senior girls wanted to make friends with her. She had become the most favourite child in the school and was loved by the Principal, the teachers and the nurses alike. Thus the twins were being brought up separately in different environment as advised by the team of doctors supposed to be the specialists on the subject under consideration. Rani, however, used to visit the Principal off and on to have a look on Shalini and also have the firsthand report about her, who had by then, started calling 'Mummy' to the Principal. Rani too was called as 'Mausi' after she was introduced to her as the cousin sister of Kamlesh Ma'am, the Principal. Of course, Dr. D'Silva had remained constantly in touch with Veer Sen's family to check the progress of the kids.

It was the last Sunday of the month. In the afternoon, Rani was going to have her post lunch nap and also trying to make her daughter sleep beside her. All of a sudden Nandini screamed and started crying with pain holding the wrist of her left hand. She immediately applied some balm to soothe the pain and gave her a chocolate bar to divert her attention. But inside her heart, she was sure that it could be due to some injury that Shalini might have sustained on her left hand, which seems to have its effect on poor Nandini. The half-hourly chiming of the clock showed it was 3.30 p.m. In order to confirm her doubt, she tried to make a phone call at the boarding school. The phone kept on ringing but there was no response. By the time Nandini had finished her chocolate. It seemed as if she had felt relief in her pain and had gone to sleep after a short while. A little later she tried once again to contact them. On hearing the voice of the lady attendant who was at the receiving end, she asked her to connect to the Manager or the Principal Ma'am.

"Sorry Ma'am, none of them is available at the moment," replied the attendant and added further, "Today, being the last Sunday of the month, the Principal Ma'am has taken the children for excursion and will be back by the evening."

"Please ask the Principal Ma'am to give me a ring as soon as she comes, as I have to talk to her very urgently," said Rani.

Rani kept on waiting eagerly and hurriedly picked up the phone as soon as it rang. It was the Principal Ma'am at the other end.

"Yes Mrs. Sen. I have just come back and received your message. Is there anything specific you wanted to talk about so urgently?" asked the Principal Ma'am.

"Well, I was a little worried about Shalini. I hope she is alright," said Rani. "As I had told you about the sensitivity of both the sisters at the time of Shalini's admission, today at about 3.30 p.m. Nandini had all of a sudden complained about severe pain in her left hand. So I was afraid that it could be the effect of any injury which Shalini might have sustained," explained Rani.

"Of course, she is alright now. In fact, we had taken the children for a short excursion today also, as we do it on the last Sunday of every month. They usually form their own small groups and play different games on the lawns of the garden. Today, a few of them were repeatedly doing their front-rolling on the lovely grass when in one such attempt Shalini lost her balance and got her left hand sprained a little. However, she was given first-aid then and there, as we always have the First-Aid-Box in our school van. Now she is quite comfortable and has just gone to sleep now. Actually, when children feel free to play with each other, sometimes minor incidents do occur but since we all are here to look after them, there's nothing to be worried about, please rest assured," said the principal Ma'am.

"Both the sisters are around four-year old now, but it seems that the strange characteristics still persist in their behavior as usual," observed Dr. D'Silva, when Rani reported to her about the Sunday's mishap of Shalini, as narrated by the Principal Ma'am. Dr. D'Silva had, however, appreciated when told that Shalini has started calling her 'Mausi' whereas Principal Kamlesh ma'am is lovingly called by her as 'Mummy'. "Well, this could be taken as some positive effect. It is, however, advisable to let the arrangement be continued till some considerable progress comes to our notice in the long run," said the doctor.

As Nandini, his sister, was still too young to play with, Mangalu had freely started enjoying the company of his fellow mates devoid of any kind of worldly concern. He could easily be termed as a spoiled brat. Having failed in a couple of classes one after the other; he had completely lost interest in his studies and also used to skip his school off and on. He would bunk his classes on one pretext or the other. Even complaints from the Principal of the school regarding his absence had not borne any fruit. Rani had kept no stone unturned to spoil the child. She just used to simply pay his school fee as well as the fine imposed by the school authorities and never bothered about his studies or the homework assignments. The irony of the fact is that though she herself happened to be well educated and could have monitored his studies yet she never showed any interest in that for lack of any motherly love or affection for him. As a consequence of such a kind of neglect on the part of his parents, as well as on his own part, the boy could clear his eighth class exams marginally, at the age of fourteen, with just passing marks.

Owing to the fat pocket money Mangalu had never cared about anything. There was nobody to check whether he had taken his meals or not. His life had become totally undisciplined to the extent that he had become more or less like a vagabond and had always preferred the company of his friends. They, however, always used to enjoy life at the expense of Mangalu who had been in the habit of spending money like anything.

"Kajara mohabbat wala, akhiyon mein aisa dala,
Kajarey ne ley lee meri jaan, Haiye re mein tere qurbaan."

.

"Wow! What a beautiful and melodious song," exclaimed Mangalu, hearing it attentively, to his friends, as soon as the lyrics of the song from a newly released film, being echoed in the air, had gone into his ears.

"It seems that some musical programme is going on somewhere nearby," said one of his friends.

The voice of the singers was really attractive to the extent that the listener, having a little taste in music, would find it hard to restrain himself and would be drawn towards it like a magnet. Mangalu, too, who happened to be walking in the company of his friends alongside the common footpath, after seeing a movie from a nearby cinema hall, was drawn towards it. Out of curiosity, all of them hurriedly took the turn in the direction the sound had been coming from. They were surprised to find that a group of young people had been performing popular dance numbers before a small crowd surrounding them. Their make-up and other physical gestures clearly revealed that all of them belonged to the Eunuch community. The gathering swelled a little with the joining of Mangalu and his friends. On a little coaxing by Mangalu, they had given a repeat performance of "Kajara mohabbat wala…" as well as a few more melodious numbers. Most of the persons amongst the gathering had full enjoyment and had offered some money to the band of the eunuchs. Mangalu also was too delighted and rewarded them with a fifty-rupee note, much to the surprise of the band which in fact comprised more than double the amount collected from the whole gathering. That was perhaps the beginning of Mangalu's friendly acquaintance with the eunuchs.

It was at that juncture, when he generally used to pass away his time in loitering aimlessly, without any specific purpose, going to see movies with his vagrant friends, etc. Thus, it was at one of those occasions when he had chanced upon having met that band of eunuchs who had been performing 'kajara mohabbat wala.....' while he had been returning with his friends after seeing a movie from a cinema hall and got acquainted with them in the first instance.

Gradually and gradually, Mangalu, being obsessed too much, was drawn towards that band of eunuchs. He used to remain on the lookout for their day-to-day performance which excited him very much. More often than not, he too would join them to have full enjoyment of the song and dance. Along with his interest in music he had possessed not very sweet but a good voice also. At times he had given them some financial help as well. Having somewhat estranged relations with his own family, he would prefer to remain in the company of those eunuchs most of the time. At times he would join them in their bouts of taking drinks also and reaching home after midnight.

Mrs. Rani, his stepmother, always remained busy with her own daughter Nandini and never bothered to care about Mangalu who had remained totally neglected. As a result, except for collecting his pocket money he had no interest in coming home. His father was too busy in his office deals as before and never cared to spare a little time at least to see even his younger child what to talk of poor Mangalu. He too had made his daily routine of coming late at night. He will then have a peg or two of scotch, and relax in his armchair. While Mrs. Rani wouldn't bother about her husband and would be having a sound sleep with her daughter Nandini, it was poor maid who would keep on waiting till Veer Sen had his dinner and retired to bed after midnight.

While everything had been just left to the maid servant, it was Mrs. Rani who ruled the roost. She had got herself freed from any kind of responsibility towards her stepson except giving him pocket money and had never asked about the expenses he used to make. He would get almost any amount just on demand because she knew it very well that it was Mangalu behind the reason that Veer Sen had agreed to accept her as his second wife. Mangalu, however, having remained in the company of the eunuchs, had never cared to return at home before midnight. Having become money-minded, Veer Sen, the so-called father, also had never tried to know about the activities of Mangalu or the household affairs and was always busy, going in pursuit of money.

Time passed by at its usual pace. On attaining the age of four-plus, Nandini too was admitted in St. Mary School of Education for Girls--- a regular private school which had its own fleet of buses and was considered as having a good standard of its own in the field of education amongst the affluent class of people in the society. A regular school-bus used to pick up Nandini from the Kothi every morning and drop her back in the afternoon after the school hours. She too possessed a sharp mind like her twin sister and was brilliant in her studies as well. With her sociable nature, she was very good in interacting with her class mates who had always been eager somehow to make friends with her. Just within a few weeks of her taking admission, she had become the most favourite child in her class.

Chapter – 12

⚭

"Hello," said Ram Nath, picking up the receiver. "Sir, this is Ganga Ram gateman speaking from the godown.

"Yes, Ganga Ram! Speak up, what's the matter?"

"Sir, Mr. Kishore has just taken out two bales of shirting code No. DS972 containing 24 bundles each, and got them loaded on a tempo to send somewhere. On my asking for the delivery challan, he says that it would be sent from the office afterwards. So, I thought that I should confirm from the office. By the way, I've noted down the number of the tempo as a precautionary measure."

"Thank you Ganga Ram. You have done a good job. I'll see to it."

Ram Nath reported the matter to Veer Sen and asked, "Was there any order so urgent to be executed today itself?"

"Well, that is not in my knowledge at least,"

"I also have checked the order book. There's no pending order on date. I wonder, how Kishore has taken out two bales and to whom he has sent the shirting without any proper order or the necessary delivery challan?"

"The matter seemed to be serious. Don't you think so? Just call him to report into the office immediately," said Veer Sen.

"Hello Kishore! Ram Nath speaking this side. Sahib wants to see you to discuss something urgently. How soon can you come?"

"In about half an hour, I think," and Kishore replaced the receiver. Half an hour later he was sitting in the office.

Mr. Kishore was the overall in-charge of the godown of the Dheeraj Spinning and Weaving Mills, where the bales of the finished cloth pertaining to the different specifications and varieties were stocked. As per the procedure whenever an order was required to be executed, a delivery challan was used to be issued from the office against the Bill. Thus the goods were supposed to be delivered as per the details mentioned in the challan concerned. But in the present case, the proper procedure hadn't been followed which was reported by the gateman at the godown. As per the general routine, an inventory was used to be prepared of all kinds of the fabric produced and the stock-taking was done bimonthly.

"I've been given to understand that two bales of shirting code No.DS972 were sent to somebody. Was there any specific order so urgent that it couldn't wait till tomorrow?" asked Veer Sen.

"In fact there was a phone call from M/s. Deepsons Textiles who needed the shirting for onward despatch by the transport leaving tonight itself," explained Mr. Kishore. "There was practically no time left to get the formal order booked and the delivery challan issued from the office which I thought, could be done later on," he added.

"But you could have at least informed the office on phone about the telephonic order before making the delivery of the goods," reprimanded Veer Sen.

Mr. Kishore felt a little embarrassed, fetched the order-book and booked the order of M/s. Deepsons Textiles. He then issued the delivery challan also for two bales of shirting code No. DS972 to straighten out the record.

As soon as Mr. Kishore left the office, Veer Sen dialed the number of Deep Chand, the proprietor of Deepsons

Textiles, for the confirmation of the order, and asked him, "Have you received the goods?"

"Yes, of course. It has just arrived. In fact I have to dispatch the same urgently by the night transport. Thanks for the same."

"Well, could you please give me the relevant delivery challan No.?" asked Veer Sen.

"Sorry, there isn't any Bill or Challan," replied Deep Chand and added, "Mr. Kishore had told me that no bills or challans are issued for such a small quantity and also insisted for cash payment which he would personally collect tomorrow in the afternoon."

"You needn't make any cash payment as none of our employees is authorized to receive any cash payment. It seems that you have been misguided. On the contrary, Bills are issued even for a small quantity which has since been done in your case also."

"Possibly, Kishore would have been scheming to pocket the money, but for the information received from the gateman," thought Veer Sen.

Next morning when Kishore reached the godown, Ram Nath was already there waiting for him. Both of them got engaged in the stock-taking process, as ordered by Veer Sen to clear his doubts about the proper handling of the stock and keeping the accounts regularly. They tallied the stock of different varieties received from the Mill and delivered against the orders. Until lunch time all went well and the tallied figures conformed to those in the stock register. But in the post lunch session, the figures refused to tally. Sometimes the necessary entries for the stocks received were missing and on another time, the goods delivered didn't tally with the figures. Both the persons had checked once again with the office stock-book as well as the delivery challans and proper entries were made wherever required to straighten out the record. All the blame was thus attributed to the slackness in performing the duties by the in-charge of the godown. At the end of the day after doing the minus-pluses and making the necessary adjustments, four bales of the shirting code No. DS972 containing 24 bundles each were found short. After adjusting two bales of Deepsons Textiles, which were not taken into the account, there remained still a difference of two bales. Mr. Kishore couldn't give any suitable explanation for the shortage. The matter was then reported to the police. Since Veer Sen was a well known figure, a prompt action was taken by the police department. Kishore was then taken into police custody. During the course of enquiry he had made the confession that the goods were sold by him to somebody against cash as he was in urgent need of the money. While the amount was recovered from him he had requested Veer Sen for his forgiveness. However, on the request of Veer Sen, the police complaint was withdrawn but Mr. Kishore was fired.

Chapter – 13

❧

The greed for amassing more and more money always brings trouble at sometime or the other. Veer Sen too couldn't save himself from the clutches of adversity befallen on him. Mr. Kishore, in order to avenge himself, after having been fired, had made a complaint to the income tax department regarding the probable tax evasion with the result that Veer Sen's office was raided at dusk when it was being closed for the day. A whole lot of unscrupulous documents pertaining to the tax evasion were seized. As soon as the news about the raid reached Veer Sen he lost no time in going underground in order to buy some precious time to make certain arrangements for his defence. He had, in fact, gone deep enough from head to toe in his scandalous operation but perhaps failed miserably to plug the loopholes.

He had never told anything to Mangalu who was good for nothing or even his wife Rani about his bussiness affairs and carried on everything on his own with the help of a couple of his most trusted employees. The irony of the fact was that Mangalu, by that time, had become completely cut off from home and fully devoted himself to that band of the eunuchs. Sometimes he even won't come home and stay with them for the night as well. Both, father and the son wouldn't find a chance to see each other face to face for weeks together. Well, it could be anybody's guess that in such a kind of situation Mangalu could hardly do anything to help his father out of the whole mess.

The maid servant had just gone to answer the door bell but came back hurriedly with a gloomy face.

"What happened?" asked Mrs. Rani, looking at her face. Her tone had become a bit harsh than usual.

"Police," uttered the maid in a frightening tone. I had looked through the 'magic-eye' fixed at the door. There stood our watchman. On opening it a little ajar, he had just told me that the Police had come at the gate to have a word with the ma'am", she added further.

The bungalow, quite famously known as 'Veer Sen ki Kothi', was situated in the heart of the city. It stood stately at the corner of one of the cross-roads at the crossing which had the honour of bearing the name 'Kothi Chowk' in bold letters, christened after the name of the bungalow. It had a permanent fixed bus-shelter just near it, commonly called the 'Kothi Chowk Bus Stand' that facilitates the bus-passengers either to board, or to alight from.

"What the Police have come for?" Mrs.Rani had felt perturbed and started speculating about the various unfounded options as to what could be the reason of their coming to see me. God willing let Veer Sen be alright and not involved in some accident or the like. It was now for her to rush towards the gate, having her maid in tow to find out as to what could be the matter. It was beyond her imagination that Police could ever dare knock at their door. As soon as she approached the gate, the watchman unlatched it keeping it a little ajar. Mrs. Rani, then asked one of the police constables:

"Yes officer! What brought you here?"

"Madam, we have been sent to look for Mr. Veer Sen as his presence is required at the police station for some urgent work. We have just been told by your watchman that 'Sahib' has not returned home yet. So we thought it better to have a word with you to enquire about him," replied the constable.

"Oh, I'm so sorry. Of course he is not available at the moment. I'm also unable to guess his probable whereabouts at this time. But rest assured, I shall let him know about your visit and pass on the message, as soon as he comes," she told the constable.

Veer Sen belonged to a respectable family which had earned a good reputation not only in the vicinity of his bungalow alone but in the whole of the Kothi chowk area as well. The presence of the Police Van at the gate of the bungalow had prompted some passersby who, out of sheer curiosity, had come up to find out the actual reason of the police commotion at the gate of the Kothi. When the crowd began to swell a little, the policemen asked them to disperse saying that it was just a courtesy call and there was nothing to know about. Soon after, the police party also left the place. However, there still remained some people who appeared to be habitual newsmongers. Having nothing else to do, they always try to poke their nose in to other's affairs. One of those mischief-monger persons had tried to coax the watchman also to extract some 'news' but was abruptly asked to mind his own business.

Mrs. Rani had kept on waiting for hours. She had tried to contact Veer Sen quite a number of times on phone which apparently was either switched off or not reachable, being out of the network area. In such a restlessness state of mind, she had drawn an armchair to the bed-side where Nandini had been sleeping comfortably. She had been constantly staring at the phone with the hope that it may ring after the midnight with some news from Veer Sen who could have been held up for the night to accomplish some most urgent work which couldn't wait for the next day.

Chapter – 14

❧

The Nurses in the hospital had been running helter-skelter from one room to the other, looking for the surgeon or for any other doctor to come in to the operation theatre at once as the victim had been bleeding profusely. Presently the nurses had tried to block it with cotton pads pressed against the wound. From the small window pane she could see Veer Sen lying on the operation table. He had been stabbed in his back quite forcefully, she was told. But no doctor seemed to be on emergency duty, a nurse had lamented. The operation was very urgent. He has been brought to the O.T. without completing any of the formalities like filling up the forms etc. which could wait. But what could be done in the absence of the doctor? The next minute all the rooms in the hospital were seen locked up and there was no O.T. nor any nurses were seen anywhere. The place looked like a haunted one. The scene then shifted to a huge cave-like place. But even there, not a soul was visible. She had been crying bitterly and thinking that in that deserted place to whom she ought to call for help. On becoming helpless she screamed out very loudly. And instantly Mrs. Rani woke up and found herself in her chair sitting beside the bed and waiting for the phone call. When had she dozed off, she didn't know. What a terrible nightmare it was. She dreaded badly to recall it, still getting nervous and perspiring profusely.

Veer Sen neither came home that night nor he tried to make any phone call as he was afraid that his phone could have been tapped to know his whereabouts or else some police personnel in plain clothes may have been keeping a close watch at his bungalow. In order to escape from his recognition he couldn't dare even look for some hotel accommodation. Instead he preferred to approach one of his confidants to ask for the shelter at that crucial hour for the night and discuss about the whole affair also. He, quite frankly, had told him about the situation he was in and also asked for his help. His friend, in view of the famous quote: "A friend in need is a friend indeed" had welcomed Veer Sen with open arms. Extending his helping hand he had made his firm promise to stand by him come what may. After the dinner both of them got settled comfortably on the bed and tried to ponder over the situation once again to find out some ways and means of coming out of the whole mess.

As a result of the discussion he had with his friend, Veer Sen had planned to avail of the services of a competent advocate and adopt a specific strategy to defend himself by fair or foul means as his honour was at stake. Having firmly made up his mind he contacted a senior advocate of the High Court, whom he had known personally while attending a few get-together parties, at just an hour before midnight and apprised him of the facts as well as about the raid of the Income Tax Officers. The advocate who had a long experience of dealing with such kind of Income Tax cases, advised him to surrender himself at the nearest police station immediately before any arrest warrant is issued. In the mean time he would file the necessary application for his anticipatory bail. Once out on bail it would become easier for him to prepare the case. Acting upon the advice of the advocate, Veer Sen surrendered himself at the police station in the wee hours of next morning.

The advocate, on his part, had first of all, informed Mrs. Rani Sen and told her about everything he knew and

Chapter – 15

❧

Misfortune had not spared Mangalu yet and kept on following him to the extent possible. While Veer Sen had been facing legal action against him, Mrs. Rani, who used to give pocket money to Mangalu with a free hand, had flatly refused to oblige him any more under the changed circumstances. Thus Mangalu too, had been compelled to compromise with the situation. Coincidently, at that time, Bhima, the head of the band of eunuchs who had received the 'Neg' for Veer Sen's first marriage, and again on his second marriage after the birth of Mangalu, told him that his real mother had died in his infancy and that Mrs. Rani happened to be his stepmother, the fact which he already had learnt from his grandma. With the passage of time, the gap in relations between mother and the son had become wider. On the other hand, the bond of friendship between Mangalu and Bhima had become stronger. Neglected by everyone, Mangalu had now become pessimistic and had no interest in keeping any relation with his family.

While remaining always in the company of eunuchs for more than two years he too had learnt their art and openly used to perform along with them. He had become so mixed up with them that he had forgotten his own identity of being a male. He too would dress and make gestures like them while performing and the onlookers believed him also to be a eunuch. By the time his body features had become to show the elements of some change which had shed the look of an adolescent boy and started the process of transforming him in to a very handsome and charming young man. In fact, Mangalu's joining had proved a boon in disguise as the band had gained much more popularity on account of his charming performance. Their earnings too had become manifold.

Mangalu had also come to know about the secret of sweet and melodious voice of Jamila, the eunuch with good looking features who had been castrated in boyhood so as to retain 'soprano' voice suitable for a female singer. Likewise, Bhima, the head of the band too happened to be a castrato viz. castrated in boyhood so as to retain his 'alto' voice fit for a male singer. With those revelations Mangalu was able to solve the riddle about such a sweet voice of Jamila and Bhima which had attracted him on listening 'Kajara mohabbat wala….' in the first instance. As far as the other members of the band were concerned, all of them happened to be eunuchs by nature, Mangalu was made to believe.

As a matter of fact, most of the eunuchs were the result of forced castration. The method adopted for the surgery was very crude, unscientific, threatening to the health of the patient and done in the most unhygienic conditions. The genitals of a normally born male baby were slashed off with a knife dipped in boiling oil. Indian legal statutes do not permit such forced castration of males and therefore utmost secrecy was maintained in conducting the operation called 'nirvaan' or 'mukti' because the act suggests a transition of the person from one life to another. The whole act is performed in the wee hours before the crack of dawn in the name of 'religious ritual' like the acceptance of 'deeksha' for a better life in the next birth, purely to conceal the barbarity and brutality of the custom and make it seem both acceptable and natural. According to a study, castrated or not, eunuchs are sexually active. As they cannot form intimate relations within the parameters of either acceptable or aberrant behavior due to lack of takers, they take to prostitution and become possible carriers of the HIV virus. Still, there are males who choose to live as eunuchs without ever undergoing the castration procedure.

Some fifteen years ago, in a police raid on a brothel in a Mumbai suburb most of the prostitutes were eunuchs. They were found to have deep gashes, cigarettes stubbed on their arms, scars of regular beatings and lashings. The police too, are no less. All eunuchs must pay 'hafta' to the police or risk being beaten up. They are rarely employed in regular jobs, though many would like to lead normal lives. They have no grudge against normal human beings because they accept their sexual identity as 'destiny'. Most of them lead a life of penitence and austerity, though not necessarily of abstinence, and practice bizarre rituals to win from God their one great wish: to be born as man or woman in their next life.

Chapter – 16

"Fetch me a cup of tea," Veer Sen ordered his maid servant as soon as he entered the room. He looked very tired due to the fatigue he had been subjected to during the past two weeks. The whole episode seemed to have deeply affected Mrs. Rani also who had been leading quite a carefree life since her marriage. Veer Sen got himself settled in the armchair lying near the window of his drawing room. He closed his eyes and began to ponder over the harrowing experience he had gone through. In a flashback he found himself how he was dead against his second marriage and how on persistent demands of his friends and other relatives he had bowed to their wishes with the hope that Mangalu would be in safe hands of his stepmother to be looked after very well to the satisfaction of one and all. Sadly enough, he himself had seldom cared to practically find about his wellbeing and had to remain contented with whatever information Mrs. Rani used to impart to him in respect of the activities of Mangalu. He had always been misguided and never knew the whereabouts of his son who had preferred to remain in the company of eunuchs rather than living with his own family at home.

Suddenly he woke up from his thoughts with a slight jerk on hearing the sound produced by placing of the plate with cup of tea on the glass-table, the maid had just brought in. The next minute, he had sent for Mrs. Rani and in no time she had showed her presence.

"I have since been given to understand that all is not well about Mangalu. Where is he?" asked Veer Sen.

Instead of replying directly, Mrs. Rani motioned towards the maid gesticulating her to handle the situation at that moment.

"He hadn't come home last night," replied the maid. "I had checked his room myself. Presumably, he had stayed with his friends for the night," she added.

"Ask him to see me as soon as he comes," roared Veer Sen rather harshly in his rage.

Fearing somewhat unpleasantness at that moment, Mrs. Rani didn't dare say anything. She had just nodded in affirmation to Veer Sen's instructions and went back to attend to her kid. In fact, neither she knew the whereabouts of Mangalu nor could anybody else. It was solely at the discretion of Mangalu if at all he may call or pay a visit to the Kothi on some errand and contact his mother in person. However, there was not the remotest chance of any such thing to happen.

The door bell had been ringing constantly and Veer Sen, sitting in his drawing room had become irritated that why nobody was attending to it. While he shouted with full throat to call the maid servant, she had already gone to answer the door bell and asked the watchman, "Who has been ringing the bell repeatedly?"

"These are the eunuchs from Bhima's band who insist upon seeing the Sahib very urgently," replied the watchman.

She then immediately rushed towards the drawing room to attend to the call of the Sahib. By the time Veer Sen himself had come out to reach the gate but met the maid halfway and asked her, "What's the matter?"

Becoming out of breath, she said, "A couple of eunuchs from Bhima's band are at the gate and wanted to talk to you very urgently."

"They must be making their routine door-to-door visit asking for alms. Just go inside and tell your Ma'am to ward them off by giving something to them," said Veer Sen.

"No, no. We haven't come for alms," said one of the eunuchs to the maid who was approaching them to give something, and added, "Ask your Sahib not to waste time as it is very urgent for us to talk to him immediately."

'There must be something serious', thought Veer Sen and asked the maid to send them in.

"Well, what is the matter so urgent you want to talk to me about?" Veer Sen asked the eunuchs.

"It is about Mangalu, your son, who, under the influence of liquor, had met with a serious accident and got admitted in the East Nursing Home located on the outskirts of the city. Looking at his precarious condition, he needs to be operated upon very urgently, the doctors had advised."

Chapter – 17

❧

As the saying goes that adversity never comes alone, it was a shock like a bolt from the blue, another addition in his woes as his income-tax case too had not been settled yet. The incident had awakened the lost love for his son whom he had neglected since his second marriage. He cursed himself for the carelessness of his duty towards his son with the result that the boy had gone astray. It had become very painful for him to learn that the boy had never taken his studies seriously. He had thought that with just paying the school fee his duty becomes over and there was no need to coax the boy at some reasonable intervals and know about the progress in his studies as well as other activities. After the water had flown over the head he found himself quite helpless and unable to compensate the loss.

However, it is better late than never. Veer Sen, with his sheer sense of repentance, had sent for the driver to come immediately. Soon the car purred in to the portico. On hearing its vibratory sound he hastily stepped out. The driver came from behind the car and opened the door for Veer Sen to enter and sit comfortably. He then returned to the driver's seat looking inquisitively for direction --- where to go?

"East Nursing Home," said Veer Sen. He was much eager to see his son and wanted to reach the hospital as early as possible to have the first hand information about the accident.

As soon as the car entered the gate of the hospital, Veer Sen jumped out of the door and rushed inside to see the doctor. A nurse introduced him to Dr. Ranjan who had attended to Mangalu earlier.

"Please come with me," said the doctor heading towards the casualty where Mangalu was lying on the bed. He had been given a heavy dose of sedatives to subside his pain.

"How about the injuries he has sustained?" asked Veer Sen.

"The preliminary examination has confirmed the nature of his injuries quite serious, rather critical which needs to be operated upon as early as possible and that's why I had sent for you to get your consent to go ahead," said the Doctor.

"Could you please brief me a little about the injuries he has sustained that require immediate operation?" asked Veer Sen once again with a visibly gloomy face.

"Unfortunately, he had the fall from such a height with an intense force getting his groin injured very badly and his genitals got literally crushed and grated, reducing them to small shreds," replied the doctor and added, "He has got a lot of damage to his lower spine also which too we have to operate upon immediately or risk his losing the movement. Please sign the consent form to enable us to take the patient into the operation theatre as the delay could pose a great risk to his life."

Poor father didn't have any option but to sign on the consent form to save the precious life of his only 'son'.

Since Veer Sen was a well known figure, a panel of senior most doctors had examined the patient once again in the presence of his father and explained the seriousness of the injury as the male organ of poor Mangalu had been crushed very badly on account of the tragic fall from such a height. The retrieval of it could be a herculean task which posed a challenge for the doctors performing the surgery. The case had been thoroughly discussed and it was decided to adopt a strategy of treatment in order to save the life as well as the damaged male organ (genitals) of the patient. They had discussed about the pros and cons of the operation also. The head of the surgical department (HOD) had appealed to the doctors performing the operation to take utmost care and make history in retrieving the totally damaged organ and saving the precious life also.

Time doesn't wait for anything to happen. It goes on its usual pace uninterrupted. So, keeping in mind the value of 'time' the doctors had hurried towards the Operation Theatre, praying in their hearts to give them strength for making the operation a great success which certainly would bring laurels to the whole team of the doctors. All of them were having hope against hope that the operation would be successful.

Chapter – 18

Veer Sen was escorted to a room, other than the common waiting hall and made to sit comfortably upon an arm-chair. Jamila, Zulfi and Massy occupied the bench lying outside the operation theatre. While the operation had been in progress, Bhima came to Veer Sen and sat beside him with a gloomy face. Narrating the whole sequence of the happening after a few minutes he explained to him, "As you know, there stands a cliff-like place on the outskirts of the city quite famous as a picnic spot. People used to come over there generally on the weekend to make enjoyment. The members of our band too had often visited the place earlier many a time to celebrate certain events. While that had always used to serve the purpose of our own enjoyment, it also had been the source of our making some extra collection of money from the persons visiting there with the sole aim of just 'drink and be merry'. But on today's fateful evening, the drinking bout had become perhaps a little heavier. Vary from anything unexpected, the members had indulged in to the dance competition among themselves. Enjoying to the extent, every one of us was so thrilled that un-cautiously, while dancing, we began to tread at the sharp edge of the cliff, showing our dancing skills and boasting about the heroic deed."

Taking a deep sigh he continued further and said, "Suddenly, under the influence of liquor, probably due to gulping down an extra peg, Mangalu had got slipped at the edge of the cliff, while dancing. Having failed to balance himself timely, he had tumbled down the cliff. All of us at once crept down the steep slope of the cliff. On reaching its base we were shocked to find him hanging upon the branch of a tree, growing out of the steep mountain side, about two-three feet above the ground, with one leg each on either side of the branch, just like riding a horse. With utmost difficulty we then dismounted him from the branch he had been hanging upon. He was totally unconscious. His trousers were torn apart at the buttock and he was bleeding profusely from the groin, the central joint of his legs. We then, immediately called a taxi and got him admitted here as this happens to be the nearest hospital from the cliff."

After a little pause he added, "The doctor attending to him had told us that the condition of the patient was very serious. He urgently needs to be operated upon to save his life for which the consent of his father was required. It had, then, become our moral duty to inform you about the accident, lest any false allegation of some foul play may creep up later on, as it generally happens in the public or the media. Unfortunately, since ours is a band of eunuchs, a speculation could become rife that the boy could have been castrated. By the time dusk seemed to be approaching. We had then decided to inform you to check and verify yourself the truthfulness of the whole event. On my suggestion, Zulfi and Massy were sent to your Kothi to apprise you of the whole situation. And Jamila had stayed here with me by the side of Mangalu's bed awaiting your arrival," concluded Bhima.

The operation was still in progress. "I never thought we'd make this one," the surgical nurse said to the anesthesiologist as they left the operating room. They had been battling for four hours to keep Mangalu's blood pressure high enough to keep him alive while they were operating on him. While the operation to repair the damaged lower spine was

Chapter – 19

❧

No sooner did Dr. Ranjan emerged from the operation theatre, than Veer Sen caught him up in the corridor itself and followed into his room.

"Please let me know about the outcome of the operation," requested Veer Sen as he was very eager to know if everything was alright.

Asking Veer Sen to sit in the chair the doctor told him, "Yes, we have been successful in saving the life of your son which was our first preference. We're also able to repair his damaged lower spine that saved him of becoming crippled." However, breaking the news about the secondary part of the operation, he added, "but we are extremely sorry that even with our best efforts, the patient's badly crushed organ couldn't be retrieved and we weren't left with any other option but to reluctantly go for its amputation to save his life."

Greatly shocked by such a bad news, Veer Sen, keeping his both hands upon his chest, fell from the chair with a thud. People, who happened to be present at the hospital premises, looked around on hearing the sound of the fall and rushed towards his room. However, by that time, the doctors had summoned for the trolley to carry the victim for examining.

Bhima and Jamila too, on hearing the sound of falling, had come to check. A little later, the doctors had revealed that on hearing the shocking news about Mangalu, his father had a minor heart attack. He had since been given an injection to overcome the shock and would be alright soon. However, after keeping him under observation for two and a half hours, Veer Sen was told that he needed a complete check-up which could be done later on, when he feels free in a few days. By the time the injection had shown its effect and Veer Sen, with the permission of the doctor, was able to walk gradually towards Mangalu's room.

Post operation, Mangalu had been kept under observation in the Intensive Care Unit (ICU) of the Nursing Home throughout the remaining hours of the night. However, as his condition remained stable, he was shifted in to a separate room in the morning.. Veer Sen, quite disheartened at the fate of his son, had taken a chair in the corner with his half-open eyes cursing himself for his misfortune. Jamila, however, had remained there by the bedside of Mangalu.

"Where am I?" Asked Mangalu, looking, a bit frightened, around his bed.

"In the Nursing Home," replied Jamila. Both, she and Bhima had lodged themselves by the side of Mangalu to look after him, post his going under the knife. Veer Sen too had got up from the chair on hearing their conversation and came along to have a look himself.

"How are you feeling son?" asked Veer Sen, caressing him affectionately. His eyes were moistened with emotion and a couple of tears rolled down his cheeks as he touched his son's forehead.

"................" There was no reply. Instead Mangalu had given utterly a blank look which had instilled some kind of fear in to the minds of all the three of them. Immediately, the doctor was summoned to check the patient's condition in order to overcome their anxiety.

"Everything is O.K.," said the doctor after reexamining the patient. He had also told them that the response towards the treatment had been quite encouraging and if the healing process continued at that pace, the patient could be discharged possibly after two-three weeks.

CHAPTER – 20

❦

Upon his part, Veer Sen had let no stone unturned in making the best available treatment. But as the bad luck would have it, Mangalu had fallen with such a force that his male organ was badly crushed. It was completely damaged to the extent that despite making all efforts it couldn't be retrieved. The doctors, as such, with the permission of his father, who had made himself available at the time of the operation, very reluctantly, had to amputate the same, keeping the urethra intact. Attending on the patient, they had very clearly opined that the amputation of his male organ was absolutely necessary to save the life of the boy. Thus poor father was left with no other choice and had to sign the form under compulsion and allow for the operation to save the precious life.

The irony of the fact was that having gone through that surgery, though his life was saved but at the same time poor Mangalu had been reduced from his male status to that of a eunuch unwillingly. For Veer Sen, it was a severe blow as apart from the twin daughters, he had Mangalu as his only son. He couldn't dare take his wife Rani into confidence about the outcome of Mangalu's operation and had kept the secret unto himself only. While the physical wounds were healed in about a month or so, it had taken Mangalu more than a year to recover from the mental shock. Ultimately, having no other option, he had to accept the reality and adjust himself with the cruelty of the fate in the absence of any other alternative whatsoever.

There was a time when Veer Sen believed that 'Money makes the mare go' and as such had never cared while indulging himself in malpractices. But he could never imagine that at certain times those 'quotes' may prove to be wrong. At such a crucial time, to save his family honour, Veer Sen had promised his lawyer to pay even some extra amount over and above his normal fee. So, his lawyer had tried his level best to prepare the case in such a manner to look as if it had escaped through an oversight on the part of the accounts officer or somebody else looking after the accounts. He had also added that the business owner had since admitted his mistake and was willing to deposit whatever the amount was payable and pleaded that being the first-time offence the omission may kindly be condoned.

Being a wise judge of men and things, the Income Tax Officer had very kindly showed some leniency towards the case. In addition to the actual amount of tax evaded by his business house, Veer Sen had to deposit some amount towards fine as well. Of course, in order to escape the trouble and hardship of imprisonment he had to lose another sum equal to the amount of fine also. Anyway, after coming out of the whole mess he had heaved a sigh of relief. He was, however, surprised to see on calculating that overall expenditure incurred on the case, including the fee of the lawyer, had become much on the higher side as compared to the amount he had been trying to save through the evasion of the tax and finally, had sworn not to indulge into any unlawful activities in future, whatsoever.

Mangalu had not yet been discharged from the Nursing Home when he was informed that Veer Sen had suffered another heart attack within a fortnight from the first one he had in the East Nursing Home and had been admitted in the Surya Hospital near Kothi Chowk. On becoming a little alarmed Veer Sen had sent for his advocate. His son Mangalu was still in the East Nursing Home and even after the assurance given by the doctors he had not been discharged as yet,. Veer Sen, as such, had asked the advocate to prepare the legal documents to give power of attorney to his wife Rani to carry on the affairs of the Cloth Mill in his absence. So far, she had been looking after the household affairs only. In the meantime he had briefed Rani to the extent possible regarding his business authorizing her to sign the documents on his behalf. While Veer Sen would be available for any guidance, she could also consult Ram Nath, his most trusted employee who had been working in association with Veer Sen for so many years since the year of his taking the charge of the Cloth mill.

After having discharged from the Nursing Home, Mangalu had gone to see his father who had a second heart attack. Veer Sen, once again had responded quite positively just like he had done on his first attack and had been treading with a good pace on the road to recovery. Doctors were very happy and satisfied about the progress shown by the patient. A full week had gone by and keeping in view the discussion Mangalu had with the doctor, he was discharged with the condition that he would take complete rest for another week at least. Mangalu then promised to take care of him and thus Veer Sen moved into the Kothi.

CHAPTER – 21

Years had gone by thereafter, and Nandini got herself promoted to the next class after class. Likewise, her mode of transport also got changed. Instead of the school-Bus she would come to the school in her father's Ford car and the driver would pick her up after the school hours in the afternoon. One could always find a couple of her friends--- specifically Marcie and Alexia sharing their seats with her in the classroom. Even outside, all the three of them would find some fun to make others laugh and enjoy the leisure time. They would have their lunch together during the recess in between the classes and would never go even to the washroom without each other's company. So much so, that a few of her classmates had started to feel a little jealousy and envied their friendship. Occasionally, their school used to organize tours for the students under the strict supervision of their teachers to visit some historical place, a museum, the zoological park, etc. which provided a good source of excursion and enjoyment to the students. While Mrs. Rani herself would seldom go out of the Kothi, Nandini, her daughter, had a very good rapport even with the parents of her both the friends--- Marcie and Alexia. Off and on they used to visit each other on some excuse. All of them would go randomly for a picnic or on a shopping spree in the market or the City Mall generally on a weekend.

Once on a holiday all the three had been to the famous botanical garden for a picnic. They had taken 'aaloo ke pranthe (Fried butter-Chapaties filled with potatoes), cheese, mixed vegetables and fried daal (Pulse) with pickle, and of course a big water-can. The garden was full of different kinds of herbal plants. There were rows of various flowers with a variety of hues and colours. The atmosphere contained fragrance which gave soothing effect to the soul. After finishing their lunch, they had a stroll in the garden chatting and laughing. Soon they had spotted a corner where an artist was busy making a tattoo on somebody's wrist. Another boy had the tattoo of a flower which looked really beautiful. All the three friends were fascinated to observe with great interest, very minutely, the process of making the tattooes with indelible ink. Encouraged, on seeing a small group of boys surrounding the tattoo walah artist, the girls decided on the spot with their mutual consent that they too should get their names tattooed as they won't be getting another opportunity like that. But then, on learning that it could be a little painful, they had opted to have only the initial letter of their names tattooed on one of their wrists. Thus, while Nandini went for 'N', Marcie and Alexia had gone for 'M' and 'A' respectively. The job was over in a few minutes and they had felt just a negligible pain. Fearing to be reprimanded by their parents, all of them had vouched to keep it a top secret for the time being. To hide the tattoo, Nandini wrapped her hanky upon her wrist over the tattoo, lest it may be seen by her mother. Marcie didn't care much and left it bare to dry while Alexia needn't bother at all as she was already wearing a full-sleeve shirt to cover it.

"Hello, May I know your good name please?" asked the maid after picking up the phone.

"I'm Raja Ram from Vikram Boarding School of Education, lavale. I want to talk to Mrs. Rani Sen please," said the Manager.

"Mem Saab! Your phone from School," the maid called with full throat.

"Hello, who's calling please?" asked Mrs. Rani.

"Good afternoon Ma'am, I'm Raja Ram, Manager, Vikram Boarding School. I've just received a call from the hostel. Ma'am Principal wants to know about Nandini's welfare as Shalini had complained about some pain in her hand, though on the surface nothing was visible. Of course the pain had subsided after a short while I'm told. However, we do hope, Nandini is quite hale and hearty," replied Raja Ram.

"Well, Mr. Raja Ram! I'm sorry, Nandini is not at home just now. She has gone for picnic with her friends at botanical garden. Now I'm also worried about her. Anyway, I'll call back as soon as she comes home, please tell Ma'am," replied Mrs. Rani.

No sooner did Nandini reach home, than the maid rushed towards Mrs. Rani's room and informed her, "Bibi ji has come."

"Nandini, my darling, please come here." She called her and hugging her with utmost love she said, "I was much eager to see you. How was your picnic? I hope all of you must have enjoyed it. Or, had something gone wrong in the garden?"

"No Mamma, Everything was O.K." replied Nandini.

"I see. By the way, what is it you have to hide by wrapping the hanky upon your wrist? Just show me. Are you hurt?" asked Mrs. Rani.

"It's nothing Mamma," saying this she tried to keep her hand behind her back. But her mother caught hold of her hand and very cautiously removed the hanky to unwrap her wrist. There, she saw a fresh wound that depicted the letter 'N' tattooed on the skin. Owing to her guilty conscience Nandini didn't dare see into the eyes of her Mamma. Mrs. Rani got very much annoyed on seeing the wound but she controlled her rage as there was no use of scolding her, fearing that her reaction may have effect on poor Shalini as well. However she simply asked her, "You must have suffered the pain on account of the tattoo. Anyway, henceforth you have to strictly bear in mind not to let anything happen to you that gives some kind of pain, as it hurts me also." Thus she politely warned her to avoid doing such things in future.

"Hello, Mr. Raja Ram, Mrs. Rani speaking this side. Nandini has just come home and I noticed that she had got a small one-letter tattoo made on her wrist which could have been the cause of some pain, poor Shalini had to bear. I've, however, strictly warned her not to indulge in any kind of such things in future which may hurt or give some kind of pain. Please explain this fact with my apologies to Kamlesh Ma'am," she told Raja Ram thanking him for the trouble he had taken to sort out the things.

This happening was also reported to Dr. D'Siva who had discussed with the team of doctors once again to have their opinion. They too got very much disappointed to learn that even at this stage when both the girls are about to cross the threshold of adolescent age and are ready to enter in their youth, the strange characteristics in their behavior still persists. Although the chances of any change seemed bleak yet they looked a little satisfied that the number of sensitiveness related incidence had reduced appreciably during all those years. That again gave them hope against hope that any further reduction in their sensitiveness may prove beneficial to some extent in the near future. So their combined verdict was to let the experiment continue for the time being.

CHAPTER – 22

"Mamma, this birthday I must have my new dress like this one," said Nandini, pointing to the photograph of a model in a fashion magazine wearing a designer silken dress that really looked attractive but at the same time seemed to be quite expensive as well.

"Of course, my darling," said her mother, adding, "I'll ask your Papa to buy you a nice dress from the City Mall, as you know that I seldom go out myself anywhere."

"No, Mamma," protested Nandini. "You too know it quite well Papa neither has time nor any taste for such things." She also added further, "I think I could go on my own with my friends Marcie and Alexia, like we had been to the City mall many a time before. They will also help me in selecting a nice dress suitable for the occasion."

"Alright honey, since only four days are left now, there's no point in delaying it any further," said Mrs. Rani showing much affection towards her daughter. I'll ask the driver to drop you with your friends at the City Mall on your way back home tomorrow after the school hours, she added.

"As far as I could remember, your birthday falls in December which must be approaching, isn't it? By the way, on what day it is?" Manisha asked, putting her arm around Shalini's waist, while coming out of the classroom.

"Oh my God, it's on the 7th, just four days to go, and I have yet to purchase my new dress for the occasion," replied Shalini, becoming a little panicky. "I'm very much in doubt if Mummy would allow us to go to the City Mall to buy my dress," she added.

"But, I think it otherwise. She would definitely give you permission to visit the Mall but most probably with the only condition that you will have to take along your class teacher with you," said Anita. "At the moment she must be in her office. Just go and ask for her permission. Don't hesitate and move a little fast lest she leaves the office," she advised her further.

"May I come in Mummy?" asked Shalini before entering the office.

"Yes my child, come in," said Kamlesh Ma'am. "What's the matter? Is there something wrong?" caressing her she asked further.

"No, Mummy. Everything is alright. In fact, I have just come to seek your permission to visit the City Mall, as I wanted to buy a dress for my birthday, Mummy, coming on the 7th, just after four days.

"No, my child, I can't allow you to go alone to the City Mall on your own," said Kamlesh Ma'am.

"Mummy, if you permit, I could take along my friends Manisha and Anita also," pleaded Shalini.

"Well, who is your class teacher? Is it Miss Sarika?" She asked. And getting the nod from Shalini, she further added, "O.K. I'll ask her to accompany you with your friends tomorrow, in the afternoon, after your last period is over."

As soon as the girls entered the Mall Sarika madam enquired about the ladies garment section for which they were directed to go upstairs at the second floor. Reaching there, Shalini asked her friends to look for a suitable dress for her, while she herself just got excused and hurriedly entered the ladies washroom.

"How come Shalini, wearing a new dress, where's your school uniform? Asked bewildered Manisha, interrupting the girl, who had just come out of the washroom and heading toward the ladies garment section.

"Excuse me. I'm not Shalini. You must be mistaking me for somebody else. A case of mistaken identity perhaps." explained the girl. Sarika madam too looked awfully surprised and tried to think logically. She was very much in doubt and then asked the girls, *How it could be possible that in just a couple of minutes Shalini could change herself like that, and that too sans her school uniform? Is it some kind of a prank Shalini was playing on all of us, just for the sake of making fun?* The girl, however, was still pleading that she was not Shalini but Manisha and Anita won't listen to her. In fact nobody would believe the girl. Anita then told her with folded hands--- "O.K. Baba, we all agree that you are really a remarkable prankster. Anyway, I think it is enough for today. Now please don't make a scene here and come into your original-self as we have yet to buy the dress. Please hasten up a little in making your selection otherwise we would certainly be getting late." Sarika madam also chided her saying, "Shalini, enough is enough. Now behave yourself and don't waste any more time lest we may be reprimanded for being late by the Principal Ma'am." Interestingly, a good number of customers present at the sales counter also came along to find out the cause of such a commotion in the garment section of the Mall.

And suddenly there happened a miracle when a girl, wearing the same to same face of the girl still held by Manisha, was seen coming out of the washroom. She stood there as if looking for somebody.

"Hi, Nandini, what happened? Are you O.K., taken so much time in the washroom?" asked another couple of young girls who appeared from nowhere and hastily rushed toward the washroom and caught hold of the girl. Taken a little aback, she retorted them, "Sorry girls, there seems to be some mistake. For your kind information, I'm Shalini and not Nandini which you guys may be looking for."

"What are you talking nonsense? You think we won't recognize you just because you got yourself dressed in the school uniform and pronounce yourself with a different name? And by the way where from did you get this bloody uniform?" asked Marcie who was a little older than her friend Alexia.

The 'scene' made by these girls too, had got the attention of some other customers as well. Incidentally, a few of them happened to be those who had, minutes before, witnessed another scene like this one, and were baffled to see two girls with identical faces. Both the girls were surrounded by a crowd of onlookers gathered in the garment section at the Mall. All of them got surprised to see when both the girls stood there gazing at each other face to face in great astonishment as if they were looking into the mirror.

And then, as it usually happens on such occasions, very soon all the confusion was over when it became into the notice of the people gathered in the garment section that it purely was a case of mistaken identity. The commotion, however, had attracted the people so much so that both the groups of the girls were drawn toward each other in no time and were seen in high spirits and deep conversation thereafter.

CHAPTER – 23

❧

"Hi, girls, this is Shalini from Vikram Boarding School of Education, Lavale, whom you mistook for Nandini," said Manisha, introducing her. She further added, "Well, myself is Manisha and this is Anita. All the three of us are classmate-friends and our group is commonly referred to as the 'Trio'. I'm extremely sorry for the utter confusion that all of us had witnessed just a few moments before, on account of the mistaken identity of both the girls which, to the great surprise of everybody, are miraculously the look-alikes to such an extent that it is virtually quite difficult to distinguish between them. This, certainly, is a rare phenomenon indeed." Shalini then did a warm handshake with Nandini and instantly both of them became friends. Sarika madam too had felt a little embarrassed and was sorry for having scolded her without any fault due to the mistaken identity.

And now was the turn of Nandini who with a warm handshake introduced herself to Shalini's friends as well. Then pointing toward her own classmate-friends she said, "These are Marcie and Alexia and we are from St. Mary School of Education for girls. They have come just to accompany me as also help me in selecting a suitable dress for my birthday which falls on this weekend." While both of her friends were busy in making a selection from various kinds of dresses with a large variety of designs and colours, Nandini herself was keenly looking for the dress just like she had seen in her drawing room on the cover-page of the fashion magazine. The other group consisting of Shalini, including Sarika madam was looking for the dress at the separate counter at the other end just opposite the first one. Generally everyone thinks in a different way and has a choice of her own. However, wary of getting late Shalini, with the help of Manisha, was able to select a beautiful dress and hastily slipped into the trial-room in order to check its fitting. She appeared to be all the more beautiful in that dress on looking into the mirror. On her coming out, Sarika madam too appreciated and gave her approval for the dress. Strangely enough, in a few moments, she looked at Nandini who too was coming out from the other trial-room located at the other corner, wearing the same to same dress as that of Shalini. Coincidently, while Nandini had to take pains to look for her choice as per the replica of the dress she had seen on the magazine-cover, Shalini could find it easily without looking for anything else selected by her friends. She too was surprised to know that not only their faces but even their choices as well as liking for the dress was the same despite the fact that both of them had their shopping at separate counters without any knowledge or consultation with each other about the design or the colour of the dress.

"May I have your attention please?" The girls looked around. It was Nandini holding a ball-pen before her mouth like a microphone and making the announcement with a smiling face, as soon as all of them came out of the Mall. "My dear friends, it would be my pleasure to have your gracious presence on the occasion of my birthday celebration at our home at 7.00 P.M. sharp, to be followed by dinner. All of you, including Shalini and her friends are cordially invited. The Venue is my home--- Veer Sen ki kothi and the date--- the 7th of December."

"The 7th of December? Oh my God, that's my birthday too," screamed Shalini with her full throat to the astonishment of Nandini and her friends, "and that's why I have come all the way from Lavale to buy a nice dress," she added.

"How come, there is such a degree of resemblance in both of us?" said Nandini. She further added, "not only our identical face but also our tastes and liking about choosing the same dress, and now sharing even our date of birth; can all these things be termed as a mere coincidence? There seems to be definitely some kind of link between us which I think could possibly be related to our previous births but couldn't be recalled in our present rebirth."

"Well, many many happy returns of the day," said Shalini, congratulating Nandini in advance, adding, "I would have loved to join you but for my own birthday falling on the same date." Of course, Nandini too reciprocated the birthday greetings to Shalini as well, citing the same reason with their mutual understanding. Both the groups, then, dispersed bearing in their minds somewhat strange feelings about the rare phenomenon just witnessed or rather practically experienced by all of them.

"As soon as she heard the sound of the car purring in the porch, Mrs. Rani hurried toward the door. She was quite eager to see the dress Nandini was supposed to have purchased from the City Mall. She took the cardboard box containing the dress from Nandini and then hastily unpacked it.

"My God, It's so beautiful," she exclaimed adding, "It seems to be the exact replica of the dress you showed me in that magazine yesterday." I'll show it to your Papa when he comes and then she started to repack the dress for the occasion in the same box.

By the time it had become almost difficult for Nandini to hold herself any longer to narrate the strange incidence that everybody had witnessed at the Mall. She caught her mother unawares and asked, "Mamma, just like this dress of mine appears to be exact replica of another one; could it be possible for a living person to be the exact replica of another person?"

"Darling, where from such a silly question like this, has propped up in your mind? May be it could be possible or maybe not. I think it solely depends upon some kind of biological properties of a human being which seems to be a rare phenomenon indeed," replied her mother.

"Well, Mamma, today there happened to be a strange coincidence at the Mall," said Nandini. She added further, "While I had selected my dress from a counter in the garment section, another girl too selected from another counter the same dress as mine. And before that, both my friends Marcie and Alexia caught hold of that girl while she was coming out of the washroom mistaking her as "ME". Whereas, her friends had mistook me as "HER". There had been utter confusion which had created a scene at the Mall. It was, however, for the customers, who too were taken aback on seeing such a pair of lookalike girls. Anyway, the overall confusion was over after the exchange of both the girls with each other. But Mamma, of course, as we had seen, that two persons could be lookalike to each other, just like we see a duplicate of some hero doing stunts in a film, but one question still remains to be answered. Could it also be just a coincidence that the date of birth of both the lookalikes too coincides with that of each other?"

"Believe me dear; my knowledge on the subject is too poor to answer the question like this. Human mind is not capable of even speculating these things. God alone knows about such kind of His unheard mysteries," concluded her mother.

CHAPTER – 24

⚮

As soon as Nandini got settled herself comfortably on the back seat of her car, just behind the driver-seat, she saw a piece of paper folded like a hand-note, lying in the corner of her seat, just below the rear windowpane. In a split second she stealthily grabbed it before the driver uncle could take notice of it. She instantly became a bit nervous. And with her heartbeat throbbing a little fast, she hastily inserted it carefully in one of her books fearing that the driver uncle might see it in the 'rear-view-mirror' fixed in the centre above the dashboard of the car. Her mind began to work overtime with the thoughts that who could have thrown that 'note' into the car which definitely was meant for her only. Her first and foremost thought was that one of her classmate-friends could have mischievously dropped it through the slightly opened window for the sake of making some fun. However speculating further she presumed that the person, either *he* or *she*, must be somebody else, other than any of her friends. Naturally, her curiosity was arising minute by minute, as the car raced towards the Kothi, to know he contents of that note. It could be that of a mere adoration of her, or most probably expressing his or her liking or love or something like that. She was finding it hard to control her urge to know its contents. At the moment her state of mind was in such an emotional disorder that, to her, it looked as if the car was running at a snail's pace. She further unnecessarily got agitated feeling utmost frustration, thinking that why it was taking the time much longer than usual to reach home, despite the fact, that there was literally no traffic jam. Ultimately they entered the porch of the Kothi and Nandini heaved a sigh of relief.

That day she didn't wait for the driver uncle to come around and fetch her books as per his daily routine. Instead she helped herself and opened the door in a jiffy and while hastily stepping out of the car, dropped her books in the process. Ultimately driver uncle had to help her in collecting them. As if something had gone wrong, she unmindfully snatched the books from him and went inside. Saying good afternoon to her mother, she hurriedly stepped upon the stairs, leaping on two at a time, as she was much eager to be in her room. Instead of keeping them upon the table in the usual way, she haphazardly threw her books upon her bed. In quick succession she then fished out that note from a book after thoroughly searching in more than a couple of her books. Though it was written on just half-a-page of paper yet it contained four folds most probably in order to decrease in dimensions. By the time she had become too nervous. Her heart was pounding heavily when she unfolded the note and did a rapid reading of the same. She then reread it once again with gusto. Still not satisfied she read it over and over again, which was clearly a love-letter from someone expressing his feelings in the note which read:

"Dear......, sorry, for I've yet to find out your name, but I see you daily in your car on my way back from my college on my bike in the afternoon. Even if we haven't met, it appears to me as if we know each other from the time immemorial. I fell in love instantly on seeing you for the first time on a morning when once your car had to stop over the red light alongside my bike at the crossing just before your St. Mary School. Moments later on getting the green signal, your car moved a little forward and entered the school premises. Since then I use to keep on waiting

at the gate beside your car after the school hours just to have a glimpse before you get in. Possibly you too must have noticed me on my red bike parked by the left side of your car. Today is the Valentine's Day which prompted me to write this note. Please feel free to check my Bullet 'Royal Enfield' bike PNM-B 1690."

Only yours--- Vinay.

It was on the mere mention of the 'red bike' referred to, in the note, that she could instantly recollect from her memory of having noticed the same quite a number of times but never bothered about it anymore. Of course the driver uncle had asked the boy two-three times to park his bike a little beyond allowing some reasonable space required to open the door of the car which he willingly obliged without making any fuss like the youngsters are prone to do these days. She then remembered of having thrown once a casual look also at the boy when he was taking the bike off its stand and then trying to re-park it at some distance, first towards right and then reversed it towards left side facing the door of the car. "*The fellow has gone crazy,*" she thought at once without caring much.

Next morning as soon as the car entered the school premises, Nandini tried to look for the red bike through its windscreen in anticipation of her stepping out of the car. However, throwing a casual look even outside the gate, the said bike wasn't seen anywhere in the vicinity. Disheartened a little she headed for her classroom. Having come of age, it was but natural for her to be attracted towards the opposite sex. She was curious enough to have a close look of the boy though vaguely he seemed to be just good looking at the time of her first casual look. She couldn't concentrate upon her studies throughout the day. Though physically she was very much present in the class room but mentally she was roaming elsewhere. She was curiously waiting for the last period to be over so that she could see the boy on his red bike before it comes into the notice of the driver uncle. Her classmate-friends had noticed that there happens to be something upon her mind. Alexia had tried to coax her in order to find the reason behind her limited conversation the whole daylong, which didn't go beyond 'yes' or 'no'. "You don't look to be in your usual-self today. Is there something wrong with you?" asked Marcie. But she didn't want to open her mind or share anything with her friends yet.

"Here goes the last bell," cheered Nandini to her friends and raced towards outside, saying, "I'll be waiting for you at the gate." Usually all the three of them used to come out with their smiling faces chatting and discussing on some topic or the other, analyzing the day's happenings after the last period is over. Both, Marcie and Alexia were all the more anxious to find out the real cause of her behaving in such a manner throughout the day. There was, however, no sign of any bike bearing the description given in the note when Nandini reached the gate. Thus poor girl once again got disappointed like it happened in the morning itself. And just at that moment, she spotted the red Bullet 1691. With a close look she was too pleased to find that its rider, of course, was a handsome collegiate boy who was busy in making its way through the traffic to reach the gate. By that time, her friends too had arrived there. That was the time she thought to share her state of mind with her friends. While Vinay was in the process of parking his bike, Nandini showed the boy to her friends for their approval tentatively. She had surely borne in her mind that it wouldn't be any easier to make friends with Vinay without taking their help for which she would have to take them into confidence. She couldn't keep

CHAPTER – 25

∽

"Hi girls, If I'm not wrong, both of you are perhaps the classmates of your friend who has just left in the car. Well, let me introduce myself first. I'm Vinay, a staunch admirer of her and studying in the S.D. College, located on the outskirts at Lavale. Frankly speaking, I use to keep on waiting here to have a glimpse of her after the school hours. Though I do not know her name, yet I dared express my feelings in a small note dropped in her car just yesterday, it being the Valentine's Day. I do hope that she must have got that note of mine and I'm eagerly looking for a favourable reply on which my life solely depends upon," said Vinay.

"Yes, you guessed it right. We both are classmate-friends of Nandini. Anyway, come tomorrow and we'll talk to her meanwhile," Marcie told to Vinay.

"So, that could be the reason behind Nandini's unusual behavior, in the classroom today," said Alexia to Marcie as soon as Vinay left on his bike. "She also must have got that friendship note of Vinay in her car but didn't speak a word about it. I'd tried to coax her number of times but she strictly had refrained to tell anything about that note. Anyway, the boy seems to be O.K. He is good looking and appears to be sober enough and worthy of friendship perhaps," she added further.

"Sorry, I'm late. The bloody car had come to a halt just in the middle of the road," explained Nandini to her friends as soon as she entered the classroom. "However with the help of the passersby, the car was pushed aside and the driver uncle opened the bonnet to look for the probable cause, and after casually examining the engine, he opined, replacing the bonnet of the car, that there could, either be a mechanical problem or some fault in the electrical wiring." Strangely, as if that was not enough, there was no other vehicle in sight for conveyance, and believe me, I had to walk a good half-a-kilometre distance on foot to reach the school.

"Now please just forget about the driver uncle and come to the point. Where's that note? Surely we would like to see, that Vinay was talking about," asked Alexia.

"Oh, you rogues; how did you come to know his name and about that note of his? It means you had a long conversation with him. Isn't it?

"Of course baby, he himself had approached, assuming us as your friends and opened up his mind. But before you ask for anything about him, hand over, first, that note to us," demanded Marcie. "At least we too should see what the boy has written, as I think half of a person's intention could perhaps be judged from the language and the style of his writing," she added.

"Well, here it is," said Nandini and then succumbing to their demand, she searched her schoolbag and fished out that note of Vinay from the pages of a book, and handed it over to her friends.

"It's just a simple note expressing one's love. What's in there to hide about?" asked alexia after giving a quick reading to the note and added, "Yes, we had a talk with the boy. He too studies in S.D. College at Lavale. As you have seen, he is good looking and from the little conversation we had with him, he appeared to be quite intelligent and sober in his behavior. He would be seeing you after the school, today itself. Talk to him as much as you like, but don't ever give him your phone no. for which he may persist upon. One thing more, as a word of caution, be sure not to give anything in writing. I think, if you liked him we could fix up a meeting with him on a holiday on some pretext to know more about each other, for a better rapport in the near future," suggested Marcie. Thus the stage was set for the ensuing meeting.

"Hello Mamma, the driver uncle hasn't come yet. Most probably the trouble in the car couldn't be set right and it must have been towed to the workshop. Anyway, I may be a little late as I'll come by bus with my friends. So, you needn't worry at all about me," Nandini informed her mother on telephone.

"Here he comes," said Alexia cheerly to Nandini, seeing Vinay parking his bike outside the gate, adding, "Since your car hasn't come, you have plenty of time to have a heart to heart talk with the boy if you like."

"Hi, Vinay, meet our friend Nandini," said Marcie introducing both of them to each other with a warm handshake. Acting as the spokesperson of Nandini, she told Vinay, "She is the daughter of Mr. Veer Sen who owns the 'Dheeraj Spinning and Weaving Mills' and her mother is a housewife." Reciprocating about himself, Vinay too had taken it easy to speak that his father was also a businessman running his own showroom--- 'Prakash Motors & Automobiles and his mother too was a housewife.

"Incidentally, the car had developed a snag in the morning while coming to the school, and that's why the driver uncle couldn't come to take me home," explained Nandini to Vinay. "Well, I did receive your note and have since been contemplating about the things. Thanks for the little compliments you have made therein. No doubt, I also used to see your red bike but frankly speaking, had never cared to look beyond that. Anyway, now that we've become acquainted with each other, I hope our friendship may go a long way. Both these girls are my fast friends and we share everything with each other. You too, now, are welcome to our group," she added further with an inviting gesture.

"Well, this is no place to chat with and discuss the views of each other freely and leisurely," said Vinay. "Can't we go somewhere to sit a bit comfortably and talk for a while?" He asked in a polite way.

"Not today," said Alexia. "We don't want to be late as our parents would be looking for us to reach home at our usual time. We may chalk out some programme at another time. So, let the today's meeting be over now," she added, to which both her friends gave a firm nod.

It was just the beginning of their friendship. Thereafter they would meet off and on in a garden or a restaurant on one pretext or the other. Month after month had gone by and every year they had been promoted into the next higher class. A period of more than two years was elapsed by then. While Vinay was now in the final year of his graduation, Nandini had joined the first year course along with her friends Marcie and Alexia.

"I've noticed that you have started coming late by almost an hour daily. Are there any extra classes held daily in the College?" asked Vinay's mother.

"No Mom, to tell you the truth, there is a girl Nandini whom I love too much. We see each other daily after the College with her other friends for a little chat. She too loves me. I would like to invite her with her friends and introduce to you on my birthday next week. She is the beauty personified, awfully loveable, to fall in love with," replied Vinay.

"Happy birthday to you, happy birthday to Vinay, happy birthday to you." The room echoed with the chanting of the birthday wishes of the guests and the hosts equally as the candles at the birthday-cake blue off. A small function was arranged at Vinay's residence where he had invited Nandini and her friends also. That was the right occasion for Vinay to introduce Nandini to his parents who were too happy to meet her. They had appreciated the choice of their son and were not averse to their friendship. Shortly, after the cake ceremony was over, some light refreshment was served followed by hot coffee. All of them got mixed up as if they were known to each other since ages. And then started a music session wherein everybody had participated. While Marcie and Alexia entertained them with their dance performance, Nandini made them enjoy with the sweet melodies of old film songs of Lata and Asha. Likewise Vinay, on his turn, offered his favourite songs of Rafi and Mukesh. His mother also participated with a bhajan. His father Mr. Prakash remained a patient listener but was later on persuaded to offer a few of his good collection of jokes making everybody burst into peels of laughter. With the assurance of seeing very soon all the friends dispersed for fear of becoming late.

CHAPTER – 26

"You look beautiful in this dress," told Vinay to the girl on spotting her at the Mall, mistaking her for Nandini. She was taken aback on hearing the compliments from a total stranger who seemed to be a college student.

"Well. You too look smart in that jacket of yours," reciprocated the girl blushing with a smile. Gazing on him for a while she found him quite handsome and was much impressed with his manners. So much so that she wished in her heart to befriend him. She took fancy of him and instantly fell in love at first sight.

"Your friends didn't accompany you?" asked Vinay.

"No, I've come with our teacher who has been to the washroom. She must be coming out and I'm afraid I won't be able to talk to you in front of her. We can meet here tomorrow afternoon," she told Vinay, on seeing her teacher coming toward them.

"Who was the guy you were in conversation with? asked the teacher.

"Just a stranger complimenting my dress," Shalini told her teacher with a smile on her face.

The next afternoon at the Mall, Vinay was looking for her in the ladies garment section. Not finding her there he went upstairs on the third and then even on the fourth floor, but the whole exercise went in vain as she was nowhere to be seen. Disappointed and also feeling a little hungry, he entered the cafeteria and ordered for some snacks and a cup of coffee. While looking for a chair to sit upon, he spotted the girl occupying a table. He too dragged his chair beside her and said, "Hi, you are so comfortably enjoying your coffee here and I had been going up and down from floor to floor looking for you."

"Never mind, have your coffee first and then we'll go out," she said to Vinay. A short while after, both of them were seen, sitting in each other's company in the park adjacent to the Mall enjoying chit-chat.

"What a lovely day. I'm absolutely thrilled. You look really graceful. I love you very much and would like to make the honest confession of my love. What kind of magic is this which you have spelt over me? I can't think about anything else but you and you only," said the girl.

"*She seemed to be in good mood today,*" thought Vinay. All the time, only she was saying something or the other to express her feelings about her love. Poor Vinay didn't have the chance of speaking even a word or two, to reciprocate his share of love to her. While listening to her, he had started recollecting the numerous love-talks that had taken place between them, where Nandini had expressed her love, time and again, thus her today's confession was just a repetition of the previous ones made, off and on. She was, in fact, in the habit of making such confessions as she pleased. Of course, there was no doubt that both of them had gone mad in love with each other.

"How come, you, here, at Mata Rajeshwari College?" asked Vinay, mistaking her for Nandini.

"Why, I've joined the first year course here after finishing my school. By the way, what brought 'you' here at our College? asked the girl.

"Oh, me, it's per chance that I spotted you on my way to my College and stopped just to say good morning to you," explained Vinay.

"Ah, very good morning, O.K.? now will you please just leave, as I'll be late for my class," replied the girl.

It had, then, become almost a routine for Vinay to look for her and say good morning on his way to College during the ensuing week. On another occasion they had even bunked their last class to spend time together but were cautious enough to reach home in-time to avoid unnecessary queries for coming late.

"Strange are the ways of God that I fell in love at first sight, the moment I saw you. And see, with just a week's acquaintance, it seems to me as if we know each other since our birth after birth," said the girl.

"What are you talking dear? Does our love seem to you the result of just a week's acquaintance?" asked Vinay.

"Why, my love, it was only last week when I saw you at the Mall for the first time and you complimented me for my new dress, explained the girl.

"Oh my God, what happened to your memory?" asked Vinay patting upon his forehead. "Please, for heaven's sake, don't make any more fun of me. Are you feeling alright?" asked Vinay touching her forehead. "I hope it has got nothing to do with the Alzhimer. Just put some stress upon your mind and try to recollect as to when we had met for the first time," added Vinay.

"I'm sorry my love. I don't remember anything other than that," lamented the girl.

"To me it seems to be some kind of lack of concentration. I would suggest you to take an auto and go home. You ought to take complete rest. Can you go alone or should I accompany you?" asked Vinay.

"No, my love, it's O.K. with me," said the girl and left in an auto.

CHAPTER – 27

"It's more than a week now since the vacations were over and yet your friend hasn't turned up even once. Is there any message from Vinay?" asked Marcie.

"No. Possibly he could either have gone out of the city, during the vacations or may not be feeling well. I'm also worried a bit about him," replied Nandini.

"Why don't we take a round of his College?" suggested Alexia. The suggestion was found worth consideration. It was then and there decided that they'll take an auto and visit his College, immediately after the last period is over.

All the three had just alighted from the auto and started looking intently towards the students coming out of the College premises in small groups of three's or four's chatting with each other. Among the crowd they had spotted Vinay also coming out and waving to them.

"What a great surprise. All of you together like making a raid. I hope all is well," said Vinay approaching them. He ushered all of them into the lawn of the College and made them sit there comfortably to have some chitchat for a while.

"In fact we have been worrying about you and have come to know about your welfare," said Alexia, breaking the silence.

"My God, have you people gone mad? Amn't I looking quite hale and hearty to all of you?" asked Vinay in a bit annoying tone.

"Then what on earth had kept you that much busy. It's now more than a week since you haven't bothered even once to see me," asked Nandini a little vehemently.

"What nonsense are you talking Nandini? I'm going to lose my temper now. Tell me frankly, is it a joke of some kind, just to embarrass me for a while or is it to make some fun of me? asked Vinay.

"Nothing is either of the two. Believe us. We had truly missed you for the whole week and that's what brought all of us here. We were really worried about you. It could only have been fair upon your part to give us some valid reason for your absence. Anyway, would you still mind to give some kind of explanation for not turning up for such a long period?" enquired the girls.

"My dear Nandini, why are you so shy of telling the truth before your friends? Or otherwise, don't you remember that I used to say you 'hello' every morning on my way to College? We had even bunked our last class day before yesterday, to be together in the park behind your Mata Rajeshwari College," reminded Vinay.

"What? Mata Rajeshwari College for Women, but that's not our College. Ours is the St. Mary School of Education for Girls," told Nandini to Vinay. She thought about something and then added further, "Oh my God, if I'm not wrong, you must have been seeing my lookalike 'Shalini'. It's really difficult to distinguish between the two of us except that I have my initial 'N' tattooed upon my sleeve. Saying that she flaunted her tattoo for him to see it. Both her friends Marcie and Alexia gave their firm nod to Nandini's statement.

Poor Vinay now looked very much embarrassed to know about the fact. But he didn't consider himself at fault as anybody in his place wouldn't have done anything different.

"Hello Mamma, please come to my room. I've to talk to you about something very serious" said Nandini to her mother.

"What's the matter so serious you wanted to talk about? asked her mother.

"Mamma, I'm so sorry, for I should have taken you into confidence much earlier. In fact, I've a boy friend and I'm very much in love with him. We have been seeing each other for over two years now. Mamma, remember? Sometime back I had told you about a girl I met with at the City Mall who was not only my lookalike but she also shared with me her tastes and my date of birth as well. And you thought, that was just a coincidence. Mamma, I've just come to know that she too loves the same boy and was seeing him for over a week now. Mamma, could you still term it as just a coincidence?" asked Nandini.

"Well, this could hardly be termed as mere a coincidence, I agree. Anyway, I think for such a strange phenomenon I shall have to consult some psychologist to find an answer to the question as well as some remedy for such kind of problem," replied her mother.

"Hello, May I talk to Dr. D'Silva please," asked Mrs. Rani Sen.

"She is in the Operation Theatre at the moment. May I know who is calling please?" asked the Nurse.

"Well, this is Mrs. Rani Sen. Please ask her to call me back as soon as she comes out of the O.T. as I have to talk to her something. It's very urgent," replied Mrs. Sen.

"Hello, Mrs. Sen, Dr. D'Silva speaking this side. I understand there is something very urgent to talk about. Could you please explain it? I hope it has got nothing to do with the twins, or is it?" asked Dr. D'Silva.

"Yes, Dr. D'Silva. That problem of the twins still persists even after so many years. As luck would have it, both the girls are in love with the same boy and poor Nandini is very upset. She is now after me to answer her queries and I don't know how to cope with the situation. As you know I don't have any other person to go to, but you, and thus approach you for a sincere and correct advice on the matter, once again," explained Mrs. Rani Sen.

"Mrs. Sen, here you will kindly agree with me that so far, the experiment has been quite successful as there was no major problem for the kids even after their attaining the age of adolescence and then stepping into adulthood. As far as I understand, now it has become the most crucial stage which would need some planning. So I'll, once again, have to consult our panel of doctors on the subject, like we have been doing before, and would inform you about the strategy they are likely to advise for us to act accordingly," replied Dr. D'Silva.

CHAPTER – 28

‹❦›

B ut as the saying goes, 'None could really predict what was lying in store for him'. Just a week after, in the middle of the night Mangalu was lying in bed with his eyes shut when he heard a loud crash from his father's room. He opened his eyes and listened. There was another sound. He hurriedly got out of bed and ran towards the closed door of his father's room. Through the closed door he could hear strange sounds. His heart pounding wildly he pushed the door open. His father lay on the floor. His face and body contorted. One eye was closed and the other looked repulsively distorted. He was trying to speak. And the words came out as slobbering sounds. Immediately an ambulance was called to take him to the Surya Nursing Home.

His eyes opened to a bright, white light. He was in an unfamiliar room, a white room. The wall beside him was covered in long vertical blinds; over his head, the glaring lights blinded him. He was propped up on a hard, uneven bed---- a bed with rails. The pillows were flat and lumpy. There was an annoying beeping sound somewhere close by. His hands were all twisted up with clear tubes and something was taped across his face under his nose. He lifted his hand to rip it off but the doctor attending on him caught his hand. Resting on the edge of his pillow he realized that he was alive.

On examining the patient, the doctor said to Mangalu, "I'm afraid, the news is bad. Your father has had a severe stroke. There is a fifty-fifty chance he will live." That again was a great blow which had wrecked Mangalu completely. However, on reexamining, the doctors had finally declared, "Only his right side had been affected. The patient had to remain for long under the treatment for the same." It had been over a week since then. They had possibly done whatever they could. They had ultimately prescribed some medicines and suggested that the patient may take rest at home. "Of course, somebody has to attend to his needs as he can not do anything on his own. With the help of medicines and the requisite massage, as well as some exercises suggested by the physiotherapist, he will surely recover. It may take some time but please remember that miracles do happen, sooner or later," said the doctor when the patient was being discharged.

Having lost his male identity Mangalu had remained perturbed for a long time. Since he was born a perfect male child, he didn't look like a eunuch at all and could dress up like a normal male person. However, day in and day out he used to curse his fate. "*The accident possibly, wouldn't have occurred had I not drunk so heavily to lose my senses to the extent of not keeping my balance while dancing on the cliff,*" he lamented and also realized, "*My habit of access drinking is responsible for ruining my whole life which has compelled me to live the life of a eunuch instead of a man.*" On one hand he felt sympathy for his father and wanted to look after him and on the other hand his heart moaned for the company of Bhima, Jamila, Zulfi, Massy etc. He had virtually become double minded and could not decide which way to go.

Ultimately, good sense had prevailed upon him and like an obedient son he had resolved, "*Come what may, I would remain in the Kothi and look after my father.*" He cared for his father, tended to all his needs and remained by his side day and night. During the day he would prop him into the wheelchair and take him outside in the lawn of the Kothi. He would timely administer to him the medicines and also make him do the essential exercises as per the instructions of the physiotherapist. He would give him the required massage, make him bathe like a child, dress him up neatly, make him eat his meals and always look for any other comfort he may require. Day and night he had been serving him devotedly. Outwardly Veer Sen looked very much pleased as he ws being taken care of but inwardly his heart did bleed for the unfortunate state of his son for which he would curse himself for having shirked from his responsibility as a father and not cared for him when he needed him most.

And look! The miracle did happen truly. Veer Sen, having felt thirsty on an afternoon, wanted to reach the glass of water kept on the small bed-side table lying nearby on the right side of his bed. In the absence of Mangalu who had gone to the washroom, he had tried himself to reach the glass of water with his left hand as usual, like he had done before many a time. But he couldn't make it this time, as, per chance the table had been kept a little far that day while sweeping his room. Finding it beyond his reach, he unmindfully made an attempt and suddenly extended his right hand a little. And to his great astonishment he could see that he was holding the glass in his shaky hand. In the process he had got some water spilled over the bed also. Veer Sen had cried out loudly with surprise. Mangalu, on hearing such a loud cry, rushed towards his father's room fearing some mishap. But the scene over there was unbelievable. Seeing his father holding the glass of water in his right hand happened to be a great miracle indeed. He then thanked God a hundred times for His mercy and was pleased that he had been amply rewarded for serving his father devotedly and selflessly. Encouraged on seeing a definite ray of hope Mangalu had almost doubled, henceforth, his efforts like giving the massage and exercise twice a day instead of doing once in the morning only. That had helped Veer Sen making a more quick recovery and in about a month and a half, he was able to walk with the support of crutches under his arms. In due course of time, he could be seen walking on the terrace with a stick only. In his heart of hearts he had felt really indebted to his son who, with his selfless service, had given him a new lease of life and making him stand on his own once again.

In another month, Veer Sen had started walking, sans any support of stick, as well as attending to his office also. However to safeguard him from any untoward difficulty, Mangalu too used to accompany him for any support he may require. He wouldn't leave him unguarded even for a minute as he was still on the process of recouping his lost health and vigour, still prone to have any kind of mishap whatsoever. Veer Sen too had the feeling of safety and security on having his by his side. Remaining uneducated had become Mangalu's major drawback which had deterred him in becoming helpful in any manner in the office work. Contrary to that Mrs. Rani, having been well educated, had been managing the entire office work as well as the various other responsibilities relating to the cloth mill, quite efficiently during Veer Sen's absence to the complete satisfaction of one and all. Ram Nath too had been all praise for Mrs. Rani's efforts towards running the Mill, of course with the help of his valuable suggestions, and taking him into confidence from time to time. On Veer Sen's joining the office, Ram Nath's as well as Mrs. Rani's burden had become slightly reduced, though not fully over yet.

CHAPTER – 29

❧

On a Sunday morning, both, Dr. D'Silva and Mrs. Kamlesh, Principal, Vikram Boarding School of Education, as well as the guardian (Mummy) of Shalini, were invited to the Veer Sen-ki-Kothi on the pretext of celebrating the marriage anniversary of Mr. and Mrs. Sen. Shalini had also accompanied her Mummy, the Principal Ma'am and was overwhelmed with joy on seeing her lookalike friend Nandini. All of them were given a red carpet welcome. Both the friends, Shalini and Nandini hugged each other. Marcie and Alexia also joined them. And as per the next step in accordance with the plan, now was the most appropriate moment when Dr. D'Silva and Mrs. Kamlesh came forward and introduced Nandini and Shalini with each other as the *'twin sisters'*. Full of uncontrolled emotions of love, both the sisters hugged each other once again. Shalini too was taken aback when introduced with her real mother Mrs. Rani Sen as well as her father Mr. Veer Sen. They also thanked Mrs. Kamlesh, the Principal who had very sincerely played the role of a foster mother (Mummy) of Shalini for so many years.

Dr. D'Silva then briefly explained to both the sisters about their sensitive behavior and the strange characteristics of each other. She further added, "A good number of physicians, doctors and psychologists were consulted. Under their expert opinion your parents weren't left with any other option but to bring up the kids separately. So, both of you were kept in different environment. Periodically your cases were reviewed and various strategies were adopted to keep an eye over your growth. With the grace of God you were able to cross the minor hurdles coming your way. You have now reached on the threshold of youth and are capable of retaining your separate individuality and enjoy the life as it comes."

"Yes, of course, we aren't so small kids anymore who would quarrel with each other for toys or frocks. We are now mature enough and grownup loving sisters who would love to do anything for the sake of happiness of the other," said Shalini.

"Lunch is served," said the maid servant and then Mrs Rani Sen, the host of her supposed marriage anniversary ushered everybody toward the main hall. At the entrance the guests were treated with appetizers and starters followed by certain kinds of beverages. Then there was the main course comprising a variety of foods like naan, puries, cheese, fried daal (pulzes) and vegetables, salads, fruit-chat, various kinds of pickles. Then there were aalu-pranthas (wheat-chapati with potatoes stuffed inside). Bhaturey (of fermented flour) with Kabuli-gram were also there. For desert Ice-cream was served. The meal was followed by hot coffee.

And after their happy union and a delicious lunch, both the sisters enjoyed a cup of coffee each and then went upstairs in Nandini's room. Getting settled comfortably upon the sofa, Nandini told Shalini, "Till now, this was 'my' room, but henceforth it will be 'our' room and we both the sisters will share it. This is the wardrobe and that's my bookshelf. By the way, how is life at the hostel?" asked Nandini.

"While living at home you can enjoy your freedom. You could go freely anywhere you like, see anybody and talk to your friends anywhere anytime. But that is not the case with me. We can't go against the rules of the hostel as we have a disciplined life. The accommodation there isn't bad.

Food is good and we have got all kinds of modern amenities. Flush type washrooms, mineral water for drinking, etc. A watchman is always there patrolling at night and a security guard remains at the main gate," replied Shalini.

"Well, now you needn't worry about all these things. You won't be living in the hostel anymore. Come as soon as your terminal exams are over which is only a matter of days now. But then, why wait for the terminal exams? You could come immediately. I'll ask Mamma to get you relieved from your school at the earliest possible," said Nandini.

After a little pause, she added, "Shalini dear, I've a little secret of mine which I would very much like to share with you. There's a boy whom I'm extremely in love with. We have been seeing each other for over two years now. He is quite sober and handsome doing his final year. They have their own bungalow and his father owns an auto showroom."

"I see. You must be having his photograph, isn't it?" asked Shalini teasing her with a cheering smile.

"Sorry, I don't have one just now. But don't worry I'll let you see him in person. I've already told Mamma about our friendship of a couple of years. Once, on his birthday, I've met with his parents also. As far as I know Mamma, she is one of the best mothers of the world. Till date, I've got everything just for the asking. She is very fond of me, and is always on the look out to fulfill each of my wishes with the sole purpose of keeping me happy. In fact her happiness lies in my happiness which is linked with your happiness as well, as explained by Dr. D'Silva. And as such, there shouldn't be any kind of hindrance in giving her acceptance when he comes to see Mamma. Yet Shalini, my dear-dear sister, please give me your firm promise that you will definitely speak to Mamma in my favour. I shall be depending solely upon your full support whatsoever," pleaded Nandini.

CHAPTER – 30

Seeing Mr. Veer Sen in a jolly mood, Mrs. Rani had very cleverly brought the subject about Nandini telling him that she has come of age now. Being a woman herself she was able to explain to him something about the anxieties of a girl when she reaches the age of an adolescent. Her attraction to the opposite sex is also quite a natural phenomenon. She becomes curious enough to know and learn about various kinds of things exploring the fields hitherto unknown to her and being in love with somebody certainly helps to a great extent in her search for answers to the queries arising in her mind from time to time. She had further told him that Nandini has been in love with a boy named Vinay a student of final year adding that they have been seeing each other for the last couple of years. The revelation had prompted Veer Sen to ask Mr. Ram Nath, his Office Assistant to make enquiries about Vinay's family as well as their auto business.

A big sign board of 'Prakash Motors & Automobiles' adored above the head of a large ground floor of a huge building which had a basement also to accommodate over a dozen four-wheeled vehicles. It boasts of being the biggest auto showroom in the city. The proprietor Mr. Prakash Chand was a clean-shaven man with handsome features, blue eyes and pitch dark black hair. A staunch believer in the small family norms he didn't go for another child after having been blessed with a son Vinay of which he was very proud of. He too had inherited the same handsome features of his father imbibed with just his other qualities like soberness, good manners, politeness etc. which normally are very rarely found in the present crop of the young generation. Mrs. Prakash too was a house wife like Mrs. Rani Sen. The fact-finding report was given to Mr. Veer Sen by Mr. Ram Nath which seemed to have met with the standard of Mr. Veer Sen's family. After the discussion a decision was taken and accordingly Vinay's family was invited for which a small get-together was arranged at the kothi itself.

Shalini was still in the hostel as certain formalities were yet to be completed before she is relieved. Mrs. Rani Sen had to make a phone call, as such, to ask Mrs. Kamlesh to kindly make it convenient to attend to the get-together along with Shalini. Shalini was too happy and got very much excited to learn about the get-together as she was very anxious to see Nandini's beloved boy whom her sister had been seeing for more than two years. In accordance with the sensitive characteristics of the twins she was feeling immense happiness inside her with just a happy thought about Nandini. She had further speculated as to how he looked like, and that if the things came up as expected, she would have a brother-in-law. And then, how will she address him--- 'Jeeja ji' or 'Jeeju' as was the trend to call in the modern society?

"Mr. and Mrs. Prakash Chand, Mr. and Mrs. Veer Sen," said Ram Nath introducing them to each other. "And this is Vinay," he added. Welcoming the hon'ble guests, Mr. Veer Sen ushered them into the drawing room. While Mrs. Kamlesh too joined the gathering, Shalini rushed towards upstairs to see Nandini.

"Where are the girls?" asked Veer Sen.

Both Nandini and Shalini could be seen hugging each other in Nandini's room. And that was the crucial moment when Shalini, once again, was reminded of her promise.

Both of them were having a hearty laugh upon something. Soon they were summoned and the next moment they entered the drawing room. Before taking their seats they were looking for the boy who was well groomed and suited booted beyond recognition. While both the sisters looked happy, a little later, Shalini could recognize the boy. It was a great surprise for her but since Nandini looked awfully happy, her heart too had to feel happy according to their sensitive characteristics. Of course, a little later, she had learned that the boy had mistaken her for Nandini while seeing her. Thus the confusion was over and the boy for whom she too had a feeling of love under the sensitive behavior and characteristics of the twin sisters was gladly accepted as her would-be-brother-in-law.

Soon, pleasantries were exchanged and the general conversation ensued while tea and snacks were served. After the personalized information the discussion was shifted to the business matters. While the mini-party was in progress, Ram Nath was engaged with his camera, taking the photographs. Both Mr. Prakash and Veer Sen gave their consent and approved the conjugal relationship of Vinay and Nandini. Both the parties, however, were agreed to perform the necessary religious formalities for their engagement etc., only after their final examinations are over.

CHAPTER – 31

❦

Mangalu's oozed sympathy and selfless service had touched the core of his father's heart. He had seriously started contemplating about recompensing the life of his son. Gradually, Veer Sen had started moving independently after feeling to have recovered from physical stress whatsoever. To begin with, he had made it a daily routine of going for a stroll, starting first in the lawn of the Kothi. Then it was extended to the nearby park in the morning as well as in the evening regularly. He would make a few rounds of a reasonable distance with brisk walking and do some physical exercise also which he used to do with the help of his son, for about half an hour, before returning home. Such a busy daily schedule of morning as well as in the evening had definitely helped him in forgetting the bitter memories of his fit of palsy and other ailments. The whole course of such activities had, in fact, rejuvenated him, strengthening his faith and making him an optimistic once again.

"Doctor Sahib! there is a phone call for you, I have put it on hold in the office of the Medical Superintendent," said the Nurse, while leaving the hospital, after becoming off duty, at the East Nursing Home where Mangalu had been operated upon after having a fall from the cliff.

"By the way, who is on the line," asked the doctor.

"Somebody, by the name of Veer Sen," replied the Nurse.

"Veer Sen? That owner of the Cloth Mill?" asked the doctor once again.

"May be, I don't know," replied the Nurse and left immediately.

Doctor Sahib then rushed towards the Medical Superintendent's room to attend to the phone call. Picking up the receiver he said, "Hello, Doctor Ranjan speaking this side."

"Good afternoon Doctor Sahib, My name is Veer Sen, if you could recollect, the most unfortunate father of Mangalu, who had a fall from the cliff and was operated upon in your Nursing Home a few years back, precisely in the year 1975."

"Oh, yes. I do remember it very well, the boy who had got to be castrated quite reluctantly, in order to save his life. That was the first and the last case in my life where that kind of surgery had to be performed. By the way, how has he been pulling on?" asked the Doctor.

"Outwardly, he pretends to be all right but inwardly he looked very depressed. I am much worried about him and would like to have an appointment to discuss about his case. I'm confident that you would certainly help me by suggesting some way or the other to solve the problem," requested Veer Sen.

"Well, let me check my diary first. Yes, tomorrow would be the day fixed for operations. What about the day after tomorrow? I may be free in the morning and you may come at my clinic, located at the back of the Nursing Home between 9.30 a nd 10.00 o'clock. Would that be O.K.?" asked the Doctor.

"Yes doctor, that suits me. I would definitely be coming to see you before 10.00 A.M. at the clinic, day after tomorrow," replied Veer Sen.

In fact, Off and on, there had been news in the newspapers, that such-and-such person had gone through the 'change of sex' which had aroused a ray of hope in Veer

Sen's mind that something perhaps could be done in the case of poor Mangalu as well, who had been slowly and steadily suffering quite silently and sadly with his unexplainable grief.

On the day of appointment, Dr. Ranjan kept on waiting in his clinic to see Mr. Veer Sen who didn't turn up even by 10.00 o'clock. *'Supposedly, he might have been held up in the traffic jam, as it happens with me also many a time,'* thought Doctor Ranjan. However, on reaching the clinic at quarter past ten, Veer Sen had apologized for the late coming, due to the traffic jam, at not one but two places. In fact, the Nursing Home was located on the outskirts of the city, on the highway, which was prone to the traffic jam, specifically at peak hours, in the morning as well as in the evening, making the vehicles move at a snail's pace. Well, better late than never.

"Please be seated," said Doctor Sahib to Veer Sen who by the time had got extended his hand for the handshake. Soon after the warm-hearted handshake, Veer Sen, without wasting any time, had briefed the doctor about the whole case of Mangalu. He had also told him how he had served his father selflessly and devotedly when he had been totally bed ridden with palsy, for so many months, thus giving him a new lease of life. Coming to the point he said further, "I understand that the technology may not have advanced by that time when Mangalu was operated upon, a few years back, but now with the help of advanced technology in the field of surgery, is it possible to restore the loss of the male organ of a person at a later stage? Day in and day out, I hear about the cases of sex change from male to female and vice versa reported in medical journals as well as in newspapers. Couldn't my son be also helped out thus making him benefited with the latest technology?"

"Of course there had been remarkable progress in this direction but it certainly depends upon various other factors also which are considered with relation to each individual case. Let me explain to you something in detail: According to the diagnostic systems used in Indian Medical establishment, transsexualism is defined as a 'gender identity disorder'. The doctors usually prescribe a 'sexual reassignment surgery (SRS), which currently resorts to hormone therapy and surgical reconstruction and may include electrolysis, speech therapy and counseling as well. Surgical construction could include the removal of male sex organs and the construction of female ones. There are two 'stages' of surgery in the most respected procedures. The first stage is all the internal work that creates the vagina. The second stage is 'labiaplasty' that brings together the two sides of vaginal lips at the top to make a more 'authentic' appearance. Since government hospitals and qualified private practitioners do not usually perform SRS, many eunuchs go to quacks, thus placing themselves at serious risk. Neither the Indian Council for Medical Research (ICMR) nor the Medical Council of India (MCI) has formulated any guidelines to be followed in SRS. The attitude of the medical establishment has only reinforced the low sense of self-worth that many eunuchs have at various moments in their lives." He had further added: "It would be absolutely necessary to directly discuss with Mangalu all the details whether at any given time he had a strong feeling like having a female body trapped in his male body. Would he really like to go for a sex change and become a woman to enjoy the life of a female body after transformation? And of course various other kinds of questions and answers relating to the subject are required to be discussed."

CHAPTER – 32

❦

Disheartened, initially, Veer Sen seemed to have lost any hope of his son's starting a new life, yet, he wanted Mangalu to have at least a meeting with Doctor Ranjan for proper guidance on the matter which he wouldn't be able to discuss with him directly. He had, thus, once again got an appointment fixed with Doctor Sahib and asked Mangalu to visit his clinic in the back of the East Nursing Home at the appointed time the next day and see Doctor Ranjan as he wanted to discuss something important with you. Since Mangalu didn't have to do any specific work, he had reached the clinic half an hour earlier against the appointed time and had to wait till the arrival of Doctor Sahib.

A little later, the doctor's Assistant, a Nurse, had asked him to go and see Doctor Sahib in his cabin. After the exchange of pleasantries, Doctor Sahib had straight away asked Mangalu.

"There have been so many years since you had gone under the knife. How have you been feeling throughout all these years?"

"I have been feeling very much depressed, always living in gloom on the thought of having an unbearable and aimless life of a eunuch since then, except for a few months I had been serving my father when he had a sudden attack of paralyses. I, then, had a purpose to live, looking after my helpless ailing father. I had always been thinking, on what sins of mine, I had been targeted to receive that kind of punishment and become a victim at the cruel hands of the destiny," replied Mangalu.

"Have you ever experienced some woman-like feelings during this long period of so many years viz. dressing like a woman, interest in work relating to kitchen etc.? Have you ever wanted to become a woman and appraised by some male? These could be a few of the basic requirements before going for a sex change," said the doctor.

"No, I had never experienced the slightest feelings of any such kind. I had always wished to be a male and live like a macho man. Only a woman body could attract me, but for my state of helplessness of being a eunuch. I had never wanted, nor would ever like to go for the change of sex and become a woman," replied Mangalu firmly and decisively. So, Veer Sen's wish couldn't be fulfilled which seemed to have a bad effect on his mental as well as physical health. That had made him to live with a heavy burden upon his heart once again. He had been again advised for complete rest and consciously to take care of his health.

Taking advantage of poor Veer Sen's helplessness, Mrs. Rani had ceased to play the role of becoming benevolent anymore and had started behaving like a sovereign of an empire. Mangalu had made up his mind many a time to leave the Kothi but for his father. So far, his stepmother had no knowledge about his castration. He used to bear the brunt of even her own wrongdoings and get the scolding for no fault of his. He had tried his level best to adjust with the changed circumstances and always refrained from making any complaints to his father, lest he may feel sorrow or become somewhat mentally disturbed. So, even at the cost of the ill-treatment that was being meted out to him on one pretext or the other, Mangalu had always tried to maintain his cool and ignored certain kind of abuses hurled upon him without any valid reason. After all, there is a limit when things become completely unbearable. He had, by that time, fully understood that after his becoming a eunuch, he didn't have any future while living in the Kothi. Still, he didn't dare leave his ailing father. Yet he had to make the fateful decision.

Once on a night, when his stepmother was asleep in her room with her daughter Nandini in her cradle, it was Mangalu who had to administer the night-doze to his father as a daily routine, before retiring to his own room. Just after midnight, he was awakened by the sound of his bedroom door opening. Moments later he felt a soft, naked body next to his. Mangalu sat up in alarm.

"Hold me," his stepmother whispered. "I'm afraid of thunder."

"It – it isn't thundering," Mangalu stammered.

"But it *could* be. The newspaper said rain." She pressed her body close to his and said, "Make love to me baby."

Poor Mangalu was in a panic. "Sure. Can we do it in your bed?" he asked.

"O.K." She laughed.

"I'll be right there just after peeing," Mangalu promised.

She slid out of the bed and went upstairs into her bedroom, waiting for him. Poor Mangalu had never dressed faster in his life. He went out of the Kothi saying his final 'good bye' with a heavy heart and headed straightaway to his pal Bhima, never to look back.

CHAPTER – 33

❧

And that was the day of rejoicing once again when Mangalu regained his entry in the group of Bhima. Perhaps Mangalu had been destined to join the eunuchs and his earlier acquaintance with them, had proved to be just a prelude. With the joining of Mangalu once again the earnings had begun to soar to the previous level, e.g. before his accident. Having become the centre of attraction at each performance, Mangalu had become beloved of one and all. After almost a couple of years Bhima, on account of his old age, had willingly taken his retirement and with the general consensus Mangalu had become the head of the Band and ascended the coveted post vacated by Bhima. Thus the honour of 'Mukhiya ji' had been bestowed upon him in the year 1979 at the age of twenty one only.

Earlier, they used to have drinking sessions generally at weekends, but the sequence of those bouts had changed with the increased income. Henceforth, they would be looking for even a lame excuse to enjoy the occasion whatsoever. During one of those drinking bouts Bhima, in his inebriated state, had recalled about the happy occasion when Mangalu was born. He told him, "as soon as Veer Sen came to know of having become the father of a baby boy, his joy knew no bounds. All of us had visited the Kothi in the forenoon and began to sing and dance before anybody could take notice of our arrival. It was, however, your father who had received us at the gate. He had quickly offered us some amount and requested to revisit in the evening of coming Sunday, falling on a couple of days later, as both, the mother and the child had just come back from the hospital and taking rest. He had also informed us that while a number of messages of congratulations are being received on phone, there would be a good gathering of our relatives and well-wishers on Sunday being a holiday. So, please do come on Sunday again, Veer Sen had insisted."

Continuing further, Bhima had added, "come Sunday and we were surprised on reaching the Kothi. It had been ostentatiously decorated as if a marriage ceremony was going to take place. As Veer Sen's family had its first child, he had arranged for some light refreshment as well for the visiting guests. Of course, a host of relatives had come to congratulate the couple. Everybody was seen rejoicing on the happy occasion. Holding you lovingly in our lap turn by turn, all of us sang and danced on the tunes of the most popular film songs as well as the 'Badhai Geet' with our blessings. A few of the guests too had participated in the dancing bouts. Quite amusingly, Veer Sen too had joined them on their persistent requests. While your father had rewarded us quite handsomely, who-so-ever was present there had also given us reward with open hand. In fact, that had happened to be the only occasion in the whole of my life when the collection had surpassed all the previous such occasions till that day, the sweet memory of which all of us still cherish very proudly. Since then we always hold your father in great esteem."

CHAPTER – 34

❧

Constant knocking at the door had made Mukhiya ji a bit irritated. After a hectic schedule since morning, he had just been trying to have a nap on reaching his so-called home. It consisted of two small rooms quite adjacent to each other. The house also had some covered space, say about half of its courtyard, in front of both the rooms, commonly known as verandah. So, both the rooms had their entrance through that verandah. The small wooden gate of the house that opened in the street didn't have any name plate fixed upon it and had a marginal width to allow just one person at a time to enter the courtyard. Though, the not so soothing voice, as well as the tone of the person calling at the door, appeared to be somewhat familiar, yet it had taken a few seconds for Mukhiya ji to recollect before he opened the door.

The visitor's name was Rang Nath known by his nick name Ranga who too belonged to the same community of eunuchs as that of Mukhiya ji but was from another area of the city after he had parted ways a couple of years ago. He was of a normal height, with medium built structure, a clean shaven face adorned with pierced ear-lobes wearing a pair of small gold rings in them. The colour of his eyes was brown which didn't support any eyebrows at the base of his forehead. He had kept fashionably cut a little long black hair falling upon his shoulders. A thin golden chain was seen worn around his neck. His yellowish teeth and the red-black 'M' shaped lips were clearly suggestive of his habit of chewing *pan, tobacco and smoking of bidies* as well.

He had come wearing a Neta-ji type dress of a white kurta pyjama and a pair of slippers. From his attire he didn't look like a eunuch. Soon after the exchange of pleasantries, both of them got settled on the wooden bench lying in the verandah itself.

In fact, Mukhiya ji was hardly in a mood to welcome anybody at that hour of the day. However, he had to call, rather half-heartedly, the tea vendor, popularly known by his nick name Babu, in the neighbourhood and ordered for the tea. Rangnath, had, at first, pretended to have made just a courtesy call but it didn't take long for Mukhiya ji to guess that the real purpose of the so called courtesy call at that hour of the day, could be something else which had surfaced after a short while when their conversation appeared to have taken an uncomfortable turn over the bout of tea.

"This is the gross violation of our verbal commitment to each other," the visitor was complaining, upon which Mukhiya ji retorted:

"What kind of violation are you talking about? In these two years, since our parting, we have hardly met each other face to face, say about not more than half a dozen times. As far as I can remember, we always had maintained very cordial relations with each other enjoying our fate of earnings within our territories as settled with our mutual consent and never bothered to make any disgraceful attempt to let down the other, come what may. Even today, at the moment, you happen to be my honoured guest and it is my privilege to welcome you as an old pal in this small cottage of mine. Here, you may just feel at home. Open up your mind and let me know clearly without any hitch, as to what kind of grudge you seem to have against me or my people."

Soon, the effect of Mukhiya ji's soothing words was instantly visible upon the face of the visitor. However, with much hesitation, and after giving a second thought to what he wanted to say, Ranga had tried to mention in brief the kind of humiliation his people had been subjected to, the previous week.

"Well, if my guess is not wrong, you are perhaps talking about that newly built portion of Chaudhary Sahib's house, located at the extreme corner of the street which has now been closed at the other end. The irony of the fact, as you know, is that the lane in question had virtually been considered to be a common passage and used by the general public as thorough fare over the years. However, Chaudhary Sahib, with his political influence, has made forcible occupancy of the place at the north end of the lane and has also built a portion upon it making an extension of his already existing house adjacent to the newly occupied place. This has blocked the street completely making it a dead-end lane henceforth," said Mukhiya ji.

Ranga nodded in affirmation and hastened to narrate in detail as to what actually had happened in the case of that particular house of Chaudhary Sahib: "As we all know, the house in question had been under construction for quite a long time. Not only the construction of the house is illegal but even the public land, forcibly usurped by the person, is illegal which has fraudulently been shown as a vacant plot in the map submitted to the authorities. Though, this is well within the knowledge of the officers concerned who have been handling the case, yet nobody dares to point out a finger. While some of the officers concerned could have been forced upon keeping their mouths shut by making lucrative offers of one kind or the other to them, there could be another lot who didn't dare to speak a word against the whole scam just out of fear of being harmed at a later stage."

Being a habitual smoker, Ranga, after a little pause, had asked for a 'bidi'. Mukhiya ji immediately fetched a small bundle of 'bidies' of 501 from his room adjacent to the verandah. As per the general practice which prevailed among the habitual smokers, Ranga held a pair of bidies together between the fore finger and middle finger of his right hand, since he happened to be a left-hander, lit them up and offered one bidi to Mukhiya ji who willingly took it with a smile. After drawing two-three large puffs through his long 'M' shaped lips, Ranga had continued with his narration:

"The electrification job with the underground wiring was also done side by side as the construction work progressed, I was told. Moreover, almost all the modern amenities had been provided by the builder. That included the fixing of fire extinguishers also on all the floors as required under the law. But even after giving the final touches, all his efforts to get the required 'completion certificate' from the concerned authorities had become futile. They had been raising one objection or the other, time and again, thereby resulting in an inordinate delay. While Chaudhary Sahib had been putting immense pressure upon the builder to hasten the job, he, on his part, showed his helplessness to meet the unscrupulous demands of the officers and was completely at a loss to know, for what to do in the kind of situation he was in. Per chance I had come to know from a reliable source that somebody by the name of Mr. Dua, I don't know his full name, was at the helm of it which had been instrumental in making all the fuss."

"Could it be the same Mr. Dua whose son….. I have forgotten his name, was involved in an accident last year?" asked Mukhiya ji. The case was reported in all the newspapers I remember, where his name had come up as an accused."

"Yes, you got it absolutely right. Now the twist in the story is that it was 'me' on whose behind-the-scene efforts, the boy had escaped the verdict of being sent to the prison," said Ranga.

"Well, it looks quite interesting. By the way, how did you come in to the picture?" asked Mukhiya ji once again.

"It so happened that one of our members in our group 'Maskari' had revealed a top secret to me which had prompted me to ponder over the whole matter and make some solid alibi in defence of the boy which had ultimately paved the way to his release and thus saved him from going behind the bars as well," replied Ranga and added, "Of course I had to run from pillar to post to strengthen the evidence which in the end had worked to the delight of all concerned. While arranging the whole sequence, I had taken in to confidence the advocate who had been engaged to represent the case, and suggested him to just prepare the case on the lines that the boy, accused of the offence, was not at the steering wheel of the car and had been virtually sitting at the police station at the time of the accident to report about his missing car, which later on, had been found lying abandoned at a far off place and not anywhere near, in the vicinity of that area."

"I had also assured him that money would be no constraint at any stage as I had already discussed with Mr. Dua, and his job would be to prove and make the Court believe that the car in question had been stolen by someone else about an hour before the reported time of the accident. That the owner of the car had been asking the people whether anybody had seen any police-crane which might have picked up his vehicle for parking it in a 'No-parking' zone or for some other offence. But soon, after getting no response to his queries, the boy had straight away headed for the police station to lodge the first information report (FIR) of his missing car. However, the constable on duty at the police station had made him sit and wait for the S.H.O. who was supposed to be on his way to reach the police station in a few minutes."

"He could also add that the news about the boy's stolen car had just been received in the police station itself which had prompted the constable to detain the boy on the pretext to wait for registering the complaint which the boy had already given in writing showing the registration number of his vehicle. In fact the registration number of the car supposed to have met with the accident, had matched with that of the car for which the complaint had been received and lying before the constable who had stealthily checked it without the boy's knowledge. By the time, the S.H.O. too had arrived. The constable on duty then explained the whole thing to the S.H.O. who, as per their routine procedure, had taken the boy in to a solitary room for questioning as is customary for these police wallahs, and tried to force him to confess the crime, despite knowing the fact that the boy had already been physically present and sitting in the police station much before the reported accident of his vehicle. The boy had tried his level best to convince the S.H.O. about his innocence but nobody paid any heed to his pleadings and was thrown in to the lock-up. There he was forced to sign some blank papers also, with the mala fide intention to make use of them against the boy at some later stage."

CHAPTER – 35

❦

"Apparently, seeing no way out, the boy had to reveal, during the questioning, his real identity. As soon as the S.H.O. came to know that the boy's name was 'Kundan Dua' who happens to be the only son of Mr. Dua, the top most senior officer in a Government department, his attitude got changed in no time. In the light of his vast knowledge and experience of having dealt with a number of such cases, he immediately had sensed a big scope of making some easy bucks and ordered some light refreshment with coffee for the boy, who had been abruptly refused and not allowed to make even a phone call before the questioning. With the sudden change in the tense atmosphere at the police station, the boy was allowed to take it easy and make as many calls he wishes to make but strictly on the condition, not to mention anything about the harsh treatment he had been subjected to. Kundan was so scared that he didn't dare call his father himself about his car accident. Instead, the first phone-call he made from the police station was received by 'Maskari' a member of our group who had passed on the detailed information to me. I was also told about his getting a V.I.P. treatment and enjoying some light refreshment at the expense of the police department. That could have happened only after he gave his identity as the only son of Mr. Dua."

"And what is that top secret you have still been holding on to your chest?" asked Mukhiya ji.

"Just wait and have a little patience," continued Ranga. "You may feel a little surprised that Mr. Dua, in fact, has been holding the post of a senior most officer in his department and has made a lot of money on account of a number of scams also. His modus operandi seems to be quite foolproof. Being the head of his branch he has made a group of his trusted juniors under the oath of confidentiality that they would never disclose anything to anyone about their operating system. He had cleverly made a strategy of allotting certain kinds of lucrative jobs relating to his branch to a few of his most trusted officers and proportionately fixed some hidden service charges over and above the actual fee to be charged from the public for doing their work."

"The system worked wonderfully to the satisfaction of both, the public as well as the officers doing the job. In order to save their time and energy in visiting the office, off and on and getting their work delayed upon one pretext or the other, the people didn't mind paying some extra bucks for getting their work done without any kind of hitch. The enormous additional amount of service charges thus collected over a period of time, say quarterly or half-yearly in the pool, is fairly distributed among the officers according to their position and rank without any fuss whatsoever. However, it could be anybody's guess that while the junior officers get their meagre share, a large portion of the booty goes to Mr. Dua."

"My patience has now crossed its limit and 'am still waiting to listen to the so-called 'top secret' of yours. For God's sake, let Mr. Dua stay where he is for the time being and tell me about that top secret to the satisfaction of my curiosity which I can't hold anymore," said Mukhiya ji.

"O.K., O.K., now, just hold on your breath and listen. The boy Kundan, that wretched son of Mr. Dua, is gay," revealed Ranga.

"So what?" asked Mukhiya ji. "There could be unimaginable number of 'gay' persons in our society. How does his gayness relate to that accident? There seems to be no link at all between the two."

"Well, let me explain the whole thing in detail," said Ranga and continued: "As you also must be aware of the fact that Mr. Dua had thrown a lavish party on the New Year Eve at his farm house located at just walking distance at the back of his bungalow. Needless to say that most of the honoured guests comprised of the persons who attended the party, had some kind of business links with Mr. Dua who had been benefited from his scams at one time or the other. Though all efforts had been made to make the party a secret affair, yet our band was able to sense it as it was being organized in the area that falls in our territory. Consequently, I myself, along with our group members, barged in to the party at around midnight when it was running at full swing. While eatables of different varieties, veg. as well as non-veg. had been displayed on the counters decoratively on the two sides of the 'Pandal' with the chefs in attendance inviting the guests, nobody seemed to care to at least have a glance over them. All the hustle and bustle could be seen only towards the north side which was reserved for 'The Bar'. Here, one could have his share of liquor of any brand he preferred to choose from. Our presence at the party, however, was a great surprise to one and all."

〜

CHAPTER – 36

"The scene at the party venue, however, looked somewhat different. Almost all the guests, reaching the gate seemed to be quite like gentlemen while alighting from their limousines, marutis, ambassadors, wagon-Rs etc. etc. But as soon as they entered the 'Pandal' their first and foremost task was to look around to find 'The Bar' and run straightaway in that direction. In their quest to reach the 'Bar' Counter, they could hardly recognize any acquaintances while heading hurriedly towards 'The Bar.' And as soon as they were able to lay their hands upon their favourite brand and manage to get hold of a large peg, they would feel themselves like in heaven. Only after that they would start recognizing other guests which belonged to the business community. Of course there could be some who, after having a peg or two, are able to keep themselves quite sober. Yet, there happen to be others who would gulp down their throats an unlimited quantity of liquor, since it was available free of cost, irrespective of it being of any damn brand, and in their inebriated state of mind, would make fun and expose themselves with some kind of beast-like behavior."

"Please don't tell me all that. I, myself have attended such parties many a time and am quite aware of the things you have been explaining to me. But my dear friend, don't you feel that you have gone astray from the main subject? I'm still eager to listen to the details," retorted Mukhiya ji once again.

Ranga nodded to the comments of Mukhiya ji and said, "O.K., here I come directly to the main point. While everybody at the party had been dancing and enjoying the occasion, certain guests had been eagerly waiting the clock to strike the 'Zero Hour'. Only a few minutes were left to welcome the 'New Year' when 'Maskari', the young and beautiful member of our band wanted to go to the washroom. A young man from the party who had been dancing at every movement of Maskari and trying to follow her steps, offered to accompany her and show the way to the washroom located in the bungalow, which Maskari had willingly agreed to. I could see both of them going towards the bungalow holding their hands together and disappearing after a short while."

Here, Ranga paused for a minute and asked for a 'bidi' once again to which, Mukhiya ji gave him the whole bundle to enjoy as many puffs as he liked. Just like before Ranga again didn't forget the custom of offering one from the pair of bidis he had lit and continued with the next part of his story, a little later.

"Suddenly the chiming of the clock was heard when it's both the hands touched the figure '12' striking a dozen times to announce that the previous year had bade 'good bye' to all of them who happened to be present over there and elsewhere, thus vacating the throne it had been occupying for the last twelve months and making room to welcome the New Year. Though the other young members of our band had participated in singing and dancing at the popular numbers of film songs on the constant demands of the honourable guests as well as the host Mr. Dua, yet, there were a few others who had tried to display wads of currency notes in their hands demanding the dance of Maskari once again. No doubt we had already received a handsome reward for participating in the event."

"By the time, Maskari too had returned from the bungalow, sans the young man, who had accompanied her to the washroom", added Ranga. "She was trying to whisper something in to my ears, but the 'gathering' didn't allow her to speak a word and forced her to dance and sing once more for their amusement even against her wishes. Mr. Dua, the host too, by the time had joined the bandwagon to make a final request which we couldn't dare refuse. Anyway, after having a buffet dinner to their fill, the guests left one by one and the party ended on a happy note wishing each other a happy and prosperous New Year."

"On our way, back home, Maskari had taken me in to confidence telling that on entering the bungalow, both of them, she and her companion, noticed some commotion in the room adjacent to the washroom itself. In her own words: 'the first thought which had come to our mind was that since the people had been busy in enjoying the party, somebody could be trying to steal something from the bungalow. So very cautiously we stepped forward to reach the door and found that it was a little ajar through which we could see on peeping through the narrow opening, as to what was supposed to be happening inside the room. Unfortunately, there was no light inside that room and both of us could only make a guess as to what could be happening there.'

Continuing further, Maskari had added: "Soon our eyesight became a bit familiar to the darkness of the room and making a vague imagination we could see a couple of human male figures indulging in some unnatural act which instantly had given us a shock. While I was still managing to recover, the young boy accompanying me, who must have already been familiar to the place, had, out of sheer curiosity, entered the room and put the light on. And then we were doubly shocked to see that one of those boys was Kundan Dua alias 'Kundu Bhai', the only son of the host, who had become the passive partner in the act. Interestingly, instead of feeling somewhat guilty for being caught red-handed with their shameful act, they had invited my companion also to share the activity, who too had joined them with a smiling face to have some fun whatsoever. Even us, the so-called eunuchs, have to think twice before indulging in such kind of sexual behaviour," said Maskari.

"It could have been possible that the host, Mr. Dua, himself, was quite unaware of the fact that his only son was 'gay'. That portion of bungalow had been given a secret code name 'G' house, I was told and was commonly known among all the gay acquaintances of Kundu Bhai which had been frequently used as 'gay bar' by his homosexual friends. I have since advised Maskari to forget the whole thing as if that was a bad dream", said Ranga.

"But I'm still baffled to find out the relevance of all this, with the car accident," Mukhiya ji had asked once again with somewhat annoyance.

"Being a gay himself," replied Ranga, "Kundu Bhai had a large number of his gay acquaintances of which, a few of them had always been on the look for some more fun-loving persons like them. Having access to easy money Kundu Bhai was always surrounded by his so-called friends upon whom he used to spend lavishly just for the asking. On the day of the car accident, the whole gay party had been travelling in that car and Kundu Bhai himself was at the driving seat. All of a sudden the car jerked to one side and the occupants had tumbled one after the other from their respective seats. Least caring about any injuries they could have sustained in the fall, all of them had forced themselves to leave the place in no time and fled in to different directions before getting noticed by someone. The site of the accident was at a short distance from our dwelling place."

Ranga further told: "Since Kundu Bhai had already developed some kind of intimacy with Maskari and often used to come to our place, he had preferred to get in to my house before anybody could find his whereabouts. He had become very nervous and was breathing heavily. Maskari had fetched him a glass of water. Soon he appeared to have cooled down a bit and then narrated that his car had met with an accident just nearby and while all his so called friends have fled immediately from the scene of the accident, he couldn't think of a safer place other than my house to take shelter for some time at least. He had also requested me if we could be of any help to him in case of a police report etc. It could be anybody's guess that Kundu Bhai had approached us because of his gayness. On my advice, then, he had to run straightaway to the police station to lodge first information report (FIR) that his car had been stolen."

"And here comes the second part of the story," continued Ranga. "Immediately after dispatching Kundu Bhai to the police station, I contacted Mr. Dua and introduced myself as one of his great well-wishers. On giving the reference of his New Year party, he was able to recognize me and then I briefly explained to him about the car accident. I Could, also make him believe that the honour of Dua family was at stake on account of Kundu Bhai's involvement in the accident as he had been on the steering-wheel. Since the car belonged to the respected Dua family, the case is prone to be reported to the 'press' and all the newspapers are likely to carry the details of the car accident the very next day."

"By the way, I didn't forget to mention about the barbarous attitude of the so-called police department, notorious enough about their way of working as well as the evil designs they could adopt in order to serve the purpose to their own advantage and trying to extract as much money from the parties involved in such cases on one plea or the other. Further when he was told that his son was in police custody, he appeared to be a little scared. At that juncture, I did quote an old saying: 'Money makes the mare go' and convinced him that in order to save the family honour, Mr. Dua ought not to hesitate in spending money to the extent possible and that too without any hitch whatsoever. And with that firm assurance from Mr. Dua, I had proceeded further and approached the lawyer, S.H.O. etc. and got the case settled which has now become history. Needless to say that one and all, associated or connected in any manner with the case, got benefited in some way or the other and myself was not an exception who had been rewarded handsomely for taking so much pain that resulted in a happy ending note."

"But what about that 'Completion Certificate' you were referring to, before Mr. Dua's story?" Mukhiya ji reminded.

"The builder had received it the very next day on the instructions of Mr. Dua, after his son was acquitted by the court and the case was cleared."

"Well, now coming back to the main topic we had been conversing with, before the story of Mr. Dua came up in-between, let me explain the whole thing. It was on Wednesday last week when all of a sudden we got the information that Chaudhary Sahib's family would be having the religious ritual, commonly known as 'Griha Pravesh' on the very next day viz. Thursday since that was declared as the most auspicious day by their family-Pandit ji. The performance of the ritual, in fact, used to have been carried on since the time immemorial which is considered to be beneficial not only to the present occupants of the house but for the coming generations as well. It is believed that this kind of 'yajna' or 'havan' brings peace, prosperity and longevity to the inhabitants of the house. Since the so-called 'haven' was supposed to be performed in the morning itself, our band had called at Chaudhary Sahib's house in the evening for our 'neg' (reward) on their 'Griha Pravesh'. But were abruptly told that a hefty amount had already been paid to your band which happened to have called upon them the same afternoon before our reaching there," said Ranga.

"Yes, we do acknowledge of having received the 'neg'. So, what is wrong with that?" asked Mukhiya ji.

"But you ought to appreciate the fact that the new construction has come up at the dead end of the common passage which consists of the common 'dividing line' of our territories of operation. Accordingly, we too are entitled to at least fifty percent share of the reward received by your group, in cash or kind," argued Ranga.

"I am sorry, I can't buy your argument on that account", said Mukhiya ji. He had further clarified: "The newly built structure, in fact, has become the extended portion of the house which already exists in our area of operation. In other words, the already existing house of Chaudhary Sahib on our side has now covered some more area to look like a bungalow which doesn't have a separate entity. So, the question of sharing the 'neg' doesn't arise at all. Had that been an independent house, both of us could have called upon them together and got an equal share of the so-called 'neg'. I do hope that you have now understood the whole situation as I have explained to you. So, my dear friend, the matter now stands settled that way and you should make your people understand the simple logic for the sake of keeping peace and harmony. There should be no ill will of any kind between both of us," said Mukhiya ji. Though it seemed as if Rang Nath still remained unconvinced, yet he had to return without gaining any monetary benefit against his wishes.

CHAPTER – 37

ᴄ⁄ᴏ

L ike other bands of eunuchs in the city, Mangalu's band too had their daily schedule fixed for visiting different streets, Mohallas or bazaars of the localities which came under their domain as decided with the mutual consent of Bhima, the then Mukhiya and Rang Nath's band of eunuchs, long back. In fact, the ill conceived suggestion of parting their ways at that time, had come from Ranga who had been contemplating for long to win the title of 'Mukhiya' but could not succeed due to the indignation of some members of the band. However, he was able to convince the other likeminded ones with whom he had formed his own band and shifted to another part of the city, as was mutually agreed upon. Had he not left the Bhima's band, it could be him, who would have become the Mukhiya after the voluntary retirement of Bhima on becoming incapacitated on account of his old age.

Anyway, it so happened that on a certain morning, going on the band's scheduled daily beat, Mangalu and party had just entered a street from the main bazaar when he suddenly caught sight of a big poster with Shri Sai Baba's photo printed in the centre which had a caption in bold letters announcing that a programme of Shri Sai Baba's Bhajan Sandhya (an evening of Sai Baba's devotional songs) was being organized at some nearby place on such-and-such date. That, instantly had reminded him of his own promise made to his grandma years before, while she was on her deathbed and told him about the vow of his mother to pay her obeisance to Shri Sai Baba which had not been fulfilled as yet. He had felt very much ashamed and to some extent had cursed himself for such kind of forgetfulness and wondered how such an important thing had gone out of his mind for so long. Presumably, the lapse could be attributed to certain unforeseen circumstances like his own accident of becoming a eunuch and the grave illness of his father etc. Well, there is a saying: 'Better late than never.' He had resolved there and then to pay a visit to Shirdi on the first available opportunity to pay his homage.

Once, having made up his mind he had a talk with Bhima about his planned visit to Shirdi. Shedding the attire of choli and ghaghra usually worn by the eunuch community while performing, as a general routine, Mangalu got himself dressed in dhoti-kurta, like a normal man for the holy journey. Keeping in view that it wouldn't take him more than a couple of days for the 'to and fro' journey, he tucked one set of a fresh dhoti-kurta in his bag along with a bed-sheet which he may require either to lie down upon or use it as a safety-cover from the mosquitoes at night. Of course he didn't forget to put other essentials like a small cake of soap, tooth-paste, tooth-brush, a towel, etc. He had to travel by train up to Manmad railway station. And from Manmad he had to board a direct Bus for Shirdi situated at a short distance of merely 60 Kms. by road. Most of the passengers in the bus were bound for Shirdi, like Mangalu who were busy in having an informal chat among themselves about social incidents. The bus reached Shirdi in the late hours of the evening and Mangalu along with a few other co-passengers headed towards the Samadhi Mandir direct from the bus-terminal. At the Mandir, since the evening prayer was already over, they were told about the timings of the next prayer (Aarti) of Sai Baba which is held daily in the early morning at 04.30 a.m. Outside the Samadhi

Mandir, he could very easily find a place of accommodation that looked like a Dharmshala where the pilgrims visiting Shirdi used to stay. Having no other option Mangalu had decided to participate in the morning-prayer positively. And to stay for the night he was able to get accommodation on a nominal rent in the vicinity of the Samadhi Mandir.

It was a small room that contained a wooden cot with a mattress and a bed-sheet spread over it. No pillow. A bucket for water and a plastic mug was also provided. A running water-tap was there just outside the row of four rooms to be commonly used by the other occupants as well. Likewise a set of four lavatories cleaned by water and connected to a sewage system, was also there in the extreme corner. He had heard about the canteen from his neighbour and accompanied him to have his dinner. That way he had a chance to take his meals in the huge canteen which could cater a thousand persons in one go. The food was very good and low-priced, available through the coupon-system. There were tens of rows of long wooden tables for keeping large steel-plates of meals upon them, coupled with an equal number of wooden benches put alongside for the convenience of the people to sit upon and eat their meals. There was great rush and it appeared as if the whole of inhabitants of Shirdi don't have kitchen at their dwelling place and come to that huge canteen for their meals which is both qualitative as well as quantitative and also affordable by one and all. After the dinner, Mangalu returned to his room, laid upon the bed to ward off his tiredness and went to sleep in no time

In spite of having a comfortable place to stay for the night, Mangalu couldn't have a sound sleep fearing he may not wake up in time. Incidentally, he had a wrist-watch with radium dial which enabled him to see the time even in darkness. Being of an old model it didn't have the facility of alarm. So, poor fellow kept on waking up at short intervals throughout the night, lest he may remain dozed off and miss the early morning prayers. It was 03.05 a.m. by his watch when Mangalu got up. After answering the nature-call, he brushed his teeth. Then fetched a bucketful of water from the tap outside the room and had a quick bath. Putting on the fresh dhoti-kurta which he had specially brought for the purpose he made a run towards the Samadhi Mandir. He was awestruck to see the huge silver statue of Shri Sai Baba, dressed beautifully and installed upon a raised platform. It contained a large silver umbrella over its head. The devotees thronged into the hall to have a glimpse of Shri Sai Baba but the priests would literally lead them on to the walking spree and won't let them have a contented look at Shri Sai Baba for more than a few seconds. There was an assembly hall in front of it which had the capacity to accommodate around 600 devotees at a time. The prayers were sung in chorus by the devotees in Gujarati language. Though Mangalu didn't understand anything of it, yet he felt immensely pleased while participating in it.

He had also made himself acquainted with one of the priests performing the *aarti pooja*. Taking him in to confidence he explained to him about his late mother's vow and under his advice, Mangalu had paid his obeisance with full devotion as directed. Thus the vow of his mother as well as his own promise, made to his Daadi-ma, had been fulfilled. He had also prayed for peace, prosperity and health for his father and other family members including his siblings, stepmother, Bhima and the other members of their band. In an enclosure adjacent to the Samadhi Mandir there was a fire-place that constantly keeps on burning heavy logs of wood producing ash-powder called sacred

Bhabhooti or Bhasm. The same is packed in tiny sealed sachets for distribution amongst the devotees who opt for taking a sachet or two for their home. Mangalu too had taken a sachet of the sacred Bhabhooti to be kept at the place of worship in his room where he too had placed, like his grandma, the statuette of the deity on the small triangular wooden plate fixed in the north corner of his room.

He had visited Dwarkamai as well situated towards the right side of the Samadhi Mandir. It is said that once, It was, in fact, a mosque in a very dilapidated condition. Baba turned it into Dwarkamai and proved that God is one. "*Sab ka maalik Ek*" He had also seen there a grinding stone (*chakki*) and a wooden vessel in which Baba used to keep the *Bhiksha* (alms) brought from the village. On taking a round of the bazaar he had observed that the inhabitants of Shirdi had been engaged in the only profession of selling material like pictures, statues, calendars, books etc. relating to the life and teachings of Sai Baba. On the whole, Mangalu had been feeling quite happy for having paid his obeisance to Sai Baba, and fulfilled the *vow* his mother had made to Him, as also his own promise made to his grandma. And thus the purpose of the journey could be accomplished on a happy note in 1980, after about twenty two years of the vow taken by his mother.

On his return journey Mangalu again came to Manmad by Bus. He had to wait for the train which was supposed to be running late by an hour or so. As soon as the train entered the platform coolies jumped on to the gates of the compartments to fetch the luggage of the passengers de-boarding at Manmad station. Mangalu too tried and jumped into one of the compartments when the train slowed down a bit before coming to halt. He then looked for an empty upper berth. Having found one he occupied the same and lay there with his eyes closed as if sleeping. However, at the very next station another passenger had come up to share the berth with him as the compartment had become fully crowded.

Failed to be woken up by the hustle and bustle of the boarding or de-boarding of passengers at almost every station, Mangalu did have a sound sleep. He didn't stir a bit and was quite unaware of even when his co-passenger, who had shared his berth, got off the train mid-way on reaching his destination. However, tired of lying for a long time on his back, Mangalu, with his eyes still closed, was having a great difficulty in trying to change his body posture towards his left side. He cursed the railways for providing such narrow berths which could have been a little wider to lie down upon them a bit comfortably. He could never think beyond, that those upper berths were actually meant for keeping the luggage of the passengers. In fact, people like him seldom care about the problems of their co-passengers. It has been a common sight at railway stations that as soon as a person, like Mangalu, gets inside the train, his first and foremost task becomes to look for a vacant upper berth. On finding one, he occupies the same by hook or by crook. He, then, spreads a sheet of cloth and lies down upon it with his eyes closed, pretending to be a sick person, sleeping there since ages.

While changing his posture, Mangalu suddenly realized that the stoppage of the train had become somewhat longer than usual. Out of curiosity, he opened his eyes, lifted his head a little and leaned at the edge of his berth towards the floor of the compartment to ask somebody as to which station that was. To his great dismay, there was not a soul in sight. He became a little panicky and immediately got alighted from the berth. Looking out through the window he found that the train had already reached its terminus. Only then he could realize that he had slept for so long.

⌒⌒

CHAPTER – 38

Fearing that the empty train would soon be taken into the railway yard for cleaning etc., Mangalu collected his bag that served as pillow and got down from his berth. Running in the aisle of the compartment he had hurriedly rushed towards the door and in the haste got his foot struck with something that made him stumble. He could have become injured badly, had he not caught hold of a side-berth while falling in the aisle. Having a narrow escape, he stood up quickly and found a pair of legs of a little child protruding from beneath a lower berth of the compartment, his foot had struck with. Poor child, had unknowingly, extended his legs, during the sleep, towards the common passage in the aisle. Out of sheer compassion, Mangalu, lovingly dragged the child from below the seats, lifted it in his lap and brought it out on the platform. He then looked for a vacant space on one of the wooden benches at the platform. Finding one, he sat upon one of them and made the child too sit beside him. Scantily clad in an over-sized frock, the child, happened to be a female one, aged just about 2-3 years only. She looked beautiful and had distinctive features of her face, with regard to the shape and visual effect, supported by a pointed nose. The colour of her eyes was blue and she was barefooted.

"What's your name, beta!" asked Mangalu.

".. .. .. .."

Giving just a blank look, she didn't speak a word. Mangalu tried repeatedly to coax her to say something but that too proved a futile attempt. Perhaps the child was too small to understand or speak something worthwhile, or she didn't know the language Mangalu was talking in. Suddenly he noticed that she had been constantly staring at a moving cart selling rice-meals to the passengers at the platform. Guessing that she could be hungry, Mangalu made some eating-like gesture pointing his hands towards his mouth. That instantly brought a big smile on her face. He fetched a plate of rice immediately. He was going to feed the child with his own hand but, to his amusement, she attacked her meal with such gusto as if she had never eaten anything since her birth.

It was a matter of great speculation as to what would have made her parents to abandon such a lovely, innocent and beautiful child of that tender age in the railway compartment. Had there been any compulsion, they could have offered the child for adoption to some issue-less couple. Though Mangalu himself didn't have much knowledge on the subject, yet he thought that at least some efforts could have been made in that direction. Perhaps, they could have approached some maternity hospital for help explaining their inability to take care of the child in the absence of having some regular means of living. Possibly, some non-governmental organization (NGO) could have come forward to take the child under their umbrella and arrange for keeping her in the safe custody of somebody who could assure to look after the child. Long ago, Mangalu had heard about the doctrine of communism, advocating a society in which everything is publically owned. Every body works and is paid according to his needs and abilities. Where the Govt. was supposed to take the liability of the children for their education, as well as look after them till they come of age. That form of society was established in the former USSR and elsewhere. And therefore, cases like abandoning the children seldom happen in those countries. But, here in India, there is no dearth of such cases. Precisely, not a day goes by, when news like abandoning or kidnapping or even raping of children, are not reported in the media.

Another thing, that had come to his mind was, that sometimes, the person, after committing such kind of odious act, becomes compunctious, on pricking of his conscience, after giving a second thought to his odious deed. Likewise, there could be a bleak chance of the probability that the child's parents might have realized that their unkind act amounted to betraying their own flesh and blood and may have some feeling of repentance as well later on. But, the irremediable loss can't be recouped, as the popular saying goes: It's no use, crying over spilt milk'. There was no way to find out as to when and at what station, they left the child sleeping and stealthily sneaked out of the train. Since the act was supposed to have been done deliberately with the malicious thinking to get rid of the child, any hopeful wait of returning her parents to make good the loss was absolutely meaningless.

Mangalu indeed possessed a heart of gold. With utmost sympathy towards the child he began to ponder upon some ways and means regarding her safety. The first step he could think of was to approach the Station Master (SM).

Looking through his spectacles, fitted with the large-sized thick lenses in a black frame, which rested upon his head, instead of nose, the SM put a glance over the visitor, holding the hand of a child and entering his cabin, which was located at almost the centre of the railway platform. He possessed a lean and frail figure with the bald head at the centre, but a few white-hair-strands still adored alongside his both the ears. His clean-shaved wrinkled face suggested that he must be running into fifties and looked at the verge of retirement. From the way he was collecting his papers, lying unevenly scattered before him, and hurriedly putting them in the drawer of his big table which had a wireless set fitted at one of its corners it appeared as if he was going off duty.

Shifting immediately the specs from his head and placing the same on his nose, he looked inquisitively towards Mangalu and waved them to sit upon a couple of chairs placed across the big table.

"What brought you here?" He asked Mangalu, before letting him sit on the chair.

"It's this little child I'm worried about," replied Mangalu. "I noticed her sleeping under the seats of a compartment of the train which has just terminated at this platform a little while ago. As you see, she is about 2-3 years of age which appears to have been abandoned by her parents deliberately to get rid of the liability to look after her. She can't understand anything and gives a blank look when asked about her name etc. I didn't want to leave her alone at the platform itself for the fear of her falling into some wrong hands and as such I have brought her here to hand her over to you. For the sake of humanity, now, it should be the responsibility of the railway authorities to take care of her or make some suitable arrangement for her safety," he added.

The S.M., however, didn't have the patience to listen to anything, poor Mangalu had been trying to explain. Instead, he took him into another room, next to his own and handed over the bunch of papers he had just collected from his table to the person sitting over there and said, "Since my duty is over, the Asstt. Station Master (ASM) would be on duty now". The outgoing SM then introduced Mangalu to the ASM. So, Mangalu, once again had to explain and apprise the ASM of the situation he was in. In response, the ASM gave a sorrowful look towards the child but at the same time regretted his inability to do anything in the matter. Instead, with a piece of advice he said to Mangalu, 'Why don't you take her to the police for help where she could be kept in to their safe custody, at least till some alternate arrangement is made to accommodate her somewhere. Hopefully, efforts could also be made to find out her parents or a lawful guardian. That way, the child, with her sheer luck, could be restored to her family as well'.

"Thank you for your kind suggestion," replied Mangalu indignantly, adding, "Me too, had already thought of that but had to reject out-rightly the idea, in the light of not-so-good experience, I had, with the so called police department. The confidence of the common people upon the police department had shattered long back, as is evident from the day-to-day press reports. Heaps of files of such unsolved cases, lying there, are piled up and the counting is increased day by day. Sometimes, innocent people too, are subjected to harsh treatment in their custody. Even the women's cell can't boast of the safety of its inmates. I understand that small children are usually sent to the 'Children's Home' or 'Bal Griha. But cases of maltreatment of some kind or the other are also common over there which keep on pouring in the newspapers, off and on. In view of these foregoing facts, I can't dare approach them and am quite at a loss to know as to what to do".

In fact, Mangalu was well aware of a number of dreadful stories about kidnapping of children. He had heard about the gangs operating in the city who always remain on the lookout for an abandoned child or else, lure the vulnerable children by offering them money who could easily fall prey to their evil designs. Once in their clutches, they wouldn't be allowed to escape. Gradually, they would be forced to learn the art of pick-pocketing. The boys, on becoming trained, would roam about the city in small groups of four or five. The teen-aged boys, in their adolescent age, would carry on their pick-pocketing business with quite an ease in Buses, trains or some other crowded places, as nobody would ever suspect them. The menace has become so rampant that even the female children were not spared to join them.

The fearful part of such stories running around was all the more horrible where able-bodied children were kidnapped and sold for hefty amounts. While some of them were maimed, the others were made blind. Having lost their limbs and becoming crippled they were supposed to be quite eligible and stand fit for begging. That way, they would earn for their boss which is necessary for their own survival as well. Every beggar child has a fixed place, called 'adda' where he would be left in the morning by the leader of the gang. Sometimes they were forced to skip their meal also. They would be picked up by the evening at the time of sunset. Reaching their 'den' they were supposed to give the account of the day's earning and only after that they were allowed to take the dinner that would consist of just 'daal and rice' or 'daal and roti', and nothing else, except water. According to another version of the story, it is added that the children were supposed to get punishment also if their target of daily earnings is not completed for which they couldn't be held at fault. Poor Mangalu couldn't bear in his mind such evil thoughts any more.

CHAPTER – 39

F ed up with living alone, in a sort of self-exiled state, from his step mother's family, for so many years, Mangalu had, occasionally, a secret longing, in some corner of his mind, to have his 'own' family and often lamented on his helplessness on account of his physical disability of becoming a eunuch at the cruel hands of the destiny. He often used to have some varying thoughts and wished that there ought to be some remedy to kill his loneliness. While all the other members of his community had a common dwelling place to live in, Mangalu, being the 'Mukhiya ji' or the head of their 'band' had, from the very beginning, maintained his separate entity and lived in a small accommodation at some walk-able distance from the main residence of the Band. None could ever have imagined that one day, that separate abode of Mukhiya ji, would prove to him as a boon in disguise.

Since there seemed to be no hope of getting some positive response from anywhere, Mangalu had to think hard, once again, to find out some way to solve the problem. And suddenly something struck into his mind and he could recollect from his deep memory about his longing to have his 'own' family in order to ward off his loneliness. Having no other valid option to choose from, he made up his mind to keep the child himself and take her to his home to fill his self-created void in his life. It is quite easy to plan something in one's mind, but to implement the same practically is difficult enough. However, with the help of his strong willpower Mangalu had become adamant and resolved to face the consequences whatsoever. That was really a bold decision which gave him enough strength to overcome any hindrance that may come in his way to deter him from his resolve.

On coming out of the station Mangalu headed towards the main bazaar carrying the child in his lap. Acting upon the first phase of his unique plan he started looking for a barber's shop. Soon he was able to locate one, displaying a signboard –'Hair Cutting Salon'-- around the curve of a street at the intersection of the main road. In anticipation of his fears that the child may not like the barber and try to prevent him from trimming her hair, he had bought a pair of chocolate sticks to overcome that kind of hindrance and entered the shop.

They had to wait for some time before the child was made to sit on a flat wooden board, fitted upon both the arms of the chair. That had substantially raised the height of the seat, almost parallel to the dash-board fixed against the huge mirror. The child gave a lovely smile on looking her own image in to the mirror. The barber was, then, told of trimming her hair fashionably making the 'boy-cut' hairdo as per the latest modern trend. The child looked frightened and began to cry at the sight of a pair of scissors in the hands of the barber and wouldn't allow him to come near her.

To comfort her initially proved to be a hell of a job. However, the chocolates had become handy to calm down the child. To distract her attention, Mangalu gave the chocolate bars to her, one in each hand. Only then he was able to hold her head with great difficulty. But, as the trimming progressed a little, the sobbing of the child subsided on feeling it a quite painless procedure. She tried to put a glance as well in to the mirror off and on from the corner of her eyes, watching what was happening. The barber, with his expertise, surely had done a good job.

The second phase of the plan consisted of looking for a ready-made garments shop. A 'Kid's Corner' board of the size of a large hoarding could be seen at the far end of the same street, on stepping over the pavement outside the 'salon'. It had taken about five minutes to reach the shop. It was a big store, beautifully decorated and displaying all sorts of readymade garments. Large wooden shelves on all the three sides of the store were full to their capacity. A revolving stand adored the centre of the store which had dozens of hangers upon it displaying kid's baba-suits, panties, socks, frocks, shirts, T-shirts, trousers, half-pants, under-wears, leather-belts, etc. all for children in various sizes, hues and colours. The store had a variety of men's-wear also. Night gowns and casual suits like salwar-kameez for ladies were available too. Mangalu preferred to buy just half a dozen baba-suits of the size to fit the child comprising of half-pant with shirt, under-wears, and socks.

There was a 'trial room' of the size of a big cupboard. Mangalu took the child inside it and changed her dress. Surprisingly, she looked one hundred percent like a kindergarten 'Boy', after the change. Even Mangalu could hardly recognize her.

Having satisfied with the outcome on the completion of the second phase of his unique plan, it was the time to give a proper and some meaningful name also to the child. Per chance, that day happened to be Monday, e.g. 'SOM-vaar', which Mangalu thought is mythologically attributed to 'Lord Siva'. Hence she was instantly given the boy's name as 'SOMnath'. His nick name however could be 'SOMI'. That way, her real outwardly identity was completely changed and thus "SOMI" was transformed to look like a male child with the boy-cut hairdo and supported with baba-suit. That was the third phase of the plan.

And here comes the next phase. There was still lack of one more thing, e.g. shoes. Any business house dealing in footwear couldn't be seen in the vicinity they had been roaming about. However, a roadside hawker told him that there was a "Bunty Shoe Store" beyond a local market on the back of the theatre building. Having no other option Mangalu hurried to fetch a pair of shoes for Somi. On reaching there a small cardboard placard, hung at the door, greeted them with the inscription—'Closed for Lunch': 1.00 p.m. to 1.30 p.m. Only then Mangalu could realize that they too hadn't taken anything since morning. Poor Somi also must be feeling hungry. There was a small 'dhaaba' across the street with two long wooden benches spread by the side of the road. The lower bench was meant for the customers to sit upon, while the other bench was used to place the food-plates etc. Mangalu ordered for a plate of 'daal and rice' which he shared with Somi. By the time they finished their lunch, the shoe store had opened. Mangalu bought a pair of black tiny shoes, sans laces, for Somi. He had to help her by putting on the pair of socks first, and then getting her wear the shoes, in her tiny feet. On successful completion of the second last phase, he was full of self-praise for the unique plan of overcoming the gloomy situation he was in, ever since de-boarding from the train.

CHAPTER – 40

⌘

The crucial moment came when they reached home. Mangalu asked Babu, the tea-vender, in his neighbour, to fetch the keys of the house from Bhima. Instead, Bhima himself came running to see Mangalu, alias Mukhiya ji, out of sheer curiosity to know as to how he would be feeling, on his return from the pilgrimage of Shirdi after paying his obeisance to Shri Sai Baba and learn all the other details of the 'yatra' (holy journey). On asking about the child, Mukhiya ji told him the whole story of finding the child in the railway compartment. Of course, he strictly had kept the most essential 'secret' to himself and never revealed the real identity of the child which would be living in the garb of a 'boy'. He told him his name as Som Nath but affectionately would call him by his nick name 'Somi'. That way, Somi was always regarded as a male child throughout the years to come. Mukhiya ji had to remain very cautious. He never allowed anybody to enter the house when Somi needed to have a bath or change her dress. Mukhiya ji practically had become both, her mother as well as father. He always had looked after Somi as his own legitimate child and regarded her as his 'son'. In addition, owing to the great sense of responsibility, he had become parsimonious, strictly adopting utmost carefulness in the use of money or other resources. He then opened a savings bank account also and started depositing regularly the major part of his earnings. In due course of time it had become manifold which gave him some inner satisfaction. Thus on becoming a little contented, he vowed to give Somi 'the best'.

Years passed by and it looked as if Somi had been growing up at a faster pace than the other boys of her age. From the very beginning she was taught to converse masculinely, like: jaata hoon (means going) and khaata hoon (means eating) instead of jaati hoon, khaati hoon, etc. which denote femininity. She had started showing her talent at an early age. Under the proper guidance of her father, she had, by the time, fully understood about her sex. She had become aware of the fact that she was not a boy and happened to be somewhat different in physique and body structure as compared to the other inmates of the community. In order to hide her real identity, Somi always dressed up like a boy. Having become aware of her surroundings she used to keep a safe distance from her companions on one pretext or the other. She had strictly followed the instructions of her father for not to give any response to who-so-ever knocks at the door except the Mukhiya ji himself. The arrangement made as such, had considerably helped Mukhiya ji in building up his confidence about her safety and he continued to go with his band of eunuchs on their routine of daily beats for the alms.

She was then about four years old when once in the middle of a fistfight with a boy who had dared tease her on some account. Per chance Mangal Sen appeared in the street. On seeing him, the boy ran away. Somi started to chase him but her father grabbed her. "Hold it Somi. You have got to learn to control your temper. Young girls don't get into fistfights."

"I'm not a young girl," Somi snapped. "Let go of me." Her father released her.

Her collared boy-shirt she was wearing was muddied and torn, and her cheek was bruised.

"I'd better get you cleaned up before your friends see you," Mangal Sen told her.

Somi looked after the retreating boy with regret. "I could have licked him if you had left me alone."

Mangal Sen looked down into the passionate little face and laughed. "You probably could have."

Pacified, Somi allowed him to pick her up and carry her into the house. She liked being in her father's arms. She liked everything about him. He was the father who understood her. When he was at home, he spent time with her. In relaxed moments he would tell stories to her.

She was stubborn and willful and impossible. At times, she refused to obey even her father. If he chose a dress for her to wear, Somi would discard it for another. She would not eat properly. She ate what she wanted to, when she wanted to and no threat or bribe could sway her. She always spent her time playing rugby with teenage boys.

Till then, everything had been going on smoothly for more than a couple of years when Mukhiya ji once again looked worried. He was thinking that in a few years time, Somi would be leaving her childhood appearance and entering the next phase of her age to become an adolescent. The very thought had prompted him to think that in the coming years it may become very difficult to hide the identity of Somi, any further. He had thus been contemplating to send her to some far off place but practically that had proved very difficult on account of sheer love between Somi the daughter and the father.

Though Mukhiya ji himself had not studied beyond primary level yet he knew very well about the importance of education. For the time being Mukhiya ji started to teach her the alphabets from the primers, e.g. the elementary text books for teaching children, at home, which he bought from a nearby book-shop. Surprisingly, Somi was very good in learning and quickly picked up whatever was taught. That way, she got the basic knowledge of Hindi and English simultaneously which in fact had contributed in paving the way for her to get admission in some school.

But in order to keep the secret of Somi's identity, Mukhiya ji could neither get her admitted in a girls' school on account of being publically known as a male child nor in a boy's school with her female identity. He was, thus, left with no other option but to arrange for a well learned private tutor to give her lessons at home in all the required subjects. However, on giving a second thought he observed that the feasibility of even that proposal couldn't be taken for granted as safe and foolproof. He then started looking for a co-educational school especially with the boarding house facility. Ultimately, his efforts bore fruit and within a week he had succeeded in locating one at a distance, far off the highway from the town. It was a famous school commonly known as Nanda Boarding School of Co-education.

CHAPTER – 41

It was high time that Mangal Sen, alias Mangalu, seriously gave a thought about his relinquishing the title of 'Mukhiya ji' owing to the feeling of the great responsibility towards the future of Somi. Till that time, she used to play in the garb of a 'boy' with her friends or team-mates without hesitation. So far nobody could ever have become doubtful about her identity. Owing to the confidence imposed in him about the non-vulnerability of 'Somi', Mukhiya ji still used to go with his band on daily beats of their area as per their routine for alms as usual. But on having her become grown up, Mukhiya ji would have to remain more vigilant to safeguard her identity. The problem was genuine and the best course he could ever thought of was to make some dependable arrangement which could be possible only if he was able to get her admitted somehow or the other in the Nanda Boarding School of Co-education, he had just learnt about. That way her identity would surely remain safeguarded from the outside world and that she would carry on with her studies as well. With that resolve he strongly felt the need of her shedding the garb of a boy and join the School as a girl student in keeping her real identity. He was quite hopeful to be able to convince his eunuch community that the boy had been sent to a Boarding School for studies.

Early next morning after having done with his daily routine like brushing, taking his bath etc., Mangal Sen changed his attire of eunuch and put on a normal dress--- shirt and trousers, like a gentleman. Asking Somi to bolt the door from inside, as usual, he set out to see the Principal of the School to enquire about her admission. On reaching the gate of the school, he felt a little embarrassment when he was confronted with a person supposed to be the security guard that looked as a muscleman in uniform flaunting his apps like a body-builder. The double-door rectangular gate fixed with vertical iron-grills was big enough to let the four-wheeled vehicles pass through it quite easily. Generally it remained closed and one had to enter or make an exit through the 'window-gate'--- a small door carved out from one of the main doors which the security guard had to latch or unlatch off and on when required.

"Yes please! Can I help you?" asked the security guard.

"I have to see the Principal regarding the admission of my child," replied Mangal Sen.

"Please go straight and turn towards left side of the block and you will find ma'am Principal's room right at the corner," said the security guard, while letting him enter through the window-gate.

And Mangal Sen found himself at the office of the Principal soon after.

"Can I go inside to see the Principal ma'am?" Mangal Sen asked the peon sitting outside the office.

"In what connection do you want to see her?" The peon made a counter question.

"This is regarding the admission of my child," replied Mangal Sen.

"Please wait a little for your turn as Ma'am is already busy with somebody. You would be able to see her in a few minutes, as soon as she is done with," said the peon and added, giving him a slip, "please write down your name for the Ma'am to call you."

Mangal Sen already knew about the probable questions which are generally asked in such kind of interviews and had come prepared having done his home-work for the same. In about half an hour, Mangal Sen was ushered in to her room and he found himself seated upon an armchair in the office of the Principal, talking face to face with the bespectacled lady on the opposite side of the table. She looked quite graceful and possessed a fine personality, not very young, as was evident from her artificially coloured black hair. While talking, Mangal Sen noticed that she had milk-white teeth with a melodious voice and probably a pleasant nature also.

"Well, Mr. Mangal Sen! What can I do for you?" asked Ma'am Principal staring over the slip.

"Ma'am, I have a daughter now running in the fifth year of her age. I've come to seek her admission in your boarding school as unfortunately, my circumstances don't allow me to keep her with me. Ma'am she is very brilliant even at that age. So, I want to give her the best education and that's why I came to have recourse to you for help," told Mangal Sen.

"Well, if you'll excuse me! I don't have, in fact, that much time to listen to the whole story as I have to see the other visitors also waiting outside. So, please collect the necessary Admission form available at the counter and fill up the details," she told him.

Without getting any kind of assurance he came out of the room and approached the lady at the counter.

"One Admission form please," requested Mangal Sen.

"Here's one," said the lady at the counter, adding further, "This form is to be submitted into the school in a week's time for admission of your ward along with the required documents."

"What documents?"

"Like, the birth-certificate of the child; three passport-size photographs; proof of address etc. as enlisted in the form itself."

"While all the other documents are available, I don't have her birth-certificate."

"Oh, in that case, you will have to submit an affidavit showing his date of birth on a Court's non-judicial stamp-paper as required under the rules."

The very next day Mangal Sen went to the District Court where a host of advocates and notary public keep on waiting for the clients like Mangal Sen. He found himself surrounded by the agents of the so-called lawyers as soon as he made his entry in to the premises. Anyway, he sidelined all of them and approached one 'Munshi ji' who looked busy in typing something on his very old-fashioned typewriter. On his looking towards Mangal Sen inquisitively, he told him, "I need an affidavit regarding the date of birth of my child for submitting in her school for admission."

"Just go and purchase a two-rupee non-judicial stamp-paper," said Munshi ji pointing towards the nearby shop of the stamp-vendor."

"For what purpose the stamp-paper is required," the stamp-vendor shot the question as soon as Mangal Sen approached him.

"For Affidavit," he shot back.

The stamp-vendor who was sitting cross-legged upon a small wooden 4' x 3' size bench, fished out the required paper from a steel-trunk placed before him which he used as a table also. After incorporating the necessary entries of the affidavit for keeping the record in the Register kept for the purpose on the lid of that trunk, he made Mangal Sen also to sign against the entries before handing over the paper to him.

In a few minutes Mangal Sen returned to Munshi ji with the stamp-paper. When he asked for the necessary details, as also the date of birth of the child, to be recorded in the affidavit, Mangal Sen had to manipulate. He could then recollect having visited Shirdi in the year 1980 when he had found the child in the railway compartment which at that time was supposed to be two-year old. So, he simply calculated roughly two years before the date she was found by him and fixed her date of birth at nineteenth April, nineteen hundred and seventy eight (19-04-1978). The other details were also provided to Munshi ji who instantly got the affidavit typed and hurried in to the chamber of some Magistrate 1st class. And in about half an hour or so the same was handed over to Mangal Sen duly stamped and verified by the 1st class Magistrate as required in the admission form. Munshi ji was however seemed to be contented with a nominal amount paid by Mangal Sen for the whole job.

Filling up the admission form, he gave the Student's name: Somi which on its first look denotes the name of a girl child. To fill in the gender column, he had to think twice and then without hesitation as well as any kind of nervousness he filled up her real identity: 'female'. Father's name: Mangal Sen. Occupation: Self-employed. Date of birth: 19-04-1978; (The necessary Affidavit on a non-judicial stamp-paper from the court specifying the date of birth of the student is attached herewith); Proof of address: and three photographs: submitted herewith. And after filling in all the required information, he put the form and all the documents, including photographs and the affidavit etc., in an envelope and submitted to the school personally on the very next day. He also noted the date and time of the interview of his ward from the Notice-board.

And that was the time for Somi to change back to her real identity of a girl child after disguising herself as a boy, all those years. She had been playing the role with such competency that none could ever have any doubt about her sex. Mangal Sen was busy in shopping. He was well aware that there must be some kind of uniform Somi would be wearing at the school, yet he had been visualizing about some suitable dresses for her to wear casually as well. So, he had selected very carefully a couple of dresses she was supposed to wear while going to school for interview the next morning.

CHAPTER – 42

On the day of the final interview, Mangal Sen had to take along Somi in the early hours of the morning in order to escape the watchful eyes of his neighbours. No doubt she was looking awfully charming in the female dress she had worn for the first time after so many years of living as a boy in baba-suits. Mangal Sen was taken aback to observe that how confidently and fearlessly the child had spoken before the Principal and the members of the Management in reply to a few simple questions as if they were her playmates. That made her all the more endearing to one and all, sitting over there. Mangal Sen too had the opportunity of briefing the story about Somi and Madam Principal indeed had given a patience hearing to the circumstances explained by him. Requesting for at least some fee concession, he had offered to deposit a lump sum amount towards the tuition fee plus the reasonable Boarding & lodging expenses as required under the rules.

Asking him to await outside for a while, the members reviewed the whole case conferencing amongst themselves. He was, then, told that keeping in view his pathetic condition and an unreliable source of income, the School management had decided to provide whatever was required to help them. In fact a 'Welfare Fund' had been created by the school management a few years back for the benefit of such needy students. However cases like that of Somi seldom came. He was further assured that henceforth it had become the sole responsibility of the school management to take care of Somi. He had also learnt that unlike other institutions, the school is unique in a way which runs in various blocks. While separate classes are run for boys and girls, the boarding and lodging arrangements are also made separately. So, there was hardly anything to be worried about. The bond of love between father and daughter was so strong that it looked impossible for both of them to depart from each other. But then, what was needed to be done would have to be done.

Two days later Somi shifted to the Boarding School with tearful eyes. She had been there earlier just once for the interview and that too only to see the Principal ma'am. The school was like most other things, far off the highway. It was not obvious that it was a school; only the sign, which declared it to be the Nanda Boarding School of Co-education. It looked like a collection of matching houses, built with maroon-coloured bricks. There were so many trees and shrubs by the sides of a large compound. She couldn't see its size at first and wondered as to where was the feel of the institution. She walked down the little stone-path lined with green hedges and took a deep breath before opening the door of the office.

The office was small and brightly lit inside. It had a little waiting area with padded folding chairs, a navy-blue commercial carpet, notices and awards cluttering the walls, and a big clock ticking loudly. Plastic pots with plants were lined alongside the walls. The room was cut in one-third of its size by a long counter cluttered with wires, baskets full of papers and brightly coloured files. There were two desks behind the counter one of which was manned by a middle aged black haired woman with a sky-blue shirt, wearing glasses. She looked up and asked Somi: "Can I help you?"

"My name is Somi, daughter of Mangal Sen."

"Oh! Of course," she said and dug through a pile of documents sacked precariously on her table, till she found the ones she was looking for. "Yes, I have your schedule right here," and sent for the peon to take her to the room allotted to her which she was supposed to share with another girl of her age and the class as well. She smiled at her and said: "I hope that you would like it here." Somi smiled back as convincingly as she could.

Mangal Sen too, was beginning to feel lonely once again on account of the void created by the absence of Somi who had become his heart and soul, an un-separable part of his existence. Outwardly he looked aggrieved to find himself once again in the same state when he used to live alone a few years back. He started visualizing in his mind: How Somi had come into his life as a God-given gift, which had changed the course of his living altogether. He was very kindly provided with a cause to live for that child. However, inwardly, at that stage, he had felt a little happiness and contentment, thinking, that at least with the grace of God he was able to fulfill his vows of getting his daughter the best of education. In the next few years she would be joining the college for graduation. Thus she would make her father proud among the whole of the eunuch community.'

Feeling a bit relieved after sending his daughter to the Boarding School, his decision of taking retirement had to be reversed and Mukhiya ji rejoined the band resuming the daily beats after a gap of about three weeks. Of course, the routine had continued in the years that followed and Mukhiya ji used to make occasional visits to see Somi. He had noted her date of birth as mentioned in the Affidavit and inscribed it, to keep permanent, on the inner wall of his room. That way he never forgot her 'Birth day' and to celebrate it, out of his sheer love, he always used to visit in person to wish her 'Happy birth day' and carried a lovely gift for her as well as sweets for her classmates.

During all those years, Mukhiya ji always used to tell his fellow members of the band that Somi, the 'boy' was never allowed to go out and had been living under strict discipline of the Boarding House. By the way, Somi did prove her mettle in her studies. She had been a brilliant student throughout her academic period that resulted in her promotion every time to the next higher class. So, until she finished her studies, everybody had presumed that the 'boy' must have entered the age of his youth by that time and were curious to see how he would be looking like. Mukhiya ji too was trying to visualize the scene when suddenly all of them would be awestruck to meet Somi and find that she was, in fact, a 'girl' who had been playing the role of a boy for so many years before going to the Boarding house. That surely will surprise them and prove to be a real fun.

Chapter – 43

∽

TWELVE YEARS LATER

That was the day of convocation. The formal ceremony for the conferment of the university degrees were to be awarded to the successful students of the 1994 batch of the college. It's needless to add that Somi too was one of them who had become a graduate. Mangal Sen, her father, was also invited at the occasion and when Somi's name was announced, his eyes had become wet with emotional intensity on account of happiness. She had proved herself the most talented child in the eunuch community who had graduated at the age of 16 years of which Mangalu, now Mangal Sen, was really very proud of.

Soon after the convocation was over, Mangal Sen, who had always insisted on seeing Madam Principal whenever he came to meet Somi, entered her office. He thanked her and bowed with a sense of gratitude and also offered a packet of sweets he had brought with him. Madam too congratulated him for having come through the long struggle they had in their lives and wished them all the best.

As was anticipated, all the members of the eunuch community were awfully surprised to learn that Somi was, in fact, the 'daughter' of Mukhiya ji who used to live in the garb of a 'boy' for so many years before joining the Boarding School. It was Bhima who had broken the news after Mangal Sen had taken him into confidence. It definitely was a matter of great pride for all of them that a daughter of a eunuch had become the first graduate which was a fit occasion that called for a little celebration. So, all the members of their band were invited to the party which Mukhiya ji had thrown, and everybody had enjoyed till it was over by just after midnight.

Having come of age, Somi had occupied one of the two rooms of their house. She had kept that exclusively for herself as she needed some privacy at least which Mukhiya ji certainly had quite easily understood. Behind the closed doors of her room, she would just stand in front of the mirror and admire herself as the signs of youth had begun to appear in her well developed figure. She, in her heart, had wished her beauty to be appraised. Mukhiya ji used to go on beats as usual and in his absence she started feeling loneliness. At times she felt herself like a prisoner kept within the confines of the four walls of her room and had a strict longing for going out. In fact she had always lived under discipline for so many years as the rules at the boarding house were very strict. The students were never allowed to go outside the school premises and as such her longing for going out to see the world outside the boarding house had to be suppressed.

The long cherished dream of flying a little free which had been buried somewhere deep below in Somi's mind, came up on the surface and started compelling her to find some way out. It had been well within her knowledge that her father was very strict and would never allow her to go out under any circumstances. So she would have to contemplate thoughtfully upon the problem and find out some solution. Thinking upon the matter over and over, she made up her mind to discuss it with her father. Apprising him about the state of her mind on the subject, she was able to convince him that merely theoretical knowledge through books is not enough. She needs to go out to gain some practical knowledge as well, of the outside world in socializing and asked for his permission to let her become at least a member of the 'Public Library' located at a little distance from their locality. That way she would no longer be sitting idle at home after her father leaves for his usual daily routine. Building up her self-confidence, she was able to convince him that she had become quite capable of taking care of herself and that there was nothing to be worried about. Mukhiya ji, then, felt a sense of pride about his daughter and the permission was granted.

And thus, a few months after her becoming graduate, she became a member of the public library. She would often make a visit to the 'library' in the afternoon after finishing her house-hold chores like sweeping, cleaning, cooking meals, washing the dishes, etc. Full of self confidence, she would be straight away heading towards the 'library'. That way she would have the chance to breathe some fresh air in the open. While going out she would always try to remain alert of her surroundings, taking strict precaution of not being followed by someone. She would look like a respectable woman wearing a simple dress and her graceful gait would attract many a passersby to have a glance at her. But she never bothered about such things any more.

In order to update herself with the knowledge of the day-to-day happenings, she would, first of all, look for a copy of the daily newspaper. She would draw a chair to one of the extreme corners of the huge table placed in the middle of the library hall. Sitting over there in a comfortable posture, she would hurriedly go through the headlines first, skipping the pages containing ads in plenty. She could concentrate on something only if that seemed interesting to her. She never bothered about the fashion magazines lying on the table which generally attract the women visiting the library. Visit to the library had proved a good pastime to her and in due course of time it had changed in to a daily routine. She had become very friendly with the Librarian as well and often used to borrow a book or two and take them home, to be returned later. Of course there was another category of some rare books, which do not have their prints available in the market. Such books couldn't be borrowed and had to be studied only in the library itself.

CHAPTER – 44

"Excuse me! Could I have the cover-page please?" Looking up, Somi found a young man stretching his hand and pointing towards the newspaper, she had been reading, spread before her. Immediately, without any hesitation, she took out the page from below the pages of the newspaper and handed it over to the young man.

"Thank you," the guy said with a smile.

That, perhaps, was the first time, since her coming back from the college after so long when somebody, other than her father, had addressed her like that. The request had come in a very polite way from the man who had just drawn a chair quite opposite, across that table where Somi had been busy in going through the contents of some interesting news. She had become now a regular visitor to the library and coincidently used to occupy the same place in a lonely corner of that huge table. She had very carefully selected that corner to enjoy her readings uninterruptedly and without any disturbance. She had got somewhat surprised on hearing such kind of request all of a sudden. Instantly, she had blushed, and feeling a little shy her face glowed with some kind of pride. While looking in to the eyes of the young man she had handed over the page.

Pretending to be looking for some news in to the paper, now spread before him, the man had been constantly staring at her face. She, however, had lowered her eyes, looking sheepishly down upon the table waiting for the return of the page. After a while she noticed that instead of giving it back to Somi, he had just kept the paper aside, upon the table and she had to pick it up herself. The request to see the paper, she had been reading, was surely a lame excuse to have a little acquaintance with her which seemed to be the case of natural attraction towards the opposite sex. But Somi didn't care a bit and became engrossed in looking for more news in the rest of the pages of the newspaper.

The young man happened to be a tourist. He had long, glossy black hair pulled back with a rubber band at the nape of his neck. His skin was beautiful, silky reddish-brown coloured; his eyes were dark, set deep above the high planes of his cheek-bones. Altogether a very pretty face, his name was 'Bob', as incorporated in the visitor's register, maintained in the library. It was mandatory for all the persons visiting the library to make entries in to the register e.g. their name, address, occupation, purpose of the visit, etc. in the respective columns provided therein. The address he had given in the column was that of a five-star hotel situated opposite the famous 'Subhash Garden' at a walk-able distance on the backside of the building of the library. A few other persons who were present at the time of the foreigner's visit were also looked curious to know about him and were pleased to learn the purpose of his visiting India--- a great country, as a 'tourist', to have the first-hand knowledge about the Indian culture, as written in the register in his own handwriting with his signatures and the date of visit.

Bob had learnt from a staff-member of the hotel, he had checked in, about the big library located nearby. He purposely got ready in no time to pay a visit and talk to the Librarian who was supposed to give him all the Information he required. Entering the library hall he noticed that the place was far bigger than he had imagined. It was full of wooden shelves in so many rows containing such a large collection of books on numerous subjects placed in various categories and marked on the small placards nicely placed on each row. There was a large wooden table placed in the middle of the hall surrounded by over two dozens of wooden chairs for visitors to sit upon. Very much impressed with such a big library that too at a short distance from his hotel, he approached the Librarian in his office.

Mr. Shyam Prasad, the librarian, was a highly educated and learned man, well versed in almost every subject worth mentioning over here. He had a good physique and a presentable personality to look at. Elegantly dressed with the golden framed specs resting upon his nose, he looked too busy, engrossed in preparing a list of the books lying on his table. On seeing Bob entering the room, Mr. Prasad looked at him inquisitively saying: "What can I do for you?"

With a warm hand-shake Bob took a chair across that of the Librarian and very politely said: "Sir, you seem to be awfully busy yet I would very much appreciate if you could kindly lend me just five minutes of your valuable time please."

The request was made very politely and in such a manner that it had a positive effect on the Librarian who instantly gave a nod, allowing Bob to continue:

"My name is Bob. My ancestors e.g. my grandfather and great grandfather belonged to Buckinghamshire (England) but my father, being a businessman used to travel all over the world. Once in India he fell in love with an Indian woman. Both of them took a fancy to each other but since they belonged to different faiths and culture, there were very remote chances of the marriage. Yet, as I have been told by my mother, both of them had vowed not to object to, or interfere in to the faith of each other come what may. As a result they got married in India in accordance with the

Hindu rituals and were settled in greater London (England) later on."

"My father is kind of a very liberal person and even after so many years of marriage he still keeps his promise of not to interfere, to this day. To me, perhaps this happens to be a rare example of respecting each other's religious faiths after the King Akbar the great and his Rajput wife queen Jodha Bai, a world famous historical fact of respecting each other's religious faith, I'm told. Even having born in India and settled in England after her marriage, she still adores and seems to be very proud of India, her native country. She is a religious minded and God-fearing lady at heart, and says her daily prayers to the deities. She would observe 'fast' on certain days in accordance with the Hindu rituals and won't take her meals. Me too, while graduating from a foreign University, have read a great deal about India, the native country of my mother whom I love very much."

"Even though born and reared in England, yet inwardly, I feel myself very much Indian, so much so, that I too consider it as 'my' motherland. The stories of the great Hindu epics and important events and festivals of 'her India' which my mother always used to tell me about, off and on, had a strong impact upon my mind and soul. With that feeling I had taken 'Hindi' as an optional subject to learn while doing my graduation."

"By the time I finished my studies, my inner urge to visit India, the land of my dreams, had become strong enough that doubly enhanced my curiosity to know more about its heritage, its people, its customs and culture, its religion, and the most famous places to visit, as well as, learn about everything within the short span of time I have at my disposal. I have checked in to the Rajshree hotel opposite Subhash Garden, located in the back of the library building, last night. I was having a brief talk with them when a member of the staff told me about this library. He knew your name as well and asked me to contact you for any help I may require. So I've come to seek your valuable guidance and help in the matter. I would appreciate if you could suggest me a comprehensive guide containing all the information about India from the huge collection of about a hundred thousand books arranged so conspicuously in the library."

It was a great pleasure for Shyam Prasad, the Librarian, to learn from a foreigner about the curiosity with which he had approached him. Feeling the intensity of the matter he immediately suggested some books like 'The Discovery of India'—by Jawaharlal Nehru, etc. scribbling them on a piece of paper and handed it over to Bob. He also told him where to look for them under the different headings and categories of subjects displayed over there. Keeping that small piece of paper enlisting the titles of the reference books in his pocket Bob entered the long rows of the shelves, putting a quick glance at each of the placards. Within a few minutes he was able to locate a couple of books and smiled to himself unknowingly.

Quite anxious to go through the list of the contents given just after the title page of the books, he looked for a vacant chair to sit upon. With sheer luck he could find one. But he didn't dare to drag the chair fearing that its dragging sound on the floor of the library would disturb the other people absorbed in their studies and lifted it to the place in the corner of the hall where per chance Somi happened to be already sitting at her usual place, across the table, engrossed in a newspaper spread before her.

Being a good looking young girl like her, it was hardly a matter of surprise if somebody admired her on account of her charms and the youthful complexion with an enviable figure. Spellbound with her fascination, Bob was drawn to her like a magnet and wanted to make friends with her. Being a tourist he knew it that he wouldn't be staying in India for too long yet he couldn't restrain himself from gazing at her. In the first instance, he had hesitated a bit, to talk to her. The request to lend the newspaper was made totally with the idea of making friendship with her. He too had started to visit the library daily and tried to occupy the seat just opposite Somi. Pretending to be engrossed in his book, he was very consciously looking intently towards Somi for hours.

Bob had bright blue eyes that shone with a kind expression and sandy blond hair. He had sharply etched masculine features and a noticeably square chin. He was wearing grey slacks, a blazer, blue shirt and a dark blue tie, and his black leather shoes had been perfectly shined before he left his hotel, he had checked in the previous night. There was a subtle elegance about him, he was well dressed without wearing anything remarkable or showy. And as he opened the newspaper to read in the library, Somi would have noticed that he had beautiful hands and he was wearing a 'Rolex' watch. Everything about him, and that he wore, had a subtlety and quiet elegance to it that drew the right kind of attention to him. For the first time in his life, Bob believed that he was in love. Though fully knowing that he won't be living in India for long yet he had decided to take the life as it comes.

Chapter – 45

❦

Somi was just seventeen years old then. She was utterly charming, enchanting, intelligent, discreet and affectionate. She too had noticed Bob gazing at her. He would come daily without fail in the forenoon itself and eagerly wait for her, staring constantly towards the entrance to see her coming and taking her seat in the usual corner. Initially their acquaintance remained restricted to just seeing each other, sitting across the table. A little conversation between them didn't show any specific progress except the usual 'hi' and 'hello'. On another day, Bob, intentionally had selected a Hindi version of a guide book on India and occasionally would ask her to explain the meaning of some word or a phrase. While Bob seemed to be interested in making some advances towards her, she didn't have the courage to give him any positive response, in spite of the fact that, by the time, on having a few visual meetings, she too couldn't remain unaffected for long and owing to her soft corner, had started liking him as well. Gradually, her feelings for him, quite unknowingly had secretly changed into love in her heart. Yet during the casual meetings, they used to have in the library hall, she had never encouraged Bob to talk freely or going for an outing. But despite making up her mind a number of times she couldn't dare share the secret of her love with her father.

Other than her visits to the library, Somi always remained at home, on account of unavoidable circumstances. She felt herself like a prisoner kept within the confines of the four walls of her room only. Behind the closed doors at night before going to bed, she looked into the mirror that hung on the wall. She had no illusions about her looks and didn't consider herself pretty enough, yet she was interesting-looking with nice eyes, high cheekbones and a good figure. She drew nearer to the mirror. What had Bob seen when he looked at her. She blushed just at the thought of Bob visualizing his presence in the room with her. She began getting undressed and stood naked. Her hands slowly caressed the swell of her breasts and felt her hardening nipples. Her fingers slid down across her flat belly and her hands became twined with each other slowly moving downwards. They were between her legs now, gently touching, stroking, rubbing harder now, faster and faster until she was caught up in a frantic whirlpool of sensation that finally exploded inside her and she gasped his name and fell to the bed.

Awaiting her positive response, Bob still didn't lose his patience. Having firmly resolved to open up his mind before Somi and seek her response whatsoever, Bob, on a certain morning, had managed to come to the library a bit earlier than usual. Occupying his usual seat he kept on waiting for her to come. The long wait was over at last. Soon, entering the hall Somi straight away went to the Book-counter, got the book renewed she had been reading and turned to her usual chair which being a regular visitor was supposed to be reserved for her in that corner. Though Bob had greeted her as usual, yet she didn't fail to notice that his mood looked somewhat different. Anyway, giving a sweet smile she said, whispering in barely audible tone:

"How come, you are here so early?"

"I've been sitting here since morning and didn't move till now."

"I know that and I'm happy to see you Bob."

"Me too," Bob said admiringly. Each time he saw her, he was struck how beautiful she was. Looking at her it was hard to believe she had a care in the world. She always had a warm and welcoming smile. Just seeing Bob, there was a joy and excitement in her eyes.

"By the way, how did 'you' come to know?" Bob whispered back.

"The uncle at the book counter has just told me. I hope there is nothing wrong with you. Is there any specific reason for coming so early and waiting for so long?"

"Yes. In fact I have been suffering from some mental stress."

"Why don't you see some doctor?"

"I also had thought of seeing the doctor and that's why I have kept on waiting here since morning."

"Are you mad? Waiting for the doctor to come to the library?"

"Yes. The doctor has just arrived and taken her chair as well," replied Bob, pointing his forefinger towards Somi and that had prompted her to have a hearty laugh. Of course, Bob too joined her. However, guessing her in a good mood Bob had finally expressed his love for her and said, "I'm in love with you. I swore to myself I was going to say those words to you. It is quite fair and I want you to know about it."

"I know," she whispered as she looked up at him. "I've loved you since the first time we met. But there is nothing we can do about it." They both knew that. And she had never wanted to say those words to him, she knew it would complicate everything, but neither of them could stop now.

As a result of meeting daily and chatting upon some topic or the other for countless hours, Somi too had started to feel the intensity of her love towards Bob but had not dared yet to admit it to him. She, in fact, had been still under the influence of her father and couldn't think beyond that how he would react on knowing about her love affair with someone without having proper knowledge about his back ground. More specifically, if that person happens to be a foreigner, where would that love affair lead to.

Chapter – 46

That was perhaps the right moment when Somi too had confessed her liking for Bob. She had told him about her back ground including her unknown parentage, how she was rescued by a kind-hearted person and looked after like his own legitimate daughter. In the first place, she had deliberately avoided mentioning anything about her father becoming a eunuch. As also, had kept to herself the 'secret' about the eunuch community she belonged to. For some obvious reason, she had refrained from telling the truth and out-rightly rejected the idea fearing that after his learning the fact about her family of eunuch, she may become an object of laughing stock and invite his hatred. She didn't want to be despised of for no fault of her. Strangely, she was even afraid to think that on the other hand Bob may feel himself betrayed on my hiding the fact about my father. But after giving it a second thought, she had taken the bold decision and told him that his father had actually met with an accident in his youth and had become a eunuch for the rest of his life. On the contrary, however, she herself was eager to know everything about Bob. So far she didn't know anything about him except his name and the country of origion. Bob too, on his part, hadn't so far bothered a bit to tell anything about his parentage, nationality, occupation, etc. Of course, he had appreciated the role of her father who, even being a eunuch himself had looked after her, so lovingly, as his own legitimate daughter and cared for her safety as well as education for so many years.

This time, Mangal Sen, once again had taken the final decision to get retirement and relinquished the coveted title of 'Mukhiya ji' in favour of a young eunuch elected from their band unanimously. Despite the cruel joke his destiny had played on him in his youth, he had the satisfaction of having saved, loved and reared a precious life. He was happy with the contentment that his little Somi had become of age and is capable of looking after self in this cruel world. The years, that followed, had seen many ups and downs of life. Mangal Sen's health had started deteriorating day by day as old age seemed to have been telling upon him. By that time, Somi had been dutifully looking after her father very well. She understandably knew that a father's love is to be cherished and respected. It's rare. With the kind of devotion and selfless service being done to each other, the bond of love between both of them had been further strengthened. Mangal Sen, in his heart of hearts, thanked God innumerous times for having blessed with such an intelligent, obedient, talented and dutiful daughter. He often, in his prayers, used to thank God for the kindness bestowed in his heart, years ago, which had prompted him to take the child into his 'own' care instead of looking towards someone else. The noble deed, he thought, had now started giving its reward in the form of true love and the selfless service being rendered lovingly by Somi while looking after him in that time of stress.

Soon, Bob and Somi would often meet at a restaurant or in a park. Their love for each other had grown up and changed into deep intimacy. Everyone watched them as they walked together in to the park. The day looked better because it was not raining. It was easier for Somi because she knew what to expect of her day. Bob came and sat beside her on the bench. Somi, however, noticed that Bob no longer angled to sit a little far, so that they could face each other while talking. Instead, he sat quite close beside her, their arms almost touching. Up until that moment, they had no doubt having enjoyed their staying with each other and spending a few interim hours off and on, in real world of romance. Though it was still the grey light of a cloudy day yet it was just beginning to drizzle. They emerged hastily from the park. It had taken much less time than they had thought. There was a raised platform in the park roofed with asbestos sheets. Bob caught hold of Somi's hand and ran towards the shedded platform to take shelter under it. About half a dozen other people sitting in the park at that time, also rushed towards the shed to take shelter escaping the drizzling that changed into the downpour after a short while. Soon it became a little scantier that prompted the crowd to disperse. Bob and Somi too left with the promise to meet the next day.

It was three in the afternoon. "I've just been sitting here," said Bob, seeing Somi coming toward him. She smiled shyly and then, there was a moment's pause. He was anxious to see her. She too was excited to see him, and he could hear it in her voice. Their meetings always filled them both with anticipation, and when they met, they talked endlessly for hours. There was never any awkwardness between them no matter how long it had been since they last met.

"I'm happy to see you Bob." said Somi. She meant something to him that he couldn't have explained. She was like an unexpected gift in his life, as he was in hers. She was what he had always thought girls should be, but couldn't have defined if he'd had to put it into words. Her creamy skin faintly flushed, her long dark hair brushed and gleaming as it hung past her shoulders and her eyes looked straight into his.

"You look wonderful," said Bob. One of the things he loved about her, was the way she opened up with him. He knew her every emotion, every reaction, every thought, and she had no hesitation anymore in sharing her deepest secrets with him. Each time he saw her, he was struck by how beautiful she was. He was captivated by her looks and instantly noticed the chic black suit, the Perry's bag, and the elegant high-heeled shoes. She wore only a ring, and on her ears a pair of small studs. She had a warm, welcoming smile, and just seeing him, there was joy and excitement in her eyes.

On another morning she woke up at dawn; when she opened her eyes, something was different. She could feel it was too early. It was not quite six. Somi lay against her soft pillow and watched the dawn through the window; pale peach light streaking against the blue; the promise of more fair weather. She knew she was getting the schedule of her days and nights slowly reversed. She lay in her bed and listened to the quiet voices coming from outside. They were loud enough for her to hear at all. She slipped out of bed, rolled her bare feet till they touched the floor and then staggered outside the room. She went to take her bath. Her thoughts ran over the meeting with Bob last evening and felt extremely pleasant calmness. Having done with the household chores she got ready to go out. Wearing a yellow suit she looked gorgeous. And as per her habit before going out she looked into the mirror. *'It seems to be O.K.'* she thought and then left for the library.

Bob was in the habit of smoking cigarettes which Somi didn't like at all, despite the fact that her own father used to smoke 'bidis'. However, Bob's intensity of love had risen to such an extent that he gave up his smoking habit, honouring the wishes of his beloved. As a matter of fact, he had further surprised her when she, all of a sudden, noticed a tremendous change in his personality. He had shed his fashionable English-style clothes and started dressing in simple Kurta-pyjama suit by adapting a correlation with the Indian culture. Somi was too pleased and looked charmed by Bob's new look. In course of time, she apprised him of other virtues of life such as truthfulness, justice, kindness, moral excellence, patience, chastity, uprightness etc. as well.

Bob had come to India on a tourist visa to meet with the curiosity of seeing the 'incredible India' of his dreams. He had thoroughly done his home work and came fully prepared about his mission. He had succeeded in getting, from Shyam Prasad, the Librarian uncle, the necessary route-map of the famous places of interest like the Taj Mahal of Agra, Qutub Minar of Delhi etc. He had heard about the sacred river 'Ganga' (Ganges) that flows through Haridwar, pilgrimage of 'char dham' viz. Badrinath, Kedarnath, Gangotri and Yamunotri, the abode of Lord Shiva--- Shri Amarnath ji, Tirupati Bala ji, Vaishno Devi, the beautiful state of Jammu and Kashmir, said to be the heaven on earth, the metro cities like Delhi, Bombay, Kolkata, Kanpur, Madras and the like. He could visualize that he could see only a few of the selected places as the time of his visa was too short as he had been staying just at one place for weeks together on account of Somi, his beloved. It happens to be such a vast country, that even the full life span of a person may fall short of seeing the whole of India. Keeping that point in view, Bob ought to have made a very careful selection of the places to be visited by him.

Incidentally, Somi had once, per chance, quite unintentionally, mentioned about her desire to go on a tour of 'Bharat Darshan'. She had been cherishing that dream of her, since the time she was studying in the Boarding school. But after becoming a little matured she had fully understood that to fulfill such a dream practically would be next to impossible in her life. That wish of his beloved had perturbed Bob to such an extent that he had decisively made up his mind to take along Somi also while leaving for the tour of Bharat Darshan.

The irony of the fact was that Somi hadn't taken her father into confidence yet about his love affair with Bob, a foreigner. It would be out of speculation that she would be allowed to go with an unknown stranger like Bob whom he had never met or even heard of him, till that time. It had become too late to explain everything, keeping it in the right perspective and convince him about the whole matter. How could, then, the problem of her father be solved. She also couldn't leave him alone at that old age. Bob too had showed his helplessness in that matter. She didn't dare to talk to him face to face, instead, she would just write a letter to him about the tour. With that thought in her mind it was presumed that he would engage some 'help', to assist him in his day-to-day house-hold affairs, from the eunuch community itself, till her return from the tour.

Chapter – 47

A rumour had been taking the rounds since evening about an altercation between two rival groups in the main market over some petty matter that later on had changed into the violent contentions. It was heard that about half a dozen people were badly injured and taken to the hospital. While one of them was supposedly fighting for life and put on oxygen, others too had been heavily bandaged and kept in the Emergency ward for observation. Consequently, a night long curfew from dusk to dawn had been imposed by the competent authority in the whole of the eastern part of the city. Unfortunately, Mangal Sen's locality too had come in the area under the curfew. Poor fellow had kept on worrying as Somi had not returned home yet from the library where she was supposed to have gone, as usual. Since, people, under the restriction, were required to remain indoors between the specified hours of the curfew he could very well understand that Somi's return to home during the curfew hours was not possible. She must have managed to stay somewhere for the night and would come in the morning after the curfew is lifted. Consoling himself with the thought, and after waiting for some more time, he ultimately went to bed.

He couldn't know for how long he had slept when suddenly he woke up with a jerk and found himself quite O.K. lying upon his bed. He was perspiring and had become very nervous. "A very bad dream indeed" he murmured with his eyes wide open. Giving a quick look by the side of his bed he tried to search for the bundle of 'bidis'. Picking it up, he had drawn the only 'bidi' that was left in the bundle and then looked for the matches to light it which couldn't be seen anywhere. Ultimately, he had to get up. Wearing his slippers he went towards the corner of the room which was being used for years to serve the purpose of kitchen and fetched the matchbox which too had just three-four sticks in it.

With a gloomy face he had lit the 'bidi', drawn two-three puffs in quick succession and tried to recollect the horrible dream he had a little before. In his dream he had seen that Somi was being carried away by the strong currents of a heavily flooded river. She was crying badly and shouting for help, keeping her both hands above the water level. Thereafter, Mangal Sen had seen himself running towards the river but by that time Somi had become out of sight and disappeared. He didn't wait for Somi to come up again and plunged himself into the water. He was going down and down when all of a sudden he woke up,

He couldn't sleep thereafter. He was afraid that he may have another bad dream like the one he had just been through. His stock of 'bidis' had exhausted after his drawing the last one from the bundle. In order to keep himself awake, he once again went towards the kitchen to prepare some tea. Since it had been Somi's prerogative for years, he had to try afresh to prepare tea after a very long time. He still had so much effect of such a bad dream upon his mind that he had forgotten to add sugar while preparing the tea.

At the daybreak he had come into the open. Drawing the wooden bench from the veranda, he had settled down in the courtyard of his house, anxiously waiting for Somi to come. He had kept on staring at the main door that opened into the street but that was all in vain. The 'bird' had already flown and poor father was left at his wit's end. Dreading about some kind of mishap to his daughter, during the curfew hours of the previous night, Mangal Sen prayed for her safety and then set out to find the library Somi used to visit. It came out to be a little farther than it was supposed to be. However, on reaching there he found that the library had not opened yet and had to wait outside for a few minutes.

As soon as the Librarian got settled in his office, Mangal Sen approached him, introducing himself as Somi's father and enquired whether he could tell him something about her whereabouts, as she hadn't returned home the previous night, perhaps on account of the curfew. He looked quite drained out with grief. The Librarian was at a loss to know how to consol the poor father for what was supposed to have happened. But ultimately, he thought that suppressing the facts, he knew about, was no solution of the problem. He too couldn't have imagined that such a nice girl would do a thing like that to her old father. Anyway he, during their conversation, had gradually apprised him about the love affair of Somi and Bob.

It was a great astonishment for Mangal Sen to learn that Somi hadn't come to the library during the last two-three days. However, the Librarian had asked him to look for them at the Rajshree hotel, opposite Subhash garden, where Bob had checked in as per the record in the library register. Poor man had further felt humiliated when told by the hotel manager that Mr. Bob had checked out early that morning. He had asked for a taxi to take him to the airport to catch a flight. Of course his girl-friend was accompanying him. That disheartening news gave him such a great shock that the poor fellow made a loud cry in a fit of hysteria which instantly made him dumb and he virtually lost his voice.

Once, the fact was established that Somi had accompanied Bob, her lover, and gone with her own sweet will, it had become useless to make any further enquiries at the airport. Lodging a complaint at the police station was also out of question as it was neither a case of missing person nor of kidnapping. It was hard to believe for all his acquaintances of the eunuch community as well. In his neighbourhood also, who-so-ever heard about it, had come to console him, but Mangal Sen, having lost his voice completely, had to keep mum. He could make only some gestures, giving a blank look in his grief. However, Bhima, his old pal, who also had retired long back, had come forward in his sympathy. Having become too old himself he had arranged for a fellow eunuch of his band to help Mangal Sen and look after him in that time of stress.

CHAPTER – 48

꧁꧂

To begin with the Bharat Darshan tour from Pune, they had planned to visit **Bombay,** by air as their first destination, now known as **Mumbai**, the capital of the state of Maharashtra. For Somi, it was her maiden flight. She had neither seen a plane in such a proximity nor had ever imagined about such a big size. It was a Boeing 737 plane. Feeling a little nervous at first, she was thrilled on getting inside climbing the steel ladder attached to its door. Once settled in their seats, Somi was amazed to see its hugeness. Incidentally, both of them had got the corner seats and Bob did make Somi occupy the window seat of the aircraft. As the plane gathered its height above in the sky, Somi felt immensely pleased to see through the window how the buildings, trees and the skyscrapers in the city below looked like becoming dwarfed second by second. As also, people and the vehicles too seemed as if crawling like small creatures on earth. As soon as the plane landed at the airport, Bob hired a Taxi and straightaway headed towards Chowpatty and stayed at a hotel in its vicinity. Being a foreigner Bob was welcomed by the Receptionist quite courteously. They were escorted to their room on the second floor. It was a large sunny suite decently decorated with flowers, blue silk curtains and antiques. Sitting comfortably upon the heavily cushioned double bed, both of them had felt quite relaxed. "So, how was the trip?" asked Bob.

"Very easy. It had to be fine since that happened to be my first ever experience of a journey made by a plane, you know? How was *yours*?"

"Mine is always fine, as I use to travel mostly by air for comfort and also to save the time," said Bob with a smile. "In fact, I seldom travel by road. Of course there's no hard and fast rule and I do travel by road in exceptional circumstances and sometimes just for fun only. By the way, don't you feel hungry?" He asked Somi.

"Not yet. I would like to have a hot bath first and become fresh." She got up instantly and reached the bathroom. Pressing the handle a little upside down, she entered therein and was delighted to see it quite neat and clean with everything in place. It was all marble inside, the floor as well as the side-walls, with designer steel taps fitted thereupon, a large-size mirror, fixed against a wall mounted steel-plate with side-bars to hold the small accessories like toothpaste, brush, comb, soap-box, etc., a full-size porcelain bathtub with the shower-bath-apparatus attached to a spiraled flexible steel pipe. Of course the other toiletries like cosmetics, talcum powder, a small bottle of fragranced oil, a soap cake clad in a pink soap-box, a comb and a hair brush with silver handle, a large plastic bucket with a steel mug too were provided. In addition, she could find even a small tooth-paste tube and a pair of fresh white towels hung upon the steel bar fixed into one of the side walls. And above all an English type modern toilet seat, of white porcelain, was also fixed therein. It was a large-size bathroom that gave it an elegant look. While Somi engaged herself into the bathroom enjoying a hot bath, Bob started unpacking the bags to fetch the dresses and other essentials, etc.

When she came out of the bathroom in her under-garments with the towel around her dampened body, Bob got stunned to look at her. He wanted to give her a kiss but restrained himself and entered the bathroom to have a quick shower himself too. And when he came out, after having a hearty bath, with the towel wrapped around his waist, Somi stood in the room, wearing tight jeans with a full-sleeve T-shirt, that fairly exposed her shapely figure. That was the first time Bob had seen her dressed in jeans and T-shirt in which she looked awful. That was, in fact, one of the 'last minute purchases' she had made for the tour. Till then she always used to wear just 'salwar-kameez' only, commonly known as the 'punjabi dress' which too suited upon her nicely. As for Bob, he dressed like his usual, with the nice grey suit, white shirt and black tie. He preferred his black shoes which always seemed as freshly polished whereas Somi had her cream sandals with matching coloured socks. In the name of ornaments Somi had only a pair of silver bangles and a pair of small earrings whereas Bob had worn a simple gold ring sans any precious stone like a ruby, pearl or a diamond. By the time they got ready, both were feeling hungry. Coming downstairs, Bob ordered for lunch sandwiches, fruit-cake, pastries, and ice-cream. Somi, however preferred chapaties, dal-fry and mixed vegetables with salad. They both shared the food equally with each other. While Bob had tried to have the taste of chapaties with dal and vegetables Somi shared with him his food. Both of them ate their bellyful and then came out to explore the Mumbai city. Before leaving, as Somi was looking for her cardigan to put it upon her shoulders, the sun was blazing down from a deep blue sky, punctuated only by a few tiny white clouds scattered across it like daisy flowers. "Oh, come on," said Bob with a smile, "we don't get weather like this everyday." He grabbed her arm and came out with her.

Bombay, now called Mumbai, is the most populated city of India with a population of over 13 million people. The financial and entertainment capital of India, Mumbai blends many communities and cultures together in perfect harmony. Among the other places they visited, were the **'Gate way of India'** and the **'Chowpatty'** as well. Both of them are located by the side of the sea shore. For Somi it was the first occasion in her life to witness the sea and that too in such proximity. There is a big wall wide enough to walk upon, that looked like a boundary line which separates the city from the sea. Crossing the wall they reached the sea shore. The vast expanse of the sea was unimaginable which could be seen up to the horizon. Sans having any kind of fear, certain people had entered the sea. However, afraid of being carried away into the sea by the strong waves, they were seen enjoying a hearty bath in the shallow waters only. Fascinated by the whole view Bob asked Somi if she too would like to have some fun in the sea. But she out-rightly had rejected the idea as she didn't know how to swim. However Bob tried to encourage and make her fearless. He held Somi's hand and both of them entered the sea just up to the knee-deep water. She was thrilled with the sight of the roaring sea-waves coming and going back into the sea after touching the shore. Soon a big wave had come to greet them that had wetted their clothing up to their waist before descending back into the sea. That had left Somi literally awestruck.

The following morning they visited the famous **'Essel World Water Park'** The entry was restricted to the ticket holders only. Here they were given a locker where they had kept their clothes and other belongings. Somi hesitated at first but on seeing a lot of other girls and boys she too joined them and entered the spa of fresh lukewarm mineral water which was just knee deep except at a particular place where one could make a dive from the platform, fixed for the purpose. They enjoyed riding the inflated rubber-boats rapidly moving in a spiral course descending at great speed through different types of winding narrow channels with water gushing down in them from enormous heights. For the purpose of safety, they were asked to grip tightly the handles provided on either side of the boats and also wear the safety-belt round their waist to support the body. That was really a great fun for Somi which she enjoyed in the company of Bob, whom she loved too much.

The Elephanta Caves happen to be the next destination in their list. These are located 10 km away from Mumbai and house a number of elegant sculptured temples cut from rock, way back to the 5th century. These rock-cut temples are dedicated to Lord Shiva, the whole of temple complex is huge, about 60000 square feet and consists of three chambers, one is main and other two are laterals. It is said that caves were used as a target practice for the Portuguese and they had constructed a fort and prepare a small army to stave off pirates. Their practices profaned most of the sculptures. Later on Britishers captured it from Portuguese and tried to lift the monolith elephant to England but couldn't lift it. It is now preserved in Bombay Museum. A large hall in the middle of temple has nine sculptured panels representing Lord Shiva in different tempers. The symmetrical temple plan with important focal point worked out in a geometric Mandala (the design that represents the energy field). Buddha, and Viharas (monasteries) used by Buddhist monks for meditation. The paintings and sculptures depict incidents from the life of the Buddha and various divinities, with the Jataka tales, illustrating stories of Bodhisattva, being the most famous. Besides the temples and monasteries, there are magnificent murals that attract visitors from all over the world. Both were very much impressed to see the marvelous structures chiseled out from the rocks. Here they had learnt from some other visitors about the Ajanta and Ellora caves also. To reach there they will have to go to Aurangabad first. And from there they would be travelling by road to the 'Ellora' caves and then to the 'Ajanta' caves which are just at 29 kms. and 105 Kms. from Aurangabad respectively, Bob was told. By the evening they had returned to Mumbai with the resolve to visit those caves as well and booked the first early morning flight to Aurangabad for the next day.

Bob had misplaced the route-map he had got from Mr. Shyam Prasad, the Librarian. Presumably he had left the same at the Rajshree Hotel, he had been staying at. He had, however, refrained from asking or taking help from anybody. So, they had been randomly travelling all over the places. As soon as the plane landed at **Aurangabad** airport, Bob hired a taxi to go to Shirdi first, situated at 144 Kms. from Aurangabad. They could reach in the afternoon at the holy *'Shrine of 'Sai Baba'* at **'Shirdi'** where they could witness the huge statute of Shri Sai Baba enthroned upon a raised platform with a large umbrella hung over it. They devotedly paid their homage into the Samadhi Mandir and then made their return journey to Aurangabad. They had to stay there in a hotel for the night and asked the Manager of the hotel to arrange a Taxi for their next day journey to witness the most famous 'Ellora Caves'.

The **'Ellora Caves'** are located at a short distance of 29 kms. only from Aurangabad. Here, they could witness that while the Buddhist caves have a vast pantheon of Buddhas, the Hindu caves are dedicated to Lord Shiva. Gods in the holy trinity: Brahma, Vishnu and Mahesh are also shown in variety of forms. A cave with a miniature of Kailasha temple is also chiseled out of a single rock of an isolated mountain. The sculptures have scenes from Ramayana and Mahabharata epics also. Bob had quite minutely looked at most of the beautifully carved sculptures and was fascinated too much to see specifically those of Lord Buddha and Lord Shiva. Bob was able to click photographs of a few of them also, like he had been doing in Mumbai of the places visited by them. It had taken them the whole day to see the sculptures in all the 29 caves with the result that they couldn't return to their hotel before sunset. Both of them got too much tired as the caves are located at varied distances from each other. Ultimately they had to postpone their programme and thus booked the taxi for the next morning to visit the Ajanta caves. Needless to say that they retired for the night immediately after having their dinner.

Ajanta caves, the world heritage site is located about 105 km from Aurangabad city. Dating from 200 BC, these caves were excavated in two distinct phases and reportedly took more than 800 years to complete. In the early 19th century (year 1819) some British soldiers were out hunting in the Deccan plateau. One of them suddenly saw, from a height, a horseshoe rock; His curiosity aroused by the entrance of a cave. The hunting party ventured across the ravine of the Waghur River. And they discovered several caves, against which bush, shrubs earth and stones had piled up. Goat herds for shelter were using a few. The Government was informed about this finding and soon the Archaeologists began to excavate them. Many experts have been restoring them during the last fifty years. The shock of discovery was worldwide. All the rock-cut caves had paintings on verandahs, inner walls and ceilings, these revealed some of the most beautiful masterpieces of world art. Actually, the truth behind how these structures were made is---Ancient Saints who were on path of enlightenment achieved powers called as "Siddhis". Some of these siddhis included seeing things in all dimensions in their mind, power to convert stones and boulders to a gel like material and revert them back to original stone through utilizing sun's rays (Long lost siddhi called Surya Vigyan or Solar Science).. The Saints used their powers to change matter and guide workers to mould the scripture. Back to Aurangabad, Bob had booked a direct flight to Hyderabad for the next day.

After the necessary clearance, the couple boarded a direct flight to **'Hyderabad'** that had taken place at its scheduled time at 13.50 hours. It had landed its destination in the evening at around 16.15 hours. Reaching there they had asked the Taxi driver to take them to the Imperial hotel near Char Minar. This was a tourist hotel with menus and prices in English and the food was appropriately superb. Bob booked a luxury suit and the couple deposited their bag and baggage in the room. In spite of having been tired enough, they looked in high spirits and none of them wanted to relax. They ordered some salad, coffee, cakes and then herbal tea. Since no time was left to visit the famous Golconda Fort, both of them preferred to walk leisurely towards the **Char Minar** and have a round of the main market quite famous for the white metal wares like bangles and other glittering ornaments, designer sarees and a good variety of ladies garments. Bob had asked Somi to take a look and on his persistent requests she had made some purchases of suitable ladies-wear dresses, light jewellery items of the white metal like earrings, tops, necklace, some bangles and two-three pairs of sandals as well. Carrying the bags, with the purchases they had made, both of them returned to the hotel and before going for dinner she had tried her dresses which made her even prettier. They were so fascinated that even after the dinner they once again had a little strolling of the market to look for any other item of interest and then retired for the night. Thus the visit to the Golconda Fort was postponed for the following day.

And the next morning Somi dressed herself neatly as usual just like she did on a normal day. She wore a red velvet dress, cut with perfect simplicity, with cream twinset--- a matching cardigan and jumper, with beautiful pearl earrings--- all the new last-night-purchases, made from the market. Her face was very attractive and didn't look like it had experienced a great deal of fun, or pleasure. And yet she seemed quite innocent.

"I think you are the most beautiful woman I have ever seen in my life," Bob said to Somi. "Even beautiful women do not essentially have that spark that raises a woman to what you are." "Beauty is not wholly on the inside, whatever the platitude may say. But it does take more than even features and a certain level of proportion in the figure. A pretty woman without a spark of grace is a cipher. And one possessing that spark will always be the one who attracts an intelligent man in real life."

Somi paused. "I think that's the loveliest thing I've ever known."

"I never thought it through until seeing you. But it is absolutely true." He took her hand in his and smiled gently at her. He was very happy indeed.

Her head lifted, and she blushed, deeply. "You don't need to lie." She smiled. "Although I admit I took my time choosing the dress."

He smiled back; it was amazing, the ease of it; he liked it immensely.

The city offers to the visitors at least two well known places. One is the **'Golconda Fort'**. It was built in (AD 1525) on a granite hill at the height of 120 metres, amazingly constructed of large rocks each weighing several tones.

One wonders that even for elephants it wouldn't have been possible to drag the huge rocks to such a height in those times in the absence of any kind of building technology available these days.

The other feat worth mention is its 'Water Supply System'. At every higher stage there is a 'well' which has a chain of small buckets that runs on a pulley. The moving chain with buckets goes down to dip into the 'well' and comes up with all the buckets filled with water and pour it in a large vessel connected by ceramic pipe lines through which the water fetched from the first 'well' is drained into the second 'well' located at the next higher stage of the Fort. From there it is again carried over the same way to the third 'well' and so on, making the water supply reach even at the highest point of the Fort.

By the time, both of them were feeling hungry and after coming out of the Fort they looked for some eatery nearby instead of wasting time in searching a good restaurant. They found one at a little distance and approached it. Though it was a small place, yet was neat and clean and a little spacious. The couple was welcome and led to a central table having its surface decently covered with a plastic sheet that showed colourful painting of flowers on it to attract their customers who care to come and dine there. The food was undoubtedly very delicious, beyond expectation, faintly scented with garlic. Crusty bread with lemon and butter was excellent. The salad was crisp and full of summer herbs. And after a hearty meal they headed for the Salarjung Museum.

The second most famous and worth a visit place is the **'Salarjung Museum'** of 'Hyderabad'. It has over 43,000 art objects and 50,000 books and manuscripts which are the third largest one-man collection of antiques in the world. It has 38 galleries but the most interesting exhibit can be seen in the gallery No.28 where a toy-figure of a watchman pushes open the door of a 'musical clock' at every hour, quickly strikes at a gong to indicate the time in exact hours and hurriedly goes back into the clock, shutting the door behind him. By the way, there also lies a 'Mummy' in a glass-box which is said to be 3000 years old. No doubt, it had turned out for both, Bob and Somi, a very exciting exhibit. They were so fascinated and absorbed in the exhibits, going from gallery to gallery, that they had virtually lost the track of the time and had to come out when the Museum was being closed for the night. Reaching the hotel they were feeling so exhausted that they didn't dare coming downstairs to have their dinner in the dining hall and as such, hurriedly ordered for the dinner to be served in their room itself

CHAPTER – 49

❧

Reaching **Calcutta** (now Kolkata) they were fascinated to see the **Howrah Bridge**. This is one of the four bridges on the <u>Hooghly River</u> and is a famous symbol of <u>Kolkata</u> and <u>West Bengal</u>. The other bridges are the <u>Vidyasagar Setu</u> (popularly called the Second Hooghly Bridge), the <u>Vivekananda Setu</u>, and the newly built <u>Nivedita Setu</u>. It weathers the storms of the <u>Bay of Bengal</u> region, carrying a daily <u>traffic</u> of approximately 100,000 vehicles and possibly more than 150,000 pedestrians easily making it the busiest cantilever bridge in the world. The third-longest inaugurated in 1921, was built to commemorate the visit of Queen Victoria, the first Empress of India. Possibly the grandest reminder of the Raj. The splendour of this Memorial hall lies in its vast collection of remnants from the British Empire's rule in India. Built in white marble and set amidst beautiful gardens, this must-visit site offers memorable old-world charm. The **Birla Planetarium** is one of the largest museums on the Asian continent. Built in 1962, this planetarium houses a large collection of paintings by prominent astronomers who were inspired by the stars. Here, the Planetarium is one of the main attractions. With a capacity of 500 spectators daily shows are held in the planetarium which is a great place to learn about life, the universe and everything in between.

In South, their first destination was Madras, now called **'Chennai'**. Bob booked a suit in a small hotel near **Marina Beach**. Somi glanced around the suit. It was certainly luxurious. There was a vast bedroom, bathrooms decked out in ivory and brass, a balcony overlooking the sea-beach, Persian rugs and large display of flowers. They visited the Marina Sea Beach. The mile-long crescent of the beach attracted many a visitor which offered a breathtaking view indeed. The water looked dark even in the sunlight, white-capped and heaving to the grey, rocky shore. The sight was quite fascinating. The waves had been coming to the sea-shore with the rhythm and having a hasty retreat after giving a cold wash to the feet of the visitors at the beach. Both, Bob and Somi had tried to have a sip of the sea-water and were really surprised to taste such an enormous amount of salt in it. The beach had only a thin border of actual sand at the water's edge. There was a brisk wind coming off the waves, cool and briny, strongly impregnated with salt. The clouds circled the sky, threatening to invade at any moment, but for now the sun shone bravely in the sky. Needless to say that both of them had full enjoyment basking in the sun.

From there they proceeded to **'Mahabalipuram'** and enjoyed the sea-beach there as well. The cave temples of Mahaballipuram built in 8th century are located in the hillock of Mahaballipuram town overlooking the coromandel coast of the Bay of Bengal (700-728 AD). Here six temples are believed to be remain submerged in the sea.

To reach the famous Temple of *'Shri Murugan'*, situated on the steep height of a hill at **'Pallani'** the devotees had to climb on foot 670 steps to have the holy darshan (glimpse) of the deity. Howevr, the pilgrims could be transported to the temple on a nominal charge by the cable-car also that consists of a small rope-train for going up and down. So, both had enjoyed the cable-car ride as well to save the time and the energy. It was a beautiful temple indeed and after paying their obeisance to the deity, they left for Madurai.

The Meenakshi Temple at **Madurai** is for its grandeur. It has four huge entrance gates, each one constructed on its all the four sides. The gates have countless idols of numerous deities beautifully carved on them producing a rare example of craftsmanship. The **Meenakshi Amman Temple** or the **Meenakshi Sundareswarar Temple** is a historic Hindu temple which is situated in the holy city of **Madurai** in **Tamil Nadu**. The temple is dedicated to **God Shiva**, seen in the form of **Sundareswarar** (Beautiful Lord) with his wife, **Goddess Parvati,** who is in the form of **Meenakshi**. This historic site is believed to be built back in 7th century and is a vital symbol of Tamil people.

At **'Tiruchirapalli'**, there was a *'Mandapam'* which had a thousand pillers they were told. The Rockfold Temple is 83 meters upwards from the surrounding plains. To reach there they had to climb 437 steps cut into the rock. Halfway up they visited another Temple dedicated to Lord Shiva. The holy shrine of **Srirangam** is situated on a tiny island formed by the bifurcation of the river Cavery. St. Lourdu's, Church built in 1812, has levered doors, which when opened, turns the church into an airy pavilion. Its excellent setting and marvelous architecture, makes it a site worth visiting. It is in the heart of the Trichy city. Also situated there is Hazrath Nathervali the ancient **Durga** more than 1000 years old. This too, like the Church, is a marvelous architecture. The dome is made up of shining marbles giving a great look to the **Durga** Mukkombu, a wonderful picnic spot, where the river Kollidam branches off from the river Cavery. It is 18 kilometers from Trichy City.

Reaching the temple at **Rameswaram** they paid their obeisance to Lord Shiva. Here, they were told that after killing Ravana, Lord Rama returned with his consort

Goddess Seeta from Lanka and wanted to offer worship to Lord Shiva, the God of Gods, to expatiate the 'dosha' of killing a Brahmin. Since there was no shrine in the island, He had despatched Sri Hanuman to Kailash to bring an idol of Lord Shiva. Thus the place was known as Rameshwaram. Both of them then straight away headed towards Kanya Kumari, 230 Kms. from Rameshwaram.

'Kanya Kumari' is the place where Arabian Sea, Indian Ocean and the Bay of Bengal meet each other. To reach **'Swami Vivekananda Temple',** situated off shore into the sea, one has to go by a motor-boat, the lone transport facility available at the site. The temple appears to be an epitome of cleanliness. It contains a big hall meant for meditation in a cool and calm atmosphere that gives 'shanti' (eternal peace) in real sense of the word. There is a pair of holy feet engraved upon a piece of rock said to be those of Swami Vivekananda himself. The visitors use to touch them with great reverence and pay their obeisance at the temple. And so did Bob and Somi also. In addition, they had witnessed the 'Sunset' at the site which was a unique experience in itself.

Next in line was **'Trivandrum'** about 60 Kms. from Kanya Kumari where they were delighted to see **'Swami Padmanabham in Anand Shayanam'.** Here, they had witnessed Lord Vishnu lying in sleeping mode on the bed of 'Sheshnag'. Also visible was the node of the lotus plant grown from his navel, at the top of which Lord Brahma ji was seated upon a Kamal (lotus flower).

'Tirupati' devasthanam, **'Lord Venkateshwara',** popularly known as Bala ji, is the presiding deity of the Tirumala hills in Andhra Pradesh. It receives on an average about 50,000 pilgrims daily. While on special occasions and festivals the number of pilgrims shoots up to 500,000, making it the most-visited holy place in the world. Thousands of persons could be seen standing in the long queues to have a glimpse of the deity. The Tirupati temple is known as the world's richest temple. Gold coins are also sold by the managing authorities of the temple to the aspiring pilgrims who wish to keep them as a memorabilia. According to one legend, the temple has a <u>murti</u> (deity) of Lord Venkateswara, which it is believed shall remain here for the entire duration of the present <u>Kali Yuga</u>.

'**Delhi**' was their next destination to arrive at. They reached there in the forenoon. Coming out at the airport, they hired a cab for Hotel Samantha on the recommendation of a co-passenger in the plane. It was cited as one of the best hotels in its class, full of ancient traditions. They were given a warm welcome as soon as they reached its front door and let themselves in. The surroundings instantly soothed them. They were offered a luxury suite on the third floor. There was a lift also apart from a spiraled flight of stairs. They had their suite set up exactly as Bob would like to; rush matting on the floors, dark red wallpaper, floor-to-ceiling windows with heavy silk curtains, decorated with flower-vases, together with antique furniture and some other gift like items which adorned the entire suite. There was attached bathroom with all the modern fittings, a geyser, a bathtub, and a mirror. The floor was fixed with glazed white tiles. A side table was also placed with the thickly cushioned double bed. So, both of them, first of all, wanted to relax for a while.

"By the way, what about our breakfast?" asked Bob. "Should I order for that on the phone itself or would you like to go in to the dining hall and get something to eat?"

"I'd love that. We can go to see the monument afterwards," replied Somi.

On coming down-stairs they entered the dining hall and instantly became the centre of attraction for one and all dining over there. Both of them were well dressed and looked elegant. They were shown a quiet table by the side of a huge floor-to-ceiling glass window where one could have a view of the well maintained beautiful garden outside.

"This is perfect," Somi smiled as she sat back in her chair and looked at Bob cheerfully. They ordered for pizza and salads followed by a cup of coffee. After the breakfast they hired a taxi and headed for Mehrauli to see the world famous Qutub Minar which Delhi is really proud of.

Located in mehrauli on the outskirts of Delhi, *'Qutub Minar'* is the most visited place among the tourists. The worth seeing monument was built by Qutub-ud-din Aibak (AD 1206 – 1210), founder of the Slave Dynasty, but completed by Iltutmish, his son-in-law who ruled (AD 1211 – 1236). The seven-storey building boasts of a real epitome of India's architectural structure of its period. Surprisingly, the artisans in those times could never have even dreamed of such an advanced technology and the heavy machinery of building-construction being used now-a-days for skyscrapers. It is embedded with convoluted carvings and verses from the holy Quran.

Initially it was a seven-storey building but later on was reduced to only five-storeys where visitors used to climb through more than two hundred stairs. But owing to a couple of mishaps, they are now allowed up to the first storey only which still is considered enormously high enough. Both, Bob and Somi, were quite fascinated to look at the Minar. As a number of other visitors were seen going up inside the Minar they too decided to follow them. And the next minute they also started climbing up the flight of stairs, moving upward in a spiral course, inside the Qutub Minar. Since no artificial lighting is allowed in the historical monuments, the visitors had to climb up the stairs in natural sunlight dimly coming from outside through the windows, carved for the purpose, into the thick wall of the Minar at short curves. Full of enthusiasm they soon reached the first storey and stepped on its balcony. It is barricaded with circular stone railing around it and has a reasonable space, wide enough to accommodate a few persons. Standing at such a great height and looking on the ground below, from its balcony, was a thrilling experience in itself as the people and the vehicles on the ground looked like small toys which both of them enjoyed very much. Climbing down the stairs one has to remain cautious enough for fear of slipping in the dark dim light. On coming down they had let themselves photographed also, as they looked a fine couple indeed. They then spotted an Ice-cream vendor and enjoyed a cup of fruit ice-cream each. It was time for lunch now. Finding no eateries in the surroundings of the Minar they agreed to have their lunch somewhere at chandni chowk. So with the idea of visiting the Red Fort also they hired a taxi to reach the famous **Chandni Chowk,** located opposite the Red Fort. Here they enjoyed the typical Indian food like 'Aaloo-ka-parantha', a kind of fried wheat-chapaati stuffed with potatoes and vegetables, served with curd and followed by sweet 'Lassi' prepared by blending the curd with water and sugar. They also had a round of the most fascinating chandni chowk bazaar and tasted various other dishes as well which both of them could never have even dreamt of, for Bob being a foreigner and Somi a hosteller.

While taking a round of the chandni chowk bazaar they had found the famous Sikh temple---'Gurdwara Sisganj' also at Bhai Mati Das chowk, quite adjacent to the police station. The structure is built in white marble and its dome is said to be of pure gold. Here, they were surprised to note that a stream of running water was flowing in the narrow water-trough at the main entrance. The devotees would dip their feet therein before going inside the gurdwara, in order to maintain the sanctity of the sacred place. Somi and Bob, out of sheer curiosity, too followed suit. That was their first opportunity of seeing a gurdwara. Once inside, they looked very much fascinated with the decoration etc. A performance of the programme of shabd-kirtan (reciting of holy hymns) was going on and the congregation of the devotees sitting inside was listening to it quite attentively. Both of them bowed and paid their homage to 'Guru Granth Sahib' placed reverently under a canopy. They came out after some time and walked towards the Red Fort as per their schedule for the day.

It was a little late in the afternoon when they visited the **'Red Fort'** a symbol of Mughal pride, in old Delhi, opposite Chandani Chowk bazaar they have just taken a round of. During the Mughal days, nobles and the public would enter the Red Fort from the western or Lahore gate, from the ramparts of which the Prime Minister addresses the nation each year on Independence Day. Unfortunately, on account of some renovation work going on in the monument, no arrow markers had yet been put up at important points. Except for a few plaques detailing the monument's history, visitors were left to their own devices which had necessitated Bob to look for a 'guide' to take them around and explain the Fort's significance. Soon he was able to find one and all the three of them entered from Lahore gate and the first place they visited was the 'Naubat Khana', the place, where drums were played to announce the arrival of special guests to the emperor, explained the guide.

Next was the **'Diwan-e-Aam'** which was originally enclosed within an arcaded court but was destroyed after the large-scale demolitions in the aftermath of the 1857 uprising but the foundations of which survive till today. Here, the emperor used to meet the general public. Then, turning left towards the *hamam*, they came to the **Diwan-e-Khas** or the 'hall of private audience' of the emperor which has been described as the finest building in the Red Fort. This is where the emperor held his special audiences with his most trusted courtiers. This is the place where he received his most important guests, sitting on the famed peacock throne, they were told. The guide had taken them to the Rang Mahal as also to the Mumtaz Mahal Museum and the Indian War Memorial Museum situated in the British Barracks of the Fort. Bob also had learnt from the guide that the 120-acre fort is recommended by UNESCO for all world heritage sites.

After fully enjoying the trip they returned quite late in the evening. Having tasted a variety of eatables in plenty at chandni chowk in the evening, both of them had their fill and declined to take dinner. Instead, they preferred to have just a glass of milk only. However, before going to bed Bob had asked the manager of the hotel to fix up a taxi to take them to Agra the next morning to visit the historical monument 'Taj Mahal'.

Chapter – 50

❦

B eing an early riser habitually, Somi got up first the
next morning, brushed her teeth and even had her
shower also. She was in the process of getting ready when
Bob woke up. Looking at his watch he hurriedly rushed
towards the washroom. Somi ended up in only skirt ---long,
khaki-coloured, still casual. She then put on the dark blue
blouse, Bob had once complemented. A quick glance in
the mirror told that her hair was entirely impossible, so she
pulled it back into a ponytail.

"Okay. I look decent now." She bounced into the room,
waiting for Bob.

"Wow," he said to Somi, coming out of the washroom
and taking a step back to admire her. She looked elegant and
far prettier than she realized herself. "You look incredible"
he said. "I don't think you need to worry about wearing
your dresses. You look lovely Somi whatever you wear," Bob
said warmly.

"I had such a good time tonight," Somi whispered softly,
acutely aware of not only of how handsome he was but of
how kind as well.

So, there next visit had been to see the historical
monument – *'Taj Mahal'* at *'Agra'*. The Taxi had come
at the appointed time to take Bob and Somi to Agra as
planned. Here, they had checked in a hotel near Raja ki
Mandi. It was a well furnished suite with a balcony on its
front that opened towards the main market. It was so lovely
that Somi couldn't restrain herself and stretched upon the
sofa. Though the journey by taxi was not uncomfortable

yet she had felt somewhat tired and wanted to relax for a while. Bob then called the room-service and asked for Tea and snacks.

They visited the monument the same evening and looked for a guide who could take them in to the monument and show all the places inside worthy of having a look. Seeing the foreigner tourist, a couple of young boys which seemed to be relaxing after the day's work rushed towards them. One of them who had some working knowledge of English was engaged for the purpose. He happened to be quite competent in his job and explained to them almost everything in detail to the entire satisfaction of both the visitors. Bob was wonderstruck and so was Somi on seeing the world famous historical monument known as 'Taj Mahal' built in AD 1631-1653 by Shahjahan, the Mughal Emperor who ascended the throne in 1627. It was built in loving memory of Begam Noor Jahan, his wife, who died in 1631. Recently the name of 'Taj Mahal' was included in 'The Seven wonders of the world' regarded in antiquity as specifically remarkable, they were told.

Since that was the day of full moon, their Guide had stressed upon them to wait till the fall of night to see the real beauty of the monument which looked magnificent on seeing in full moonlit night. And as such under compulsion they had to stay there. Needless to say, that the couple remained awestruck to witness the charming moonlight effect on the Taj Mahal, a memorable experience for them, indeed. A group of some other visitors also joined them who had specially come to see the Taj Mahal in the moonlit night. They had also got themselves photographed with the Taj Mahal in the background like they had done at Qutub Minar. For the following day, Bob had planned to return to Delhi again by road. They would stay in the Hotel Samrat for the night and leave for Jaipur by air the next morning. He had, as such, again booked a private Taxi in accordance with the programme.

Next morning she was dressed in a beautifully cut navy blue suit. She had a bright green scarf around her neck. She looked pretty and fresh and as always, utterly beautiful, very chic. Bob's eyes ran up and down, across her body, her slim curves perfectly visible through the well-cut suit. With this she had become more attractive.

"You look wonderful today," Bob commented. He wanted to gather her in to his arms, hug her and kiss the life out of her mouth. Anyway, standing very close to her while dressing himself, He caught her hands in his; for all her years, her slim, feminine hands were dwarfed inside his; he liked the look of them in there and asked, "Shouldn't we take our breakfast downstairs?"

"That would be nice," she smiled again as Bob opened the door and kissed her on her cheek. She smiled at him bravely. They walked down the stairs side by side. He looked in good spirits as they walked in to the dining room. He had called and reserved a table and ordered a huge breakfast for both of them.

"I can't eat all that," she complained. She looked at what he had ordered --- eggs, burgers, wafers, oatmeal and fruit, orange juice and coffee --- more than enough for a starving crowd, Somi commented with a smile.

"I don't know what you like for breakfast," Bob grinned at her sheepishly, "so I ordered everything. What do you usually eat?" he asked with curiosity. He liked knowing every little detail about her.

"Usually, coffee or tea with sandwich or bread-butter, but this is more than enough," she said, putting burgers and eggs on her plate, and then adding some wafers. And much to her own surprise, she ate a huge amount of what he had ordered and he finished most of the rest. And by the time they left the hotel, they were both in high spirits and teasing each other about how much they had eaten and how fat they would get.

"I'd be obese if I eat more often like that," Somi said. And Bob had been thinking how nice it would be to have breakfast with her like this every day. She was such a good company and so easy to be with. Soon after, Bob had asked the Manager at the hotel for billing as they would be checking out in a short while.

The Taxi came at 10.00 o'clock as was agreed upon and left for Delhi after Bob and Somi made themselves seated comfortably. Somi still looked under the spell of magnificent Taj Mahal and the Qutub Minar which so far she had seen in pictures only while studying at the Boarding school and was really fascinated on physically seeing them. Immersed in her thoughts she dozed off. And Bob had made himself busy in admiring the sleeping beauty throughout their journey, patting on himself to be such a lucky man.

By the time they reached Delhi both of them looked tired. On returning to the hotel Bob requested the Manager to get two air-tickets booked for Jaipur available on any Airline for the next morning. They then had their dinner and retired to their suite for the night.

"I hope you had a sound sleep as I had been watching you snoring, off and on, throughout the night but didn't dare wake you up. How are you feeling?" asked Bob next morning.

"I'm just happy to be here. I've never done anything like this. I feel so removed from all my worries here and am feeling like a bird that had escaped his cage."

Soon the phone rang and Bob spoke into the receiver: "Hello."

"Good morning Sir. This is Reception counter. Sir, your confirmed tickets for Jaipur had been booked on line for today itself on Skyway airline and the flight is scheduled to take place at 13.50 hours sharp. I would be sending you the details of the booking in a short while."

"Oh, thank you very much and please don't bother anymore. I will collect the details from your counter personally before the check-out time."

They got ready in an hour or so and ordered for a heavy breakfast as Somi was told that they would be served only some light refreshment in the aircraft. Before finishing the breakfast, Bob had also asked for the bill for payment as they would be leaving in a short while. In about half an hour they found themselves in a cab speeding towards the Delhi airport.

Chapter – 51

❦

On a Sunday, say, after about a month of disappearing of Somi, Mangal Sen, as usual, was sitting in the veranda engrossed in his thoughts when his 'help' had served his meals to him. He had taken just a few bites when he heard as if somebody had knocked at the door. He asked his 'help' to see who was knocking. To his great surprise, it was Shyam Prasad, the Librarian who had taken time to visit Mangal Sen. In fact the library, Somi used to visit, had its weekly off on Sunday. He got the address from the records kept in the library register itself. He had told Mangal Sen that during the course of making an inventory of the books he had noticed that a couple of books borrowed by Somi from the library had not been returned till that date. Mangal Sen, then, with the gestures of his hands asked his 'help' to take a look in to Somi's room and find if any book from the library was lying there. Shyam Prasad had felt very sorry on seeing the pathetic condition of Mangal Sen after having lost his voice. Soon the 'help' came out of the room with some books. He handed them over to the librarian and left. Shyam Prasad immediately sorted out the two missing library books. On a quick scrutiny of the books to look for any damaged or torn pages he found a folded piece of paper supposed to be a love letter which are very commonly found in the library books secretly placed there and forgotten thereafter.

But that was not a love letter. It was written about a month back by Somi, addressed to her father explaining everything about her intimate love with Bob, a foreigner and the Bharat Darshan tour, but she forgot to give him before leaving. Shyam Prasad had read it to Mangal Sen and also consoled him for the unfortunate happening. Mangal Sen had thus realized that poor Somi didn't dare to tell her father face to face and had informed him through that letter which per chance had been kept lying in her room but couldn't be delivered to him. Shyam Prasad also told him about the conversation he had with Bob in the library office introducing himself as the son of an Indian mother who lived in England. The information, certainly, had given much relief to the grief stricken mind of the old man.

Jaipur is popularly known as the pink city and **Hawa mahal** is one of the best tourists places in the city. Every guest and tourists are recorded to be impressed by the architecture and the history behind the establishment of royal palace of winds. The architecture of the building is so build that it concrete the shape of a pyramid with total of 953 windows uniquely carved in the Rajasthani pattern and designs.

Bharatpur Bird Sanctuary:The area is best known as the home of Keoladeo National Park, an outstanding bird refuge that is also a UNESCO World Heritage Site. In the winter it's a stopover point for migrating birds and hundreds of species have been spotted. The best way to see the park is via bicycle rickshaw. Be sure to take binoculars and a good camera! You can get to Bharatpur from Delhi also by train, or by Bus.

Shri Nathdwara (a pathway to Lord Shri Krishna) literally means the gateway to the Lord **Shri Nathji.** This great Vaishnavite shrine was built in the 17th century on spot exactly identified by the Lord himself. The legends have it that the idol of the Lord Krishna was being transferred to safer place from Vrindaban to protect it from the destructive wrath of the Mughal Emperor Aurangzeb. When the idol reached this spot, the wheels of bullock cart it was traveling in, sank axle deep in mud and refused to move further, at all. The accompanying priest realized that this was Lord's chosen spot and the Lord did not want to travel any further. Accordingly a Temple was built here. This is a temple and place of pilgrimage amongst its believers

'**Haridwar**', was their next destination to visit. Reaching there both of them had taken the holy dip in '*Ganga*' at "*Har- ki-pouri*". Here, in the evening, they had the opportunity of witnessing the famous *Ganga ji ki 'Aarti'* on the bank of the river performed by the holy priests at Har-ki-pauri. That happened to be really a spectacular sight. On reaching **Rishikesh** they were able to have a trip to '*Neel Kanth*' as well. For Gangotri and Shri Badrinath dham, they were told that the Buses and Taxis go up to the last point, from where, pilgrims had a walking distance to reach the temple, however, for Yamunotri, and Shri Kedarnath one has to go either on foot or hire a pony to reach there. But the yatra season had not commenced yet on account of heavy snowfall in the region. Moreover, there wasn't much time left for them to visit those places.

Bob had heard about the Kumbh Mela also which takes place after every twelve years at different places and regretted very much to miss the last one which was held at Prayag. He no more looked like a foreigner except for his fair skin by which he could easily be taken as a native of Kashmir. He appeared as well as behaved like a religious person and tried to perform the so called '*pooja-archana*' with Somi quite devotedly like husband and wife at almost all the places. On applying the holy dot of sandalwood paste in the centre of his forehead, Somi would mischievously address him as '*Pandit ji*'.

In metro cities like Bombay (Mumbai), Calcutta (Kolkata), etc. they couldn't stay for long. Both of them wanted to see Kashmir, famously known as 'the heaven on earth' but instead of getting a direct flight to Srinagar, they flew to **Jammu** by Jet Airways to visit *'Mata Vaishno Devi'* first. For pilgrims there was a regular Bus service to and fro between Jammu and Katra. On reaching 'Katra' they looked for a room nearby to stay for the night. Early next morning they got ready for the ascent but had to wait for their turn in accordance with the number being allotted to the pilgrims in order to put a check over the crowd. Well, after a considerable time, they were allowed to proceed towards the holy cave of Mata Vaishno Devi and were delighted to have a glimpse of the deities on reaching there. **Vaishno Devi Shrine:** It is said that around 700 years back Mata Vaishnavi appeared in Pandit Shridhar's vision (dream) and told him to search for her at the Holy Cave in the mountains and showed him the way to discover it. When he reached the Holy Cave, he found a rock form with three heads atop it. At that moment Mata Vaishno Devi appeared before him in full glory and introduced him to the three heads (now known as the holy pindies) as Mata Maha Lakshmi, Maha Mata Saraswati and Maha Mata Maha Kali. She also blessed him with a boon of four sons and a right to worship her manifestation and asked him to spread the glory of the holy shrine all over. On their return to Jammu were also delighted to visit the famous Raghunath Mandir also. Thus Bob's another wish, his mother had spoken about, was accomplished, as also various other famous attractions worth paying a visit while in India.

CHAPTER – 52

❦

Coming back to Jammu airport, they had once again found themselves lucky to board the direct flight to Srinagar which per chance had a couple of seats still lying unreserved. They reached **'Srinagar'**, the beautiful valley of Kashmir in just half an hour from Jammu and stayed at Hotel Lake View near 'Lal Chowk'. It was a three star hotel where they were greeted with a smile at the Reception. Being a foreigner Bob had an added advantage of getting special treatment wherever they had been throughout the tour. Instead of a room offered at the ground floor, adjacent to the lounge, they had preferred to book a luxury suite at the third floor with an open gallery from where one could have a view of the city and the Dal Lake as well. The room was well furnished. It had a double bed, a bit larger than the standard size with the mattress of four-inch thickness. The silken bed sheet had beautiful embroidery work on its borders. Decorated with a large sun-flower, embroidered in yellow in the centre of the bed sheet, with small replica of the flower on all the four corners was spread over neatly and a pair of pillows with beautifully embroidered matching pillow-covers placed at the head of the bed. A thickly cushioned sofa-set with covers matching the décor of the rich tapestry curtains hung upon the doors and windows gave a royal touch to the entire suite. A small vase that contained a bunch of fresh flowers adorned the central table. A pair of cushioned arm-chairs was kept in the gallery itself. A wooden cupboard was seen in one corner of the room which had a built-in-locker and a full length mirror fixed upon one of its doors. It was painted in light grey that matched the colour of the walls of the room. Using the attached washroom was another innovative experience in itself. It was wonderful: American-style, with a Western shower, hot water on demand, clean white tiles and soft towels. It was fitted with the most modern sanitary appliances like designer taps of steel instead of brass with moveable levers, a large full size ceramic porcelain bath-tub where one could easily lie in it to have a hearty bath with the help of the shower-bath-apparatus fitted with flexible spiralled steel tube attached with the water tap, a mirror was fixed just over the wash-basin. An automatic door-closer was also fixed at the door of the bathroom. Somi stood for a long time under the warm droplets, washing herself from top to toe with the French lavender soap kept in a little dish. She washed her hair. She felt glorious and took Bob's plush bathrobe and wrapped it around herself. Apart from the nice accommodation, the hotel management had to offer awfully delicious food to meet the taste of every body staying over there. They would order any thing of their choice either veg. or non-veg. Both Bob and Somi had preferred to have their dinner at the hotel on their return by the night after visiting a place or two throughout the day. However, on feeling a little hungry, they used to have just fruit and some light refreshment at any place wherever they had been by the lunch hour. They had really enjoyed their stay at the Hotel Lake View and chalked out their daily schedule to visit some place or the other for a full week.

On the very first day after their arrival, they approached the Dashnami Akhara to make enquiries about the "Amarnath yatra' but were disheartened when told that the route of the Yatra to the holy cave remains covered under the heavy snow throughout the year except in the month of July-August. Only then, the pilgrims who are medically fit to bear the strain during the yatra would be allowed to go there. Bob, then, hired a house-boat called 'Shikara'. Enjoying the thrill of boating in the *'Dal Lake'*, they had tried their hand at its 'oars' also by rowing the boat to some distance in the still waters of the Lake. They visited the 'Nehru Park' that was situated in the Lake itself. It looked like a little piece of an island surrounded by the Lake-water from all sides, approachable only by a boat. There were beautiful gardens in a row alongside the Dal Lake scheduled to be visited the next day.

On another day they had visited the famous **'Khir Bhawani'** temple. There was a 'sarover' also for the pilgrims to take a bath in it before performing 'pooja'. It was a beautiful temple indeed, worth paying a visit. On the morning, that followed, they visited the famous **'Shalimar Bagh'** and the **'Nishat Garden'**. Blooming with flowers and maintained in a superbly arranged manner, both of them looked as if they were competing against each other with envy. There was a wide artificial 'waterfall' also which had its cooling effect in the atmosphere all around it. Lush green shrubs cut and shaped in various sizes were placed in matching number on either side of their openings, giving a soothing effect to the onlookers. Last in that range was **'Harvin'**, another famous garden which could be attributed to the beauty personified, making it a heaven-like place on earth and supposed to be the heart-beat of the Kashmir valley.

The next day was fixed for tracking. After an early breakfast both of them had set out to track on the *'Gulmarg'* route. It had thickly grown trees of unconventional heights up to 40 feet, standing stately like poles fixed in the ground. These are widely used for construction of wooden houses all over the valley. The Electricity department also makes use of these trees as electricity poles to support the heavy electric wires. At Gulmarg they enjoyed the 'sledge' ride consisting of a boat-like wooden carriage without wheels which rows upon the steep slopes of the snowy hills with great speed. While returning they had the thrilling 'Cable-Trolley' ride also that ferried them downhill. The whole day was thus attributed to the adventurous rides.

The climate became quite pleasant by the night. Both Bob and Somi lay on the bed in the hotel which was reasonably warm. She was running her fingers lazily down his arm and then ran across his shoulders and down his back. And as she did, he looked at her with an air of longing and then smiled looking like a mischievous little boy.

"Why are you looking like that?" She asked, wondering if he was laughing at her.

"No, I dare not. Honestly, wanting you is driving me insane".

"What did you have in mind?"

"I want to make love to you." He had been having overpowering sensations for the past half hour. And he was so comfortable with her and wanted to make love to her for a long time but had never asked her then. But there was a hopeful look in his eyes that went straight to her heart.

"It is all right my love." It was something she wanted to do for him, even if all they did was just lie in each other's arms. She understood perfectly now what he had in mind. He had an irresistible desire for her for the last half hour and it was all he could think, of now. She stopped him for a moment, then, looking serious, she gently kissed him on the lips. I just want to tell you Bob that I love everything about you, loving each other… being together… and holding each other…

She had just removed his night gown. He had a beautiful body and he was longing for her. There was no shame between them, no modesty, they had been through so much, it was as though they had always been together, as she stroked and caressed him and he looked concerned. He felt everything she did emotionally, but he was not sure of the rest. She took her own night gown off as he held her breasts in his hands. The bodies had suddenly become active and gently, she began kissing him first on the mouth, and then she worked her way artfully down. They knew how much they loved each other and this was the last secret garden where they hadn't been. They discovered it slowly together, and he was overwhelmed by his feelings for her. She was infinitely careful as she tried to arouse him. In response, Bob too was careful not to put any weight on her, just enough in the right places, and he felt exquisite pleasure she intended for him till the desired effect took place much to their satisfaction on reaching orgasm and then he lay with his arms around her. "Wow!" she said softly afterward as she clung to him and he smiled.

'Seven Springs' was the most beautiful place that attracts the tourists. It was surrounded by large grassy, green patches of the ground covering wide area on all sides. Bob had taken their packed lunch with them and enjoyed the picnic at such a lovely place. In the evening they had visited 'Chashma-e-Shahi' and the 'Pari Mahal'. Both the places are considered beautiful marvels. At the entrance, there were earthen flower-pots painted in bottle green, suitably arranged in equal number on either side. One could see the coloured fish in Chashma which means the spring of water. Likewise, the Pari Mahal means the Palace of the Fairies. It was a beautiful place situated at such a height that one could easily have a view of the Kashmir valley.

Chapter – 53

Poor father had hardly recovered from the previous shock when the heart-rending news of her pregnancy had come to him like a bolt-from-the-blue. He couldn't believe it in the first place but was greatly shocked to learn that her daughter had gone physical with a stranger whom he didn't even know about. She had gone to such an extreme without considering the pros and cons of doing a thing like that. It had become all the more shocking when Somi told him that she didn't know about even the real identity of Bob except his name and the country he belonged to. Mangal Sen had seriously been thinking about the problem. Having been in the first stage of pregnancy it was still possible for Somi to have a safe abortion. He was of the opinion that the honour of his family was at stake which consists of not just two persons viz. the father and his daughter but the whole band of eunuchs as well. In a couple of weeks everybody in the neighbourhood would come to know about it on just putting a glance over her unmarried daughter. To go for the abortion was the only way left to save their honour and humiliation they may receive otherwise at the hands of others.

"There is hardly any other option left for you to shed away all your worries, to buy your freedom as well as your peace of mind," poor Mangal Sen told her. He had tried his best to make his daughter understand all those things repeatedly and coaxed her to go for the abortion.

"In fact, somewhere, in my heart, I still have a soft corner for Bob, even now, and I believe that one day he definitely will come to India and meet me," she argued and flatly, rather forcefully, had refused to go for the abortion.

"This is the question of your whole life," persuaded her father once again. But Somi had become adamant about her decision to keep the child come what may. Ultimately, poor father had got very much disappointed and finally had to succumb to her wishes.

It was quite impractical for an unmarried pregnant girl to live here. How would they explain to people living in their neighbourhood? The whole of the eunuch community would laugh at them. Afraid of facing the Librarian uncle, she had forsaken her urge of going to the library any more. In view of the seriousness of the situation, they had made up their mind to shift their residence to somewhere else. Another suggestion was to send her to some faraway place remotely connected with their native town as money was no constraint for Mangal Sen. But practically, on giving it a second thought, it didn't seem to be that easy at all. So he had to think about some other solution to the problem which had kept on ticking in his mind day and night.

On a Sunday morning Mangal Sen was going to the market on some errand. Passing by the Church in the vicinity he thought of something and went inside to join the 'Sunday service', which was in progress. He too got himself seated like others on a pew and listened to the sermon. After the 'service' was over, he approached 'the Father' and opened his mind. He explained to him about the problem of his daughter in brief, and the eunuch community he belonged to, and looked for some guidance or any help he could give in the matter. Somehow he knew that people who have their faith in Christianity are very liberal minded both in word and deed. He had also heard about Christian hospitals somewhere who give help in cases of children in distress like his daughter.

Listening to Mangal Sen's problem 'The Father' directed him towards a Clergyman of the Church where he had to narrate his problem once again. The Clergyman had noted down the facts of the case and assured him that he would certainly look into the matter. He was also asked to keep in touch with the Church for the probable solution to his problem. Presumably the Clergyman must have contacted their numerous diocese established all over the world. And within a week's time Mangal Sen was asked to contact St. John Hospital at London. Somi was glad to learn all about it and was happy that she would at last be able to give birth to her child. As the time was running, both of them were eager to leave the country as soon as possible.

Meanwhile, Mangal Sen had contacted a Travelling Agency for the necessary Passport and visa required for the purpose. He had sent for his pal Bhima too, like he had been doing earlier also to discuss about Somi. On his coming after an hour or so, Mangal Sen told him, "Somi wanted to go for an advanced course in one of the subjects she had studied so far, from a foreign university which may help her to stand on her own feet, earn her living and live a life of comfort on her own. Just imagine and give a serious thought to the fact that for how long I would be going to live with the old age ailments?" He had become a bit emotional and added: "As you know, I don't have anybody else in the world except Somi. I live for her only. My happiness lies in her happiness. I would certainly do whatever she wants me to do. My sole object is to make her happy as long as I live."

Bhima felt very much impressed and appreciated the utter devotion and such a fatherly love for his daughter. Mangal Sen also told him that he had already applied for the necessary Passport and visa and would leave for London as soon as it comes. He further had asked him to take care of his house till he returns.

Chapter – 54

"Where have you been since morning?" Asked Somi, adding: "I thought you had gone to see your pal Bhima after the breakfast."

"No, I had been to the office of the travel agent to find out the status of our passports which we have applied for. I was told by his Assistant that he could be available only in an hour or so, as he was supposed to have left for the Passport Office as per his daily routine for necessary pushing-up of the papers they had already submitted and see the officers concerned as well, for a quick follow-up of the cases. He might be back soon, I was assured. In fact, I myself was so curious about the information that instead of coming back home I preferred to stay there and wait for a little while till his return," replied her father.

"And what is the outcome of all that exercise?"

"It may still take some more time, say another two-three days, though the required scrutiny and such other necessary formalities like police verification etc. have already been completed, I'm told. Now we have to wait for the postman as the passports are delivered only by the registered post at the address given therein."

"What about the Visa?"

"Soon, after receiving our passports we have to apply for the necessary Visa to the foreign Embassy. As I don't know the exact procedure, our travel agent has promised me to do the needful and help us in procuring the same for our visit to London as early as could be possible. It is high time to make the necessary arrangements for the journey to the foreign land."

"What kind of preparations do we need to make our journey comfortable?"

"How do I know? Being the in-charge of all the household affairs it should be your prerogative to give it a bit serious thinking on the matter. At the least I could suggest only a thing or two which seem to be of some importance, as suggested by the travel agent. First of all, you ought to make a comprehensive list of important things of daily use. Then strike out the less important ones we could manage without, as we are supposed to keep our luggage to the minimum possible, in the flight. I understand that there we would likely to have a little change of climate on account of the cold weather as compared to that of, in India. It is, therefore advisable to have some warm clothing which I needn't go in to the detail. A small bag, like purse, would also be required to keep the air-tickets and other important papers handy to present at the airport-counter for quick verification of the same."

"What are you searching for?" Asked Somi, as her father seemed to be very tense, looking for something, making all the things upside down.

"I can't see my specs, placed somewhere here."

Somi motioned herself towards her father. Seeing in his face she found herself in a peel of laughter. Controlling herself a moment later, she said to him, making a loving gesture, "My dear Papa! Just feel around your ears instead of eyes," and she had a hearty laugh once again. Mangal Sen, in fact, had already worn the pair of his spectacles he had been searching for. Touching upon his ears amusingly and having found the specs, he too had joined Somi in her laughter. However, after a little while, he added, "I use to forget something or the other very often. It appears as if the old age has been telling upon me."

Mangal Sen, then, very cautiously handed over the visa he had just received in the morning, to Somi along with the air-tickets, booked earlier through their travelling agent, to keep them safely. She had been busy in her packing for the travel. Mangal Sen had already asked her to keep it to the minimum for easy and safe travelling. He too had checked and satisfied himself that everything of his day-to-day use was taken care of. While Somi already had the opportunity of travelling by air many a time with Bob on their tour of Bharat Darshan, Mangal Sen was too excited to imagine about boarding the aircraft instead of some bus or a railway compartment. How it would look like from above in the sky. He had a host of questions about flying in the air to which he would find the answers only after reaching the airport and boarding the plane.

All the international flights are usually scheduled to take place at night. As the passengers were supposed to reach the airport at least two hours before the departure time of the flight, both, father and the daughter, left just after the dusk, on the day of their flight, leaving their house to the care of Bhima, the most trusted friend of Mangalu (Mangal Sen) whom he had already taken in to confidence. Although everything had already been arranged quite carefully, as per the plan, yet it had taken a quarter to an hour in getting the immigration papers checked and verified to the entire satisfaction of the airport authorities. It had taken some more time in marking, labeling etc. on the luggage of the passengers and then depositing it in to the plane as per the usual routine. After obtaining the necessary 'clearance' both of them headed towards the lounge to wait for the necessary announcement regarding their flight. As Somi knew that her father has the habit of smoking, she told him that smoking in those premises, was strictly prohibited. A small sign-board depicting 'No Smoking Area' was fixed at a prominent place in the lounge. The announcement came after a short while.

"May we have your attention please!" a female voice blared at the Public Announcement (P.A.) system in the waiting lounge. "Bon Bon Airways welcome all its patrons. Flight No. BB 9899 to London is ready for departure. Passengers are requested to please proceed towards the runway to board the plane. Thank you."

A coach was kept waiting there for the passengers to take them to the place by the side of the plane. With the help of a small ladder the passengers were made to reach the door of the craft. While Somi had taken it easy, it was her father who was startled to look inside the huge aircraft with dazzling lights. One of the air-hostesses approached them and guided them to their respective seats. They just then, heaved a sigh of relief and grinned towards each other with smiles lit up on their faces after having occupied their seats comfortably.

Within a few minutes, on seeing that all the passengers were settled in their seats, an Air hostess was seen standing in the front portion of the plane near the cockpit inviting the attention of the passengers. Giving a quick demonstration of safety drill she, in fact, was guiding the passengers about the safety-rules like: fastening their seat-belts, switching off their cell-phones, how to use a mask at the time of an emergency and caution them against any eventuality. She also did assure them that the Air-jackets were kept handy and placed just below each seat to be used if there need be. She then practically exercised with her hands to make everybody understand and follow the instructions. The whole course of exercise was repeated at the centre of the craft and lastly in the rear portion also. And immediately, there came an announcement: "The plane is taking off. Please fasten your seat-belts if not already done. Thank you."

With that announcement the plane had gone afloat into the sky.

Since it had become a matter of routine for Somi to travel by air in the company of Bob, she didn't feel any kind of excitement. However, for Mangal Sen, that was his maiden flight which proved to be an awful and thrilling experience he could ever have expected or even imagined in his life. He was delighted to find that the plane was fully air-conditioned and the seats were comfortable enough where he could stretch his body from head to toe in a relaxed position. A knitted nylon pocket of a reasonable size was provided on the back of every seat of its front row which contained newspaper, magazine, pamphlets, brochures or some other useful information about the flying craft etc. As also a very small folding table that could be opened in front of him, was attached therewith for placing eatables on it. There was a duct provided above every seat which is meant for the passengers for keeping in it their small bags and other miscellaneous handy items. Along with a wide range of paraphernalia, a small light was also fixed at the base of the duct above their heads which they could make use of, for reading etc., as the main lights would go off after a reasonable time and only a dim light at the centre of the craft would remain 'on' to facilitate the passengers wishing to doze off when they feel like, or some other activities like going to washroom etc. Incidentally, both of them had got the corner seats and Somi could make her father sit by the side of the window of the huge aircraft. As the plane gathered its height above in the sky, Mangal Sen, felt immensely pleased to see through the window how the buildings, trees and the skyscrapers in the city below looked like becoming dwarfed second by second. As also, people and the vehicles too seemed as if crawling like small creatures on earth. He was fascinated to gaze upon the colourful neon-lights whirling around below as well as the rows of street-lighting running on the sides of the roads, visible from above the sky, which really looked awful from the window. In a short while they were flying over the sea and a little later everything on earth became invisible due to the great height. Instead, he could see below mass of clouds as the plane had possibly shot itself at extreme height, quite above the clouds. The whole scene was unique in itself. And then, when there were no clouds in between, he enjoyed the night-sky full of beautiful and glittering stars shining luminously in a variety of sizes and colours. The flight was very smooth and Mangal Sen literally felt like floating on the surface of water on the sea-bed. Outside, nothing could be seen thereafter, in the most part of the night, except the whirling galaxy of millions and millions of shining stars. Though outwardly, both of them looked to be happy and enjoying their journey, yet inside their minds they had been very tense about the next course of situation they would be going to face on reaching their destination. They didn't know how to react to certain awkward queries supposed to be made by the Management Committee or the In-charge of the hospital they were going to meet. However, they had full faith in God the Almighty and prayed in their hearts with utmost reverence. That made them much more confident that everything would be going to be alright. In about half an hour or so, some eatables and drinks were served during the flight. And then stretching himself comfortably in his seat Mangal Sen started yawning and dozed off in no time. Somi too followed suit a little later.

Chapter – 55

‿‿

It was almost dawn when Somi woke up on hearing the announcement. The flight had arrived at London's Heathrow airport. It was delayed by about an hour and a half as the craft had landed for filling the fuel somewhere en-route. In nutshell the overall journey looked enjoyable. On reaching London, their destination, they had to go through more or less the same exercise as in India where their luggage was supposed to be searched thoroughly for the reason to put a check on any kind of unwanted substance like drugs or smuggled goods etc. Well, both of them didn't have any difficulty of such kind and were allowed to pass through the green channel, meant for the passengers who didn't have to declare anything illegal. On coming out of the airport, the first and foremost thought that came to their mind was to go and look for some inexpensive place to take shelter temporarily for the time being to keep their bag and baggage, but on an afterthought, they decided to straightaway go to the hospital first. Possibly, Mangal Sen was hoping against hope that somebody at the hospital may become helpful in finding them some suitable place not far away from the hospital. Thus, with the well considered decision they made up their mind to hire a taxi for the hospital.

Unlike the international airport in India, they found the well disciplined gentry outside the airport. The taxis were lined up in rows to take the passengers to their destinations turn by turn irrespective of a long or short distance. Meters were installed on each of them and the rate-cards were also fixed showing the distance and the amount chargeable. The drivers wore their uniforms with a badge displaying their name along with the number allotted to them. Soon a Taxi driver standing ahead in the queue approached them and asked about the name and place of destination.

"Saint John Hospital," Somi told him.

"O.K. be seated please," said the taxi driver. He then turned towards the rear of the taxi and put their baggage into the dickey.

St. John hospital appeared to be quite at a distance. On the way, watching the taxi sometimes going underneath a foot-over bridge and at other times crossing fly-over bridges one after the other, Mangal Sen once became a little suspicious as to whether they were being taken to the hospital or some other secluded place. Ultimately, after winding through a good number of alleyways and backstreets, they finally reached the hospital. They paid the taxi fare and entered the gate of the hospital with their baggage.

The bedlam had begun even at that early hour of the morning. Inside the front entrance of the main building of the hospital, there was a large waiting hall, with hard wooden benches to sit upon for patients and visitors alike. Saint John hospital was perhaps the oldest hospital in London. The old building complex was in a dilapidated condition made in brick and red stone which had occupied more than half a dozen blocks. It looked like a city within a city. The construction of a new building, quite adjacent to the old one, had also started in order to accommodate more patients as well as introduce and provide the most modern medical facilities to them in the times to come.

An unimaginable number of people had been employed with various duties of different kind assigned to them. There were doctors, surgeons, physicians, nurses, anesthesiologists, technicians, unit aides etc. etc. Other than the large operating rooms, accommodating a heart monitor, a heart lung machine, and an array of other paraphernalia, there were rooms marked 'cardiology', 'Dermatology', 'Nephrology', 'Neurology' etc. There were separate 'Dressing rooms' for doctors and nurses to change, the physiotherapy section, a blood bank, a bone bank, emergency wards and roughly about eight hundred beds. And above all, there was a 'public announcement' (P.A.) system which operated all the twenty four hours. Occasionally one could hear it blaring something like: 'Dr. Patricia! Please rush to emergency room 2 (E.R. 2) etc.

A wooden plate also hung there bearing the word ENQUIRY in bold letters that adored the uppermost place of a large-sized window towards the left side of the waiting hall where a few patients were seen lined up. There wasn't any separate queue for women or the senior citizens. There were long corridors in every block which had rooms on either side of them, for X-Ray, Echo-cardiology, Ear-Nose & Throat (E.N.T.) department, as well as for the diagnosis and treatment of various other kinds of diseases. Appreciably, cleanliness was being given top priority as the entire premises of the complex looked neat and clean even at that early hour of the morning. One could find the casualty department just adjacent to the main entrance gate of the hospital which had been constantly busy to cope with the rush as the patients had been coming in all night, arriving in ambulances, and police cars and on foot, broken and bleeding, victims of stabbings and shootings and automobile accidents, etc. wounded in flesh and spirit.

Dr. W.F. Clifford liked working in obstetrics as, to her, it was a ward filled with new life and new hope, in a timeless, joyful ritual. Women in their early stage of pregnancy were supposed to get registered and then go through a battery of tests from time to time as had been the general practice. The maternity ward had been spread to four large rooms occupying six beds in each room. All the six of them were equipped with modern medical and surgical facilities as were generally required to make the safe deliveries. Dr. Clifford had been working in the hospital for the last sixteen years and had earned a name and fame for her sincere and dedicated services which enhanced the reputation of the hospital even in the remote areas of London city. Women in the middle of their pregnancy would prefer to register themselves with St. John Hospital only instead of going elsewhere irrespective of the distance involved between the hospital and their dwelling place. An upper floor of one of the blocks in the vicinity of the maternity ward had been reserved to accommodate the relatives accompanying the would-be mothers so that they could be easily sent for in case of an emergency. A canteen was also being run nearby within the complex where eatables were made available to them at subsidized rates by the hospital authorities.

Hesitating a bit, both, the father and daughter found themselves settled upon the corner of a bench in the waiting hall. Being a literate and well educated girl, Somi did have enough courage to face the situation they were in. Having asked Mangal Sen to take care of their baggage she herself got up to just take a round of the hospital premises in front of her. Making her way through the hall, she entered the long corridor looking on either side upon various name-plates hung over the doors displaying the department they belong to, with the name of the doctor on duty. At the far end of it she was able to find a room marked 'Obstetrics', quite adjacent to the Maternity Ward on the ground floor. The name plate hung over there showed the name as: 'Dr. W.F.

Clifford' on morning duty. Somi stood there and looked around for a while. The door of the room was kept ajar and as soon as the lady attendant, standing there, stepped a little aside, Somi hurriedly peeped through the door to have a look inside the room. There were half a dozen beds in that particular room of which just four were duly occupied by the would-be mothers and looked much eager and apprehensive. One of them had started getting labour-pain and was being attended to by the veterans. Somi heard one of the women, who was about to deliver, saying to Dr. Clifford: 'Thank God! I'll be able to see my feet again.' Thinking something on the spur of the moment Somi made a hasty retreat into the corridor.

By the time she returned to the waiting hall, Mangal Sen had already made himself acquainted with a stranger. Sitting idly in the waiting hall he minutely observed a person that seemed to be of Indian origin, as the colour of his face didn't match, like his own, with the natives around them. On asking, the man factually happened to be the person from India. He introduced himself as Mr. Partho Ghosh and told that he hailed from Bengal. Somi too joined them in the mean time. During the conversation with him it was further revealed that even with 'Bengali' being his mother-tongue, he had a fair knowledge of Hindi language as well. He also told them that his wife has been under the treatment at that hospital and that God has very kindly blessed them with a son the previous night. That happened to be the first delivery of his wife, and that both, the mother and the child were doing fairly well. In a short while they looked as if all the three of them were known to each other since ages. However, when Mr. Ghosh asked about them, both, the father and the daughter declined to reveal anything. Instead, Mangal Sen then simply concocted a story and said, "Somi's

259

husband 'Bob' had gone on a business tour some time back. His last phone-call was received from London. Since then, say about two and a half months, we neither have heard from him nor got any kind of information regarding his whereabouts. That is why we have come here. We are so much worried about him. Poor Somi has even lost her sleep since then".

"To search a person in a big city like London, and that too without any proper address, is next to impossible," said Mr. Ghosh.

On having come to know the name of the doctor in-charge of the obstetrics department, Somi instantly scribbled briefly on a slip of paper something about herself expressing her desire to see Dr. W.F. Clifford. To her, the man inside the Enquiry window seemed to be in the forties with a slightly bald head but quite sober looking. He might be of some help, Somi thought, and just after five minutes she found herself at the Enquiry window.

"Yes please! What can I do for you?" The man at the counter asked.

"I would be obliged to see Dr. W.F. Clifford please," replied Somi. And while saying that, she just put her hand through the 'hole' of the glass-window and handed over the slip of paper to him that read:

"I have come all the way from India this morning with my father and am in urgent need of seeing the Doctor. Where could I find her? Please help me."

"This isn't possible at the moment," said the counter clerk, on seeing the long queue of patients lined up behind the counter, and added: "Please wait for a little while. Let me finish with the queue first." That made Somi a bit hopeful of getting at least some help or guidance from him.

As soon as the last person in the queue left the counter, she said to Mr. Ghosh, 'Excuse me," and hurriedly approached the Enquiry clerk, looking curiously towards his face. She didn't need to say anything.

"Dr. Clifford is presently busy with her morning round in the obstetrics ward, in accordance with her daily routine, to enquire about and see the reports of the patients under her treatment." He told Somi, and further added: "However, I think she could make herself available after about an hour or so in her office room no. 203 on the 2nd floor."

Mr. Ghosh sympathized with them on listening to their tale of woe about the missing husband of Somi but showed his utter helplessness in doing anything in that respect. Telling about himself, he said, "I have been working with a multinational company and though I have been posted here in London about six months back yet, unfortunately, I do not know much about this place."

They had about an hour's time at their disposal. Feeling a little hungry Somi asked, "Shouldn't we have some breakfast before seeing the doctor?"

"Of course, you have plenty of time. Let me show you the way to the Canteen," said Mr. Ghosh. He then himself accompanied them to the Canteen where they were offered sandwiches, bread & butter with tea or coffee, for breakfast. Since the customers had little option, they got to satisfy themselves with the food-stuff, whatever was just available there. Even with that little acquaintance of half an hour or so, Mr. Ghosh offered to pay the bill but Somi didn't let him do that. She, however, was faintly touched by his friendly gesture. As Somi started towards room no. 203 to see Dr. Clifford on 2nd floor, Mr. Ghosh took leave with the promise to see them the next day.

Chapter – 56

"May I come in please?" Hearing someone addressing her, Dr. Clifford motioned towards the door and politely said to the visitors, "Yes, please come in." She had just stepped into her office a few minutes before, after finishing her morning round of the wards. Both, Somi and her father entered the office leaving their baggage at the door itself. They were made to sit upon a couple of chairs lying over there. Somi was hesitant to explain about herself in front of her father and asked the doctor if she could spare a few minutes to listen to her in some privacy. Being a woman of substance and having much understanding and experience, Dr. Clifford looked towards Mangal Sen and politely asked him to wait outside. That gave an opportunity to Somi to talk freely. Dr. Clifford listened to her with utmost patience. She briefly narrated her harrowing tale and said, in her own words:

"Ma'am, to begin with, I happened to be an abandoned child left somewhere in a railway compartment and do not know who my real parents are, and why they had become so heartless to leave me unsecured without the care of somebody. Well, the person, I've come with, now sitting outside, is my godfather. His name is Mangal Sen who happened to be one of the passengers in the same compartment of that train. He found me lying under a seat and took me under his care, loved me as a father since my early childhood and looked after me as his own real daughter till date. It may look strange enough to you Ma'am, that fate had been very unkind to him. Unfortunately, God too had played a serious joke upon him. Per chance he himself, in an accident, had become a 'Eunuch' in his early youth by misfortune after having a fall from the cliff of a mountain and yet he was such a kind hearted person to run the risk of adopting a female child. Till my adolescent age, I used to pretend to be a boy on the strict instructions of my father and had to live in the garb of a male to hide my real identity of a female child in order to protect myself from the evils of the society in the neighbourhood. To me he is not any less than God and I owe him my whole life."

Coming to the second part of her story she said, "Though my father himself attended the school up to primary level only yet he arranged for my higher education that could have been beyond his means at that time. Even being a eunuch he worked hard, toiled throughout his life for my sake. But adversity never comes with the warning. A foreigner had come into my life. We remained together for some time and suddenly one day he vanished in to thin air. Only after his disappearing I did come to know that I was pregnant. Had he knew it before he left, he could possibly have stayed because he really loved me. God knows under what compulsion or circumstances he was forced to do a thing like that."

"Ma'am, as you might be aware of the fact that In India, an unmarried mother is always despised by the society and there is no place to live with keeping her head high. With the firm belief that this was a gift from God, I never wanted an abortion. Ma'am, this is the child of the man I still love, the best thing that ever happened to me. A clergyman at the Church then had suggested the name of St. John hospital of London to my father. And therefore, I've come here all the way from India to give birth to my child because I am dead sure that his father too loves me and God willing, he will definitely think seriously upon his doing and come back to me one day. I have nowhere to go to Ma'am. I beg you. Please help me."

Tears rolled down her cheeks while narrating her pathetic story. Dr. Clifford was a religious woman. She used to go to Church to listen to the holy sermons on Sundays and being a kind hearted lady she never refrained from helping somebody in distress, within her means. She felt very much touched and asked Somi, "Where are you staying?"

"We have just landed here this morning and straight away have come from the Airport with our bag and baggage," replied Somi.

Taking pity on them Dr. Clifford told Somi that they could stay for the time being in the waiting hall meant for the relatives of the women admitted for the delivery. She also assured them that she would have to talk to the hospital In-charge and discuss about their case with the members of the Managing Committee of the hospital. A guard on duty was summoned to lead them to the waiting hall located on the upper floor of the maternity ward.

CHAPTER – 57

❧

Lying in her bed at night, Dr. Clifford stayed awake for quite a long time and couldn't put away her thoughts about the plight of poor Somi who had become the victim at the cruel hands of her fate. The Committee didn't approve the idea of admitting an unmarried woman from a foreign country and she was coaxed away to leave. She gave birth to an ugly looking eunuch child at the gate of the hospital and was horrified to look at him. She then ran away from the scene quite naked and jumped into the deep well nearby with a thud. Dr. Clifford woke up all of a sudden, screaming and sweating profusely. At just that moment the wall clock chimed. It struck only once showing the time half past three A.M. Sitting in the bed, she pondered about what a horrible dream that was.

Early next morning after finishing her usual morning round, Dr. Clifford sent for Somi to appear before the Committee members. Dr. Clifford had already briefed them about the case and requested to kindly refrain from asking any embarrassing questions as the victim already had suffered a lot. The members were totally moved on having come to know about their plight that how her father who himself had become a eunuch by misfortune had dared adopt an unclaimed female child, kept her disguised in the garb of a boy for so many years, got her educated and looked after her as his own legitimate daughter till she had come of age. During the interview Somi did show her willingness to work, if she could be of any service to the hospital.

"Being an educated girl and also having been in good health, she could surely be made to do some kind of job till the time of her delivery," said Dr. Clifford. The members considered the case most sympathetically and then unanimously agreed to help them. They also accepted the proposal of Dr. Clifford to give her some job at the hospital itself for the time being. The necessary formalities like filling up of admission forms etc. were completed as per rules and the initial charges for admission were deposited by Mangal Sen, her father. However, he was told that since St. John was a charity hospital, all the other expenses, henceforth, will, as a special case, be taken care of by the hospital authorities, till the safe delivery of the child and as such there was nothing for them to be worried about. That happened to be a matter of great relief to both of them.

Being in the process of having to expand its activities, the hospital was always in need of more funds, especially for construction of another building, and as such, is always open to accept donations from the general public as well as big business houses. Keeping in mind the gesture of the hospital people to accommodate and take Somi under their care, Mangal Sen too, very generously, donated some amount for the Welfare Fund of the hospital. In the next couple of days, Somi was shifted from waiting hall to share a room with Annie, a resident nurse in the hospital. She was a few years older than Somi yet she looked beautiful, had blonde hair, a pointed nose and always wore a sweet smile on her face. And above all, she greeted Somi quite warmly as her room-mate friend. On having fully satisfied himself with the arrangement, Mangal Sen boarded the next available flight to India.

Mr. Ghosh had continued visiting the hospital during the whole of the week that followed, after the delivery of his wife, to see her and the new-born child as usual. He also had looked quite anxious to know as to what could have happened to poor Somi and her father with whom he had got acquainted the previous day. He had tried to look for them in the waiting hall. Then thinking that her father might be relaxing outside on the grassy lawns, he had taken a round of the park, in front of the Hall where some relatives of the patients were seen gossiping. Disappointed, he had returned towards the hall once again when by sheer luck, he had met Somi in the long corridor itself. She was accompanying the nurse Annie, her roommate, as she had an appointment with Dr. Harney for medical checkup. After the exchange of pleasantries Somi introduced him with her roommate also. Mr. Ghosh looked very anxious about her meeting with Dr. Clifford the previous day. So, Somi asked him to wait in the park for a while, till she returns after seeing Dr. Harney.

Asking Somi to 'just wait a minute' Annie hastily entered the Dr.'s room. On seeing him busy in examining a patient she just informed him about the coming of 'Somi' for the check up, as Dr. Clifford had already had a word with the Dr. in the morning itself. Coming out of the room she tapped on Somi's shoulder and said, 'Dr. Harney will see you in five minutes'.

Dr. Harney was around forty-year old but still looked young and quite handsome man with an adorable good personality. Dressed in the white coat over his blue shirt, he appeared with a smiling face and said to Somi, "Come in, you look quite tired".

"I am fine doctor". She lied. No one watching her would have guessed that she was depressed of having once loved Bob with all her heart.

"Any way, be seated please. This won't take long. In fact, it's quite normal to feel tired sometimes in the early stage of pregnancy. I would estimate you are about three months gone. We'll have to do a scan to be sure if everything is alright". On having been told that she was perfectly 'normal' she had been speculating to request Dr. Clifford to get some work assigned to her as she didn't want to sit idle.

In half an hour, Somi found herself in the park, chatting with Mr. Ghosh. She told him briefly about the meeting as well as the decision of the Managing Committee of the hospital and also that she had been sharing the room with Annie. Later Mr. Ghosh had taken her in to the maternity ward to introduce her with his wife. Her name was Deepti. Though, not very fair in colour, yet she looked beautiful with her sharp features. Even after having become a mother she had really an enviable figure. She too was delighted to meet Somi as she had already learned about her Indian origin, and also her pathetic story, from her husband. They liked each other so well that in no time they had become good friends. Likewise, both Somi and Mr. Ghosh had also taken each other as brother and sister. In fact, while on a foreign land, it happens to be a matter of great pleasure when two strangers come to know that both of them belong to the same country of origin and then to have the friendly relation between them becomes inevitable, which is quite a natural phenomenon.

Deepti was discharged and relieved from the hospital that afternoon with her new-born. Before leaving she had told Somi that in accordance with their family tradition in Bengal, they would have to perform a 'havan and pooja' of 'Goddess Kaali'—a kind of sacred religious rituals, at their bungalow to celebrate the birth of the child, in the next week. She had invited her with the humble request to come and grace the occasion with her presence and give her blessings to the new-born. She also gave her address and the contact number as well. When Somi had very politely regretted that it wouldn't be possible for her to leave the hospital, Mr. Ghosh had offered that he would come to take her home with the permission of the hospital authorities.

CHAPTER – 58

⁓

"Why don't you go for the Nurses' Training Course"? Asked Annie, while going to bed. 'You still have got six months approximately. Why not make use of that period to your benefit'. Somi looked at her inquisitively if that could be possible for her. In fact she was thinking of doing some job in the hospital itself. Annie told her that she could do the course by joining the Nurses' Training Institute which was being run by a subsidiary of the hospital. She had coaxed her to request the Management to grant you the necessary permission and also ask Dr. Clifford to help you in joining the course. That way, Annie had played the role of a real friend indeed which may help Somi to make 'Nursing' as her career. Being a graduate she was quite eligible to join the course.

The very next morning, Somi had approached her benefactress Dr. Clifford when she was getting ready to go on her usual morning round in the wards.

"How come my dear?, it's very nice to see you. By the way, what brought you here at such an early hour of the morning? I hope everything is alright".

"Yes Ma'am, I'm fine. Everything is O.K."

"Don't be hesitant my child. Speak it up if anything is there on your mind".

"Ma'am, I'm already very much indebted to you for your kind gesture and sympathy which has helped me in restoring my life on the right track. Yet once again I have come to seek your help. Ma'am, I've come to know about the Nurses' Training Course being run by a subsidiary of the hospital. I have a keen desire to become a Nurse which, to my mind, is the most sacred and respectful profession in the world. I wish to make my career in 'Nursing' and as such earnestly request you to please help me in joining the 'Course'. Being a graduate from an Indian University I could be hopeful of my eligibility for the Course. In that way I shall be able to utilize the period left in between the time of my delivery as also to become benefitted by making my career in Nursing. After the class, I could attend to some part-time job in the hospital as well if there need be".

"It is quite heartening and I'm pleased to know about your wish. I'm sure this will enable you to secure your future and help you stand on your own feet as well. I shall definitely have a talk with the concerned persons and see that there shouldn't be any kind of hindrance in your joining the Nurses' Training course".

Dr. W.F. Clifford was perhaps the senior most Doctor in the St. John Hospital of London. She was equally respected by one and all and as such her expert advice, opinion, suggestion or recommendation are always valued the most and carried ample weight in every important matter what-so-ever. So, with her strong recommendation Somi had got admission in the Nurses' Training course.

Chapter – 59

The night before the function at Deepti's, fixed to celebrate the birth of her child, Somi had visited a number of stores along with Annie to buy a good dress. But there weren't all that many good choices and she had to content herself with a deep V-neck and black, ornamented with circular spangles on it, a far cry from anything she had ever imagined wearing. She'd filed and painted her nails on her own, taking her time, pleased that she hadn't smeared any of the polish.

Seeing her reflection in the mirror she tugged at her dress, adjusting it slightly. She looked pretty good, she had to admit. She smiled. And definitely good enough for the occasion. She slipped into her shoes when Annie moved nearer to inspect her more closely. "You look wonderful," she said quickly.

Surprising herself, Somi breathed a sigh of relief. "Is the dress okay?"

"It's perfect," Annie answered.

"And my shoes? I'm not sure they go with the dress."

"They're just right."

"I tried to do my makeup and my nails….."

Before she even finished, Annie shook her head. "You've never been more beautiful," she said. "In fact, I don't know if there's anyone more beautiful in the entire world."

Once, having satisfied herself with her dressing etc. and becoming ready to go out, she headed towards the office of Dr. Clifford. It gave her a little surprise, when Somi entered the office to see that Mr. Ghosh had already been sitting there. Presumably he had apprised the Doctor beforehand about their having a religious ceremony at their home and had come to take Somi whom he regarded as his sister, to attend the same. He had also told her about his wife Deepti and that God had very kindly blessed them with a son a fortnight back. At that moment Dr. Clifford could recollect having seen Deepti in the maternity ward. She congratulated Mr. Ghosh and gave the permission to take Somi with the condition that she must be back in the hospital by the same evening positively.

The place was as spectacular as a movie set. There were flowers everywhere. The hedge was trimmed to perfection, and even the brick-and-stucco wall that surrounded the property, had been freshly painted. When they finally made their way to the central roundabout, Somi stared at the bungalow which looked as if growing larger in the foreground. Eventually, Mr. Ghosh motioned towards her when she exclaimed, "What a lovely place for a celebration." The car stopped in the portico and Mr. Ghosh came out first. Before she knew it, it was her turn to get out, Mr. Ghosh swung open her door and offered his hand to help her out. She peeked in the mirror one last time before emerging from the car. Once she was out, she adjusted her dress, thinking it was easier to breathe now that she was standing. In fact, her dress obviously was not designed to wear while sitting; it was digging into her ribs, making it hard to breathe. Then again, may be she was just too nervous to breathe. The porch railings were decorated with lilies and tulips and as they made their way up the steps towards the door, it suddenly swung open.

Inside, Somi had received a red carpet welcome. "You look incredible," Said Mrs. Deepti Ghosh, and at those words, she felt herself relax. Others, present on the occasion, were mostly the office colleagues of Mr. Ghosh, and a few other acquaintances of Deepti from the neighbourhood. The parents of both Mr. Ghosh and Deepti had regretted their inability to come to London, being a far off place which required a passport and visa. However, thanks to the latest communication technology, they were able to see their newborn grandson as well as witness the whole ceremony on the television screen through the 'Internet'. In fact they had special equipment with Cameras fixed to their television sets having connectivity to the 'Internet' which had given the feeling as if the persons seen or being talked to, were looked as virtually present over the T.V. screen. The ceremony was elegant and yet surprisingly intimate.

As soon as the pooja ceremony was over, the guests enjoyed a rich feast where Indian food was served. Somi was surprised to know that no cook or chef was engaged to prepare the food. In fact, both Mr. as well as Mrs. Ghosh proved to be excellent cooks. They were busy in cooking since early morning. Mr. Partho Ghosh, the husband was good enough in cooking mix-vegetables, rice, black-gram, cheese, potatoes, etc. A couple of his colleagues also helped in chopping up salads, onions, etc. Curd and ice-cream too was there sufficed with coffee. Everything was made ready before the starting of pooja ceremony except the chapaties. After the pooja ceremony Deepti had showed her expertise in rolling out chapaties with great speed and thus the warm food was served to the guests. "You really did a wonderful job getting all this organized. It is quite beautiful here," Somi told the hosts.

All the guests and the host, thereafter, had comforted themselves in a comparatively large-sized room where a 'musical evening' had been arranged. No particular artist or singer was invited. The office colleagues of Mr. Ghosh looked quite frank and without showing any kind of hesitation or shyness, contributed their might in entertaining the whole gathering. A couple of boys among them were really very good singers. Apart from Bengali songs, there were a few Hindi songs also. Mr. Ghosh had tried his best that she should feel at home but Somi didn't dare sing before the strangers. The celebration ended by the evening on a happy note and Mr. Ghosh had to take Somi back to the hospital. On the way she had told Mr. Ghosh about her joining the Nurses' Training Course and also asked him to visit her off and on whenever possible. He had given her his phone number also to make a call if anything was required of him.

It was almost a year back when Somi had attended a 'musical fest' at the Boarding School in India. She could still visualize what a beautiful evening that was. A stage was set up in a big hall. A good number of students had given their names to perform one thing or the other. Somi too was persuaded to give at least a short performance. While there had been a singing competition consisting of film-songs and folk songs, a couple of interesting plays were also staged and applauded by the whole gathering.

In the flashback she could see a girl-student playing the role of a barber whose wife coaxed him to get her a silken 'lehnga', a garment, just like a skirt-type petticoat, worn from the waist downward (with a matching blouse) irrespective of being a costly one or a damn cheap. In reply, the barber shows his inability to meet her demand by making a variety of lame excuses but at the end had to surrender when the wife threatens to leave him and go back to her parents' home. And she also remembered how on her own turn she too wanted to skip the same with a couple of excuses but ultimately had to sing a popular film-song and received the clapping of the audience.

Chapter – 60

❧

Somi had woken up around five in the morning with fairly mild contractions, and insisted on waiting a further two hours before she would let Annie, her room-mate, to take her to the maternity unit. Annie was at her bed side when Somi was wheeled into it and was looking a bit nervous whereas Somi was astonishingly calm. "Try to relax" she said to Annie, "I'm having a baby. Women do this every day here. Don't worry, I'll be fine".

"Now you just bear down," The doctor instructed. "Nature'll do the rest."

The first pain brought a smile to Somi's lips. She was bringing her child in to the world, and he would have a name. The labour went on, hour after hour.

"Is it going to be a boy?" Somi gasped.

A nurse mopped Somi's brow with a damp cloth. "I'll let you know as soon as I check it. Now press down. Real hard! Hard! Harder!"

The contractions began to come closer together and the pain tore through Somi's body. Oh my God, something's wrong, Somi thought.

"Bear down!" the doctor said. And suddenly there was a note of alarm in her voice. "It's twisted around," she cried. "I – I can't get it out!"

Through the blurring of her sight Somi saw the doctor bend down and twist her body, and the room began to fade out, and suddenly there was no more pain. She was floating in space and there was a bright light at the end of a tunnel.

She heard a voice saying, "It's almost over," and there was a tearing inside her, and the pain made her scream aloud.

"Now!" the doctor said. "It's coming."

And a second later, Somi felt a wet rush between her legs and there was a triumphant cry from the doctor. She held up a red bundle and said, "Welcome to London of the 1996. Honey, you got yourself a daughter."

In the maternity unit at the hospital, The Staff Nurse watched Somi, the beautiful young mother take her newborn child in her arms for the first time. She was gazing at the baby girl, oblivious to everything around her. The Staff Nurse thought: "She's thinking how beautiful she is".

A midwife for more than a decade, she was pleasantly plump with a round open face and a ready smile that accentuated the twin lines around her eyes. She had seen that moment played out thousands of times---hundreds of them in that very room---but she was never tired of that. Stupefied mothers, their eyes lighting up with love, the purest love they would ever know. Moments like those made midwifery worthwhile---Worth the grinding hours--- Worth the crappy pay. Worth the patronizing male obstetricians who thought of themselves as gods just because they had a medical degree.

She gently caressed the baby's cheeks and said, 'By God, 'she's so like her mother'. That was true. The little girl's skin was the same delicate, translucent peach as her mother's. Her big inquisitive eyes were the same pale grey like dawn mist of the mountains. Even her dimpled chin was her mother in miniature. For a split second, Somi's heart leaped at the sight of her, an involuntary smile playing around her lips.

"Congratulations, Somi had become the mother of a beautiful female child". The telegram was received in the morning and the name of the sender was Dr. W.F. Clifford.

"I have become grandfather" murmured Mangal Sen to himself. He had felt too happy on receiving the news and wanted to share it with his friend Bhima. But suddenly he changed his mind and decided to keep the news to himself fearing any untoward repercussion. In fact he hadn't taken Bhima, in to confidence about the pregnancy of Somi, while leaving for London. Instead, he had simply told him that she wanted to do an advanced course from a foreign university to enable her to stand on her own feet and earn her living in the long run.

All the nurses at St. John hospital had become very fond of Somi's baby because of her sweet smile she gave to who-so-ever takes her in her lap. In fact they always were on the look for an excuse to have a glimpse of the child. Her resemblance with that of her mother was so perfect that she looked just like her pocket edition. The hospital staff as a token of their love had unanimously decided to give her a name as beautiful as she herself appeared to be. And with utmost affection, they had started calling her 'Jennet'. Within a few days she would respond to her name. Somi had quite a normal delivery and as such within a week after giving birth to healthy child, had to leave the maternity ward. While Dr. Clifford had sent a telegram to her father, Somi herself had broken the news to Mr. Ghosh, who had maintained brotherly relation with her and used to keep in touch with her, off and on.

Both, Mr. and Mrs. Ghosh had come to congratulate her. Deepti looked too happy to see Jennet. While Mr. Ghosh didn't have much to talk about and remained a silent spectator most of the time, both the ladies had a long heart to heart talk with each other. As she had been told in the beginning that all her expenses will be borne by the hospital authorities till the safe delivery of the child, it is time for her to arrange for some inexpensive accommodation. Somi, as such had requested Deepti to help her in looking for some suitable place where she could shift with her child after she is relieved from the hospital.

Indebted to the kind hospitality of the hospital authorities and also having passed the half-yearly examination of the Nurse's Training Course, Somi had requested for a suitable job in the very hospital itself to serve as a Nurse which would enable her to make a living by herself and also to pursue her remaining half year's course. She was quite hopeful of getting a suitable small accommodation somewhere near the hospital either with the help of a staff member or with the efforts of Mr. Ghosh whom she had already approached and apprised him of the situation she was in, after the safe delivery of the child.

Chapter – 61

꩜

Annie, her room-mate had become very much upset as soon as she came to know of Somi's leaving the hospital and trying to find out some suitable dwelling place outside the hospital. She had always treated Somi as her younger sister and loved her to the extent that she became panicky just with the thought of her leaving. Going off-duty at around 8.00 P.M. she hurriedly reached her staff quarter to see Somi who was busy in breast feeding her child. She gave her a sweet smile and entered the bathroom to have a shower which had been her daily routine on coming after the long hours of duty. Changing her hospital uniform and becoming fresh she came out in a normal dress consisting of a printed salwar-kameez suit and sat beside Somi on the bed. She was quite eager to talk to her and was fumbling for proper words to convince and impress upon her to change her decision of leaving the hospital for the time being. She then further coaxed her to approach the Managing Committee once again with the request to allow her to share her staff quarter for another six months e.g. till the completion of her remaining half year's Nurses' training course. Undoubtedly the advice and the suggestion that came from Annie were quite significant with reference to the circumstances poor Somi had to deal with. She pondered for long over the proposal and firmly made up her mind to talk to Dr. Clifford the next morning and seek her help to sort out the accommodation problem. Hopefully the required permission of staying at the staff quarter could be granted to her that will enable her to attend to her hospital duties as well as pursue her remaining six month's Nurses' training course side by side.

The strategy had been chalked out wisely and consciously that had worked very well quite favourably. Dr. Clifford was all praise about Somi and pleased to see her in the office after a long time since the delivery of her new born. Somi, first of all hesitated a bit to say anything. However, seeing Dr. Clifford in a happy mood she explained to her about the accommodation problem adding that she still had to complete the remaining half year's course of Nurses' training which could be possible only if the necessary permission is given to share the staff quarter with Annie. That way she would be able to continue to attend to the hospital duty as well. Of course she didn't forget to add that some alternate arrangement would be made to look after the baby in her absence.

While Mr. Ghosh used to attend to his office, Mrs. Deepti Ghosh had started to make rounds of her own locality as well as in her neighbourhood to explore the possibility of getting at least a single-room accommodation but all her efforts of searching bore no fruit. At times she became very much disheartened and ultimately decided to accommodate Somi and offered her to come to live with the family at least till some other suitable arrangement is made. Somi had felt very much obliged and was really touched at heart with such a generous offer.

It was, however, Dr. Clifford who once again had come to her rescue. She was able to convince the members of the Managing Committee logically with her solid and reasonable arguments and succeeded in making them agree to give the required permission to Somi to stay and share the staff quarter as usual with her room-mate Annie for another six months. While Somi was very happy to know about the decision of the Committee, she considered it was in fact the trump of Annie who happened to be at the base of all that ultimately had been achieved with the proper strategy. With the help of Annie, a Nurse-maid was engaged to look after the baby Jennet in her absence.

Mr. and Mrs. Ghosh heaved a sigh of relief on hearing from Somi that her accommodation problem was ultimately got solved. Annie took the lead saying that the occasion seems to be quite fit to have a little celebration and asked Somi to also invite her brother Mr. Ghosh with family. Dr. Clifford was approached to be the Guest of Honour. Initially she was hesitant to accept the invitation but had to agree later on the request of other Nurses from the staff quarters of the same block. There was a small gathering of 8-10 persons including Mr. & Mrs. Ghosh who had made it a point to come and grace the occasion with 'Vaasu' their new-born son. The refreshment had been arranged in Annie's room. Somi played the role of the 'host'. A warm welcome was given to the Guest of Honour Dr. W.F. Clifford. But the main attraction of one and all was baby 'Jennet' resting upon a swing in one corner of the room giving sweet smiles to who-so-ever tried to make a goodwill gesture to her. After the refreshment was served, the gathering was asked by the host to make it a musical evening as is customary on such occasions. Dr. Clifford seconded the proposal. It was Annie who broke the ice first to encourage everybody else to come forward and perform anything like singing or dancing. After Annie's beautiful song, all the other Nurses had shed their shyness and performed quite boldly even in the presence of Dr. Clifford who otherwise could never had known about the hidden talent that existed in the Staff Nurses. While departing at the end everybody had offered something to 'Jennet' with love.

CHAPTER – 62

ﾟ

Time had flown upon its wings as quietly that nobody could notice as to when its flight had taken place. All of a sudden Somi had realized that the half-yearly examinations of Nurses' training course were fast approaching and that only a couple of weeks are left to appear for the same. Till then she had been busy with her hospital job and nursing 'Jennet', her baby. Only occasionally she had the chance of making a random look into the study-books as also skipping her training classes on one plea or the other. Yet she had been confident to make up her studies and pass out the examinations come what may. At the time of going to bed she had a heart to heart talk once more with Annie who always had a remedy for all the problems what-so-ever.

"You look very tense, what's wrong with you?" asked Annie.

"I'm worried about my half-yearly examinations. In fact I haven't been able to go through the text books except for a few chapters off and on. I had always taken it lightly postponing the studies to make it up at the weekends which could never materialize. Now I'm in a fix and don't know how to overcome such a lapse on my part," replied Somi.

"My dear little sister, there could be an easy solution to your problem if you care to do as I say." Annie said.

"You know, I don't have any option. Speak it up what you suggest," asked Somi.

"O.K.. Apply for a two weeks' leave and go ahead with your studies. That is the only way left for you if you wish to get through the Examinations," suggested Annie.

Nevertheless the suggestion that came from Annie could only be a possible solution to Somi's problem which didn't need giving a second thought. 'For me, the first and foremost task tomorrow morning would be to apply for two week's leave,' resolved Somi while going to bed.

Since the leave application submitted by Somi contained a valid reason, the hospital authorities didn't object to her going on leave to prepare for the Nurses' training course examinations scheduled to be held in two weeks' time. The training classes had also been over giving ample time to students to revise the course and get prepared for the examinations. Thus, Somi could fully avail of the period lying at her disposal. She totally absorbed herself in studies except for breast feeding the baby. The other house-hold jobs were taken care of by Annie.

Acting like an elder sister, Annie got up early in the morning on the very day of the examination. Asking Somi to get ready, she kept herself busy in preparing the breakfast for her. Somi got ready well in time after having her breakfast and left for the Examination Centre. Annie wished her 'all the best' and prayed for her success too. And that had become the daily routine till the last day of the examination. According to Somi, all the papers had gone fairly well as per her expectation yet she sometimes used to feel nervous fearing the result which was supposed to be declared by the end of next month. Annie always tried to remain by her side keeping a watchful eye upon her assuring that everything would be all right and that she didn't need to be worried about.

And Look! It was again Annie who happened to be the first to break the news to Somi that she had been declared successful and that too with the first division. Of course that called for another occasion to celebrate like they had done six months back. Needless to add, that Somi remained busy for a good part of the day receiving messages congratulating her from almost the entire class of Nurses at the hospital. Dr. W.F. Clifford was all the more happy with such heartening news among the doctors, whom Somi used to assist while on duty.

Now that the grace period of her staying in the staff quarter was going to end, after the examinations were over, she became more worried once again about shifting somewhere else. Presently, she had been counting upon Annie for any kind of help who used to assist her in looking after the baby as well. But once out, who would take care of her. Seriously thinking ahead over the problem she had always been on the look for some charitable home that takes care of young children. Alternatively, even if a small accommodation could be made available to her, she would keep the Nurse-maid and be able to manage somehow or the other.

Among all the other staff members, it was perhaps Dr. W.F. Clifford who had a very soft corner for Somi since the day she had come to St. John hospital. Thinking about the six-month period granted to her to share the staff quarter with her room-mate would be over in a few days, Dr. Clifford had already sent a word to all her acquaintances to search for some inexpensive small dwelling place for Somi. In addition, since she had been settled in London for more than twenty years, she had an overall knowledge about various charitable homes, hospitals, societies, N.G.O.s etc. engaged in some kind of social work. Among them there could also be one or two who take care of young children. Dr. Clifford was a well known figure and she didn't have any difficulty in contacting one namely 'Jesus Christ Child Care Home' run under the aegis of the Christian Charitable welfare Society.

She got them apprised about the pathetic condition of poor Somi and her child. Like everybody else Manager of the Society too was touched at heart.

And thus, with the kind help of Dr. Clifford who had strongly recommended Somi's case, her worries about looking after the baby were unfounded, especially since the baby's lactation period was already over by then. Annie too was pleased to hear the news. After a couple of days, the six months old baby Jennet was got admitted in the Jesus Christ Child Care Home where she would be taken care of by the 'Home' management. As far as the expenditure was concerned, it was agreed upon that a nominal fixed amount would be required to be deposited quarterly or half-yearly, as would be convenient, in the Society's account. Of course the initial registration amount and other expenses had to be deposited at the time of admission.

Once feeling free from the burden of studying after the result of her Nurses' training course and having satisfied with the arrangement with regard to the looking after the baby Jennet, she tried to focus her thoughts imagining about the condition of her father who could be living quite isolated from the society on account of her stubbornness. Having become old enough he must be having it quite difficult to manage the house-hold jobs on his own. Possibly his old pal Bhima could have been able to arrange for a 'help' to attend to poor Mangal Sen's day-to-day needs.

On her successful completion of Nurses' training course, Somi too was promoted to work as full-fledged 'Nurse' like Annie thereby becoming eligible to draw regular pay-scale that had substantially enhanced her income. She had continued to stay with Annie and opened a deposit-account also with a local Bank with the advice and introduction given by Annie. Mr. Ghosh used to visit her often. Likewise she too had made it a routine to visit the 'Home' once a week to see Jennet. That used to give her mental satisfaction to see her progress and was pleased to find that she was being looked after quite well. She also didn't forget to check her bank-balance every now and then and refrained from making undue expenses. Her sole aim had been focused on planning to return to her homeland as early as possible and wanted to save sufficient amount to deposit at least two half-yearly installments in the Society's account in advance as also to pay for the air-ticket to India. Annie had become very sad after Jennet had been admitted in to the Home. So, on her next off-day Somi had taken her to Home to meet Jennet. She had also introduced her to the Management and asked them to allow her to see Jennet whenever she comes.

It had taken her approximately six months since she started planning to return to India, her homeland. She had deposited two half-yearly advance installments in the Society's account. She further had authorized her bank to transfer the amount of next installment into the Society's account, when it becomes due every six months, from her account which could be recouped by her remitting the funds from India. Mr. Ghosh had helped her in arranging the Air-ticket to India. In between she had once taken Mr. Ghosh also to see Jennet and introduced him to the Home management with the sole idea that he too could visit them occasionally to enquire about the welfare of Jennet. At the time of leaving the hospital, the staff nurses and doctors bade her farewell. Dr. Clifford and Annie with tearful eyes wished her a happy journey with the promise that she would write to them on reaching India.

CHAPTER – 63

At London's Heathrow Airport also she had to go through the same procedure like one they had experienced while coming from India. She reached the airport one and a half hour before the departure time of her flight. She had only a small bag as her luggage and after scanning the same she was allowed to take it into the plane. In a short while a small bus had ferried the passengers toward the aircraft where a ladder was attached to the door of the plane. That too was a huge plane like which they had boarded while coming from India. She was ushered to her seat No. by the air hostess. On occupying her seat she deposited her bag into the luggage duct. Soon an airhostess appeared in the centre of the aircraft and apprised the passengers about the safety measures to be taken during the flight, like fastening of belts etc. And minutes after, the plane had gone afloat in the sky.

The seats were really quite comfortable. She got herself stretched from head to toe and started visualizing what her father would be doing at that time. Being an early riser he must have got up by now as in India it could be dawn, the time of day-break. It was more than a year since she saw him at the St. John hospital and leaving for India after satisfying himself with the arrangement made for her stay in London. Various kinds of thoughts became coming to her mind one after the other and she couldn't remember when she had dozed off.

Landing on the Indian soil had given Somi an immense pleasure for that was her homeland. As she had nothing to declare, it didn't take her long to come out through the green channel. Taking a Taxi she headed toward her house and wished that she had wings to reach there in no time. Thinking about her father she could see, that after all, his long wait to see his daughter was going to end in an hour or so. How would he react on seeing her? He would be awestruck when she appears before him all of a sudden. He could never have imagined that his daughter had just landed in India and would be meeting him very soon.

Mangal Sen, on the other hand, had always used to speculate about his granddaughter. How would she be looking like? She must be quite beautiful like her mother. She must have a very fair complexion. She would be about one year old and must have started crawling upon her hands and knees. Somi could have sent at least a photograph of her to comfort my eyes. In his daily prayer he always used to wish for the welfare of both, his daughter and the granddaughter.

He had awakened on hearing the sound of 'tick-tick' as if someone was knocking at the door. It was still some dark outside, awaiting the daybreak. He got up, still half-asleep and unlatched the door but couldn't see anybody. Disregarding the sound as his mere imagination in sleep, he turned back toward the courtyard. All of a sudden he found himself hugged from behind. He became really awestruck to see that it was Somi, his beloved daughter. She had deliberately stepped a little aside when her father had just peeked out of the door and entered quietly behind him to give a great surprise with her sudden appearance before him. Tears rolled down his cheeks with happiness. At that moment his joy knew no bounds and out of sheer love and affection he caressed her and planted kisses upon her forehead.

It gave Mangal Sen utmost contentment to learn about the arrangements made for his granddaughter. She is lovingly called 'Jennet' and admitted in Jesus Christ Child Care Home run by the Christian Charitable Welfare Society, he was told. He was further informed that only a nominal fixed amount would be needed to meet the expenses, what-so-ever, to be deposited half-yearly in the Society's account for which she had already given standing instructions to her Bank in London, from her account with them, to be recouped by her from India from time to time. On his asking about how his granddaughter looked like, Somi had fished out of her handbag some photographs of the one-year old Jennet she had taken of her, a week before. Mangal Sen too was delighted to see the little angel's resemblance with Somi, her mother.

Since his return from London after lodging his daughter for the safe delivery in the St. John hospital, Mangal Sen had remained constantly in touch with the 'Father' and used to visit the Church to attend the Sunday Service regularly. He had already gone to see the 'Father' immediately on reaching India to thank him and express his gratitude for the guidance and kind help to overcome the problem he had been facing at that time. He had also didn't forget to explain about the helping attitude of the Managing Committee and was all praise for the St. John hospital.

CHAPTER – 64

❦

"This is Somi, my daughter, who has just returned from St. John hospital, London," said Mangal Sen, introducing her to the reverend 'Father' at the Church as soon as the Sunday Service was over. 'Father' gave his blessings and asked about the child as well. She then explained everything briefly about the safe delivery of the baby named 'Jennet' and her admission in the Jesus Christ Child Care Home for which she has to send a nominal fixed amount to bear the rearing expenses for her. She had also told him that in order to utilize the time she had at her disposal, she had joined the coveted 'Nurses' Training Course of one year run by a subsidiary of the hospital. She further added that after successfully passing the course in first division she had remained with the same hospital for six months working as full-fledged 'Nurse'.

'Father' was pleased and showed his happiness to see that with the grace of God everything had turned out to be in their favour, as explained by Somi. He also had asked her not to hesitate in approaching him again if any kind of further help is needed, to which she promptly asked if she could be helped in seeking the job of a Trained and Qualified Nurse with the six months' job experience at her credit in some reputed hospital. She was then assured by 'Father' that he will be doing his best to help her and asked Mangal Sen to keep in touch with him as usual.

Having retired long back from his profession and shedding the tag of 'Mangalu', he had become 'Mangal Sen', a proud father of Somi, but sans any source of income. In fact, a considerable portion of his savings had been spent on travelling on different occasions like air-tickets for their going abroad e.g. to London and his returning back to India, depositing the required initial registration and admission charges of Somi in the St. John hospital, expenditure made on the things like pre- and post delivery of the child as well as a generous donation given to the St. John hospital in London. Moreover, since the day he had returned from London, he had been managing his day-to-day expenses from his savings account for the past one year most economically.

Somi too had spent her earnings from Nurses' job on depositing the initial registration charges with the Christian Charitable Welfare Society at the time of admission of Jennet in the Jesus Christ Child Care Home. She also had to bear the day-to-day expenditure for her own survival for six months. While coming back to India she had managed to deposit two half-yearly advance installments in the Society's account and also paid for her air-ticket to India. Thus, both, father and daughter had been in dire need of finding some source of income to make both ends meet.

Sitting idle at home could neither be of any use, nor advisable. To earn the daily bread one has to do some work. Fully knowing that there could be no chance in getting a job in a Govt. hospital, Somi, on her part, had applied with her resume to 3-4 privately run hospitals but there was no response from any of them. She was as such quite disheartened and a little depressed as well. There was a time when, like her father, Somi also, on having lived in the company of her eunuch inmates for so many years, had learned how to sing and dance of which she used to practice regularly when alone in her room behind the doors, just for self-enjoyment. Mangal Sen knew about that talent of her. One night, after dinner, he had a heart to heart talk with her and asked, that pending any offer coming her way for the post of Nurse, if she was willing to make use of that talent in earning her livelihood. Keeping in mind her father's old age weakness and deteriorating health day by day, she had to agree, seeing no other option but with the condition to do only a respectable programme like participating in a marriage party or giving a stage performance etc. Accordingly, Mangal Sen had talked to his pal Bhima about her willingness to perform. He had asked him to extend the invitation of the programme, when received if any, to him also.

However, her stars seemed to be quite favourable as pending receipt of any invitation from Bhima even after a fortnight, Somi was called for an interview at St. Stevenson Hospital run by a Diocese. Though she had sent her application to that hospital as well, yet she was sure enough that 'Father' must have had a word with the hospital authorities. The interview had gone very well. Her testimonials, Certificates from St. John hospital, London and six months' experience of working as a full-fledged Nurse had a good impression on the members of the Medical Board. Nobody had asked for any reference. She was selected there and then and was asked to join her duty the very next day with the assurance that the requisite Appointment Letter would be issued in due course. Thus, to Mangal Sen's mind, the problem of earning and to run the kitchen was solved.

She would regularly attend to her duties in the hospital and in order to save more money would always remain on the lookout for the double shift. Occasionally she had even opted for night shifts also if there need be and with that she had considerably gained her popularity among the doctors and the staff alike. As compared to the other Nurses in the hospital, she was considered one of the most beautiful, charming and graceful lady as also well versed in her job. Outwardly everybody seemed to be very keen to make friends with her. But Somi, as the popular saying goes: 'Once bitten twice shy', had never encouraged the attempts of any kind of advances of her colleagues. Of course, in just a couple of days, after her joining the hospital, she was welcomed to join a popular, like-minded, little group of Nurses.

There was a 'Recreation room' of the size of a hall equipped with a large dining table and a dozen chairs which was commonly used by the staff Nurses. Here they could have their lunch and also while away their spare time in-between their duty-hours. They would sit there comfortably gossiping with each other about persons or social incidents related to the inside or outside the hospital. Nurses under some kind of distress, would discuss their problems also in order to find a solution. Talking about their personal matters generally helped them in sorting out the things amicably. On other occasions, one could hear fits of laughter in the room or a singing competition going on amongst the Nurses present in the hall. Just like Annie, her room-mate friend in St. John hospital in London, here too she had the longing to have a well-wisher like her.

'Come the right time and everything will fall in line', is the general conception. Accordingly, Somi had once opened her mind before 'Sadhana', her coordinator Nurse, with which, she used to be on duty, off and on. During the course of conversation she told her about Annie, her London room-mate friend, who was ever-ready to help her, come what may, like a real elder sister and was still in touch with her on phone. Sadhana was very much impressed with her story and offered to be her friend, in word and spirit, no less than Annie, in anyway. With that kind of assurance Somi felt really comfortable at heart.

Chapter – 65

Baby Jennet was being looked after extremely well at the 'Home'. However Somi hardly had any link throughout Jennet's childhood. Of course she always remained in touch on phone with the Home management to find about her progress and from the conversation she often had with them she could visualize that Jennet surely had all the features of her mother and had become literally a replica of her. While Mr. and Mrs. Ghosh used to visit Jennet once in a month, Annie couldn't wait for more than a couple of weeks and would rush to meet Jennet on a weekend so much so, that Jennet had started to recognize as if she were her mother. She would invariably speak to Somi also and give her the first information report. Somi would also talk to Deepti Ghosh to enquire about Vaasu's progress. Both, Jennet and Vaasu must have reached the age of entering the Kindergarten. At that juncture, after a long period, say about four years, she had developed a kind of yearned longing and a strong desire of seeing her daughter. She wanted to physically see whether Jennet would be coming up a beautiful lass like her and that she still would resemble with her mother as the Nurses at the hospital had told about her. In accordance with her tenet once she had made up her mind it becomes next to impossible to deter from her resolve. She had started preparing for her journey and made the necessary arrangements like booking of Air-tickets and purchasing certain gifts for Jennet and Vaasu. Mangal Sen too had a keen desire to accompany Somi to see his grand-daughter but for his ill health and to some extent the financial constraint as well. By the way, Bhima was again kept in the dark and was told, "A special one-week tour is being organized by the St. Stevenson Hospital for the Nurses and Somi too is selected to join the group leaving for London in a couple of days." So, obviously Bhima was supposed to take the responsibility of looking after Mangal Sen in her absence.

For Jennet it was indeed a red-letter day when she was told that her mother would be coming from India to see her. The flight had reached the London's Heathrow airport at its scheduled time. Like on the previous occasion, Somi didn't have to declare anything objectionable and crossed through the green channel. She had only two small bags with her. One of them had two-three pairs of her clothes and a few other items of daily use and the other contained some toys and a few children's books of legendary tales or fables which she had brought specially from India for Jennet and Vaasu, son of Mr. Ghosh who had been in touch with Somi and had the requisite information about her coming to London. As Somi had already faxed the necessary message to the Principal of the school, giving the date, time and other necessary details about her flight, one Mr. James Wilson, a senior teacher from the Jennet's school was deputed to make suitable arrangement to receive Somi. Strangely enough, instead of sending someone else for the job, he preferred to go himself at the airport to receive her. As soon as she came out, Mr. Wilson immediately approached her with a sweet smile. He introduced himself as the teacher from Jennet's school and had come to receive her. He had come a bit earlier than the scheduled arrival time of her flight and had kept on waiting eagerly at the check-out point. He didn't have any difficulty in recognizing her as he was astonished to note that the face of both, the daughter and her mother, did amazingly resemble with each other. This time she didn't have to look for the 'taxi' as Mr. Wilson had ushered her in to the staff car, he himself had come in.

A rousing grand reception had awaited her at the school premises as if some V.I.P. was coming from a foreign country. Somi was quite impressed on reaching there and was welcomed by the Principal and her staff. There happened to be a small gathering in a hall-like room where a few grown-up students and teachers had assembled. The Principal, in fact, appeared to be a good orator. In her brief speech she had introduced Somi to all of them. Some teachers as well as members of the staff looked very keen to have a hand-shake with her and were delighted to do the same. Mr. Wilson was only too happy for having a brief conversation also with her on their way from airport to the School. Soon, accompanying her class teacher, little Jennet had also come to see her mother. The whole gathering was busy in gazing at both, the mother and the daughter, as same to same, comparing them feature by feature and finding their resemblance as no less than a miracle. Having seen her mother for the first time, she looked somewhat bewildered. However, when her mother affectionately embraced her with tearful eyes, she too had hugged her tightly enough, as if saying not to leave her anymore. The meeting of both, the mother and the daughter was really a spectacular moment and the whole event was worthy of catching in the camera which was done by a staff member, and on her return to India, later on, had adorned her room occupying a prominent place to meet the eyes of the visitors, if any.

Somi had taken the Principal in to confidence and told her that she had planned her stay in London just for one week only and wished to make most of it during that short spell of the time she had at her disposal. So, in order to make her stay more comfortable, as also to let her daughter feel the closeness of her mother, the school authorities, as a special gesture, had got a room of the hostel opened for her. Jennet too was allowed to stay with her mother during the ensuing week. That being the weekend, the next day happened to be Sunday when Mr. and Mrs. Ghosh had visited the hostel to see Somi. Master Vaasu had become all the more happy to receive his gifts of toys and the fable-books. Annie, however, couldn't stay back at her apartment and rushed the same evening to see Somi on the day of her arrival and tried her level best to take both of them to her staff quarter to which she had promised to visit her in a day or two just for a short while.

Jennet was overwhelmed to meet her mother, even though she had been receiving motherly love from the hostel warden as well as her teachers alike. The beautiful and loveable lass, like her, could become the centre of attraction anywhere. Even at that tender age, she looked smart and intelligent. At night, she would ask her mother, to make her listen, a story or two, from one of the children's books she had brought from India and gifted to her. With the feeling of immense love she would share the bed with her mother and would keep hugging her time and again.

CHAPTER – 66

✺

During her short stay Somi had taken Jennet twice on an outing. In the first instance, she had taken her to a 'Circus' show. What to say of seeing it, perhaps Jennet hadn't even heard about such a thing. Here, Jennet had enjoyed the live performance of the various trained animals, where a jockey would ride standing and keeping his either foot upon the back of a pair of the horses running together simultaneously side by side in the ring; dogs riding a wooden rolling barrel as also jumping through the ring of burning fire. She had also seen with interest and enjoyed the various feats of elephants as also the tigers and the lions; young girls in glittering costumes riding the 'single wheel' cycles in the ring; as also their riding on about eight feet high tension steel wire tied on the poles holding small colourful umbrellas for balancing; jumping mid-air on swings across the ring from one side to the other and vice versa; acrobatic feats, etc. Somi was pleased to watch Jennet clapping with joy every few minutes. Coming out of the 'show' she asked Jennet, "How did you like the show?"

"It was very good Mamma. I liked it and enjoyed it too much. You see! How the girls were riding on single-wheel cycles with their umbrellas. It was awful. And the girls swinging above in the air jumping from one swing to the other across the ring without any fear of falling down. And that little doggy riding the wooden roller and another who jumped through that ring burning with fire. Mamma! This is the first time I have seen 'real' tiger, lion and elephant.

So far, I had seen only their pictures in the book." replied Jennet who looked much in high spirit.

Somi looked up in the sky that was overcast with clouds but at the same time the weather was very fine which Jennet seemed to be enjoying after sitting for hours in the show. Somi then decided to take Jennet to some restaurant for dinner, skipping the hostel meal, as it would be a little late reaching there. She found one just nearby and both of them walked towards the same. The place was nice, well maintained and not very crowded. Both, mother and the daughter were ushered towards a table by the side of a huge floor-to-ceiling window from where Jennet could see with interest people running helter-skelter on the pavement looking for cover as it had started drizzling outside making the weather all the more beautiful. Soon they were settled in their chairs comfortably. Picking up the menu card she started scanning it and asked Jennet, "What would you like to eat, beta!?"

"Bread-roll stuffed with cheese and potato crisp; orange juice and ice-cream," replied Jennet making her choice very carefully as she wanted to have something to eat other than the usual nutritious stuff the children were served in the hostel. With the clear Intention to share the meal with her lovely daughter, for the first time, Somi became a bit emotional and with a little excitement she doubled her order. Till the food was served, Jennet didn't stop talking about the circus show she had just witnessed, the joy of which had a lasting effect on her mind. The food smelled good and was delicious as well. During the course of eating, while mother was putting a bite into the daughter's mouth, Jennet was doing the same to her mother. The scene was spectacular indeed for the random onlookers who happened to be dining there at that time. It was the day Jennet would never forget. Even in the taxi, on their way to the hostel, Jennet continued asking something or the other about the daring feats she had seen in the circus. In the night too, she kept on thinking about the circus show for some time and then gone to sleep rolling over and hugging her mother with love.

On another day Jennet was taken to the famous river Thames where she looked at various types of Big and small boats going in or coming out at the bank of the river. She had seen fishermen with huge nets used to catch the fish. Some tourists were seen riding and sailing in the shallow waters near the bank. Jennet too had a thrill and enjoyed a motor-boat ride as well. She didn't feel any kind of fear and enjoyed the company of her mother. Here they also visited London's eye which is the 3rd largest wheel – Ferris wheel of the world located on the bank of the river Thames and is one of the main attractions in London with 135 meters of height. It provides a magnificent view of the capital city. They could see the Big Ben (clock) also which is the most representative symbol of London the great. On their way back to the hostel they had visited Annie too but regretted that the visit to Deepti Ghosh couldn't be made in the late hours at night.

The full week had gone by and nobody could ever realize that. The day at last had come when Somi had to leave for India, her homeland. She had been lamenting how quickly the time had passed. While leaving she had deposited some extra amount for Jennet, over and above the actual fee. She had expressed her gratitude to the Principal and the staff for their hospitality. Poor Jennet had been constantly crying and pleading with mother to take her along. No plea, what-so-ever would work to console her. However, it was Annie who had come to their rescue. Acting just like her second mother, she could make Jennet believe that mamma would be coming back very soon with a host of gifts next time and would go on the outings also like before. Mr. Ghosh had made it convenient to come with Somi at the airport to send her off.

Mangal Sen had been eagerly awaiting Somi's return. A wild thought had once come up in his mind that owing to the immense love and affection for her child, Somi might resolve to stay in London with her daughter. However, he had quite forcefully discarded away such an ugly and wicked thought. He had further pondered over the fact that since she had booked a return ticket while going, there couldn't be, even remotely, any chance or possibility of her over staying in London. Just to pass his time, he would argue with himself for nothing, keeping in view such kind of baseless speculations.

Ultimately, with a heavy heart, Somi had to return to India. She looked depressed and reached home with a sullen frame of mind. While her body was here in India, her mind and soul were still in London, always thinking about Jennet. Such a kind of her state of mind had developed only after physically seeing Jennet. Before that she had never bothered to think that much about her and used to live with just a faint imagination of her in mind. In the next couple of days she had become a little talkative and would talk nothing but about Jennet. She had told her father even the minute details of her daughter especially her resemblance with her mother showing a close-up of her photographs. He was further told about her welcome fete as well as the comforts her daughter had been enjoying. While looking after her health, the Society had been taking care of her education also. At the time of her coming back to India, she didn't forget to collect the photographs taken during her stay, especially those of Jennet which anybody would be pleased to look at. Mangal

Sen too, on seeing the photographs, was surprised to note the cent-percent resemblance of Jennet with Somi. He had, for the first time, appreciated from the core of his heart, her decision of going against the abortion and keeping the child.

There had been no news about Bob, the biological father of Jennet, for so many years. At times Mangal Sen had told Somi that having become too old he wouldn't be living for long on account of his persistent ailments and poor health and tried to persuade her for marriage. But owing to her decisive nature she had never agreed with him for the reason that in spite of having been left in the lurch many years back she still loved Bob and secretly cherished the sweet memories of the short spell of time she had enjoyed with him. Moreover, there was Jennet, her sweet daughter, the consequence of their love, adding that she still had hope against hope that Bob will definitely come back to her one day. Till then she had solid reason to live alone for the sake of her lovely daughter. Thus the question of getting married didn't arise at all.

CHAPTER – 67

❦

S timulated by her earlier success in accomplishing the task of visiting London she was dying to see her daughter again. She had become all the more restless with the passing of year after year nourishing her keen desire to repeat her fete once more at least. She had tried in between once and planned her tour well in advance to coincide with the school holidays when there would be no classes and as such Jennet would have free time to seek full enjoyment in the company of her mother but had to postpone the same on account of sudden illness of her father when he had to be admitted in to the hospital. The fragile state of health of her father had become now constant phenomena which she couldn't dare ignore. That had been a valid cause to keep her at bay from making the unmindful resolve every now and then. However, following the footsteps of her father who always used to come to the Boarding school with her 'birthday' gift every year, Somi too had never failed in sending the pretty little 'birth-day' gifts for her daughter from India.

Jennet and Vaasu, both, by the time, had become grownup children. They had crossed the age of childhood and subsequently stepped on the threshold of adolescence. Likewise, in the field of education also, it looked as if both had some kind of a competition between them with the result that they had succeeded in achieving higher grades one after the other. Of course Vaasu happened to be senior to Jennet by a year or so and as such one class ahead of her. But on account of her outstanding performance in her exams she was once promoted to a higher class thereby becoming equal to Vaasu. While reaching the pre-graduation level, signs of youth had become clearly visible in them.

It was a matter of chance when suddenly Somi had found a couple of white hair strands while combing her hair. Taking it as a signal she had become a little more worried about her own age. She pondered over the fact that old age would, gradually, be drawing upon each one of us, sooner or later, which happens to be a natural process and as such was inevitable. Simultaneously, in her thoughts, she would be thinking about Jennet who had been growing a little fast and ready to join some college for higher studies as per the latest information she had received from Mr. Ghosh who had never forgot to give her a phone-call on such kind of important matters. With a little influence of his official position he had been running from pillar to post to see that both, Jennet and Vaasu, join the same college, as they already had remained in touch with each other since their school days while studying even separately. That way it would be much easier for him to watch the progress of both and pass on the first hand report to Somi as well.

"It is more than six years when I had last seen my daughter. Now is the high time to pay another visit to London come what may", resolved Somi. The more she would contemplate on the subject the stronger her resolve would become. Ultimately, unable to bear the extreme mental agony she had to succumb to the pressure coming from within. She then had a heart to heart talk with her father who still had been confined to bed and needed some more time to recover from his ailment. However, on realizing the situation, her daughter was in, he too, was left with no option but to give his consent for the trip to go abroad like before. But they had to think of a suitable and valid excuse one more time for leaving the country.

On his next routine visit to come and have a chat with his pal, Bhima was pleased to find Somi also at home since that was her weekly off. During the ensuing conversation, Somi had, quite tactfully, broached the subject, telling him, "A conference relating to the medical field is being held by the fraternity of doctors in the Trinity College of Medicine, in collaboration with the St. John hospital in London where I had served for about half a year after completing my Nurses' training course. Our St. Stevenson Hospital has also received the invitation with the request to send a team of prominent doctors to attend the same where they would be apprised of the latest techniques developed recently as well as the break-through happened in the field of surgery". She also didn't forget to add, "Out of the whole lot of Nurses serving at the hospital, I have been lucky enough to be selected to join the team to assist the doctors during the conference. We may be leaving as such in a couple of days and I don't have anybody else to approach but yourself to take care of your pal in my absence".

And thus, once again poor Bhima, acceding to the request of Somi, had to arrange for a 'help' to look after Mangal Sen, from the band of eunuchs, like he had done on the previous occasions, and manage the household chores till she returns after a week or so.

CHAPTER – 68

❦

On her previous visit, Mr. James Wilson, a senior teacher from Jennet's school had come to receive Somi at the London's Heathrow airport. However, this time, she had planned to give surprise to everybody. Instead of going direct to the Jesus Christ Child Care Home, she, after de-boarding at the airport, telephoned to Mr. Ghosh who, in the first place, couldn't believe his ears. It was, in fact beyond his imagination that Somi could come to London all of a sudden. Well, he took leave from his office and hurriedly reached the airport to receive her. On his persistent requests, Somi had to agree to his proposal and straightaway they headed to meet Mrs. Deepti Ghosh. She too had been waiting passionately to see her as Mr. Ghosh had already informed her on phone about the arrival of Somi before leaving for the airport.

Both the ladies hugged each other after the initial hi hello. While Mr. Ghosh and Somi got themselves settled comfortably on the sofa lying in the drawing room, Deepti rushed towards the kitchen to fetch something like cold drink to which Somi told her that in view of the cold weather outside, just a cup of hot tea would suffice. Sipping the tea, a little later, Somi also apologized for having not been able to visit her while leaving for India on her previous trip due to the shortage of time. On asking about Vaasu, she was told that his classes must be over by that time and that he might be on his way and would be reaching home in a short while. She had further learnt that with the great efforts of Mr. Ghosh, both Vaasu and Jennet had got admission in the same St. Xavier's College, known as the most prestigious college of London.

Soon, the roaring sound of a motorbike was heard from outside to which Deepti had responded, declaring that Vaasu has come. He too was surprised like his father to meet Somi Aunty after so many years. He had also briefed a little about Jennet and their everlasting friendship of so many years. Somi was really pleased and tried to visualize that Jennet too must have attained that much height like Vaasu and also become even prettier than she had seen her last, about six years back. She then asked Mr.Ghosh to take her to Jennet's 'Home' as she seemed to be quite eager to meet her daughter. The very thought of seeing her after so many years had instantly made her a little nervous. Whether she would recognize her mother, as the gap of more than six years happens to be such a period that possibly would be quite difficult for a child to remember.

The lady In-charge of the 'Home' was also pleased to learn that Somi, the mother of Jennet had come from India to see her daughter. She had already returned from the college, Somi was told and must be in her hostel-room. With the permission from the In-charge, both of them were allowed to meet Jennet in the hostel itself. Unbelievably that particular moment of both mother and daughter hugging each other had become spectacular indeed in every sense of the word. Their joy knew no bounds so much so that tears rolled down their cheeks. To the great astonishment of Mr. Ghosh, Jennet had instantly recognized her mother and told her that in fact it was like having a dream come true. Till then she had been seeing her mother very often in her dreams only and was really happy to see her physically touching and hugging her.

Like on previous occasion about six years back, this time too she was allowed to stay with her daughter for the whole week but with the condition that Jennet wouldn't be allowed to bunk her classes. Of course they could enjoy their outings on week-end when the college remains closed. To begin with, they had chalked out the programme for the very next day. It was decided that immediately on returning from college, they would make a surprise visit to Annie's apartment. In a quick response to the door-bell, Annie hastily opened the door and couldn't believe her eyes. She had rubbed them twice as if she had been half-asleep seeing a dream. Here too the scene of hugging each other was repeated once again as both the room-mates had met each other after almost six years or so. After the tea and snacks were served, both the ladies had become busy in exchanging their accumulated sweet memories of the past, piled up since the time they lived together as room-mates, in the hostel of St. John Hospital, before the birth of Jennet. And Jennet was listening quite attentively, to whom Annie Aunty had proved no less than her mother who always used to come and see her on very short intervals in the absence of her mother.

All of a sudden Somi realized that the short spell of the week would be over by that night and she wouldn't have any option but to leave the next day positively as she had already booked her return-air-ticket while coming to London. In her heart, though, she had wished if by some miracle she could stay there for a little more time which even remotely wouldn't be possible. Since Jennet had to attend to her college every morning, they could avail of just half of the day. However, even with that short time at their disposal they could make maximum out of that. They were able to visit the tower of London, the Royal Botanic Gardens,

Kew, and St. James's Park where they have pelicans as well as Madame Tussauds. Here one comes face to face with the life-size statues of world's famous persons including the Bollywood stars. There were a host of other places also worth paying a visit e.g. St. Paul's Cathedral, Buckingham Palace, Shakespeare's Globe as also a few museums like Science Museum, British Museum, Natural History Museum etc. but so far, Jennet could hardly get time to see all those places.

Chapter – 69

❦

Somi had not shared so far the story of her life with her daughter and always found herself in a dilemma in taking a decision. Now, that jennet had crossed the threshold of adulthood, she was supposed to have become mature enough to understand things in the right perspective. Hence, that was perhaps the right time to take her in to the confidence instead of waiting further for a few more years. Till then Jennet had simply known that her maternal grandfather had settled in India. He is too old to do anything on his own and her mother had to look after him. About her father she had been told that he had gone on a world tour and had not returned yet. Her mother had been working in a well reputed hospital in India to take care of everything whatsoever. Once having made up her mind firmly, Somi had preferred not to go in to the minute details and simply briefed her about the events. In her own words:

"Originally your grandpa—Mangal Sen happened to be the only son of the owner of a big cloth mill. Unfortunately, he had met with a terrible accident in his youth and became a eunuch. He had then, left his family and joined the band of eunuchs."

That was indeed a great shock for Jennet to listen about the tragedy. However, Somi had continued further to tell her:

"Once, while returning from Shirdi, after paying his obeisance to Shri Sai Baba in the Samadhi Mandir, to honour the 'vow' of his late mother, he had found an abandoned female child of hardly two-three years in age, sleeping beneath a berth of the train which your grandpa was going to alight from. Being a kind-hearted person he had a little dreadful feeling that the child may fall in to some wrong hands. So, even being a eunuch himself, he had decided to take the child under his care and looked after her like his own legitimate daughter for so many years. Can you imagine that she had to live in the garb of a boy to safeguard her real identity of a girl, all those years till her joining the co-educational boarding school? Now just guess, who could be that child? It was 'me' – your mother."

Jennet was really touched at heart and surprised to hear about all the revealing facts and instantly hugged her mother out of instinct emotional feelings. After a little pause, Somi added:

"He had toiled himself day and night for my sake to get me proper education and provide all the comforts of life he could, within his means. After my graduation, I had become a member of a nearby public library where I had met Bob, your father. He was a foreigner, yet we took a fancy to each other and left for the Bharat Darshan tour. At the end of the tour he had left for his native country all of a sudden. The irony of the fact is that after his disappearance I found myself pregnant. However, I didn't go for the abortion and your grandpa had managed to get me admitted here in the St. John hospital in London. In due course of time I had completed my Nurses' Training Course, and had some work experience also in the hospital. Then after your admission in the Jesus Christ Child Care Home, I returned to India, our native country. I hope you already know about the rest of the story".

Needless to say that Jennet had felt really proud of her grandpa as well as the sacrifice and the struggle her mother had gone through all those twenty years and was still hopeful about the return of Bob, her father.

Both, Mr. Ghosh and Deepti had come to the airport to see her off. In fact Mr. Ghosh had made the offer that he would drop her at the airport in his office car. That would not only save her time but also give her one more opportunity to have a chat with Deepti on the way to the airport whom she adores very much. They had reached an hour before the departure time which had been made mandatory for one and all. Anyway, the flight had taken place at its scheduled time and Somi, stretching herself comfortably in her seat, tried to visualize about the scene at home thinking what her father would be doing at that time. He must be eagerly waiting for her return. Soon her mind had a flash back about Jennet. On the previous occasion, some six years back, being just a kid, it had become very difficult to console her and it was Annie Aunty who was able to comfort her. But this time she didn't make any fuss and thoughtfully tried to understand the circumstances as well as the compulsion of her mother for going to India.

"There was a day when Somi, just a two-year old kid, had come to this house," Mangal Sen had been contemplating in his thoughts, while sitting in the verandah. "Then there happened to be another day when Somi had gone to college and in due course had become a graduate, of whom I am really very proud of, and hold my head high in the society. And see, this time, even my granddaughter has joined the College, that too in London. God has been really kind who always showers his blessings even on people like me. Now I understand that my earlier sufferings, whatsoever, in my youth, were in fact, could be of my own doings." Comforting himself a little with such thoughts, he lay on his cot gazing on the clouds in the sky.

Unlike her previous return-visit to India from London, Somi looked quite cheerful this time, as compared to her sullen mood when she had landed at Indian soil some six years back. She was full of sweet memories and the pride of having a daughter like Jennet. She was occasionally looked absorbed in her thoughts about the lovely conversations she had with Jennet. She had appreciated her resemblance with herself. Both, the mother and daughter weren't merely the lookalikes but were positively same to same. She showed her photographs to Mangal Sen. Looking at the photographs of Jennet, his college-going granddaughter, Mangal Sen had felt much delighted. He would have taken her as that of Somi, on account of the utmost resemblance with her mother but for the age-difference which had become more visible with the passing of time. Somi had also told him about Vaasu, son of Mr. Ghosh, whom Mangal Sen still remembered as his first acquaintance in London hospital. He had remained in touch with Jennet since their school days and had joined the same college with Jennet. He too had become quite handsome just like a hero, she had added further. Bhima still hadn't known anything about Jennet as the utmost secrecy had been maintained by both, the father and the daughter. As Somi had returned after attending to the so called conference, the 'help' had been relieved of doing the household chores.

CHAPTER – 70

B hima, the ex–mukhiya of the band of eunuchs, who had, years back, taken leave and bestowed the title of Mukhiya upon Mangal Sen, often used to come and see his old pal. He had called on him last evening also. Both of them had seated themselves side by side upon the old wooden bench which had been lying permanently in the verandah. They had been discussing about the difficulties being faced by them day in and day out. The gist of the discussion was to find out ways and means of making some extra income as even the daily routine of door to door roaming could fetch these days only a nominal amount which was quite insufficient for them to survive. As far as their community profession was concerned Bhima had told that there was hardly any scope for improvement, as more or less all the members of the band had become old.

Carrying on the conversation further, Bhima had informed Mangal Sen:

"It is rumoured that elsewhere, eunuchs have been compelled to change their profession to survive. It is, however, beyond any doubt a historical fact that transgender community in India is dated since more than 4000 years in ancient Hinduism and Islam, where eunuchs used to serve in harems of the Mughal rulers. According to a rough estimate, there are not less than a lakh transgender or eunuchs in the four major metropolitan cities of India, roaming from one place to the other, within the cities as well as outside, to earn their livelihood, giving their blessings and greetings to individuals, couples and families on special occasions.

While a few have become professional 'bar' dancers in the city like Mumbai, still there are others who go for begging from shop to shop, at the road signals on the highway or on the streets. It is also heard that a few of them had taken up the oldest profession of prostitution, as seeking alms from well-to-do families, house construction sites and the so called 'bakhshish' from businessmen, road-siders, etc. don't help anymore in running the kitchen. On account of dearness, the prices of all the things including those of the household commodities have reached sky high. Moreover, due to the urbanization, our profession had become from bad to worse. By the way, there are still others who had been crying hoarse to have voting rights as also the assertion of an additional category of 'eunuch' along with 'male' and 'female' columns in the identity cards."

"What is the news about Zulfi, Massy, Jamila etc.?" asked Mangal Sen, enquiring about all of them by name.

"All of them have become old like us. Putting their faces on, they have become even uglier than before with the excessive use of sub-standard make-up material," replied Bhima, making his face.

"What about Maskari, the youngest of all, in Ranga's band? Is there any news of her? I understand that she happened to be the prominent member of their group and had been the main attraction at the parties," asked Mangal Sen.

"I have heard about her. Sailing in the same boat, even her condition is no better. She had become too weak now and is quite unfit to walk around by herself. She, however, often enquires about your health, I was told," replied Bhima.

"Yes. Maskari, though, had been Ranga's favourite for a good number of years, yet she had a good rapport with me as well. I also remember her off and on. Perhaps you may recollect that it was Maskari who had once told Ranga about that wretched son of Mr. Dua. He too must have got his retirement by now," said Mangal Sen.

"Retirement, what are you talking man? For your kind information, Mr. Dua had gone behind the bars some three or four years ago and has yet to complete his term in jail," Bhima told Mangal Sen.

"What charges he has been sentenced on?" Mangal Sen had asked quite curiously.

"It was some kind of over cleverness on the part of Mr. Dua," continued Bhima. "There was a general perception that Mr. Dua had developed a foolproof method of making money."

"Yes, yes. I knew about his foolproof method of charging some extra bucks over and above the actual charges which his trusted subordinate staff used to collect from the clients. The excess amount thus collected would be kept in a pool and distributed amongst them after short intervals according to their rank and position," confirmed Mangal Sen who had still remembered the case of his gay son Kundan Dua.

Bhima had nodded to the assertion of Mangal Sen and added, "In fact one of his trusted men, Charanjit, had a grudge against Mr. Dua who, on a previous occasion, had refused to pay his share of the unscrupulous amount on the plea that he had gone on leave for a full week without any intimation. Charanjit, though, mentally hurt, had kept quiet at that moment but vowed to avenge the kind of insult and humiliation he had been subjected to, before his colleagues. Keeping that in mind, he had henceforth, started eyeing up the transactions being carried on for a month or so in order to gain some time required for the normalization of the things. In between, he had contacted Vijay, one of his acquaintances in the vigilance department who also was at loggerheads with Mr. Dua for some reason and asked for his help in teaching him a lesson.

"Yes, what can I do for you?" Asked the man, sitting across the table which had a wooden plate with the word Enquiry inscribed on it.

"My name is Sanjeev," replied the gentleman, occupying one of the chairs kept there for the visitors and continued to explain, "A person, supposedly an Inspector from your office had visited our premises where presently some construction work had been going on the first floor. He had stopped the work and asked about the permission for the construction. On his demand we had shown him the requisite sanctioned plan to which he had pointed out that the same had been obtained for constructing the ground floor only. He had further advised to get the revised sanctioned plan before constructing the first floor as early as possible to save any penalty charges as also to avoid the demolition of the additional portion of the building which had been constructed till now." He had, then, handed over the requisite application for the revised sanctioned plan, as advised by the so-called Inspector along with the existing sanctioned plan of the ground floor.

After giving a patient listening to Sanjeev, the Enquiry clerk had looked scantily at the application and directed him to see the officer in his cabin at the extreme corner of the office, assuring him that he would look into the matter and do the needful. However, the next minute, Sanjeev was back to tell him that the cabin was empty and nobody was there. The Enquiry clerk then directly contacted his Boss Mr. Dua and also briefed him about the case of Sanjeev regarding the revised sanctioned plan. Seeing an ample scope of making some extra bucks in sanctioning the revised plan, Mr. Dua told the Enquiry clerk to send the man direct to him. Though

Mr. Dua had already been briefed by the Enquiry clerk, yet he himself had gone through the application as well as the previously sanctioned plan. He then said to Sanjeev, "You are required to submit the revised plan afresh for approval of the same." He had further added, "It is in your own interest to see that the revised plan is submitted as early as possible. Let me warn you that any unnecessary delay on your part may attract the penalty clause on the subject for making changes in the already sanctioned plan including the demolition of the structure."

"I shall definitely get the revised plan prepared in a couple of days or so," replied Sanjeev. Mr. Dua, by the way, didn't forget to mention that in addition to the actual fee charged for the revised plan, Sanjeev will have to pay service charges that would save his precious time and energy as well as fatigue of making repeated visits to the office to get his work done without making any fuss. That way he would get the revised sanctioned plan in just two days flat and carry on the construction without any hindrance whatsoever. Sanjeev had got very much impressed with the clear and frank talk he had with Mr. Dua and left with the promise of seeing him very shortly.

❧

CHAPTER – 71

Charanjit, who had since been keeping a watch with utmost interest on each and everything, had immediately sensed that there must be some fishy deal going on between Sanjeev and Mr. Dua. Taking his friend Mr. Vijay into confidence he had quickly jotted down the address from Sanjeev's application. He had firmly told Mr. Vijay not to miss the opportunity and be prepared to catch Mr. Dua red-handed in a couple of days. In the evening, after the office hours, Charanjit had accompanied Vijay on his motorbike and called on Mr. Sanjeev. He had welcomed them after the formal introduction. All the three had then got themselves settled in the drawing room. During the chit-chat while sipping the tea, they had broached the subject of the revised plan to which Mr. Sanjeev said, "Mr. Dua has demanded so much amount over and above the actual fee payable for the sanction of the revised plan, giving me the assurance that I would be getting it in two days flat from the date of its submission." He had further added, "While I would be getting the revised plan prepared in a couple of days, I haven't been able to arrange that much extra amount demanded by Mr. Dua and am at a loss to know what to do. Just place yourselves in my position and suggest some solution to my problem please. I shall feel very much obliged and shall ever remain indebted to both of you for your kind help at this juncture."

Having remembered the famous quote 'Strike while the iron is hot' both the friends had looked in to each other's face. Charanjit then had very carefully said to Sanjeev, "You are not the first and only victim of such kind of blackmailing and harassment. This practice has been rampant over the years in this department but the neo-rich people don't worry or hackle over shedding a few extra bucks to save the trouble of visiting off and on to get their work done. He, honestly, is in dire need to be taught a lesson to refrain from such nefarious dealings and in a way robbing the poor people who had to pay under compulsion."

The effect of Charanjit's sermon-like lecture had become visible upon Sanjeev's face. Lamenting his state of mind, Vijay then put a proposal by which Sanjeev could save the extra amount demanded by Mr. Dua. Initially Mr. Sanjeev had looked quite hesitant to accept the idea but in view of charanjit's reprimanding Mr. Dua, he couldn't find any option but to agree to the proposal. He had, thus, been coaxed to write a complaint, as dictated by them about the bribe demanded by Mr. Dua in the name of service charges over and above the actual fee fixed for sanctioning the revised plan. Both the friends then shook their hands with Sanjeev and returned with the firm belief in making their plan a success.

In accordance with the strict implementation of the plan, Sanjeev had come to Mr. Dua's office after three days' gap to submit the revised plan as had been directed on his previous visit. He, straightaway, had gone to the Enquiry clerk and asked for Mr. Dua. The man had recognized him instantly and talked to Mr. Dua on phone. Mr. Sanjeev was then told that Mr. Dua would see him in five minutes. That 'five-minute-wait' had made him a bit nervous putting him in a dilemma. But before he could make an undesirable decision, he was called in Mr. Dua's cabin where he had firmly acted upon the plan chalked out earlier, shedding all his fears, whatsoever.

Mr. Sanjeev had just entered the cabin, when Charanjit gave his signal to Vijay. Soon a couple of vigilance officers had dropped from nowhere and rushed into the cabin of Mr. Dua. On hearing some hot exchanges other staff members also rushed in to Mr. Dua's cabin and were looked surprised to witness the scene over there. A wad of currency notes was lying upon Mr. Dua's table who had been pleading innocent with his folded hands. But the vigilance officers wouldn't listen to him and ultimately had taken him away to take the legal action whatsoever. Thus, both the friends had got avenged. In fact, it were they who had arranged the money meant for Mr. Dua and also got the wad of the currency notes signed by the head of the vigilance department beforehand. Needless to say that Mr. Sanjeev got his revised sanction on payment of actual fee only. The plan, however, could materialize only because of handling the case by Mr. Dua himself and not by any of his trusted subordinates, who too must have learnt the lesson for not indulging in such kind of unscrupulous deals henceforth. With the catch, Vijay had got his promotion to the higher rank.

"I'm so sorry to hear all that about Mr. Dua," said Mangal Sen. Carrying on the conversation further, as he hardly would get any chance to talk to somebody to ward off his loneliness, he had added, "By the way, is there any news about the band of Rangnath? Have they been pulling on together like before? I've not heard about them since long. A good many number of years have gone by when Ranga, once, had come to see me in connection with the 'neg' from Chaudhary Sahib, on the occasion of the extension of his house. We used to have the chance of seeing each other very often before that episode of Chaudhary Sahib. He too, must have become very old like us by now, along with the other members of his band".

Chapter – 72

❧

"**J**ennet dear, Just go and attend to that guy at the counter No.3. By the way, where is Rosy? I hope nothing is wrong with her. In a minute she is seen here and in the next minute she disappears in a jiff like a ghost in the air. I'm fed up and don't know how to manage that girl. Ask her to see me as soon as she comes." Giving a pretty smile to her Boss, Jennet quietly proceeded to the counter no. 3, as directed.

"Hello Sir! Looking for something special?"

Engrossed in his quest over the multiple rows of hangers of different shapes and sizes delicately displayed at the Mall in countless hues, styles and varieties along with glittering steel-racks full of unimaginable number of commodities, the gentleman, on hearing some commotion behind him, turned around and became face to face with Jennet standing at the other side of the counter. The guy happened to be a really good looking or rather a handsome man of normal height, with a stoutly built enviable physique and dressed up in an off white suit. He looked all the more attractive with his clean shaven face and small moustaches. However, as far as his fair complexion was concerned, it hardly matched the other folks at the Mall which in fact had distinguished him from the natives of the country he had been roaming about. His age, though couldn't be easily guessed, yet it could be placed in his mid forties or he must have celebrated his fortieth birthday at least.

On having a glimpse of Jennet, the gentleman became momentarily confounded in his mind. He rubbed his eyes not twice but thrice to confirm whether he was awake or, all that he had seen across the counter was just a dream which invariably he had got used to see off and on in his sleep for years. Jennet, while attending to the other buyers, as well, at the counter, asked the gentleman once again, "May I help you Sir?"

"No, I'm not looking for anything in particular," replied the gentleman who, by the time, had recovered from the initial shock, appeared to be quite impressed not only with her sweet voice but her manners as well while in conversation with the customers asking for something or the other at the counter.

"In fact, the Mall happens to be on my way to the Hotel Regent I have been staying at, and just out of curiosity I thought to have a short look inside the Mall and find if there is anything which may be of some interest to me," said the gentleman.

"Well, if you could name at least one or two things you are interested in, May be I could direct you where to find them," asked Jennet. "Anyway, just enjoy your visit to the city's biggest Mall," she added.

Totally confused over Jennet's facial looks as well as her physical appearance, poor Bob, the gentleman, strolled up and down through the Mall a good number of times. In his thought of thoughts he forcefully stressed upon his mind to ward off the general conception of 'lookalike' persons. How it could be? Is it possible? In a flash back Bob could see himself in India, sitting with Somi across the big library table, some twenty years back where he had found his sweetheart for the first time engrossed in reading a newspaper. How could he forget that innocent face of a simple girl which had changed his lifestyle in entirety? The whole of the library staff had known about their friendship which in due course of time had become a deep intimacy.

Having been more or less of the same age, both Jennet and Rosy had developed a unique kind of relationship between them. The bond of their friendship had become stronger with the passing of time consecutively in spite of the fact that both of them were poles apart in their nature. Yet both of them used to share their secrets in sheer confidence with each other. While Jennet happened to be simple lass, still in her teens, working as a Salesgirl to earn her living, Rosy could be termed quite her opposite in comparison, being the blue eyed child of her father, the Boss, at the Mall.

CHAPTER – 73

Jennet, whose face resembled with that of her mother, had inherited her other characters also. Following the footsteps of her mother, she too had started looking for a job to earn her living and stand on her own feet, after completing her academic education. The Principal of her college had a very soft corner for her and wanted to help her in finding a respectable job. But since Jennet couldn't wait for long she could recommend her to join as a 'Salesgirl' for the time being at the city's biggest Mall. Here she had become the subject of Bob's attention and as such he had started taking rounds at the Mall on one pretext or the other. While making some purchases on two or three occasions he had befriended Jennet. With the little acquaintance, on a certain afternoon, seeing nobody around, Bob had a piece of conversation with her and asked her, "How come, at such a tender age you have to work so hard?"

"Well, one has to do something for survival in a foreign country like this. In anticipation of getting some suitable job, I thought it better to make use of even a small opportunity coming my way. In fact, I have just graduated from St. Xavier's College and am looking for a good offer from somewhere. Working here as a Salesgirl in the Mall is only a temporary assignment that I had to accept for the time being. You may agree with me that sitting idle at home won't help to make both ends meet these days."

"What is your father, by the way?"

"My father is a foreigner, supposed to have gone on a world tour in connection with his business, some twenty years back and never returned so far, I've learnt from my mom".

"I'm so sorry to know that, anyway, what about your mom?"

"Still living in India to look after my old and ailing grandpa, as well as waiting for my dad to return. She hasn't lost her patience yet even after so many years. She had still been living in the same house with its dilapidated condition and never thought of shifting elsewhere fearing that my dad may get disappointed on not finding her at that old residence when he comes. She is cent-percent hopeful that 'Bob', well that is the name of my father, will definitely come to India one day to see her, come what may. She happens to be very much optimistic, and so am I."

The conversation had ended abruptly as a small group of a family had come at the counter asking for some merchandise.

Bob had listened to Jennet with utmost patience about her plight in brief and was touched at heart. On knowing that she was the daughter of Somi, he, instantly, had come to know about the secret of her resemblance with his sweetheart. It had been a matter of great surprise for Bob to find that Indian women have the characteristics of true love to the extent of remaining unmarried for so many years, especially when she hadn't been in the know of anything about him. Repenting in his heart, he had felt too much ashamed of himself and dared not give his actual introduction to Jennet and reveal about his real identity of being her legitimate father, who had deserted her innocent mother for no fault of her and never looked back for so many years.

Strange are the ways of God who does such kind of miracles which are beyond the imagination of the human beings. Nobody could ever have thought that after such a long time, suddenly Bob would appear out of oblivion and have the chance of seeing his own daughter born of his first love. He was also at a loss to know that after refusing out-rightly for the abortion how Somi could have faced the world. What explanation she could have given to the piercing sights of the onlookers on showing her pregnancy. The foremost worry that had come to his mind was that she belonged to the eunuch community, so people must have poured innumerable questions to her, like—how come! a eunuch becoming pregnant? How could she have been able to cope with the miseries associated with the pre- and post delivery of the child? It must have been a heavy burden for her to bear the enormous expenditure on foreign tours and he had failed to understand how she could have managed for the same.

After returning to his suit in the Hotel Regent, where he had been staying, he couldn't feel like taking his dinner. His conscious was pricking him. He had started cursing himself and feeling very uncomfortable. He had strolled in his room for quite a long time and ultimately dropped himself in to the armchair lying beside his bed. There was a knock for room-service at the door to which he abruptly had refused to attend. He, in fact, didn't know what to do to console himself of the agony he had been going through his mind. He then had tried to take a shower to cool himself a bit, but for how long? Strangely enough, the idea of having a drink was absolutely out of question as Somi, his sweetheart, had once made him take a vow, while in India, many years back and since then he had become a teetotaller and most sincerely had kept his promise of not having a drink, come what may. Though his business had taken him to a host of countries the world over where he used to attend many a party meeting with high ranked officials, yet he had never joined them in having a bout of drinks whatsoever. The Himalayan blunder on his part was only for not chanced upon making another visit to India after his first one when he had befriended Somi who was able to change his life pattern and made him look like an Indian.

Making up his mind he then vouched to do penance for the wrong he had done to Somi whom he too still loved even after such a long period. Actually it was Jennet who had brought to the surface the diminished sweet memories, with her resemblance to her mother, as well as her self-revealing, after so many years. Bob had a reason for maintaining his unmarried status as he could never stay at a place for long and as such had always shirked from shouldering the responsibilities of having a family. That too must have been one of the factors which had contributed in his leaving Somi under the compelling circumstances. Anyway, in order to make good the loss, both of them had suffered, Bob had resolved to tell the truth to Jennet about his fatherhood the very next morning. Feeling a little relieved with his decision, he had gone to bed.

Come next day and he had started becoming a bit nervous the moment he got up. The matter of his concern was how to tell his side of the story to prove the truthfulness of his statement claiming that it was he, who happened to be the real culprit of having fathered her and leaving her mother under such unfavourable conditions. He had further pondered over the situation thinking himself as "how would I apologize for my wrong doings in the absence of any proof of my being Jennet's father?" Then, all of a sudden, an idea had struck to him. "I must look for some photographs I had got clicked with Somi during our tour of Bharat Darshan. But, where could I find them after so many years? Though it may seem a bit doubtful, yet, I don't have any other option but to search for them." He couldn't see any other alternative beyond that decision for which he would have to go to his native town. In the light of that resolve, it had become very difficult for him to wait for long. He had got ready immediately and left for the Mall to see Jennet.

At the Mall, Bob had to wait for some time as Jennet had been busy with some of the customers. Soon, she too had spotted him standing beside the counter No.2. She then asked Rosy to take care of her counter also for a while. Approaching Bob she had asked him if he needed her help in looking for something in particular from the Mall. Replying in negative Bob said, "I have to leave very urgently for my native town for which I have to catch the flight in an hour or so, adding to be sure that I would be back definitely in a couple of days with a too good surprising news for which you will have to wait till my return." Jennet had tried to coax him for any hint or a clue about the news, to which she was told that being the top secret it would be revealed only on his coming back. Ultimately she had to give up opting quite anxiously to wait for his return.

CHAPTER – 74

◦

The maid servant had announced, "Sahib has come back from the tour". As Bob had reached home quite unexpectedly, his mother had immediately rushed towards his room. He had scheduled a month-long tour as usual whereas he had come back within a week and that too without any intimation which he usually used to give before his returning to home. In fact, she had become a little worried that why he had cut short his tour in between.

Touching his forehead and caressing him lovingly, she had asked him if he had been feeling O.K. Bob, then, taking his mother in to confidence, had started telling her about everything. Sitting beside her on the sofa, he had asked his mother:

"How would you like to have a beautiful, young and grownup granddaughter of your own"?

"What kind of a riddle is this? Are you kidding?" asked his mother adding: "a granddaughter before even a daughter-in-law. A great confusion, I really don't understand."

"I hope you could still recollect from your memory, when some twenty years back, right after doing my graduation, I had been to India, your native country. If you remember, you have been persuading me off and on to go and see the incredible India of my dreams about which I had read a lot. And in accordance with your wishes I had successfully accomplished my tour in three months sharp. I was fascinated enough to know everything which you had specifically mentioned at the time of my leaving. On my return I had showed you an album of photographs of the places I had visited and the people I had met with. I had also frankly told you about a beautiful girl who had accompanied me throughout the tour." Adding further, he said:

"You will be surprised to know that after twenty long years, I did meet my daughter in London, just three days back, at a big Mall. Born of my beloved Somi, she resembles cent-percent with her mother whom I had met in India almost twenty years ago. She was pregnant at the time of my leaving India. Unfortunately, I didn't have a chance to make another visit all these years. But she still has not lost her hope and kept on waiting to see me, I'm told".

"God is great", exclaimed his mother and said, "Year after year had passed by and whenever I had broached the subject about your marriage, you never listened to me making one excuse or the other. I had told you a thousand times that doing business is not the only purpose to live one's life. One should respect God's creation of this world as well. In Indian mythology one is supposed to get married and repay the 'debt' one owed to his father, by becoming a father himself. In simple language it is called the 'Pitree-Rin' (father's debt). That way it was God's Will that you had repaid your 'Pitree-Rin' twenty years back and that too without any knowledge. By the way, if you were so sure about your finding, as you claim, why didn't you bring her along"?

She had become extremely excited to learn that Bob, her son, had become father of a sweet daughter many years before and that she too had become a proud grandma of a grownup granddaughter. Being an Indian herself and settled in England after marrying a foreigner, she had become all the more happy on knowing that her granddaughter too belonged to India, her native country, the ever sweet memories of which she still loved and cherished. It was, in fact, she who had, long time back, aroused the curiosity in Bob, after completing his graduation, to see her native country, the incredible India, just once at least. There is hardly any need to add that Bob had really been got fascinated with his Bharat Darshan tour and enjoyed the company of her beloved Somi as well.

"There seems to be a problem about my own identification" said Bob. "While I have recognized her at the first sight, it won't be easy for my daughter to accept me as her father in the absence of a solid proof. In fact, I need to have something in support of my claim to prove myself'. The solution of such a problem lies in that album which contains our old photographs taken together where I could be seen with her mother at a number of famous places and monuments in India", added Bob. He had then asked the maid servant as well as his mother to look for the album all over the house.

Stressing upon the urgency of the matter, Bob himself began to look for the photo-album without wasting a minute. He had tried to look at all the probable places where he remotely could hope to find the same. Strangely, he had, always, been in the habit of boasting, off and on, about his sharp memory. How such an important thing could slip from his mind, had become a matter of speculation. The maid servant had been asked to leave all the other household jobs of her daily routine and give priority to look for any photographs whatsoever. Poor mother too had joined them to see if she could find any of them.

So far, the whole exercise of searching the album had proved futile as Bob, in spite of his best efforts, couldn't recollect anything as to where he could have placed that album, as so many years had elapsed since those photographs were taken. All the cupboards and shelves had been turned upside down but to no avail. It had been the general practice to keep the photographs in an album. There had been half a dozen old albums which Bob's mother used to have a look upon them in Bob's absence. Bob had looked through all of them turn by turn but couldn't find anything he had been looking for. He had, then, stressed upon the fact that there should be at least one more album which seemed to be missing from the whole lot. He had further emphasized that only the missing album was supposed to have contained those photographs. Hence, everybody, including his mother as well as the maid servant had been pressed in to the search expedition once again. In his thoughts, Bob could visualize his failure in proving himself as jennet's father, in the absence of those photographs, where both Bob and Somi, Jennet's mother, could be seen together.

Chapter – 75

The night had fallen and Bob's heart had also sunk with gloom. He could never have imagined that a thing like photo-album could go missing from his room. Shouting at the maid or anybody else wasn't the solution of the problem. His mother also had been feeling very sorry for the missing album. However, the next morning, the 'operation search' had begun once again. Each and every place, all the corners, underneath the beds and bed-sheets, suitcases, drawers, etc. had been thoroughly searched once again. Poor mother had got herself seated before the deity, placed in their house for worshipping, and prayed to get the missing album found. The maid servant had thoroughly searched the scrap-house viz. the store room also, located in the basement where all the waste material and things which had been discarded and not in use, were dumped haphazardly and the practice of dumping like that had been carried on for as many years together as one could remember.

Suddenly, while searching in the scrap-house, the maid servant had observed a very small heap of tiniest pieces of paper that looked the handiwork of some mice beside an old and badly worn out handbag. She, out of curiosity had opened its flap but dropped the same instantly, screaming for help and running towards the stairs. On hearing her shouts Bob had rushed towards the basement fearing some mishap and asked the maid as to what had happened. She then simply pointed towards the worn-out handbag and told that there were very small creatures lying in the bag which look like tiny offsprings of a mouse. She had further added that there lies a book-like thing also, from which those tiny pieces of paper were supposed to have been torn and eaten up by the mice. On observing minutely, Bob had found a big hole on just one side of the bag which must have been made by the mice to gain entry in to it. Anyway, lifting the flap carefully, Bob had, hurriedly took out that book-like thing from the bag and jumped like a spring with joy.

Finally, the latest discovery of the book-like thing fished out of the badly worn-out bag from the scrap-house was found to be the actual missing album which they had been searching for, since the previous morning. Though the upper portion of the album had been badly eaten up by the mice, yet the other photographs lying in the bag on the lower side of the album touching the floor, had remained intact. Leaving the bag to be used by the mice family, Bob had come running upstairs with the maid coming in tow and told his mother that her prayers had been answered favourably. The missing album had been found from the scrap-house. Only then he could faintly remember that most probably he himself had placed that album in the bag for keeping it in his own personal custody. But as the years passed by, the bag had become worn-out and hadn't been in use for quite a long time. Ultimately, without looking in to its contents, owing to sheer carelessness, it was dumped in to the scrap-house, as per the general practice, along with other unused things.

Bob had then retrieved from the album some of the photographs which appeared to be in good condition. Even after so many years, a few of them had not lost their freshness. He showed the photographs of 'Somi' once again to his mother who had felt herself to be very proud of becoming the mother-in-law of such a beautiful Indian wife of Bob. While some of the photos showed close-up of both, Somi and Bob together, in a few others, both of them looked enjoying each other's company holding their hands at various different locations. Pleased with the 'mission accomplished' he had taken leave of her mother. Coming out of their mansion he had hired a taxi to reach the airport as quickly as possible to catch the next available flight to London. While on board in the aircraft, he just tried to visualize as to how Jennet would feel surprised and react on seeing the photographs of her mother with Bob. How she would hug him on recognizing him as her real father who had met per chance by the grace of God after so many years.

He had been engrossed in his thoughts, coming to his mind one after the other, with his eyes closed, and woke up only when the plane had landed at the Heathrow airport. It had taken him a few minutes to cross through the green channel as he didn't have anything to declare. While it had started just drizzling inside at the time of landing of the aircraft, it had begun pouring heavily outside the airport, so much so that he had to wait for another few minutes to get into the taxi who had come quite reluctantly to fetch him in that heavy downpour. Instead of going to the Hotel Regent where he had been staying, Bob had straightaway headed towards the Mall to see Jennet. He had asked the taxi driver to speed up a little fast. Curiously enough, he had wished to have wings to fly and reach the Mall in no time, to present himself before her daughter in a wink.

Reaching the Mall, Bob paid a fifty-dollar note to the taxi driver and rushed inside without waiting for the balance from him. In fact, by that time he had completely lost his patience and wanted to break the surprising news to Jannet as quickly as possible. By the time it had become practically quite difficult for him to hold it any longer. His state of mind had become beyond any expression. He had felt himself

CHAPTER – 76

ొల

On taking leave and thus becoming off duty from the Mall, she had accompanied her father to the Hotel Regent. That day she had the opportunity of taking lunch for the first time at a five star hotel where she could have the food of her own choice from a good number of varieties. Soon after, they had retired to their luxury suite. She could never have imagined a more comfortable place in her life. Having settled down on the sofa, Jennet, very curiously had requested her father to tell about his meeting her mother when he had visited India long time ago. While telling the story about their first meeting in the Library hall, etc. he had also shown her the other photographs, which had escaped the invasion of the mice and could remain uneaten by them. Most of the photographs showed the famous places and the monuments which he, along with Somi had visited during their Bharat Darshan tour. Coincidently, even after a gap of so many years Bob had still been able to remember the names of most of the places and explained to her about their importance as well.

In the evening, Jennet had taken her father to her apartment where she used to share the place with her room-mate, a girlfriend who had accommodated poor Jennet in her room till she finds a suitable place elsewhere. Jennet had introduced her father to her. Before returning to his suite, Bob had asked Jennet to pack her bag and baggage by next day and shift in the Hotel suite. He had also wanted her to say goodbye to her Boss at the Mall as she won't need doing a job anymore. Her boss, however, had been very much impressed with the honesty and devotion of Jennet and didn't want her to leave the job but under the compelling circumstances, she couldn't continue.

After her shifting to the Hotel, Bob had asked Jennet to let her mother also know about him. With a keen desire to meet Somi personally and ask for her forgiveness apologizing for his wrong-doing, he had wanted to visit India once again along with his daughter Jennet and give Somi the greatest surprise of her life which she could hardly have imagined even in her dream. Unfortunately, Somi had always kept extreme precaution in keeping the secret of her identity lest somebody may come to find out the reality and as such hadn't given her address to anybody including her daughter Jennet. There seemed to be no way to overcome that hindrance.

But God's greatness can never be challenged under any circumstances. He certainly helps miraculously with His grace the person who has full faith in Him. Jennet, having relieved of her job, didn't have any specific work to do. So, in order to make use of her free time, she had been busy in sorting out her important papers like her birth certificate, papers relating to her educational qualifications etc. etc. to place them in a separate file for an easy access to them when required. She had still been keeping the books of her last semester even after the declaration of the result. She could visualize the occasion when the college Principal had proudly given a pat upon her shoulder for having passed the examinations attaining the second position in the college.

Arranging the books subject-wise she had noticed that while keeping them symmetrically, a small bunch of papers looked like protruding a little from one of the books. To rearrange them Jennet had drawn that book lying in an unsymmetrical position. It was a novel titled—'Far from the Madding Crowd' written by Thomas Hardy. On looking at those papers she was surprised to find that it was the xerox copy of her mother's Passport. Possibly, Somi, on her previous visit had temporarily kept that copy of her passport in that book while reading the novel and forgot to take it at the time of her leaving for India. Needless to say, that the passport had contained Somi's address in India, along with other details. That way the problem of address was solved.

Both, father and the daughter had started making preparations for the journey. Bob, with his personal influence was able to arrange for the passport of Jennet as well as the required visa for both of them. Air-tickets had been booked in advance. They had taken a round of the Mall also to make some special purchases for Somi as well as for her old father. Rosy and her father, the Boss, had been looking very sad and told Jennet that they would definitely miss her badly. Without taking Jennet in to confidence, Bob had sent a message to his mother that he would be coming home along with Jennet, her granddaughter. By the way, Bob and Jennet had paid a visit to the St. John Hospital and also to Jesus Christ Child Care Home to thank them for rendering medical help as well as looking after Jennet in her infancy. As a goodwill gesture, Bob had also donated some amount for the 'hospital fund' to help the needy patients. At St. John hospital, Jennet had come to know that Dr. W.F. Clifford had become too old and retired about a couple of months back. However, Annie Aunty was indeed very happy to meet Bob when Jennet introduced her father. The very next day, before leaving for the airport Jennet had insisted on visiting Uncle Ghosh and Deepti Aunty who happened to be the only family in a foreign land to look for any kind of help, Jennet may require. Deepti had been too pleased welcoming Jennet and her father who was supposed to have come back

CHAPTER – 77

B ob had to wake her up when they landed at the airport. On coming outside, Jennet had felt amused with the thought that ultimately she had reached India and in a short while, on reaching home she would be seeing her mother once again as well as her maternal grandfather, as she was told by Somi. She had tried to speculate how her mother would react on seeing Bob physically accompanying her daughter after so many years. Likewise, her old grandfather too would be surprised to see all the three of them together. Poor lass, however, didn't know that it was not India where they had landed. Soon, Bob had hired a taxi and directed him towards highway to reach their mansion where his mother had been eagerly waiting to receive her granddaughter. To cool down the curiosity of Jennet about India, Bob had briefed her on the way from airport that presently he had brought her to his own native town, before their leaving for India, as, he wanted to let his mother too, see her granddaughter, even after so many years.

The thought of her granddaughter being from India, her native country, had made his mother, all the more, happy. She would look towards the entrance every few minutes and was beginning to lose her patience when suddenly she heard the sound of horn. A minute later the taxi had reached the main entrance of the mansion. Immediately, Bob had come out of the taxi followed by Jennet. Bob's mother had come forward and hugged her as she didn't need any introduction. Staying there only for a couple of days, Bob took leave of his mother. They had spent those two days just roaming and visiting the best attractions in the city and enjoying the company of each other. They could have stayed for a few days more but Bob's guilty conscience won't let him delay any more his meeting with Somi. He, too, had become quite eager like Jennet to reach India as early as possible. So, once again the exercise of obtaining Visa for India was repeated on the day of their arrival itself to save the time. On receipt of the required documents both, father and daughter had boarded the plane. It was a long journey indeed. Bob had been making Jennet amused with his jokes and both had been having a chit-chat for quite a long time. That time too Jennet had dozed off after a while.

The aircraft had touched the Indian soil in the early morning. Jennet had been asleep till then and Bob had to wake her up. Coming out of the green channel they had hired a taxi to their destination viz. the address given in the passport and reached there in less than an hour. Unloading their luggage Bob, after paying the taxi fare, had requested the driver to help a little to take one of the suitcases to the street as nobody could be seen around that locality at such an early hour to help them. However, on hearing the commotion a resident of the street had peeked out of his door to find out the reason of the disturbance. On asking him, he had pointed towards the house of Mangal Sen a little further.

There was no door-bell or any name plate to indicate either the number of the house or the name of its occupant. Anyhow, Bob had the courage of knocking at the door. Since Mangal Sen had been sleeping in the verandah, he immediately had got up and opened the door. Seeing some strangers, he had enquired about the person they had been looking for. In the meantime Somi also had come out to see whom had her father been talking to. Seeing her mother,

Jennet had come forward immediately and called her mother, entering the courtyard. Bob too had followed her the same moment. Somi couldn't believe her eyes, rubbing them again and again, to find whether that was a dream. To her, that seemed to be quite impossible that after so many years, Bob too would come along with Jennet. On seeing that Bob had actually come back as she had been hoping in all those years, Somi's joy knew no bounds. In the first place Bob didn't dare to make eye contact with Somi. But later on prostrated with self-pity, he literally had apologized for his shameful act and asked to forgive him for his wrong-doing. She had also felt happy on his confession of having remained unmarried throughout, which also had helped Somi to forgive him. Needless to say that it had been really a surprise visit which neither Somi nor Mangal Sen could ever have imagined. All of them hugged each other. Since all of them looked busy in their conversation with each other, Mangal Sen had tried to help in taking the suitcases into the house which still had been lying at the doorstep in the street. Seeing poor Mangal Sen taking care of the luggage, Bob had come forward to help, feeling sorry for the old man. Mangal Sen who had seen Jennet earlier in the photographs only, had been all the more happy to find her physically present before him, along with Bob, his son-in-law, for the first time and thus had the feeling of now having a complete family of his own.

Nobody had ever seen Mangal Sen happier in the past two decades. Presently, he was busy in looking for some suitable place to make all of them sit comfortably. There was nothing which could be named as 'furniture' barring a wooden bench lying in the verandah, a cot in the courtyard and of course two beds, one each in both the rooms. A small wooden stool could also be seen in a corner of the verandah

CHAPTER – 78

⁓

It was the year 1977 when Mangal Sen had the chance of visiting Shirdi to pay his obeisance to Sai Baba. A long period of about 35 years had elapsed since then. Mangal Sen had a longing throughout his life to have a dip at the Maha Kumbh which used to be held every 12 years or the Ardh Kumbh held after every six years cyclically at Prayag, Haridwar, Nasik and Ujjain. But his compelling circumstances had never allowed him to accomplish his long desired wish. Now that he is quite contented of having a family of his own consisting of his daughter, his son-in-law and his lovely granddaughter Jennet, he felt at the helm of becoming almost free of his worldly responsibilities. He had, therefore, expressed his desire to go for the ensuing Maha Kumbh to be held in January on the occasion of Makar Sankranti on the banks of the confluence of the country's sacred rivers, Ganga, Yamuna and Sarswati and asked for their consent.

"No. I don't think It's feasible practically,", Somi said to her father, "You have done more than enough while you were young but at present, you are running into the sixtieth year of your age, old enough to restrain yourself from such fatigues any more. It now becomes the moral duty of all of us to protect you lest any mishap occurs in the melee at the 'mela' site. The festival you propose to visit would have a huge crowd that would consist of hundreds of thousands of devotees, gathering there to have the holy dip on the special occasion of the Makar Sankranti. Let the festival pass on peacefully and I promise to take you for a holy dip at Allahabad afterwards during the normal days sans any such crowd."

"Then what about my wish I have been kept waiting for years? With my ailing and fragile body like this, I can't expect to survive for another twelve years for the next Kumbh. Would you honestly prefer me to die with my unaccomplished wish?" That way, both, the father and the daughter were at loggerheads with each other. It was at this juncture, when Bob had to come forward to pacify both of them. Poor Jennet was very much confused over all the arguments and counter arguments between the two. In fact nobody was in favour of letting Mangal Sen go alone. It was, then, unanimously, agreed upon that all of them would accompany him to Allahabad for the holy dip at the Maha Kumbh. And as such, Bob had arranged the booking of air-tickets for all the four from Pune to Delhi. However the necessary railway reservation was also made on line for onward journey from Delhi to Allahabad in accordance with the programme.

Reaching Delhi airport by the evening, they had stayed at hotel Janpath for the night as their rail journey was scheduled for the following afternoon. Owing to their reservation they didn't find any difficulty in occupying their seats in the reserved railway compartment. Once again it was Jennet's maiden journey by railway like she had experienced earlier in the plane while boarding it from London. She had virtually clung to her father most of the journey narrating the stories about her school and classmates as well. Bob too seemed to be enjoying the love and warmness of his daughter. Likewise, Somi had been engaged in talking to her father to save him from becoming bore. As a pastime, some of their co-passengers were found chatting with each other about the day-today events and the news appearing in the dailies and discussing their point of view. At another time there was a run of some interesting jokes where almost everybody from both the opposite seats facing each other in the aisle, had participated contributing his share in making all others to have a hearty laugh. Soon their attention was shifted to the voice of a melodious song coming from a window-seat across the aisle, the common passage provided in the railway-compartment where a young lad was blissfully singing a devotional song that touched the very heart of the listeners around him. Having been a very good singer himself, Mangal Sen was secretly trying to make a comparison and appreciate the sweet melody he had just listened to. Encouraged with the constant persuasion from one and all, the passengers were obliged with a few more devotional songs. Occupying the rear seats near the door-opening, a group of passengers looked busy in playing some game of cards as they were shouting upon each other on short intervals

CHAPTER – 79

The Mangal Sen and party looked somewhat surprised to note that almost all of their co-passengers had something up their sleeves to make others listen to their abstract stories with interest. After listening to a couple of them, a young man of good physique and robust health having occupied the seat, next to theirs, invited the attention of his companions and told them about his participation in the previous Ardh-Kumbh snaan at Haridwar six, years back. In his own words: "A very strong desire to have a holy dip in Ganga had been persevering into my mind for a number of years which could be fulfilled only on the occasion of the previous Ardh Kumbh mela held at Haridwar. Before that, every time, whenever I chalked out my programme to visit Haridwar to have a dip it got postponed on some plea or the other. But last time, I was adamant to participate in the Kumbh come what may."

"Eager to visit the holy city, I kept on waiting for the appropriate time and the opportunity to fulfill my long desired wish. I had come to know that there was a daily Bus service from Delhi to Haridwar. I, thus, planned my pilgrimage for the holy dip in Ganga, took a week's off from my office and reached Delhi. There I stayed for the night at a hotel near Kashmere Gate and boarded the direct Bus to Haridwar next morning as planned. My joy knew no bounds when ultimately, after making a long journey, I reached my destination. There happened to be a great rush of people I could ever have imagined even in my dreams. The original Bus-terminal had been temporarily shifted to a far off place. All the incoming Buses were made to terminate at the new Bus stand with the result that pilgrims, visiting Haridwar, had to walk on foot to cover a distance of 2-3 Kms. approximately with their bag and baggage. That had proved really a horrible experience, even for the young, what to say of the old persons for whom no auto or even cycle rickshaw was made available to take them to the ghat. In order to control the heavy inflow of the public, the road, approximately ten feet wide, leading to the venue of the Kumbh mela had been barricaded on both the sides with the help of bamboo sticks and ropes. The incoming crowds were being directed to pass through the barricaded lane only. Fearing a stampede in the hustle and bustle, one had to remain very cautious as the people had been unruly pushing each other to make their way without knowing as to where they were heading to."

The young man had to pause for a while as a tea vendor had come in between the narration, offering tea only. All, except one person, declined to have it. Continuing the episode further he added, "By that time I had been feeling hungry. While, drinking water was available, there was no arrangement of any kind of food-stuff for the pilgrims. Stalls of food and eatables were located at a far off place where a few religious organizations had opened 'Bhandaras', commonly known as 'Langar' e.g. free distribution of food. Thank God, I had carried my tiffin containing some snacks etc. from Delhi with me while leaving for the pilgrimage which became handy in satisfying my hunger."

Coming to the concluding part of his pilgrimage, he said, "On reaching the ghat for the holy dip in Ganga I was awe-struck on looking at such a crowd. In order to cope with the heavy inflow of the crowds, a temporary wooden over-bridge was also constructed in addition to the two existing cemented over-bridges near 'Har ki Pouri' for the people to cross over to the opposite bank of the river. Soon a horizontal wooden beam on one side of the new foot-over-bridge gave way which caused a stampede. Some persons on falling down appeared to be carried away by the strong currents which were rescued by the 'Diving Squad' deputed there to help in such kind of mishaps. However the wooden beam was replaced in no time by the Army personnels for the people to cross over without any fear."

"The situation, however, on the opposite bank too was the same. There was nobody to take care of one's belongings. I, then, saw people carrying their bags in one hand, and taking a 'quick dip' while extending their hands above the water level to save them from getting wet. Ultimately I too followed the same course and somehow fulfilled my long desired wish."

"By the time I reached the new Bus terminal, I had become completely exhausted. There, I found people running helter-skelter. Even for a muscleman like me, boarding any Bus looked next to impossible and I had to run towards the railway station for my return journey."

"It seemed our station has come as the train appears to becoming slow and changing its tracks", said one of the passengers.

"Take care of your baggage folks! Hurry up and get ready to de-board. Be at the gate as the boarding public won't even let you get down first", warned another.

CHAPTER – 80

Mangal Sen and party fetched their bag and baggage. Seeing the heavy rush outside at the station Bob carefully had tightened his grip over his purse lest he may get his pocket picked in the crowd. Being an early bird Mangal Sen had already eased himself from bowel movement at dawn in the train as also the other members. Bob had engaged a coolie for their baggage which had helped them coming out of the station from other than the main exit. They then hired a taxi to go to a nearby hotel to take some rest as all of them had been feeling tired from the long journey. They had felt immense delight as soon as they touched the holy soil of Allahabad, commonly known as the Sangam city. Owing to the great rush, it had become a herculean task to find a suitable accommodation despite the fact that exorbitant rates were being charged even for small and shabby places. But as somebody had wisely said, "What cannot be cured must be endured", so Mangal Sen and party too, after searching two-three hotels, had to make themselves comfortable with whatever little space the hotel manager could offer.

Started in the eighth century, the Kumbh Mela propitiates the 'Kumbha', clay pitcher of nectar of immortality that was churned out of the ocean at the beginning of time. The nectar fell at four places when the gods were hurrying to take it to heaven before the asuras, demons, could get at it. The four sites were Prayag, Haridwar, Nasik and Ujjain where the Maha Kumbh is celebrated cyclically every twelve years, and the ardh Kumbh, every six years.

Finally the day had come when the world's biggest gathering of humanity had begun on Monday, the fourteenth of January, 2013, at Allahabad, where an estimated over eighty-two lakh devotees, as reported in the dailies, had taken the holy dip at Sangam on the very first day of Mahakumbh on the occasion of Makar Sankranti, the festival that visits the banks of this confluence of the country's sacred rivers, Ganga, Yamuna and Sarswati, every twelve years. All arrangements seemed to be in place except for one problem---there wasn't enough water in the Ganga for the mass ritual. There was just knee-deep water at Sangam and around three feet at the main bathing area which should be roughly three to four metres in the post monsoon season.

The Kumbh Mela as a matter of fact, is primarily dominated by a number of organizations commonly known as akharas of sages or sadhus e.g. 'Shahi' akhara, 'Satnami' akhara, etc. who use to pitch their own tents at the venue. Drenched under sodium vapour lights in the early hours of the morning, the vast area of Sangam city was fenced off for tens of thousands of people with barricades of horizontal wooden beams. Many of the akharas or groups of saints have their holy dip well before sunrise. The faithful devotees had to wait breathlessly for the groups of Sadhus and Mahants from fourteen akharas to take their 'shahi snaan' (holy bath) first. And only thereafter the general public was allowed to have the holy dip, immersing themselves in the river with prayers on their quivering lips. According to a rough estimate around ten to fifteen lakh pilgrims were already living in the Sangam city's sprawling quarters day and night with most of them in tents and make-shift shelters of Sadhus and mahants, eagerly awaiting for the opportunity to accomplish and fulfill their long-desired wish to have the sacred dip at the Maha kumbh.

Next morning, reaching the venue of the Kumbh, the Mangal Sen and party had just followed the crowd without asking any body which way to go and reached the Sangam's cordoned off area. While Bob and Mangal Sen took off their clothes, Somi and Jennet had to put them on, for bathing. It was agreed upon that while Bob and Mangal Sen would have the holy dip first, Somi and Jennet would take care of their clothes, shoes and other belongings and the vice versa. They had however observed other people looking for some place to deposit their belongings and keep them under the care of a person engaged for the purpose by a group of other pilgrims staying in the tent. Another man had put his purse that contained some money, into a small polythene bag, folded it three times and put the same inside his underwear after firmly tying it with its cord. However having relieved themselves from the worry of their baggage, both Mangal Sen and Bob headed towards the ghat for the holy dip. They had to struggle hard and try their level best to reach the bank of the river. Pushing their way through the melee of the crowd they, somehow, were able to find themselves miraculously of having entered the water. But to reach the mid-stream which was supposed to be the Sangam, e. g. the actual point of confluence of Ganga, Yamuna and the mythical as well as invisible Saraswati, happened to be far away and still looked beyond their reach. Looking behind their back they could witness a huge mass of people being pushed towards them whereas on looking ahead of them they had visualized a stampede-like position and were afraid that per chance if anyone of them slipped and fell down in the water below, he may not be able to get up, and mowed down to his watery grave under the feet of the crowd.

Ultimately, having been pushed gradually by the crowd from behind them they automatically reached the Sangam with the help of their co-pilgrims. Even returning back to the bank, after taking the holy dip, was not easier. There happened to be virtually a scuffle between the incoming crowd and the outgoing pilgrims. While pushing and counter-pushing were going on incessantly, mounted policemen cantered in, to clear the ground. Cops too reached blowing whistles, as Rapid Action Force (R.A.F.) personnel arrived with AK-47s slung from their shoulders. On their coming back at the bank of the river, it was now the turn of both the young ladies to go for the dip. But owing to the struggle men had to make, Bob offered to lead them holding their hands and thus Mangal Sen's wish was accomplished. Of course, Bob, Somi and Jennet had also been benefited by the rare sacred ritual of taking the holy dip at Sangam.

There were people virtually from every state. Those from rural areas of Uttar Pradesh, Madhya Pradesh Gujarat and Maharashtra accounted for the largest numbers. Wide-eyed tourists as well as professionals from abroad couldn't stop gushing at the sights. 'This is huge', a photo-journalist exclaimed'. 'I don't know from where to begin and where to end'. According to the newspaper-reports thirty computers, all connected to broadband and printers and scanners had been provided to the media. Uttar Pradesh Govt. had spent over one crore rupees on a dozen gigantic LED screens, which dot the mela premises at vantage points, says another report.

Soon the crowd at the main ghat were obsessed with the fragrance when sadhus emerging from water were seen rubbing themselves with sandalwood powder. When asked what the holy dip meant to him, a pilgrim, coming from as far as Andhra Pradesh said, 'There is an invisible power today between the earth and the moon. This energy helps cure disease and clears all mental blocks.' However, another devotee from Lucknow said, 'The event gives us a chance to revive our faith in spirituality, which is essential to keep our humanity alive. I think our ancestors were very far-sighted to have thought of such a ritual'.

The mela administration had divided the Sangam area spread over forty square kilo metres into seven zones. A zonal police officer along with a magistrate had been appointed in-charge of each zone. A number of organizations were complaining that their tents had been allotted too far away from the Sangam ghats and they had to walk up to three-four kilo-metres for a dip. But that couldn't be helped out since the entire land on the banks of Ganga and Yamuna had been allocated by the mela administration. Another major setback, pointed out by a foreigner, was lack of signages in the Sangam city in other languages as well especially, when people from across the world were coming for the mega event. Bob, being a foreigner, was really wonder struck to witness a sea of faces and could never had imagined such a huge gathering of over a hundred million of people at one place to have a dip at the Sangam and perform the ritual, offering their obeisance to the sacred river Ganga, Yamuna and Saraswati at the confluence.

The number of police personnel and guides in the mela also looked quite inadequate in proportion to the thronging crowds continuously all the twenty four hours of the day in the Sangam area. By the way, an appreciable gesture was noticed on the part of the Muslim community as well in the Mela. They too participated in running a couple of langars (community kitchen) for people coming to take a dip on the occasion of Makar Sankranti at Subhash crossing, Civil Lines and Mundera with the firm belief that service to mankind is the holiest of all services. Kumbh Mela, in fact, is a mirror which reflects our culture and social life.

Coming out and making their way amongst the crowd with great difficulty, all of them had made some brisk walking towards their hotel where they had a belly-full lunch. Bob then made a request to the Manager of the hotel to make arrangement for railway tickets to Delhi through some authorized travelling agent. While the required reservation could be made available for the following day, Bob had to cough up some extra bucks as service charges.

There was utter chaos inside the railway station. The train had yet to come at the platform. An unimaginable crowd with their bag and baggage had been anxiously awaiting its arrival. It would be quite difficult to board the train with such a crowd of passengers Bob thought in his mind and signaled to a porter. As soon as the train had arrived, coolies jumped at the doors of the slow moving train before its halt to fetch the luggage of the incoming pilgrims who were engaged in a tussle with the outgoing passengers by not letting them alight from the train. The porter engaged by Bob, too jumped inside a window through which Bob could hand over the baggage to him. Since Mangal Sen and party had their reservation, the porter could easily locate their seats and got them settled comfortably with the baggage. Even with the reservation, it wouldn't have been possible to board the train without the help of the porter.

Their return journey to Delhi had been quite comfortable. They once again had preferred to stay at the same hotel Janpath. Having sufficient time at their disposal Bob led them to see the Qutub Minar, a real epitome of India's architectural structure built in AD 1216 approximately by Qutub-ul-din Aibak and Iltutmish, his son in law. He had also booked a cab to take them to Agra early in the morning and return by the same night as they would be flying to Pune on following morning for which air tickets had already been arranged by the Manager as Bob had requested him immediately on reaching Delhi

Early next morning all of them headed for Agra to witness the world famous historical monument known as Taj Mahal built in Ad 1631 – 1653 by the Mughal Emperor Shahjahan in loving memory of his wife Begam Noor Jahan who died in 1631. While Bob and Somi had already seen it previously, both Mangal Sen and Jennet were wonder struck to see it. Recently its name was included in the Seven Wonders of the World. In the afternoon all of them had left for Delhi and reached hotel Janpath quite late at night as per their schedule. They had left the hotel before check out time to catch the flight and reached Pune by the evening. It was again Bhima who had been asked by Mangal Sen to take care of the house as usual till the return of the family from the holy pilgrimage of Maha Kumbh. He was sent for on their arrival and was pleased to meet all of them. On the occasion of Mangal Sen's successful accomplishment of Maha Kumbh yatra, a feast was held and all the members of the eunuch community were invited to partake in the celebration.

Chapter – 81

B ob was really touched. Foreigners too, have a heart to bleed. Somi had simply told him about her, long back that she belonged to the eunuch community, nothing more than that. However, Jennet knew all the facts when she was told by her mother on her previous trip to London. Bob didn't have even the basic knowledge of the eunuch community or anything else about their activities till Jennet had briefed him in London. It was Mangal Sen, however, who, not only told Bob his own story but had tried to enlighten him too on the subject explaining the general trend prevailing in the society. That had made Bob curious enough to ponder over the problem seriously. Being a well educated person Bob could find the ways and means of raising their voice through the media to invite the attention of the Government towards the plight of the eunuch community and stressing upon the need of making suitable laws to safeguard their interests in order to protect them.

As a first step in that direction he had decided to see the old Librarian and seek his guidance as well as help in addressing the problems of the transgender or the eunuch community. He had needed some literature also in the shape of any published books or some printed material in newspapers or magazines to enhance his knowledge on the subject which generally is considered taboo in the society. He was in doubt whether the Librarian, whom he had seen so many years back, would still be available or had retired. But as luck would have it, Bob had visited the library the very next morning and was surprised to find the

Librarian still there. Just to test the old man's memory, Bob had asked him if he could recognize him. Giving a smile on his wrinkled face, the Librarian had told him about his meeting with Somi and was pleased to know that he had once again come to India. Feeling very sorry, he had regretted his inability to provide any kind of information on the required subject. However he was directed to surf on the internet where he could find a few sites which could be having plenty of material relating to the transgender or the eunuchs.

People living in the neighbourhood had been very anxious to find something about what had been going on at Mangal Sen's residence as, for years together nobody had ever called on him except his old pal Bhima who used to come off and on, to enquire about Mangal Sen's health. Babu, the tea-vender who still had his little shop at the corner of the street, and used to serve tea to Mangal Sen long back, before the coming of Somi, had also become very weak in body structure on account of his old age. He too, out of curiosity, had wanted to get some news relating to Mangal Sen's guests but he had never entertained anybody on that account.

Soon after taking his breakfast the next morning, Bob had gone to look for some cyber café' to the main market situated at some distance from the locality, Mangal Sen had been residing in. Bob was pleased to have located one just nearby. The man at the counter had been quite courteous. He had warmly shook hands with Bob and asked what he could do for him. In reply Bob had told him that he wanted to use internet upon which he was immediately offered a seat before one of the computers lying in the cyber café'. While surfing on the internet, Bob really had found a number of websites which impart valuable information related to transgender, eunuchs, cross dressers, transvestites, etc. He could find a quote from the holy Bible as well. It says: "For there are some eunuchs, who were so, born from their mother's womb: And, there are some eunuchs, who are made eunuchs by men: And, there are eunuchs who have made themselves eunuchs for the kingdom of Heaven's sake. He that is able to receive it let him receive it," (Matt 19:12). "For in the resurrection they neither marry, nor are given in marriage, but as the angels of God in Heaven." (Matt: 22:30)

For Bob, that was a new world indeed about which he didn't have any knowledge till that day. He was very surprised to note that there have been a large number of persons living as transgender about which even their parents didn't have the slightest idea. Keeping their sufferings to themselves they do not dare to reveal their actual status of being a transgender, transvestites, etc. even to their friends, relatives or for that matter to any of the acquaintances. Bob had been really touched on going through various accounts narrated by the people on the net and had started feeling pity for them. The owner of the café' was pleased to observe that a foreigner had been showing much interest in that specific subject. On Bob's request he had obliged him by taking a few printouts of the matter from the different websites for his references. Bob was very pleased and looked satisfied for having done a good job as that was going to help him a lot, in the absence of any other literature on the subject, to ponder over the problems of the transgender or eunuch community and suggest some solution, if there could be any.

During the course of study of those printouts, the revelation of certain things had made Bob felt enlightened more and more with the personal experiences of the people who had expressed their views also on the net. For example, one of the affected persons who happened to be a transgender had written that even his migrating to a western country didn't make any difference. Being a well qualified person he had been living there peacefully and doing a good job. But unfortunately, the establishment had rejected and fired him because of his gender choice. Poor fellow had not been getting any work and living with his widowed mother just to survive. Another one had reasoned that because of discrimination the transgender suffer from the society, they can't get a suitable job to earn enough money to survive. So they would be left with no option but to go for begging, become bar dancers etc. but in majority of the cases they get involved in sex-work.

Despite the enactment of so many laws in India, there are not such hard core laws for the transgender. What to say of any recognition, they are not even treated as a living being. Though a number of Non Governmental Organizations (NGOs) have been working in that direction, yet, there seems to be no reprieve from the problem. How then could we hold our heads high? In this 21st century where we call ourselves the most civilized human beings, why do we discriminate them from the main stream? They also have the same fundamental rights which all of us do exercise. We often see them begging in trains, buses etc. where people behave like they are somewhat disgusting for the society which definitely is not fair. God has created all of us and therefore we deserve to be treated equally with respect. Not agreeing with the life style of transgender doesn't give us the right to disrespect or mistreat anyone.

Strangely enough, in spite of gender equality legislation, society still has some problems in coping with transgendered behavior and so too will some employers, although in recent years things are improving on this front. Recent gender equality legislation provides some protection against gender discrimination but experience shows that in practice there are very mixed results. As reported many a time in the newspapers, awareness rallies have been conducted in a number of cities, in Europe and elsewhere by gay and lesbian men and women demanding their recognition for homosexual marriages and equal rights to the parental or ancestral property as applicable to the heterosexual persons. So far, after a long struggle, the eunuch community has succeeded in a small measure by convincing the bureaucracy to allow them to enter "E" in forms, data-base sheets and other official documents like passport application forms on the NET in the place where they have to enter their sex instead of the routine "M" or "F" which does not apply to them.

By the way, Mr. B.R. Shetty, a former banker, had devised this unique plan of appointing eunuchs as recovery agents with the help of suspended former Mumbai deputy municipal commissioner G.R. Khairnar. Thanks to Shetty's enterprise, at least some of the three lakh eunuchs of Mumbai now have a chance to earn a decent livelihood. In fact there should be a separate provision for education of eunuchs which is the first step so that they are not forced to beg for living. But still there are many among them who choose the easy way out. The DAI Welfare Society of Mumbai caters exclusively to eunuchs across the city. DAI has provided a plot of land to eunuchs for a housing society of their own. It also has a planned programme to provide employment to some 60,000 and odd eunuchs in the city. It also has a project on paper to set up an ashram for aged eunuchs who are too feeble to earn their livelihood.

Since 2006 the government has employed eunuchs in the State of Bihar as tax collectors, singing loudly about the debt outside the defaulter's premises until they are shammed in to paying up – one of the most effective tax recovery method ever used in India. Yet for many eunuchs the method of making ends meet is prostitution.

PAIN OF PARTITION

Entitled, **Face to Face with Destiny**, the debut novel of K K Sudan throws light upon the conditions prevailing in the undivided India and thereafter. Beginning with the pre-partition and the hatred generated between the Hindus and the Muslims and the subsequent pogrom between the two communities, leading to the partition of country in 1947, has been in a way well documented in Sudan's novel.

After having undergone an open-heart surgery, the author now a septuagenarian, has truthfully recorded the hard struggle of his family in the wake of the displacement after being migrated to India. He started from scratch and rose like a phoenix from the ashes of partition.

Born in a small village of 'Araazi', he spent his early childhood in Rawalpindi. With his strong and immense power of observing things, he has depicted minute details of the city of those days, sans electricity and telephone.

The book enlightens the reader with breath-taking sequence during various pilgrimages undertaken by the author, including the holy caves of Amarnath, and depicted the events in a picturesque manner. Places of tourist importance in Kashmir Valley have also been described in graphic detail.

The youth of today can certainly draw an inspiration from the struggle the author has gone through and his craving for educational excellence which has driven him to take up higher studies 20 years after his matriculation.

This is his great feat. The book also strongly advocates the filial duties between parents and children, an important thing for the happiness in life and the well being of society in general.

It becomes all the more important considering into the fact of our degrading moral values and disintegration of the joint family system, where the importance of nuclear family has taken a centre-stage.

The book is in a way a driving force that helps a man to become a "karamyogi", who does not yield his whims and fancies.

The icing on the cake is that the narration of the author keeps reader's curiosity intact from beginning to the end.

The inclusion of various anecdotes makes the book all the more interesting.

Publishers: P & A Enterprises, 1580/G-1, Raj Block, Naveen Shahdara, Delhi- 110032. Pages: 228. Price: Rs. 195/-